About the Author

Mark Hayden is the nom de guerre of Adrian Attwood. He lives in Westmorland with his wife, Anne.

He has had a varied career working for a brewery, teaching English and being the Town Clerk in Carnforth, Lancs. He is now a part-time writer and part-time assistant in Anne's craft projects.

He is also proud to be the Mad Unky to his Great Nieces & Great Nephews.

THE ELEVENTH HOUR

The Third Book of the King's Watch

MARK HAYDEN

PAW PRESS

www.pawpress.co.uk

First Published Worldwide in 2018 by Paw Press
Paperback Edition Published 2018
Reprinted with minor corrections 08 September 2022

Cover Design – Rachel Lawston
Design Copyright © 2018 Lawston Design
www.lawstondesign.com
Cover images © Shutterstock

Paw Press – Independent publishing in Westmorland, UK.
www.pawpress.co.uk

ISBN: 1-9998212-3-8
ISBN-13: 978-1-9998212-3-4

To Anne,

For Everything, but especially for giving
Poor Conrad a second chance.

THE ELEVENTH HOUR

A Note from Conrad...

Hi,

Some of you have said that it might help if there was a guide to magickal terms and a Who's Who of the people in my stories.

Well, I thought it might help, too, and my publisher has been kind enough to put one on their website. You can find them under 'Magickal Terms (Glossary)' and 'Dramatis Personae(Who's Who)' on the Paw Press website:

www.pawpress.co.uk

I hope you enjoy the book,
Thanks,
Conrad.

1 — Homecoming

'**D**id you ever meet Prince William?'

'Eh?'

'He flew helicopters in Wales, didn't he? So did you.'

I gave my partner a pair of severely raised eyebrows. 'When he was posted to RAF Valley, I was in the middle of a double tour of Afghanistan, so no, not to talk to. Where did that come from?'

'It's hard to think about serious stuff when you've come back from the dead. Me mam brought us a copy of *Hello* magazine into the coronary care unit. I hid it when you came to visit me.'

It's funny what you learn about people when the chips are down. Up on a Welsh mountain, I'd learnt that Vicky Robson, my partner in magickal crime fighting and apocalypse avoidance can keep her head in the most extreme situation possible: imminent violent death. And now I'd learnt that she has a royal thing going on underneath. Neither of these facets makes her a better person, but the courage does make her a better partner.

'You didn't come back from the dead,' I told her. 'Your heart stopped for a bit. That's all.'

'Eight minutes! I wouldn't call that "a bit". Anyway, are we nearly there yet?'

We were driving home from a close encounter with a Dragon, and Vicky had only been discharged from hospital three hours ago. She may have been joking about *are we nearly there*, but I could see that she really, really needed to lie down and sleep.

We weren't even driving to her home — we were heading for *my* home, Elvenham House in the village of Clerkswell, just east of Cheltenham in the Gloucestershire countryside. Home for Vicky would be a flat in Camden or her parents' house in Newcastle. She's a Geordie, as you've no doubt guessed, but for reasons she'd kept to herself, convalescence on the Tyne didn't seem to be an option.

She didn't look well, not that she's a picture of health at the best of times. Vicky is young, yes, and has the unlined open glow that comes with being twenty-three and not having had to gut chickens for a living. She also has the pallor of northern genes and a life spent mostly indoors. It was too early to tell whether the experience would age her or whether her infectious smile and pointed sarcasm would bring her fully back to life. As she keeps pointing out, I'm fourteen years older than her and pretty much a physical wreck. I hadn't died on the Welsh hillside, but I'd lost what little hair I had left to a third degree burn. We both needed some time out from danger.

'We'll be home in less than five minutes,' I said. 'I wonder if the dragon will still be there.'

She looked confused. 'What dragon? I know you don't mean a real one, 'cos that would be cruel.'

Why should she remember? I only mentioned it once, in passing, ages ago. 'We think the oldest part of the house is the limestone carving of a dragon over the front doors. The rest of the house is brick. We always say hello after coming back from a long journey.'

She adjusted her seat into the upright position and blinked herself awake. 'What counts as a long journey to you lot?'

'Oh, anywhere outside the village. Mixing with strangers is always an adventure.'

'Please tell me there won't be Maypole dancing or nothing. I've never stopped in a proper village for more than hour in me life.'

'It's March, Vicky, not May, so there'll be no Maypoles, Morris dancing or cricket. Here we are.'

The road sign told us that *Clerkswell welcomes Careful Drivers*, and I slowed down to point out the Inkwell pub.

I opened my mouth, but Vicky got in first. 'The Inkwell pub, which has beer brewed with water from the original Clerk's Well at the bottom of your garden. You've told us about it enough times that I know it off by heart. I still think you live in a semi-detached with a water butt.'

I turned right at the church and drove down Elven Lane. Two hundred further yards and I turned into Elvenham House. There's an ancient yew tree by the gateless gateposts that masks the house all year, so you don't see it until you pass the tree and trip the sensor, causing three spotlights to pick out the gravel drive, Victorian Gothic tower and rampant dragon.

'Bloody hell, Conrad, it's huge. How in Nimue's name can you afford *this* on a squadron leader's salary *and* a flat in Notting Hill? What are you not telling me?'

'It's the family home, that's all. Clarkes have lived here since the first Queen Elizabeth, as my 11xGreat Grandfather will tell you when you're well enough to summon his ghost.'

There was a lot I wasn't telling her, but I'd promised to tell my girlfriend first, and a Clarke's Word is Binding. Literally binding. If I make a promise, I have to keep it.

'Was that him?' said Vicky, pointing to a window. 'Was that Spectre Thomas?'

I followed her direction. Vicky's night vision isn't as good as mine, but even so… 'He's not a cross-dresser. That's Mrs Gower.'

'Who's she, and what's she doing in your house?'

I killed the engine. 'You could call her a housekeeper. Sort of. She lives in the village and keeps an eye on things when I'm not there. Tonight, for example, she's been in to put the heating on, make your bed and put some soup in the fridge. Let's get you inside.'

I climbed out of the car and saluted the dragon. Despite having destroyed a real one last week, our mascot seemed to bear me no ill-will. I limped round to the passenger door and opened it. Vicky gave me a weak smile and stuck out her hand.

I levered her out of the car, and she rested on its roof for a second before taking a deep breath and stretching her arms. She leaned back inside and picked up her sPad tablet computer. Vicky is a Sorcerer: she can sense the Sympathetic Echo that all magick leaves in its wake. The tablet is her Focus and helps her sense even more. She used it to scan the dragon, then shook her head.

'That cannot be right. I must be really, really tired.'

'What?'

'I'll check again in the morning, but yes, there was once a complicated Work in that stone. It's been discharged for years.' She shivered. 'Does Mrs Gower not open the doors for you?'

Our front doors are big, metal-studded mock-castle doors. 'Round the side,' I said. 'Let's get in and I'll fetch the cases later.'

I led the way through a gate and round to the back door. Much of Elvenham House is due an upgrade and the kitchen is often the only warm spot. You should see my gas bill.

Mrs Gower was waiting for us. 'Welcome back, Mr Conrad. I've nearly finished.'`

'Thank you. This is Vicky, the colleague I was telling you about.'

Vicky shuffled into the kitchen, nodding to Mrs Gower who responded and cast a critical eye over the patient.

'I don't know why you let him nurse you,' she said to Vicky. 'I'd have insisted on a proper health farm. Preferably one with lots of half-naked masseurs. That'd perk you up more than this place or his cooking.'

'I, er…' Vicky didn't know where to look. At that point, Mrs Gower's excitable Jack Russell bounded into the kitchen and skittered over the flags like a novice skater, barking furiously.

'Hush, Nipper,' said Mrs Gower to the dog. 'What's up?'

I pulled out a chair and sat Vicky down while Mrs G tried to calm the dog. She gave up and turned to us. 'I'll just finish off in the living room and leave you be.'

11

I filled the kettle and put it on the Aga hotplate. When Mrs Gower was out of earshot, Vicky said, 'Why did she call you *Mr Conrad* and not *Mr Clarke*?'

'Because my father is Mr Clarke and I'm only his son. There's a few in the village who still talk like that.'

In the distance, the great bell on the front door rang. I started to get the teapot ready. 'I wonder who that is,' I said conversationally. And then I remembered: the front door bell hasn't worked for years. My heart stopped, just for a second, then re-started at full throttle, pumping adrenalin not blood. I dropped the teaspoon and ran out of the kitchen.

I had to swerve round the back stairs before I could get to the hall, and in that time Mrs Gower had opened the door.

The dog howled, Mrs Gower screamed and a silver shape shot past as I rounded the corner and took in the scene. The vast front door stood open, and Mrs Gower was cowering away from a giant, seriously huge snake which was rising up and flaring its hood: an Indian cobra. Nipper the dog was facing it down and Spectre Thomas was trying to manifest himself in defence of our home. Even I could feel the magick building up.

The cobra hissed and jabbed its venomous fangs towards Nipper. To the dog's left, Thomas Clarke had materialised enough to be opaque, and declaimed in his best Lincolnshire accent, 'Begone foul serpent!' He made a ghostly grab for the snake, which left off the dog and turned on him.

And me? I'd reached for my gun and realised that it was locked in the car, along with all my mundane weapons. Not that my gun had any bullets anyway. I dashed forward, tugging off my coat and aiming to put myself between Mrs Gower and the cobra.

Spectre Thomas put out a hand, and I could feel him drawing on his tiny reserves of magick. The snake rose up, hissed, and struck, digging its fangs into the glowing flesh of my Grandfather's calf muscle.

The snake was at least fifteen feet long, which is five times longer than a cobra should be, and it was five times thicker, too. Nipper is a true terrier: he saw the exposed flank of the snake and clamped it with his jaws.

The cobra writhed in pain, whipping round to strike at the dog, and that was my cue. I dived forward, holding my coat like a shield and aiming for the head. Have you ever tried to catch a rabbit with your hands? They're very quick, and a real cobra is even quicker – they have to be, or they wouldn't catch any rabbits. This one was thankfully a lot slower, as I'd seen when it struck at Spectre Thomas.

I got my coat on its head just before it could strike Nipper. Unfortunately, although a lot slower than a real snake, it was also a lot stronger. The cobra lashed its body, dislodging Nipper and taking my legs out from under me. The only good news was that the coat was still wrapped round its head.

'Run!' I shouted to Mrs Gower. 'Run now!'

She fled through the open door and Nipper covered her retreat. I rolled away from the snake and saw Vicky appearing, clutching the chain of Artefacts that hangs round her neck and is the store of most of her magickal power. If she tried to use offensive magick in her current state, her heart could easily stop again. I was not going to let that happen, and besides, I had a feeling that this snake's business was with me alone.

'Hold!' I shouted. 'Nāga! I know you for what you are.' The snake stopped thrashing and lay still for a moment. 'Hold still,' I said. 'I will remove the coat and you will appear in human form.'

'Conrad,' said Vicky, 'are you sure?'

I nodded and climbed to my feet, grabbing a console table for support. I saw Spectre Thomas clutching his calf and fading fast. 'Grandfather? Can we help?'

He looked at me. 'I must go. I can't be here no longer. Seek for me in the well.' He turned to Vicky, fading by the second. 'You too, sweet Witch.' And then he was gone.

The snake hissed a reminder of my promise, and I limped over to retrieve my coat, skirting a pool of snake blood and trying not to stand in the venom. I gingerly retrieved my coat and took a step back. The snake drew back, too, then raised its head.

Vicky took a panicked breath and touched her Badge of Office again. I gestured for her to hold her fire, and the snake's head rose further. Arms sprouted from its body and legs from its tail. In seconds, the cobra's hood had become the wild black hair of a woman.

She emerged from her snake form with her eyes closed, stretching out her arms and rising on her toes. As her tail finally disappeared into her lower spine, a wound appeared in her side and she staggered back as blood flowed. Vicky and I both moved to offer support, but the woman held up one hand to keep us at bay, clutching her side with the other. When she smiled, gritting her teeth, I caught a glimpse of fangs.

'It's *Nāgin*, not *Nāga*. As you can see, I'm a woman, though I can see you trying not to notice. My clothes are outside.'

I kept my eyes riveted to hers as I edged towards the door; it's hard not to stare at a naked woman who used to be a snake, especially if you're worried she might still bite. Above her deep brown eyes, I noticed the red dot of a Hindu *bindi* on her forehead. It was glowing, slightly.

There was a pool of fabric on the steps outside – the three parts of a *ghagra choli* (long skirt, top and scarf, if you're interested). There was also a pair of soft boots and a long woollen cloak. There may have been underwear somewhere inside the heap, but I just gathered it all together and chucked it through the open door.

13

I saw Vicky pick up the cloak, leaving the other garments, and pass it to the Nāgin, who was out of my sightline. I counted to three and stepped back inside.

'She needs first aid,' said Vicky. 'Unless you're gonna finish her off.'

'Is that any way to treat a guest?' said the Nāgin.

She had a point. Assaulting a guest is only one step down from breaking your word in the roster of magickal no-nos. On the other hand... 'I only attack guests who don't appear in their true shape.'

The Nāgin looked down. 'You have a Ward on this house. It didn't stop me coming in, but it stripped me of my human form.'

'I have a Ward?' I said blankly. 'That's news to me.'

'Is your King's Bounty here?' said Vicky.

'Aah...' When I became a Captain of the King's Watch, I was given a gold medallion – the King's Bounty. I was told that it would *protect your house in unexpected ways*. I hope it works more than once.

'I did not attack anyone,' said the Nāgin. 'I only defended myself.'

'True enough. What do you want?'

'My name is Pramiti, and I have come for a reckoning.'

I nodded. 'Then come in peace and be welcome. My partner will look after you until I get back.'

Vicky looked alarmed on several levels, not least because she'd twigged what the Nāgin was doing here. 'Why? Where are you going?'

A freezing draught was blowing through the door. I heaved it closed and shot home the bolts, then picked up Mrs Gower's voluminous bag from the console table and Nipper's lead from a nearby chair. 'I'm off to pour oil on troubled waters.' Thankfully, Pramiti hadn't spat venom on my nice new coat.

The walk back into the village helped ease the pain in my leg. The titanium tibia always aches like hell after a long drive, and I needed some thinking time. If you're wondering how come I'm an expert on Indian women's clothing, and how come I recognised the Nāga – sorry, the *Nāgin* – it's all because of my girlfriend.

Mina Desai's family is from Gujarat, and although she prefers western clothes most of the time, I had to give myself a crash course on the difference between a *saree* and a *salwar* so that I could buy her an ethnic outfit.

Mina and I have never been on a date, because she was married when we met, and although we did have feelings for each other, we were only free to act on them after her husband was murdered, and the reason we haven't dated yet is that she's in prison for shooting the guy who murdered him. And money laundering.

Before her trial, I know that Mina prayed to Ganesha, and I know she still does because her priest from London, Mr Joshi, has told me so. I had a feeling that the Nāgin's appearance at my door had something to do with what had happened earlier today at the prison in Cairndale, Lancashire.

Mrs Gower was locked out of her house because I had her keys (I also had her phone). She didn't invite me inside, but she did gratefully accept three months' wages in lieu of notice for distress and for agreeing not to call the RSPCA.

And the magick? She'd answered the door to a woman who turned into a snake when she crossed the threshold. Mrs Gower's brain and the magick inherent in the Nāgin had by now altered her memory. In the new version, she answered the door to a woman *who had a snake round her neck* which had escaped and attacked her and Nipper, thus avoiding awkward questions about magick.

I still needed a new housekeeper, though.

2 — A Reckoning

'We've got a problem,' said Vicky when I got back to Elvenham. She was waiting for me in the scullery, out of the cold but away from the kitchen.

'Thank the gods. I thought we had a lot more than one problem.'

She rolled her eyes. 'Give over, man. I'm not in the mood. Your snakey friend can't leave the property, and that dog did more than take a lump out of her side. She needs Lux.'

Lux. The magickal energy that allows Mages to mess with the laws of nature and allows creatures like Pramiti and Spectre Thomas to exist at all. It also plays a part in human consciousness and free will. Apparently.

The packet of cigarettes was in my hand before I knew I'd taken it out of my pocket. Vicky coughed and pointed to her chest. 'Cardiac patient,' she said. 'No smoking round me.'

'I'll have one,' came a rich Indian voice from the kitchen. 'And I can hear every word. Snakes have excellent hearing.'

I sighed. 'Let's get some food inside us before we all get too tetchy. Pramiti? Are you going to expire in the next hour?'

'No. Not unless you deny me bread. Your *baaii* can prepare the food while we smoke.'

'What did she just call me?' said Vicky, setting her jaw mutinously. She does have a long face, I'm afraid, and when she digs her metaphorical heels in, she looks like a stubborn mule. A bit.

'I'll heat the soup. You make the tea.'

Back in the kitchen, I took a good look at Pramiti now that she was fully clothed. The Nāgin's human form was that of an Indian woman, but there ended the similarity to Mina. My love is only five foot two and doesn't eat much; Pramiti was … shall we say voluptuous? Her eyes sparkled with mischief; she tilted her head to look at me and made sure that her scarf wasn't covering the front of her low-cut top. Then she flinched, hissed and grabbed her side. Her bindi wasn't glowing nearly so brightly.

I tipped the soup into a pan and put it on the low heat. Vicky was waiting for the tea to brew and stood behind Pramiti, checking something on her tablet computer. I thought she was using it as a Focus to scope out our magickal guest, but she was using the device's mundane features, something which became apparent when she leaned forwards and clipped Pramiti round the ear.

'Don't you call me a baaii again. I am not a maid. Is that clear?'

The Nāgin cowered back and scrabbled for something at her waist.

Vicky took a small jewelled dagger out of her pocket. 'Looking for this, pet?'

Time for Uncle Conrad to step in. I'm not Vicky's uncle, but it does sum up our personal relationship a lot of the time. When we're working, we both try to be professional.

'I think the tea's ready,' I said. 'It's English Breakfast, not tchai, I'm afraid.'

'Just put three sugars in it,' said Pramiti. I put the sugar bowl in front of her and Vicky poured the teas. We all settled round the old kitchen table and Vicky finally took her coat off.

'Okay, Pramiti,' I said. 'What's this all about?'

Way up north in HMP Cairndale, Mina had been on the receiving end of some nasty, racially aggravated aggression that went way beyond bullying. Earlier this evening, a fellow prisoner had used one of the many illegal phones in the prison to capture a particularly vicious example of racial assault, and that video was going to be Mina's get-out-of-jail card. I had a feeling that Pramiti's *reckoning* had something to do with that video and that the get-out-of-jail card wouldn't be free.

'For a start,' I continued, 'you can't have got here from Cairndale if you were involved in the filming. Unless you flew.'

She shook her head. 'That was Lord Ganesh. I've been waiting for you to return. May I tell you a little of my story?'

'I want me bed soon,' said Vicky. 'Keep it brief.'

Pramiti ignored her and waited for my nod before beginning. First, she delicately touched her bindi. 'This mark is the personal blessing of Lord Ganesh. It has kept me alive since my jewel was stolen. In my true form, as a serpent, I should have a ruby in my third eye. It is a source of *prana*. Lux, you call it. My jewel was stolen by an English Mage while I slept many, many decades ago.'

'Sorry to hear that.' If what she was saying was true, then I really was sorry to hear it. On the other hand, serpents don't have a great track record for truthfulness. Just ask Adam and Eve.

'Lord Ganesh found me dying on a rock by the holy Ganges. He gave me his blessing and took me with him. I have served him faithfully for one hundred and eleven years, and now I can seek my freedom.'

'Go on.'

'You know that my Lord is the lord of new beginnings, of the doorway to the future?' I nodded. 'Sometimes he opens the door and sometimes he puts an obstacle in the way. And sometimes he does both.'

'Is the soup ready?' said Vicky. 'I can't do Eastern riddles on an empty stomach.'

I stood up and pointed to the cupboard. 'Bowls and plates, Vicky.'

The soup was good, but not home-made. The nicest home-made soup I know comes from a coven of Witches near Cairndale. I have unfinished business with the Witches, too.

We ate in silence for a while, all three of us discovering how hungry we were. Pramiti's bindi was glowing a little brighter when she resumed her story.

'Lord Ganesh heard Mina's prayer, Conrad, as he hears all prayers, but as you know, he cannot always act.'

'Hmm,' I said. There is a lot that I'd love to know about the many gods, but even after working for one of them, I'm not much the wiser, and no one is in a hurry to enlighten me.

Perhaps Pramiti guessed, because she said, 'Lord Ganesh hears the prayers, and even if he cannot help in this life, he knows the supplicant's atman and guides it through Samsāra.'

It was Vicky's turn to look bemused.

'Reincarnation,' I said. 'Is that really a thing?'

'Oh, aye,' said Vicky. 'If you sign up for it.'

'What changed?' I asked Pramiti.

'You slew the Dragon.'

I rocked back in my chair. 'How did Lord Ganesh know that? Did the Allfather send him an email?'

'It was me,' said Pramiti. 'I knew Mina loved a Mage, but I thought you were a Mage of little Talent.'

'He is,' said Vicky. 'Very little Talent.'

'Hey, you two, no ganging up on me.'

'But you slew a Dragon,' said Pramiti. 'Spirits who knew I was interested rushed to tell me. I petitioned Lord Ganesh to grant Mina's prayer.'

'What did he do?'

'Mina had been trying to get that Sonia woman on video for days, but Sonia never did anything when there were witnesses. Mina's friend Stacey had the phone, and when Sonia and Kathy came to deliver the meals, Ganesh unlocked Stacey's cell so that she could get the footage.'

Mina had said in her message that there might be a debt to pay. I thought she'd bribed someone with my money, but no: this was a magickal debt.

'How much?' I asked.

The energy of Lux can be trapped and stored in Alchemical Gold. It's a sort of magickal currency, measured in Troy ounces. Pramiti shook her head.

'The price is not prana-gold. Lord Ganesh has adopted Mina. If you wish to marry her, you must return my mānik. My ruby.'

I blinked. That was unexpected. Not a price, but a challenge. I was still digesting this when Vicky had a thought.

'What if they don't want to get married? What if they just want to live together?'

'What business is it of yours?' said Pramiti.

Vicky put down her spoon. 'Answer the question. Are they forbidden each other?'

Pramiti flushed. 'No. But if Mina wishes Ganesha to bless her wedding, Conrad must meet the bride price.'

'Where is it?' I said.

Pramiti winced, groaned and grabbed her side. 'It's worse. Is there a stream near here?'

'No, but there's a well. It's definitely got some magick.'

For the first time, Pramiti looked to Vicky. 'Please help me. Help me get to the well.'

We made an odd grouping as we staggered through the drizzle. Pramiti leaned on Vicky's right arm, Vicky leaned on me, and I carried the LED lantern, lurching occasionally to my left as my leg spasmed.

'How far?' asked Vicky as we dodged the mole hills on the lawn.

'Through the shrubs, round the tennis court and past the trees.'

We nearly fell over as Vicky suddenly stopped and stamped her foot. 'Tell me you made up the tennis court. You cannot have a tennis court.'

I nudged her forward. 'Not mine. It's my sister's. She hid the net and posts when I bought the house off Mum and Dad. It's overgrown now. Round here.'

The original Clerk's Well is at the end of our gardens, just as the land rises at the start of the wooded Cotswold escarpment. The well has a four foot high stone parapet and is about six foot in diameter. Round the back is the pump that draws water on demand and pipes it to the Inkwell.

The well also has a plastic cap to keep out birds and animals. I wasn't entirely sure about dumping a fifteen foot snake into the water that makes my favourite beer. I hoped she'd only need a quick dip.

'How long will you be in there?' I asked.

'Until you propose to Mina,' said Pramiti. 'Or renounce her. Let me know either way.'

I couldn't help myself. 'What about the beer? And my Grandfather? Is he safe with you?'

'Yes to both. We'll be waiting.'

She spasmed again, and I let go of Vicky to remove the cover. When her route was clear, Pramiti relinquished Vicky's support and stood still. She raised her arms and reversed the transformation. As her limbs disappeared and her body shrank, the ghagra choli slipped away and a serpent stood before us.

She flared her hood and hissed, then her upper body sank down, her head dropping over the parapet. With a twist and a wiggle she slithered over the edge and down into the water.

Vicky moved first, unshipping her sPad. I took out my fags.

19

She walked twice round the well, flicking her eyes between the screen and the water. Finally, she lowered the tablet and just stared into the black mouth of the well. I waited.

Still staring at the water, she said, 'Have you been lying to me, Conrad?'

'Yes, I have. About what, in particular?'

'About magick. Did you really have no Gift until the Allfather enhanced you?'

'I wouldn't lie to you about that, Vicky. I wouldn't lie about anything important. Not to you.'

She picked up the lantern and stood back. 'Cover it up.'

I replaced the cap and collected Pramiti's fallen garments. 'What's up, Vic?'

'That well was the gateway to a Fae realm. Under the hill. The gateway's been closed since Thomas drowned himself in the well, and before it was closed, some serious magickal shit went down here. I'll tell you something, Uncle Conrad.'

'What?'

'I am not summoning Thomas out of that well until I'm feeling a lot better and until I've got a proper Necromancer with me for backup.'

'Fair enough. He can wait. They can both wait. I'll light the fire when we get back.'

'Not for me, thanks. I just want me bed.'

'You and me both, Vicky. Come on.'

We linked arms and made our way back to Elvenham House.

3 — *It was Nice while it Lasted*

I let Vicky sleep in on Monday morning while I took a long walk via the well, the woods and an old bridle path that snakes its way from the village up the escarpment. When I left the woods, I turned right and headed down to Clerkswell. I'd gone for a walk because I wanted to reacquaint myself with the land and because until Mr Joshi called, I wouldn't be able to stop worrying about Mina. She had sent the video of Sonia's attack to him because Mr Joshi is a retired civil servant and knows exactly who to talk to inside the system. I did feel a little put out that she didn't trust me to deal with it, but I could see her point.

I got a few funny looks in the village shop, but whether that was down to the burns on the back of my head, or whether Mrs Gower had been spreading gossip about a haunted house, I couldn't tell you.

By the time Vicky appeared, wrapped in the fluffy pink dressing gown her mother had bought for her when she was in hospital, breakfast was nearly ready. The sausages, tomatoes, mushrooms and black pudding were already cooked and keeping warm in the Aga. All I had to do was fry the eggs and bacon.

'Your house isn't half noisy,' she said. 'And it's none too clean, neither. I'd have sacked Mrs Gower ages ago.'

'Good morning to you, too, Vicky. We didn't pay her to clean, and this is genteel, country dirt. All old houses have it.'

Vicky slumped into a chair. She didn't know it, but she'd unconsciously chosen Rachael's chair. I wouldn't tell my sister. 'Rick James's house isn't dirty,' she said. 'Is that tea fresh?' She got up again, and I took a good look at her while she poured two mugs. Vicky looked a little stronger and a little livelier today, though still nowhere near her old self.

I dished up the breakfast and placed it in front of her. She pointed to her plate. 'Black pudding. You know I hate it.'

'It's a superfood. It's packed with protein, iron, zinc, potassium and magnesium. Just what you need.'

'It's boiled pig's blood. No one eats boiled pig's blood.'

'I do.' I forked the offending delicacy onto my plate and we both tucked in.

'You do have a beautiful house, Conrad, underneath the dust and cobwebs.'

'When we've eaten, I'm going to light the fire in the drawing room and tuck you up on the couch with the remote control. After we've had a chat.'

She grinned. 'Is there biscuits?'

I hadn't quite got the fire lit when Mr Joshi called. I took the call and hovered between wanting privacy and wanting to finish lighting the fire.

From the settee, Vicky leaned out an arm. She clicked her fingers and most of the logs burst into flames. I so wish I could do that.

'I am standing outside the Ministry of Justice,' said Mr Joshi as I retreated to the kitchen. 'It's a long time since I've seen an Under Secretary go quite so pale.'

'Oh.' I didn't know if that were a good thing.

'The MOJ are grooming the governor of Cairndale to take over one of the big men's prisons. If that video got out, they would have all sorts of problems.'

Sometimes, you have to be selfish. Perhaps, if the press got hold of the video there would be a scandal, an enquiry and some recommendations. Perhaps Kathy the Prison Officer would be disciplined and the Governor's career sidelined. That's not what I wanted, and that's not what Mr Joshi delivered. For the price of keeping the video secret, the Prisons Department was going to remove Sonia the inmate to Nottingham and transfer her accomplice to Liverpool, both with no warning. Sonia was already in a G4S van, her belongings in boxes on the floor, and Mina would be allowed home visits, starting this weekend.

I made a fresh pot of tea and took a packet of chocolate Hobnobs into the drawing room.

'Mina doesn't have a home, does she?' said Vicky after I'd filled her in (and threatened her with violence if she didn't turn off Homes under the Hammer).

'No,' I agreed, 'she doesn't, but I've got a plan, and talking of plans, we need to discuss where we go in terms of the Watch.'

'Do we have to? I'll miss Bargain Hunt.'

'Then it's a good job that I'm here to save you from yourself.'

She pulled the plate of Hobnobs towards her. 'Well, you did save me from the Dragon. Go on.'

I'm a Captain of the King's Watch and Vicky is an Officer. She was born to magick and my powers were god-given. Literally given by Odin. Not that he was very generous. Vicky learnt magick from adolescence and graduated from the Invisible College. I did eighteen years in the RAF. We're a good team, which is why our boss, put us together. Even so, since we started our magickal partnership, we've been nearly killed half a dozen times. That should not go with the territory, and the Boss agrees with me.

I waited until at least some of Vicky's attention wasn't focused on the biscuits. 'I sent Hannah an email and we had a long chat while you were in hospital.'

'Is that the one where you talked her into giving us a medal? Not that we don't deserve it.'

'Amongst other things. Hannah agrees that something has happened in the world of magick, and she's not the only one.'

'Who?'

'After I emailed her, she spoke to Dean Hardisty.'

Vicky put the plate of biscuits down and sat up a bit. 'Things must be serious for those two to work together.'

Our Boss is Colonel Dame Hannah Rothman, also known as the Peculier Constable and leader of the King's Watch. To others, she's the Peculier Constable; to me and Vicky, she's Hannah. She and I are not obviously the same. For a start, Hannah is a North London Jewish woman. Despite that, we share several things that make us natural allies. Both of us had non-magickal careers and neither of us studied at the Invisible College. We are not part of the magickal establishment and our futures don't depend on the good will of the College's Warden or of its Dean, Cora Hardisty. We also have war wounds, hers a lot worse than mine. That makes us slow to trust.

I laid out my argument, such as it was. 'You know there's been a rise in fatal incidents involving Watch Captains.'

'I do. You got the figures off Maxine.'

'According to Cora Hardisty, the number of established Mages who have died or dropped off the grid is on the rise, too. All this points to a new element of some description.'

'Howay, man. That's a bit vague. You don't suit vague, Conrad.'

'Hannah's not keen, either. Do you remember what Adaryn said when I asked her where she got the secret of Dragon breeding?'

'She said she'd rather gargle in bleach than tell us where she'd got the info. A bit gruesome, but she's obviously frightened of something.'

'Something. Someone. A person, a gang, a Dæmon, a coven, a temple, a god… They're all candidates, as are all kinds of Spirits, Demi-Powers, Dwarves and things no one has heard of. Don't forget, until a year ago, there had never been a giant talking mole, may he rest in peace.'

Vicky's attention drifted back to the biscuits. 'You're still doing the vague thing. Surely, between them, Hannah and Cora must have come up with something.'

'No. And that's where you and I come in.'

She put the biscuits down again. 'Why do I not like the sound of that? Adaryn stopped my heart. She tried to feed me to the Dragon. We're going after something even she's afraid of? Can we not do a few inspections or site surveys or something?'

'Relax. Until the Occult Council have authorised me to carry ammunition, Hannah doesn't want us at risk. Besides, you need to recuperate and I need a rest. Hannah has ordered us to divide our time between tying up loose ends and starting an investigation into those fatal incidents, the disappearing Mages and so on.'

'Sounds like a plan. What loose ends?'

I spread my arms. 'Everything from Elowen and Guinevere to Iestyn's funeral and Moley's legacy. From…'

'Stop! I'm not well. And don't forget Mina. You're gonna want to be in Cairndale this weekend, if Mina's allowed out of jail.'

'Yes I am, so I thought we'd start at Lunar Hall. If I pay for a decent hotel on Friday, you could spend Saturday night with the Sisters while I'm with Mina. If she'll have me.'

An evil grin appeared on her face. 'She'd better. I'll have words with her if she doesn't. Hang on – why do I have to spend the night with the Witches?'

'I'm not leaving you on your own until you've been to the cardiologist next week. I promised your parents.'

'And a Clarke's Word is Binding, I know. Can I watch Bargain Hunt now we've got a plan?'

'That's not a plan, that's … never mind. I'll go in search of some food for tonight.'

'Best idea you've had today.' She moved round a bit to take the pressure off her side. The electric shock we'd used to re-start her heart was a bit uncontrolled and she'd suffered severe burns on her upper right chest and lower left side. When she was comfier, she continued, 'Helen of Troy hasn't been seen for centuries, yet Keira and Deborah got hold of the rite of Summoning and Binding. Do you think that's part of the mix, too?'

'Probably.'

Half way through checking the cupboards and making a shopping list, I got the call I'd been praying for: Mina. She was calling me on the official prison line, so our conversation was being monitored.

'I have some good news, Conrad.'

'Oh?' I said, trying to sound surprised. We didn't want the listening Prison Officer to suspect that Mina was behind her colleague's sudden transfer to Liverpool.

'Yes. I'm getting a home visit. Saturday lunchtime to Sunday evening.'

'I'll be there. If you want me.'

There was a pause. My diaphragm seized up completely, and I couldn't breathe for anticipation.

'If I don't get a better offer.'

'I checked. Luke the hot dentist is married.'

'Then I'll have to make do with you, I suppose. Oh, Conrad, I'm scared.'

'Me too, love.'

'And what if you have to carry on looking for your dragon.'

Oops. I hadn't got round to writing that down, yet. Letters are the only way I can get in touch. 'We found it. I'm in Elvenham for the week, looking after Vicky.'

'Is she all right? Are you all right?'

24

'I'm fine. She's had a bit of a knock, but she's getting there. I'll tell you all about it on Saturday. Where and when?'

'Twelve thirty in the market square.'

'I can't wait.'

I don't know if she heard the last sentence because the line went dead.

It wasn't the greatest love scene in the history of romance, but, alone in the dining room, I did a little dance. Then I did a bigger dance, all round the twenty-six seater table until I heard a voice from the sitting room.

'What's going on? Are we under attack? Are you having a seizure?'

'No, Vicky. Everything's fine.'

By the afternoon, things were getting quite domesticated. Vicky had got bored with daytime TV, and had migrated back to the kitchen where she gave a running commentary on my efforts at cooking. Quite simply, she didn't have the energy for much else. Tomorrow, I'd start with some gentle exercise.

She was peering into the warming drawer of the Aga when I got another call – the Deputy Peculier Constable, Iain Drummond. I answer directly to the Constable, but Iain is her Deputy, and he outranks me in all sorts of ways.

'Hello, sir.'

'How's Vicky?'

'Recovering slowly, sir.'

'Good. I've called you directly because you've been avoiding Annelise, and I don't want to bother Hannah by going through the chain of command.'

Ouch. Big ouch. I stood up and left the room to continue the conversation. I've been avoiding Annelise van Kampen because Vicky doesn't like her and because talking to Annelise would mean a lot of boring work on statements, indictments and the paperwork of prosecution in the Cloister Court – the special court that tries magickal cases. For Annelise to get the Deputy PC to intervene is not a good sign, and for him to do it is a black mark against me.

'I'm sorry, sir. I'll call her right away, even though I'm on leave.'

'Never mind that now, there's been a serious development in the case against Keira Faulkner.'

'Faulkner? I never knew she had a last name.' If you've been following my story, you'll remember that Keira tried to kill me several times before I captured her at the battle of Lunar Hall.

Drummond continued. 'Yes, Faulkner. And do you know who her mother is?'

I did. Her mother had opened the gates to Lunar Hall and let in Keira and her partner. 'Her mother is a traitor called Augusta. She has blood on her hands.'

'Augusta Faulkner was a top barrister in the Cloister Court before she retired to Lunar Hall. She paid her daughter a visit this morning.'

25

'I hope you bloody well arrested her.'

Drummond snorted. 'You don't get it, do you, Clarke? Augusta Faulkner committed no crimes, and she's close to getting all the charges dropped against her daughter.'

Surely that could not be possible. Keira was caught red-handed in any number of crimes. This smacked of incompetence to me, though I wasn't about to say that over the phone.

'Is there anything I can do to make sure it doesn't come to that, sir?'

'Keira flat-out denies the murder of Sister Lika, the most obvious charge against her. It would help if we could get a straight answer out of those bloody witches in Lancashire. They won't talk to us, and I know you're keeping an eye on those Welsh kids, so is there any chance you could push them a bit?'

He meant *push them over the phone*. I think. I wasn't going to tell him we were going anyway, not when I could get brownie points for volunteering.

'I'll go there on Friday, sir. Personally.'

'Good. Give my best to Vicky. Oh, and well done with that Dragon.'

Vicky was not impressed when I told her what Drummond had had to say, even less so when I said a nurse was coming. 'She can change your dressings. They're due. And take your blood pressure.'

4 — *Scenes of Crime*

Vicky looked even happier on Wednesday morning when our plunder from Wales was delivered in the form of a Volvo XC90 to sell and a bright red Audi RS TT for Vicky to drive when she's been given the all clear by the cardiologist.

If a Watch Captain arrests (or kills) a Mage, you get to keep what they're carrying. Mostly this is magickal Artefacts, but car keys and the associated vehicles are also covered. For reasons going back centuries, the same rule doesn't apply to house keys.

The plunder was delivered by Detective Sergeant Helen Davies and her son. The lad had done it for the money we were paying him; his mother had done it because she was very concerned about a job offer from the Peculier Constable. I installed the son in the drawing room and we gathered in the kitchen. As well as being a copper, Helen is also a Druid. She'd been on our side in the fight against the other Druids who unleashed the Dragon. At my suggestion, Hannah wanted to recruit her to the King's Watch.

'I can't be a Watch Captain,' she said. 'I'd love to work in magick, and the money would be great, but I'm no Mage. I can't even make a Lightstick, never mind do proper Sorcery.'

The last Watch Captain for Wales is waiting to be buried. I've got to go to his funeral. 'You're an experienced police officer, Helen,' I said. 'You know the Druids. You speak Welsh. Hannah's going to get the Dwarves to make you a turbo-charged Badge of Office. Look at it this way: just do the job as long as it takes to sniff out a Druid you trust and train them up to take over.'

'And you'll help?'

'I'm the Watch Captain at Large. I can work anywhere to support the local officer. And you get Vicky thrown in as well.'

'Oy,' said Vicky. 'Other way round, more like. I'm the one with the magick.'

'Catch that train to London,' I urged. 'See Hannah for yourself.'

Later, I dropped mother and son at the station in Cheltenham and watched as Helen headed for the ticket office. She was catching the last non-stop train to London, to the HQ of the King's Watch in Merlyn's Tower. I headed back to Clerkswell and decided that it was time for Vicky to sample the Inkwell Bitter and the chef's special.

I put our drinks on the corner table and proposed a toast. 'To partnerships. Of all kinds.'

Vicky took a slurp from her half pint and put the glass down. 'Sorry, Conrad. I'm sure it's lovely, but I can't help imagining that I can taste snake from that well water. I know it's me imagination, but could I have a glass of chardonnay instead?'

By the time I'd bought her another drink, everyone in the bar had clocked me, my burnt head and the strange woman in the corner; one of the downsides of village life is that nothing goes unremarked. I told the captain of the cricket team – in a loud voice – that a colleague was staying with me for a few days and let them get on with it. I also ordered two steaks. Vicky needs building up, and I would be having a beef free weekend.

I expected Vicky to start with some joke about inbreeding in villages, but she turned serious. 'You remember your assessment at the Invisible College?'

'I'm not likely to forget that in a hurry. My magickal career nearly finished before it had started.'

'Aye, well, do you remember the Warden saying that there was a vacancy for Guardian.'

'I remember him saying it. I've no idea what it means, though.'

'The Guardian is head of Wards and ballistic magick. He – and it's always been a he – is responsible for the training programme for Watch Captains. The last one took a job in America two years ago. Hannah hasn't been able to appoint a new Watch Captain since, which is one of the reasons she created the post of Watch Officer, just to get some bodies through the door.'

No wonder she'd been keen to appoint me and jumped at my suggestion that we appoint Helen Davies.

'Why has there been a vacancy for two years?' I asked.

'I don't know. It's way above my head, all that stuff. Hannah trusts you. I think you should find out when we get back to London. I do know that the Peculier Constable has to sit on the appointments panel, and the panel hasn't sat since last summer when I started in Merlyn's Tower.'

'You're right. Do you think it's just lack of organisation or is someone trying to keep the post empty to affect the Watch?'

She shrugged. I took a long drink from my beer. It tasted fine.

'Enough talking shop,' I said when the steaks arrived. 'Until we get hold of the files at Merlyn's Tower, we can't actually *do* anything, and we'll go mad if we keep speculating. We're off to Lunar Hall and other places on Friday, so let's focus on the immediate problem.'

'The immediate problem is your steak. There's blood coming out of it.'

'And yours has been burnt to a crisp. The immediate problem is your wardrobe. We're going shopping for outdoor gear tomorrow. Not only will you be ready for action, you'll fit in better round here.'

'Neither of those sounds like a good idea. Are you gonna pay?'

'For the dinner? Yes. For the wardrobe, no. You've got a brown envelope in your room stuffed with twenty pound notes.'

She grinned. 'Worth a try.'

'Tell me again why we're going to a stables,' said Vicky as we left the motorway. We were in mid Lancashire, just off the Preston-Blackpool road. This was one part of our road trip I didn't think I'd have to tell you about because it was unfinished business from my time in Operation Jigsaw. I'll leave you to look that up, if you haven't already heard about it, and I'd hoped that this part of the trip could stay private.

'It's the Fylde Equine Research Centre,' I explained. 'They look after horses for a number of long-term veterinary research projects, as well as some livery business.'

'So, basically a stable with white coats. It's still a stable.'

Vicky was feeling a lot better this morning. As you can probably tell.

'Your best friend at school lived over a stables.'

'I'm not twelve, Conrad. She was a friend, yes, but I never went to her house or nothing. She used to stop with me to go to the big city. You saw me with Rover's Boy at Lunar Hall. I'm not good round horses.' Having made her point, she moved on. 'This is the woman whose dad killed himself, is that right?'

'Sir Stephen Jennings. Yes. I'm going to see his older daughter, Olivia Bentley. She owns a majority stake in Fylde Racecourse with her husband, and he's the Chief Exec. This is a grounding visit, to discharge the built up static electricity.'

'Eh? You might want to work on that metaphor, and you definitely shouldn't say anything like that to her.'

'I wasn't planning to. The Jennings family are old money, so it's stiff upper lips all round.'

'Your family's old money. Is that why you can be a callous sod sometimes, or are you just naturally heartless?'

'We're here.'

'What if she's not in?'

'It's term-time. She has two young children. She lives next to her seven-day-a-week business. She'll be here.'

She was. I took the liberty of parking next to the house rather than the stables, and she came out to see who we were and point us in the right direction. When she recognised me, she put her hands on her hips and waited.

'I wondered when you'd show up again.'

Vicky had followed slowly behind me. I pointed to her and said, 'This is my colleague. Can your head groom show her round while we talk?'

Olivia and Vicky shook hands. Olivia whistled loudly and waved to a woman in the distance who started to walk towards us. Vicky set off to meet her half way.

'Shall we keep this outside?' said Olivia. 'Let's walk along the gallops. They're the only dry bit.'

We made our way slowly up the hill until we got to Olivia's favourite spot, by a tree with views to Blackpool Tower and the Lakeland Fells. I smoked and we talked. I told her some lies and helped her see some home truths. We didn't shake hands when it was over, but we had made our peace. Why am I telling you all this? Because of what happened when we got back to the stables.

We found Vicky trying to get to grips with a curry comb. She was running it down the chestnut flanks of a powerful colt and, for the first time since her cardiac arrest, her cheeks were pink with a healthy glow and there was a smile of uncomplicated pleasure on her face.

'They've got you working,' I said when we got nearer.

'He's beautiful,' said Vicky. I couldn't argue with that. 'Becka said I'd get much more of a feel for them if I got hands-on.'

Olivia hooted. 'You mean she dumped you and went for lunch. Still, if you're happy, don't let me stop you.'

Vicky put down the comb and brushed hairs off her jeans. 'Nah. Becka gave me the full tour first and asked if I'd be OK. I didn't want to get in the way.' She pointed to a nearby stall. 'This lad's mam is a fine horse, too.' She paused. 'It's not *mam*, is it? What was the word? She's his *dam*, right?'

'Very good,' said Olivia. 'We'll make a horse-woman of you yet.'

'Or surrogate dam, to be accurate,' said Vicky, who turned round to look for her bag. That's why she didn't notice the effect her words had.

I winced. Olivia went rigid.

'Surrogacy is illegal,' she said stiffly. 'What on earth do you mean?'

Vicky looked bewildered, as well she might. 'I'm sorry, Mrs Bentley. I must be wrong.'

'You won't be,' I said. 'Trust your instincts, Vicky.' I turned to Olivia. 'Where was the mare covered? Here?'

'No. She was in foal when the owner asked me to stable her. He wanted her to be somewhere with daily vet's visits and twenty-four hour staffing.'

I breathed a huge sigh of relief: neither animal belonged to Olivia and she was clearly ignorant of any funny business. I drew her aside and said, 'You can ignore us if you want, or you can confirm it with a DNA test, but if Vicky says the mare isn't the colt's genetic mother, then she's right.'

Olivia was furious. 'How the fuck does she know that?'

'Instinct. It's not your horse, so we don't care and we won't breathe a word, but Vicky will be right. We'd better go.'

Vicky mumbled a combined thanks and apology, which Olivia returned with a stiff nod. We walked back to the car on our own.

Vicky would be the first to tell you that she is not a first rate Sorcerer, but she is a top notch Imprimatist. If she looks closely with her magickal Sight, she can sense your Imprint, the part-biological, part-spiritual ID that's a sort of record of your holistic identity.

The working method of the Invisible College is known as Quantum Magick because it tries to combine pure science with applied magick. They have their own vocabulary, and I tend to use it because Vicky does. Other magickal traditions – Witches, Druids and so on – have a different terminology. What Quantum Magick calls an *Imprint* is known by others as the *soul* or *aura*. To Vicky, those two horses would have looked as un-related as Winston Churchill and Nelson Mandela.

We headed towards the small town of Garstang for lunch. 'Will that horse business come back to bite us in the arse?' asked Vicky.

'Hopefully not. I don't have to speak to Olivia again, and it really is none of our business. Unless you sensed any magick involved, of course. No one's trying to create a race of centaurs, are they?'

Vicky shuddered. 'I hope not, and definitely not with those horses. No, I didn't sense any magick, but that's not to say there wasn't any when the embryo was implanted.'

'Let's keep our fingers crossed then.'

'Is that what you do for a plan when you're stumped? Keep your fingers crossed?'

'Absolutely. Best possible strategy in the circumstances. Now, don't have too much for lunch, we're eating at a Michelin Starred restaurant tonight.'

'Really? Really, really?'

'Yes. And I'm paying.'

The car was packed, the engine was running, and all I needed was my passenger, who couldn't tear herself away from one last gaze on Hartsford Hall, ancestral home of the Earls of Morecambe Bay and now a very fine country house hotel.

With great reluctance, she fumbled for the door and managed to climb in without taking her eyes off the ivy-clad sandstone walls. As we drove away, she craned her neck to get one last glimpse.

When the hotel was out of sight, Vicky adjusted her hair to a more comfortable position. It's very long, and today she'd put it in the elaborate Goddess braid as a mark of respect to our next stop, Lunar Hall. How women do that to their own hair is one of life's great mysteries.

'You know when I died,' she said.

When we've talked about it, we've called it the *cardiac event*. 'Un-hunh.'

'I really don't remember anything. No visions, no tunnel of light.' She leaned back and let out an enormous sigh. 'Last night, getting into bed after that meal, I really thought I was in heaven. Don't say another word until we get to Wray.'

The Lunar Sisters of Wray, a coven of Witches, have their base at Lunar Hall in the Roeburn Valley on a road to nowhere and heavily concealed by occulting magick. Even finding the driveway is a challenge, and then you need a special token to get through the Wards or you suffer terrible, nightmarish hallucinations. They don't get many visitors.

The Sisters were my first clients. Helping them got me into the King's Watch, and they took in a couple of refugees from the Dragon affair, twin eleven year old girls, only Guinevere isn't really a girl. What Surwen the Druid did to her own child is one of the most evil things I've seen, the Taliban notwithstanding. I won't repeat the details here, but trying to decide how complicit Gwyddno was in his wife's crimes is giving the Deputy Peculier Constable sleepless nights.

Surwen had also done something to Gwen's twin, Elowen. We had found a complex Artefact on Surwen's body which Vicky says echoes Elowen's Imprint. Delivering that Artefact is one of our missions today.

There are quite a few women with some or no magickal Gift who are not members of the coven but who do worship at their Sacred Grove and help out with various domestic chores. One of them, Susan, let us into the Mother's Lodge and made us welcome in the kitchen. Less welcome visitors are shown to the temple of chintz next door.

Mother Julia joined us, and we caught up over coffee. I did my best not to stare at the stump where her lower left arm used to be before she ran into Keira Faulkner. Coffee and scones digested, it was down to business. Vicky was going to a meeting in the Hall itself, with the twins, Sister Rose the Healer and a new recruit who knows something of Artefacts. After much negotiation during the week, I was seeing my sparring partner, Sister Theresa. Julia said that Theresa would be waiting for me at the monument to the Pendle Witches, half way between the Hall and the Grove.

Theresa had not wanted any man to help the Sisters, and definitely not one who aspired to the King's Watch. Many of the Circles (groups of Mages not affiliated to the Invisible College) refer to us as Witchfinders, a reputation we've been trying to shake for over three hundred years since the Occult Council declared Witchcraft fully legal. Knowing Theresa, meeting at the monument to a dozen martyred sisters was no coincidence, though to be fair, it does have some benches with a nice view.

I took the long route to the monument to stretch my leg and have a smoke. As I got nearer, I saw Theresa sitting on the bench next to Anna, the twin sister to the murdered Lika. If you're thinking three sets of twins are a coincidence (Hannah is one, too), they're not. Twindom is a feature of magickal inheritance.

Anna was bending down and playing with a dog, only it had very short legs. It wasn't a dog, it was a Labrador-sized mole, and a very frisky one at that.

'You really do try to annoy me, don't you, Mr Clarke?' said Theresa. She is a very powerful Witch, and although old age has slowed her down, it hasn't mellowed her in the slightest. She pointed at the frisky mole. 'This ... creature ... this abomination is playing havoc with my trees. Why didn't you let us put it down after the invasion of the Grove?'

I bent to look at the sole survivor of a commando team of enhanced moles who'd led the assault on Keira and Deborah. An ordinary, palm-sized mole is a vicious, territorial, eating and digging machine. This one was having its tummy tickled. I held out my hand until the mole could smell me, then let it run its nose over my hand to feel my shape. It went further and dragged itself onto the bench with its massive digging paws so that it could nose my face.

'You love him really, Sister,' said Anna, turfing the mole off the bench. 'I see you in the trees, leaving treats by his burrows. You're a hungry mole, aren't you Krecik?' She rubbed his head. 'He is too big to eat worms. I help him learn to catch mice and rats. He is better than any cat.'

'Thank you for looking after him, Anna,' I said. 'You know that his creator was unstable? He died.'

'I heard. This one will have a home here. I shall take him back to the Grove before he digs another burrow in the lawn.'

Anna lifted her skirts and gave a peculiar whistle with three fingers. Krecik the mole turned and followed her, nose flicking and searching every inch of ground. It brought a lump to my throat.

The Lunar sisters wear a sort of nun's habit – layers of cotton and wool with a brightly coloured cloak on top, which is how you can recognise them at a distance. Mother Julia wears green, blue for Sister Rose and dusky pink for Sister Anna. Sister Theresa wears black. I was already feeling nervous, and when she turned her gaze directly on me, a light sweat broke out down my back.

'I know why Victoria is here, Mr Clarke, and I hope that we can help those poor children, but I don't know why you've come back. There aren't any Dragons to slay around here.'

I decided to approach my mission from a roundabout route. 'How's Abbi bearing up?'

'She's in Glastonbury with the Daughters of the Goddess. She needed to put some distance between herself and Lunar Hall. I don't think that meeting the man who killed her mother would have done her any good, either.'

'Even if I did save her from a fate worse than death.'

'In time, I hope she feels the same way. One of the reasons I agreed to see you today is to acknowledge that my actions contributed to Lika's death.'

There was nothing I could say that wouldn't sound like a platitude, so I let her words blow away on the wind. She had, however, given me a good opening.

'Tell me about your calling, Sister. What is it exactly that a Memorialist does with magick?'

33

'You really don't know?'

I spread my hands to show that my ignorance of magick is an open book.

She sniffed. 'You know, roughly, what an Imprint is?' I nodded. 'Have you heard of the Final Projection?' This time I shook my head. She sighed and adjusted the folds of her cloak.

'When any human dies, Mage or mundane, there is Lux bound up with their Imprint. An infant or someone with a wasting disease won't have much; others have a lot. A sudden, violent death may trigger a haunting, and many offer themselves to the gods, if the gods are listening.'

It was light on specifics, but Theresa had just filled in a huge pothole of ignorance on my road to enlightenment, and there was more to come.

'You've met the Warden?'

'Of Salomon's House? Yes.'

'Chymists like him, and it's mostly been men, created the Final Projection. It allows the Imprint to survive death and become a Spirit. Even though you leave a lot behind when you leave the body, it is definitely a continuance.' She smiled at a private memory. 'I remember Roly Quinn as a young Mage. He never thought he'd be Warden, or become *Sir Roland*, but I could see it. He's waiting, you know. Waiting until he thinks he has a safe pair of hands to take over. Then he'll make the Final Projection.'

'A bit different to my parents. They bought a villa in Spain when they retired.'

She found that amusing. Perhaps she'd thought I didn't have parents.

'Here at Lunar Hall, we mostly give ourselves to the Grove, and that's where I come in.'

'This has something to do with talking trees, doesn't it?'

'Mr Clarke, you can be terribly reductive. I think you do it deliberately. They are *not* talking trees, they are the souls of our Sisters bound into living wood. My role is to help the soul migrate.'

You'll have noticed she'd switched from *Imprint* to *soul*. This was going to get very technical very quickly unless I cut to the chase. 'I've heard that Augusta Faulkner has shown herself in London, in defence of her daughter.'

Theresa shuddered. 'It's very cold, Mr Clarke. Shall we walk a little?'

I stood up and hopped around shaking my leg. With grace, Theresa accepted my hand and rose to her feet. Her fingers were a lot warmer than mine. She pointed to a path that would let us take advantage of the shelter of the trees without crossing into the Grove, something men were not supposed to do.

'Where is this heading Mr Clarke?'

'I know you're not interested in justice as dispensed by the Watch and the Cloister Court, but Keira denies killing Sister Lika. I wondered if your Art could help me find the truth.'

She walked for a few paces. 'You've come a long way to ask me that. You could have got Mother Julia to ask on your behalf.'

'There is something else.'

'I thought there might be.'

We stopped as the path approached the boundary wall. 'You know about the Dragon?' I said.

'Glastonbury is abuzz, apparently.'

So much for keeping a low profile. 'I saved lives there, Sister, including Vicky's and several innocent Welsh farmers. Along the way, I discovered that I have a very modest talent for Geomancy.'

'Indeed, Mr Clarke, you *have* surprised me. That I would not have guessed. I'll save you the bother of uttering your next sentence: you've also discovered that, freely given, the branch of a tree from a sacred grove makes the best divining rod.'

As I said, age has not dulled the Sister's edge. 'I saw the Grove, remember. I saw that Dodgson's Mirror had damaged or destroyed a fair few trees.'

She burst out laughing. 'The first rule of magick is *Be careful what you wish for*. Are you sure about this?'

Not anymore, I wasn't. If they play poker in Lunar Hall, Theresa would clean up every time. I had no idea whether this was a bluff or a genuine warning. I keep telling Vicky to trust her instincts, so I did the same. 'Yes, Sister, I am.'

'Then come with me. I never thought I'd invite a man back into the Grove, but come with me and we shall let the Goddess decide.'

The whole of the wood is magickal and constitutes the coven's sacred grove. There is also a special space inside with an altar, room for a congregation and a fire pit. That space is the Heart of the Grove. Theresa led me down a path away from the Heart, towards the river. In her presence, the trees were quiet, insofar as they didn't talk, but they did rustle ominously.

'Watch the burrow,' said Theresa.

I stopped to admire a huge hole in the ground. A Labrador-sized mole can shift a *lot* of earth, and Krecik had been a busy little worker. I moved something aside with my boot. 'Pork scratchings? Where did you get them from?'

She turned away to answer. 'Susan brings them. I only put them down to show the creature which burrows don't threaten the roots. If he digs too close, we spray the hole with skunk aerosol.'

'You're kidding.'

'I am not. We bought it off something called the Internet.'

'Very funny, Sister. I know the Lodge has Wi-Fi, and I bet the Hall has, too.'

'It does, though I don't. This way. And I wasn't joking about the skunk spray. If you're unlucky, you may get some on your shoes.'

Almost by the river, we came to a clear patch of ground with disturbed earth and a tiny mound of soil piled in the middle.

Theresa said, 'Lika is resting here until the spring. Julia selected an acorn, Sister Anna planted it and I will help it germinate and grow. The oak is the national tree of both Poland and England.'

We stayed quiet for a moment, heads bowed.

'Stand back, Mr Clarke,' said Theresa. I gave her some room. 'I won't disturb Lika, but there were plenty of witnesses.'

She loosened her cloak, lowered the hood fully and laid her nearly white Goddess braid, even longer than Vicky's, carefully down her back. She lifted her arms and I felt the magick flow around me.

'Sisters, sisters, spring approaches. See the bulbs. Listen to the birds. Feel the growth in the ground around you. Feel it in your heartwood. Sisters, listen to me.'

The hairs on the back of my neck prickled. The rustling in the trees turned to whispers, and the whispers to voices appearing straight in my head.

'Sister.'

'Sister.'

'Sister, we hear you.'

'Sister, welcome.'

'Sister! Beware! There is a man amongst us!'

'A man!'

A deeper voice from further away broke through the chorus. 'We know him.'

A simple statement, but one which carried layers of meaning that echoed through the rustling branches.

Theresa lowered her arms. 'Sisters, he comes in peace and would ask you a question. In the name of the late First Sister, now with the Goddess, and in the name of her daughter Augusta, tell me true: did Augusta's daughter take the life of this sister, of Lika?'

The rustling quickened, whispers spread out through the wood, and I felt words brushing against my mind. I think they were trying to decide whether to tell me the truth. It was the deeper voice that answered.

'She did not. The dark one who brought the Spirit amongst us. She it was who took our sister's life.'

Theresa flicked her eyes in my direction and jerked her head upwards.

'Thank you,' I said. 'You have shown me great favour.'

Theresa nodded and spoke again. 'Many of us fell or were hurt by Augusta's daughter. I will return tonight and ask if there is one amongst the fallen who would leave us and go with this man.'

The rustling swept round the Grove, chasing itself.

'Come on, Mr Clarke, let's go. I'm going to ask for your help getting up that hill. For some reason it seems to get steeper every year.'

She leaned on me until we got to the Hall and said goodbye until tomorrow. She was still smiling at some secret joke when she turned away.

There was no sign of Vicky in the Lodge, but she'd left a small gift-wrapped parcel for me with Susan. I was in a hurry to get to Cairndale, so I stuffed it in my jacket pocket.

On the drive over, I played a voicemail from Olivia that had arrived while I was off the grid in Lunar Hall.

'Hi Conrad, it's Olivia … erm … You know we've still got the fraud squad at the racecourse, yeah? Well, we have, and I'm in enough trouble with the authorities already … so … I decided to talk to the guy who sent me that mare in foal. You know the one I mean … Well, from his reaction on the phone, I think your colleague may have a point. I'm going to see him on Monday to try and get to the bottom of this. I thought you should know. Thanks. Bye.'

I wouldn't have done that. In her shoes, I'd have sent both animals back and denied all knowledge of them. You can try too hard to do the right thing.

5 — A Gift from the Gods

Two women and a penguin got off the minibus in the Market Square. The bus had no markings to say that it was from the prison, but every head in the little town of Cairndale turned to see who was being let out for the weekend.

The two women put their heads down and made a bee line for the bridge over the river Cowan and the station beyond. The penguin stood forlornly flapping its wings and looking for me.

I wasn't going to tell Mina that she looked like a penguin, of course, but she did. Most of her story is in the past, with Operation Jigsaw, but the past has left her looking almost anorexic and with a pathological aversion to cold weather. All I could see was an oversized calf length black padded jacket, boots, black gloves, a white scarf and, from underneath the fur-trimmed hood, a pointy nose.

'I'm here,' I said, stepping forward.

'I know you're here. I could see you from the bus. You are the least inconspicuous person I know.'

Charming. Maybe I would tell her she looked like a penguin. Later. Right now, we were going to kiss, and nothing was going to stop me.

Nothing except Mina, that is. She put her hands up to my chest. 'What if someone's watching.'

'Someone's always watching. If not human, then divine.'

'That's what worries me. It's cold, Conrad. Very cold.'

It wasn't, but who was I to tell her that?

She pointed across the square. 'Do you remember meeting in the library and pretending we were strangers?'

'I do. And going for a coffee and sitting at adjacent tables.'

'I could commit murder for a proper cappuccino. Let's sit inside, where it's warm.'

'If that's what you want.'

'I want you, Conrad. Just give me time, OK?'

The coffee shop has outside tables, where I'd have loved a cigarette, but we found an inside corner at the back with enough privacy. I put a large cappuccino and danish in front of Mina.

'What happened at the counter? What was in your pocket?'

'Oh, nothing. I'll tell you later.'

She finally lowered her hood. She'd done her best to hide it, but the yellow of a decaying bruise disfigured the pale brown skin all around her left eye and down her cheek.

'Mina!'

'Shh, Conrad. I'm petrified that someone will think that you did it and not that bitch, Sonia. I'm so sorry.'

'What for?'

She started crying. I went to put my arm round her, and this time she let me. I'm 6' 4" and she's 5' 2". I wrapped her right inside my arm and she burrowed against my chest until way past the point where I could feel my fingers. When she emerged, the bruise was worse because half a tube of concealer was now smeared down my coat.

She lifted her head, raised her arm and put it round my head to draw me in for a kiss. I think. I don't know because I yelped with pain. Now we were sitting down, she could see my burns.

'What happened?'

'Exploding Dragon.'

She made little fists with her gloved hands and saw the makeup on my coat. 'Conrad! I must look a sight. Go for a cigarette and get fresh coffee. I'm going to the ladies.'

I did go for a smoke, but I didn't get any more coffee. I don't plan to make a habit of it, but this was definitely the moment to put my foot down. When Mina reappeared, I picked up her holdall and said, 'Come on, we're going somewhere private.'

The drive to Hartsford Hall took half an hour because I took the long way round. The direct route is lined with signs pointing to HMP Cairndale. As soon as we left town, Mina started peering in the door pockets and the glove box. 'Why is this car so dirty and so old? And why are there mint wrappers everywhere?'

'This car is very reliable. And safe. And the mint wrappers are Vicky's. Filthy habit. She's staying at Lunar Hall tonight on King's Watch business. And also because she didn't want to play gooseberry in the dining room.'

'I'm not sure I can eat in public.'

'There's plenty of time before dinner.'

'Good. Now tell me about the Dragon. I don't want to hear about it after we get where we're going.'

Mina was as impressed as Vicky had been when we pulled up to the Hall, and also worried. 'Do I have to check in?'

'No need. I've got the room key and there's a side door we can use.'

Inside the Kirkham Suite, she turned slowly round while I put her case to one side. When she finally took her coat off, she gave me the half-smile she'd perfected before her face was rebuilt.

'You are a very patient man, Conrad Clarke. I'm surprised the suspense isn't killing you. It is me.'

We kissed for a long time before taking things further, a slow process because there was so much to take off. Before we got to the point of no return, I got out two boxes. One was the present from Vicky, the other I'd brought from London.

'What's that?' said Mina. 'And why are you getting it out now? It's too big to be a ring, and we don't need one to be together.'

'I checked the date. It's Holi today.'

'Yes it is! So what! Come here.'

I opened the box. It was full of bright green powder. 'We don't want to upset the gods, do we?' I sprinkled some on to her hair. 'Happy Holi.'

She grabbed some and threw it at me. 'Happy Holi yourself. Now shut up and kiss me again.'

It was getting dark on the Sunday afternoon when I returned to Lunar Hall. I had planned to head back to Clerkswell today until Vicky had messaged me this morning to say that she'd need an extra night with the Sisters and that I was expected for the evening devotions. She was waiting for me outside the Mother's Lodge.

'Well? How was it?' she demanded.

'We made good use of your present, thank you very much.'

She gave me an evil grin. When I'd been ordering the coffees yesterday, I'd found Vicky's gift in my pocket and unwrapped it just as the barista had asked me for my order. 'Oh,' I'd said.

The barista had looked down at my hands and saw a bright red packet of assorted condoms. He had made a suggestive noise, then asked what I wanted as if it were perfectly normal for customers to examine their prophylactics at the counter.

I stared at Vicky. 'And that is the first and last time I am going to discuss my intimate relations with you. Clear?'

'Not much of a discussion, but you should see your face, man. It matches the colour of the burns on your bald patch. I take it that you two are sexually compatible, then.'

I shrugged as eloquently as I could.

'Why have you got green stuff on your coat?'

I brushed at the Holi powder. 'Page seventeen of the Kama Sutra calls for anointing with colours.'

'You what? Don't talk rubbish, man.'

'I'm not going to tell you the truth, so you can make do with suggestive lies.'

'If you're making up stuff like that, it must have been good.' Satisfied for now, Vicky went into the Lodge. 'Apart from that, how is she?'

'Don't forget, she is in prison. The suite, the hot bath and braving the dining room for proper food would have been pretty overwhelming for her without the news about Pramiti.'

'How did she take it?'

The Eleventh Hour

'Deep down, I don't think she was surprised. She's had dreams about Ganesha and snakes for a while now. She knew there'd be a price to pay for what she got. Are we going straight to the Grove?'

'Aye. I'll tell you about it on the way.' We passed through the Lodge and headed round the Hall towards the monument and the Grove. 'You're going to be invited to the Heart for some reason that amuses Sister Theresa no end. I didn't think that anything amused her, but there you go. You won't be there long. After that, the Sisters will make their evening devotions.'

She went quiet. 'That Artefact. Surwen used it, somehow, to delay the onset of puberty in Elowen. That sort of magick is right over my head, but Sister Rose says we need to unravel it. We're going to try tonight, in the Grove. They're also going to start Gwen on hormones. Poor bairn.'

We stopped at the edge of the trees. Vicky picked up a branch from a pile next to the path and used her magick to create a Lightstick. Yet another magickal operation I can't perform. I left my torch in my pocket.

The Heart of the Grove has its own illumination, so Vicky extinguished her Lightstick and placed it on a larger pile just outside the clearing. 'You wait here.'

Keira Faulkner had used a magickal Charm called Dodgson's Mirror to keep us out of the Heart. It's a complete, impermeable barrier of magick that cut through trees, rocks and soil when Keira brought it up. Krecik the mole and his siblings had burrowed underneath the Mirror and attacked Keira, breaking her focus on the Charm and allowing us access for the final showdown. Krecik was the only moleish survivor.

Since the confrontation, the Sisters had filled in the trench, but it would take Mother Nature a few years to fully erase the traces of Keira's destructive magick.

Inside the Heart, eleven Sisters stood before the Altar. There were benches at the side, and an empty chair where the First Sister would sit when a new one was chosen by the Goddess. Julia had told me that it would be empty for at least a year.

Vicky took a seat on the benches with some other women. I recognised Susan and the twins, but none of the others. They were a complete spectrum of ages, sizes and outfits, including four girls of primary school age. Their mothers were the only ones in robes, plain white with a grey hood. These would be Witches taking leave from the coven. The only thing everyone had in common was a Goddess braid. Even the twins had adopted it.

A Sister in pale blue moved to stand with her back to the altar. With a quick lift of her hands, she cued in Sister Dawn to lead a song. It wasn't one I recognised, and not all the women had great voices, but it made me want to get in the car and drive away, not because it wasn't beautiful (it was), but because it was a song of home. I suddenly had a great urge to be in the kitchen at Elvenham House with Mum and Dad and Rachael. And Mina. Especially Mina. When the last notes died away, I had to wipe my eyes.

The coven moved to sit on the benches, leaving Mother Julia and Sister Theresa standing by the altar.

Julia used her teacher voice to say, 'Sisters, is it your will to admit the man who stands outside?'

The Sisters and the congregation responded, 'If the Goddess wills it.'

Julia turned to look at me. 'Approach, and be welcome.'

As I walked across the grass, Julia sat down. Theresa, I noticed, was using a stick to help her balance. I stopped at a respectful distance and bowed as low as I could.

Sister Theresa carefully lifted a cloth from the altar to reveal four branches from the fallen trees. A lot of utility companies still use dowsing rods, and they're made of metal. A magickal rod does not have to be forked (they're harder to stash), but it does have to be long enough to grip both ends. Theresa had chosen well – all were the right length and thick enough for my outsize hands to grip comfortably. So why the choice?

'You can look, Mr Clarke, but don't touch until you're ready to take one away.' That note of amusement was still there in Theresa's voice.

It was going to be a chilly night, and the Sisters wouldn't thank me for holding up their devotions, so I stepped right up to the altar and closed my eyes. There is more than one way of looking.

The Heart of the Grove is full of magick. It pulses with Lux. Any Mage could have told you that, but the Art of Geomancy is to sense the *flow* of Lux. I normally sense it as heat, like putting your hand near a radiator or walking underneath a patio heater. In the Heart, it flowed all round me like a sauna. I moved my hand slowly over the altar, being careful not to touch anything.

The first branch was itself full of power, useful perhaps as a source, but too strong for my limited skills. The second branch was better for me. It focused and shaped the Lux like a lens, sometimes coherently, sometimes as noise. That one would work, but would need a lot of modification (expensive). The third potential dowsing rod was completely different.

If the first was a gas burner, the third was a laser. I felt a single spot of power hit the palm of my hand, and I knew this would be the one. I quickly checked the fourth option, and it was just weak. I opened my eyes and pointed to an eighteen inch stick of what looked like willow.

Theresa kept her face deadpan, but just a flicker in her eyes told me that she hadn't been expecting this. 'Are you sure?'

Two can play at this game. 'It is as the Goddess wills it, Sister.'

'Really?' said Theresa with a sandpaper dry voice. 'Then take your gift and go with my blessing.'

'Thank you. That means a lot.'

I grasped the branch and got a jolt of magick that travelled right up to my collar bone. For a fleeting moment, four women appeared behind the altar, little more than silvery shadows. Three were wearing coven robes that could have been from any era, but the third in line, the one directly in front of me, was wearing a long, high-necked dress with puffed sleeves from the Edwardian era. She looked at me, eyes bulging, and reached out her hand to the other end of the willow branch. It was all I could do not to drop my end and run screaming from the Grove.

When her ghostly fingers met the living wood, her image flickered and collapsed, funnelling itself into the branch. The other women faded like smoke rings, and the only sounds in the whole of the Heart and beyond were my breathing and a distant scratching noise.

As one, the congregation let out a sigh and vocalised their surprise. Theresa folded her hands and stared at the willow wand. 'Goodbye, Madeleine. I hope you find peace.'

The willow had stopped pulsing and was now dense with the promise of magick. I bowed to Theresa, Julia, the altar and the congregation before nodding to Vicky and walking out of the Heart.

There was a sound behind me as I turned on my torch. 'A prayer to the Goddess,' said Julia. I quickened my steps and left the words of their prayer behind. Ahead of me, I heard that scratching sound again, somewhere in the undergrowth.

'Krecik!' I said, bending down. 'Krecik.'

The scuffling stopped, started and came nearer until a moleish snout appeared. I held out my hand, having dug in my pocket for some curried worms. They went down a treat.

6 — *Locking the Stable Door*

'I am never staying there again,' said Vicky on Monday morning when I collected her from the Mother's Lodge.

I re-set the satnav for Clerkswell and drove out of the Roeburn Valley on a cold, crisp morning. I'd enjoyed another five-star breakfast at Hartsford Hall; I doubted that Vicky had had the same. 'What is it?' I said innocently. 'The cooking? Too wholesome for you?'

'Don't get me started on the cooking. You are definitely going to buy me a bacon butty very soon. Nah, it wasn't the cooking, it was the dawn.'

'Sister Dawn? The Occulter? I thought it was me she had a problem with.'

'Howay, man. It was the dawn devotions, and they were followed by Pilates. Pilates! At that time in the morning!'

I didn't let her see me smile, because it was a smile of relief. If Sister Rose thought that Vicky was well enough for sunrise Pilates, she'd ace the cardiology exam, no problem. I concentrated on the road and said, 'I've heard that Annelise van Kampen goes to the gym at six thirty every morning.'

'That's 'cos she's a robot and goes to recharge her batteries. No human could do that.'

'How did it go with Elowen?'

Vicky frowned and tapped her thigh in thought. 'I don't know is the honest answer. Elowen's imprint did change – a bit like a stream that's been dammed, and there were bits that escaped and collapsed, as if Surwen was planning something bigger that she never finished. As far as Sister Rose could tell, Elowen is now as nature intended her. Unlike her poor sister.' She shrugged. 'Mother Julia gave me two messages this morning.'

'Oh yes?'

'Whatever happens to Gwyddno in the Cloister Court, he's not welcome at Lunar Hall just yet. They're going to keep me posted about the twins.'

'Good.'

'Also not welcome is you.'

'Me?'

'For thirteen months. Julia said that you're welcome to call or text if you need to, but, and I quote, "Tell him to keep his size 13s off our lawn until April next year." Now, enough about work. Tell us all about your weekend of passion.'

'No.'

'You know you want to.'

I had to say something. It was a long way to Gloucestershire, and I knew she'd keep on at me until I threw the dog a bone. Or threw the mole a curried worm. Not that Vicky's either a mole or a dog. Maybe, *until I threw the horse a sugar lump*. Stop it, Conrad. That's mean.

'You know what Mina said when I dropped her off yesterday?'

Vicky crossed her hands over her heart and looked up at the Volvo's roof. 'Oh, Conrad, I love you so much, I can't wait for you to take me in your arms again.'

I left a pause. 'Not even close. She said, "I have never been so happy and so scared in all of my life."'

'For some strange reason, you make her happy. I can accept that, in theory. What's she scared of, if you don't mind me asking?'

'Everything. Of surviving in prison, of coming out into the real world. Of us. Of being broke and having a criminal record. Of magick.'

'Poor bairn.'

'She's four years older than you, has a degree in finance and was a qualified accountant with a happy home life. She's also killed a man, been married and widowed, and that's at the root of it.'

Vicky had gone as serious as my face suggested. 'What do you mean?'

'Have a look in the glove box.'

After I'd dropped Mina, I'd gone to the Cairndale Pharmacy with my digital camera, printed several pictures and bought a couple of frames. From the glove box, Vicky pulled a 6x4 full-length photo of Mina, hands on hips and only the right side of her face to the camera.

'Wow! She scrubs up well. What a beautiful black tunic.'

'It's a kurti, and it's normally worn with a scarf, not a black rollneck jumper.'

'It's stunning. Is that real silver thread in the pattern?'

'Yes.'

'So, what did you mean about her being frightened?'

'Does that woman look like a bankrupt convict and disqualified accountant?'

'No. She looks gorgeous, if a little thin. Why is her hair over her face on one side?'

'Because Sonia gave her a black eye. It hasn't gone yet, but that's all she can think about. Inside, she's lost. I know she'll find her way eventually, and I hope that I'm not just a lifeboat to be used until she does.'

Vicky held the photo in her lap. I kept trying to sneak a glance at it. I'd stared at it all evening as I wrote Mina a long letter. She'd told me that I had to write, and that I had to use hotel notepaper.

'Pramiti,' said Vicky.

'Eh?'

'Pramiti bet her future on yours. If you and Mina don't work things out, if you don't get on one knee to propose, Pramiti's gonna be stuck in that well with your grandfather forever. She must know something about the way Mina really feels.'

I smiled to myself. It was a comforting thought.

'And on that note,' I said, 'it's time for your second breakfast.'

'First. Couldn't face porridge after Pilates. Yeuch.'

We were on official business, so I stopped at the eye-wateringly expensive Tickle Trout Hotel near Preston so that Vicky could satisfy her cravings for cured, salted pork and processed white bread. I stuck to coffee.

Before she crammed the first of two huge baps into her mouth, she said, 'How's Madeleine?'

'Quiet. I now find myself being polite to a stick in case it's listening. I had to buy one of the bath towels to wrap it up in. To wrap her up. Whatever.'

'Mmm. They're quality, those towels. I nicked a fluffy dressing gown to keep me warm in Lunar Hall. They have shared bathrooms. Didn't even have them at boarding school.'

'No, you didn't nick the bathrobe. You *took* one and it appeared on my bill. It can be my get-well present. Did you get any clue as to what happened in the Grove last night with that branch?'

'Oooh, these bacon rolls are champion. A bit. I can tell you that Madeleine died suddenly in 1902 at the age of thirty-nine, and that she had had a daughter. That much I got from her Imprint before she disappeared into the stick. No, you can't call it a *stick*. It's your magick wand.'

She seemed to find that funny and had nothing useful to add. Apparently, Theresa had left the Grove straight after devotions last night, and wasn't around this morning. None of the other Sisters had a clue what was going on.

We walked out of the hotel and into a cold, thin drizzle. No wonder Mina hated it up here. 'Shall I drive?' said Vicky.

'I'm rested and you're barred until Thursday. Let's not take the risk unless we have to.'

My phone rang, and if Vicky had been driving, I wouldn't have taken Olivia's call on speaker, and all our lives would have been very different. I checked the callerID and answered.

'Conrad?'

'Here.'

'Thank God. I need your help. He's dead. He died in front of me, then … the flames.'

Vicky and I were looking at each other already.

'Take it slowly, Olivia. What's happened?'

'I went to see the man who put that mare with us. I hadn't been there five minutes when he got a parcel, and … Well, he was spinning me a yarn all right. Said he'd changed his mind about registering the colt and refused to answer any questions. Then the doorbell went. He ran off to answer it and came back with a tube.'

Vicky grabbed my arm. She didn't want to speak, but she was very worried about something.

Olivia drew breath, then continued even faster. 'He opened the tube and pulled out a rolled up piece of paper. As soon as he broke the seal, he ... he just dropped dead.'

Vicky couldn't contain herself. 'I'm sorry, Mrs Bentley, but...'

'Conrad! I thought you were on your own.'

'Vicky's my partner and an expert. Carry on, Vic.'

'Mrs Bentley, did you say that there was a seal?'

'What? Yes. A black wax seal. He died, Conrad, and then he burst into flames. Not just him, his clothes, the rug, the chair and the end of my scarf that was nearest him did, too. I turned and ran. I had to call the fire brigade — his cottage is attached to the stables. They'll be here in a minute. You have to help me, Conrad. My brother said you were so deep in the secret service you'd disappeared. The police will listen to you.'

I owed Olivia nothing, not directly. On the other hand, we had started the ball rolling, and I believed that she was a completely innocent victim here. I was just reaching this conclusion when Vicky decided for us.

'We're on our way, Mrs Bentley. Where are you?'

'Cartmel. Conrad knows where it is if you don't.'

I put the Volvo in gear and headed for the M6 North, back the way we'd come. Vicky was looking at me expectantly.

'It'll take us forty-five minutes,' I said. 'Where about exactly?'

'A mile north of the village. Fellside Farm. I can hear sirens.'

'Was anyone else in the house? Could they still be in there?'

'No. He was on his own. He told me when I first got there.'

'What did you say to the emergency operator?'

'I said that I'd arrived, smelled smoke, gone in and found him slumped on the floor.'

'That's good. Stick to that story, but don't leave the site until we get there. Deep breaths, 'Livia.'

'Right. See you soon. Bye.'

The colour in Vicky's cheeks that had cheered me up when I saw it first thing had all drained away. She pointed up at an approaching gantry over the motorway. 'That says *The Lakes*. Where exactly is Cartmel?'

'Just north of Grange-over-Sands.'

'And where's that?'

Vicky's ignorance of geography is almost as total as my ignorance of magick.

'Half way between Kendal and Barrow in Furness.'

'They're in the Lakes.'

'Barrow isn't, and Kendal…'

'No, I don't care about the actual lakes. I mean, they're in the Lakeland Particular. We've got to call Hannah.'

Vicky was already reaching for the media console to dial the Constable. As gently as possible, I held out my hand to stop her. 'What do you mean, Vic? I know about Scotland and Wales, but what's so special about the Lake District? And shouldn't we call security liaison first? We'll have to deal with the local police.'

'Never mind the police, we'll have to deal with one of the Unions.'

'Vicky! Begin at the beginning.'

'Hmmph. Can you not trust me on this one?'

If she was going to put it like that…

I drew my hand away from the console, and she punched the contact for Tennille Haynes, Hannah's PA. When Tennille heard the agitation in Vicky's voice, she put her straight through.

'Vicky! How was the visit to Lunar Hall? Did they look after you?'

'It was fine, thanks. Sorry, Hannah, but I think something bad has happened in the Lakeland Particular.'

'Oy vey! I cannot turn my back on you two for a minute, even when you're on sick leave. You have been sent to test me, this I know. Is he there?'

'Ma'am?' I said.

'Good. Now, Vicky, tell me what's going on.'

'I'm not sure. Long and short, I think a Malaglyph has been used on a mundane civilian.'

There was long pause, during which I wondered whether to ask what on earth a *Malaglyph* might be. It didn't sound good.

Hannah came back on the line. 'You're on your way to … whatever. And there's been a fatality? Yes?'

'Yes.'

'So you don't know whether or not the victim is a Mage or whether it was Imprint targeting?'

'No.'

'Which Union's territory did it happen on?'

'Erm… Sorry. That's Conrad's department, and you never gave him the Lakeland briefing, so he doesn't know where the boundaries are.'

'Conrad? Do you have a location for the incident?'

'Near the village of Cartmel on the Cartmel Peninsula, ma'am.'

'Langdale and Leven,' said Hannah decisively. I'll get someone to call you.' There was a pause and change of tone. 'Vicky? Are you well enough to lead on this?'

'Yes, ma'am.'

'No! You can't start that. Enough with the *ma'ams* already. Both of you. I need to make a call. Be very, very careful, Vicky, and call me the *moment* you establish whose jurisdiction this is.'

I was happy to let Vicky lead. More than happy, but there was a massive problem looming. 'What about the police and the fire brigade, ma'am? I mean Hannah.'

'Fire brigade? What fire brigade? Ach, you two could find the Devil in the Temple. You deal with the mundane authorities, Conrad, and Vicky can deal with the Union. Right? Good. Goodbye.'

I turned to Vicky. 'You're the boss here. What on earth is going on? And don't tell me it's a long story, just give me what you can in the next twenty minutes.'

'There's just so much, Conrad, that's the problem. I wish it were all written down somewhere so you could look it up.'

'You're not just talking about the Lake District, are you?'

'No. It's everything from the Inquisition of St Michael to the Commonwealth of New England, from, I don't know, from King Arthur to the Fleet Witches.'

'It's not your fault, Vicky. So far, you've never let me go into danger through ignorance. We can cover the rest somehow, so just start with the Lakeland particular.'

'Basically, we don't have police powers up there when it comes to magick.'

'What! How did that come about?'

'Now that really is a long story. The Lake District has always been the last refuge — Druids running from the Romans, Witches hiding from the Inquisition, Gnomes and Dwarves being hunted by the Pale Horsemen. And they all settled on and under the mountains and around the lakes, and they didn't take kindly to the King's Watch. Don't forget, we've only been going since 1618 and by then there was already an organisation in the Lakes. They used to have gatherings in the valleys, and they became the Unions.'

'Hannah said something about dealing with one of them. Was it Langdale-Leven?'

'Aye. There's eight Unions, all with funny names like Watterdale and Burrowmere.'

'Right. We'll skip the geography for now. What do they do?'

'They're part council, part trade union and part police force. The last big change to our relationship with them was after the French Revolution. The then Peculier Constable forced the Unions to accept that we would investigate crimes against civilians and that the Cloister Court would try all cases, though they sit in Hawkshead not the Old Temple in London, and most of the judges are local.'

'So, Mage on Mage crimes are investigated by these Unions.'

'Aye.'

'Is there a Watch Captain in Lakeland?'

She gave a big sigh. 'The Deputy Constable in Chester should handle Lakeland. Hannah can't get anyone to apply.'

I was musing on the vulnerabilities of mundane people under this system when Vicky had something to add.

'And there's Waterhead Academy. I think it's near Ambleside. Wherever that is.'

'Go on.'

'It's a boarding school for all the kids of parents who are in the world of magick, whether they've got a Gift or not. When they leave the Academy, they never go to Salomon's House after. They do apprenticeships up here outside their home Union. I did once meet a post-grad student when I was at the Invisible College.'

We had passed Lancaster and were at the familiar turning to Cairndale; soon, we'd cross the invisible but potent boundary into the Lakeland Particular.

'Tell me about this Malaglyph business.'

'Well, the good news is that I know more about them than I did about Dragons. Oh, I should say that there's a Dragon's nest somewhere in Lakeland, though the Romans definitely sealed it.'

'They'd sealed the nest in Caerleon, but that didn't stop the Brotherhood.'

Vicky didn't get back to the subject of Malaglyphs because she got a phone call.

'Is that Watch Captain Robson?' said a slightly nasal, slightly northern man's voice.

'It's Watch Officer Robson. I'm with Watch Captain Clarke and you're on speaker.'

'Then who's in charge?'

Vicky blushed. I'd have taken the call privately, but Vicky does like to do the right thing. She obviously couldn't think of a polite way of putting me in my place, so I said, 'We're partners.'

'I'm Matthew Eldridge, Assessor for the Langdale-Leven Union. I believe there's been an incident in our area.'

'Aye. Yes. In Cartmel.'

'Could you text me the details and I'll let you know what's happened when I've finished.'

Nothing like being thrown in at the deep end. I kept my eyes on the road. This was Vicky's show.

'We have reason to believe that this involves magick being used to target at mundane civilian,' she said stiffly.

'Which I can establish quite quickly. I'm in Newby Bridge, so it's only ten minutes away.'

'And we're…' said Vicky, looking round for a clue. I pointed to the big blue exit sign. 'We're just leaving the motorway.'

'You haven't told me why you think magick may be involved and how do you know if it's a mundane victim?'

Vicky opened her mouth to give our source away. I put my fingers to my lips and made a *kill it* gesture.

She nodded enthusiastically and said, 'It's best if I text you the address, then we can discuss it on site.'

'If you insist. What should I expect when I get there?'

'Erm,' said Vicky. She raised her eyebrows to me in a clear plea for help.

'I wouldn't worry, Assessor Eldridge,' I said. 'They won't have put out the fire yet.'

'Fire? What fire?'

'I'll text you the address,' said Vicky, disconnecting the call. She shifted to her sPad. 'I'll have to look it up first. What was the name again?'

'Fellside Farm, Cartmel.'

We were off the Kendal bypass and heading west on the A590 before Vicky had finished texting and putting the postcode into our satnav. It told us we'd be there in five minutes.

'What a tosser,' I said, pointing to the phone.

'Aye, well, we'll see. I am not looking forward to meeting him or seeing Mrs Bentley again.' She looked around at the scenery. 'It's pretty flat round here.'

'With this low cloud, the fells are hidden. This road hugs the coast, pretty much.'

I started to speak a couple of times before thinking that anything like *You can do it* would sound a bit patronising. In the RAF, it was assumed that you could do it. We turned off the A590 and I stuck to the important stuff.

'Is this likely to be an ambush? Should we prepare for the worst?'

'I thought you always prepared for the worst,' she said, smiling again. 'No, Malaglyphs don't need anyone nearby to work. Whoever did this will be anywhere but Fellside Farm.'

'Good. I can leave the Hammer in its box.'

Hledjolf the Dwarf had named my Badge of Office *The Hammer*. It's an exact copy of a SIG P226 handgun and it fires magickal rounds, or it would if I were allowed to carry them. Mages can sense that the gun is empty, which is quite embarrassing, especially as I have to have it around me to act as a magickal shield. I reckoned we'd be safe enough at Fellside Farm.

'In two hundred yards, turn right,' said the satnav.

'Turn right and follow the ambulance,' added Vicky.

We got a quarter of a mile before the lane jammed up completely with flashing lights, abandoned vehicles and noise. I pulled into a field entrance to leave some room and we jogged up to the action. At first it was the smell of

Guy Fawkes' Night, distant bonfires across the fields. Soon we were coughing and trying to find a way upwind of the smoke before we needed the ambulance, too.

Two fire engines were winning the battle, but the cottage was lost, all windows blown out, roof collapsed in two places. The engines had pulled in to the stable yard and pretty much filled it. Scattered around were a couple of uncoupled horse boxes, Olivia's Range Rover, an ambulance, a police car and several miscellaneous vehicles. The incident was still at the emergency stage, so no one stopped us going into the yard, where all the non-firefighters were busy dealing with the horses under the capable direction of Olivia. Except one.

'That's Eldridge,' I said, pointing to a man in a waxed jacket standing by a fire engine.

'Are you sure?'

'Who else would be avoiding the dirty work quite so brazenly? Go get him, Vic.'

She flashed me a grin. 'I shall approach him with a spirit of mutual co-operation and knuckledusters.'

The half dozen horses had never been at risk from the fire, but if you were locked in a stall next to a burning building with added sirens and shouting, you'd panic too. In these situations, accidental self-harm is the biggest danger.

Three beasts had already been led to the safety of a field up-wind of the fire, two more were being dealt with by other helpers, leaving Olivia and a young looking policeman outside the stall of a big stallion, who was bucking and rearing so much that they couldn't get near him.

'Conrad! Thank God,' said Olivia. 'Can you get a lead rope on him if we watch the door?'

'I'm not sure it's safe in there,' said the policeman. 'We should wait for the vet.'

'Don't be so wet,' said Olivia. 'Of course it's dangerous, that's why we need to get him out. You get ready with the door.'

I took one end of the lead rope and had a wild idea. Once, to escape the police, I'd hidden in a stable and narrowly escaped a trampling. I was in no hurry to repeat the experience. I loosened my coat and reached under my shirt to touch one of the Artefacts round my neck, just enough to draw on its reserves of Lux.

'Ok. I'm going in.'

The officer pulled open the door and I dodged into the stall. As soon as I got inside, I dived into my memory of water – a mythical place of Spirits where silence reigns. From that memory, I created a magickal Silence around me and the horse. Suddenly, every noise disappeared. The horse stopped to figure out what was going on, and in that moment I had him.

I grabbed the halter and snapped the clip into place, then jumped back. The Silence dropped as soon as I stopped focusing on it, and I let go of the rope sharpish, but that was fine because Olivia had the other end and the horse was more than happy to leave his stall. The pair trotted off leaving me with the stunned policeman. Time to strike.

'Squadron Leader Conrad Clarke,' I said with a handshake.

'Oh. Hi. I'm Barney Smith.'

'That's the livestock accounted for. It's lucky that Mrs Bentley was on hand to take charge.'

I could see it playing over his face – he'd suddenly found himself out of his depth in an emergency where he should have been in charge. At least he had the courage to admit it.

'I'm not so good round big animals. I'm from Barrow, so I'm more used to humans.' He scratched his chin. 'I did once get called to an escaped lion, though. We let the handlers deal with it.'

I shuddered inside at the memory of a close encounter with some magickal lions deep under a Welsh hillside. I stepped away from the stables. 'All sorted. We can let the firefighters do their bit.'

'Yeah. Then the insurance guy is going to have a look.'

That did not compute. This was a potential crime scene. Where was the duty CID team? Where were the forensic technicians? 'Insurance guy?'

He pointed towards the tender. 'Mr Eldridge from the Langdale Union Insurance Company. We have an arrangement with them.'

'Oh yes?'

'Where a property is insured with one of the Union insurance companies, they investigate first. Saves us a lot of money.'

I'll bet it does. I didn't say anything for a moment while this sank into my understanding: the Mages of Lakeland have managed to subvert the Lancashire & Westmorland Constabulary. Quite an achievement.

It was PC Smith who spoke first. 'Funny thing is, Fellside Farm isn't on the list of Union covered properties. Must be a new policy.' He paused. 'Did that woman come with you?' he said, meaning Vicky. I could almost see the dots joining inside his head. 'And you obviously know the horsey lady who dialled 999.' He checked his phone. 'Olivia Bentley.' He left the statements hanging, expecting me to fill the gaps. This lad may not be so good with horses, but he clearly has a future in the police force.

I weighed up the risks of declaring my hand against the chance of walking away incognito. 'Mrs Bentley knew I was in the area and called me to help her. She lives on the Fylde, so no one else was near and she knew I was good with horses.'

He couldn't argue with that, so I took it a step further and denied all knowledge of my partner. 'The other one flagged me down. I think she put her car in a ditch to avoid the ambulance and she said she had to get here urgently. It looks like she's working with Mr Eldridge.'

I dug out one of my business cards and offered it to PC Smith, who accepted it and took a glance. There was no mention of the King's Watch, Merlyn's Tower or magick, just my name, rank, contact details, the RAF badge and the shield for 7 Squadron.

'Sorry sir,' he said. 'I didn't realise you were a serving officer.'

'Why should you? If you'll excuse me, I'll check on the horses.'

'Thanks.'

Thanks? Poor lad thought I was doing him a favour. I've broken enough laws to know that he shouldn't be allowing me anywhere near Olivia, that my appearance should be treated as suspicious and that he should know I was giving him yards of RAF blue flannel. I wasn't going to blame him, though. When you outsource fatal accidents to a mysterious insurance company, you've already let your standards slip so far that a bit of witness collusion is nothing.

7 — *From the Ashes*

When I tracked her down, Olivia had the horses calm enough to leave them be in the field. Two of the equine rescue party had been passing motorists who'd stopped to help out; the other was a very nervous stable girl. The motorists went back to their journey with Olivia's thanks, and we left the stable girl near the beasts and moved to the middle of the field to compare notes.

'Thank you so much, Conrad. This is above and beyond. Ooh, can I nick a cigarette?'

I lit two and said, 'I think everything's in hand as far as you're concerned, Olivia.'

'I wish I'd never clapped eyes on that mare. What's going to happen to her and her foal?'

'Carry on looking after them and bill the estate. The bigger problem is the horse's owner. Let's start with his name.'

'Rod Bristow.'

'Tell me everything you know about the late Mr Bristow.'

She tipped her head to the side. 'Why are you bothered?'

'I'm just collecting information. It'll get passed upstairs, then someone will be on the hunt for Mr Bristow's killer.'

'He was murdered?'

'Well, what do you think?'

'I … well, I don't know. So long as you don't think that I had anything to do with it.'

'Me? No, but the more you can tell me about him, the more leads will point elsewhere when my boss looks at the file.'

'Your boss?'

She went a little paler under her outdoor tan, and I left her question hanging.

'Right,' she said. 'I'd never heard of him until he sent me an email enquiry, said he'd heard of the Research Centre and looked us up. It's common enough.'

'Go on.'

'I rang him, we talked numbers, I emailed our terms and he brought the mare. He came a few times before she foaled and a few times after.'

'Alone?'

She pointed to the stable girl. 'Sophie usually came with him.'

I had no idea what Vicky was going to discover in the cottage, especially with the Langdale Assessor looking over her shoulder, but we play to our strengths: hers is Sorcery, mine is horses.

'Who did the sampling and microchipping?'

All horses have to have a passport, and they have to be microchipped and have their DNA sampled before they're thirty days old.

'I have no idea,' said Olivia. 'Rod Bristow got his own vet to come down and do it. She turned up at the yard when I was in Oxford and I never met her.'

'Then, if I were you, I'd get myself down to that ambulance and get checked over for shock and smoke inhalation. It'll keep PC Barney Smith off your back while I talk to Sophie.'

'Thanks, Conrad, I will.' She walked down the field, shoulders a lot more slumped than when we'd met on Friday. She turned around. 'Would you be offended if I asked not to be kept informed?'

'Me? No. I'm just a tradesman, Olivia.'

'I … Oh. Right.' She turned back and shoved her hands in her coat pockets.

I made my way over to the horses and their minder. 'It's Sophie, isn't it?'

The girl looked cold, frightened and completely lost. She had a round, slightly flat face with big eyes that were shedding tears. She nodded and wiped the back of her hand over her face. I took out a half packet of tissues and offered her one. They were in my coat because I'd known I'd need them for Mina. Sophie choked out a thank-you and I gave her a moment.

I pointed to Olivia's back, now crossing the yard. 'Did Mrs Bentley tell you that Mr Bristow was dead when she arrived?'

'Yeah. Poor Rod. I can't believe it. He looked fine this morning.'

'You work here?'

'I'm doing a year here before I go to Myerscough College to do equine studies. I didn't get all me GCSEs.'

I circled my arms around. 'This isn't a racing stables, so what did Mr Bristow do?'

'Oh, he farms. Sheep mostly. Well, it's only sheep. There's four horses in livery and he was trying to breed off the others.'

It was time to put things on a more formal footing. 'I'm not just a friend of Mrs Bentley.'

Sophie blushed. 'I've met her husband. I thought from the way you watched her you had something going on.'

Oops. That was not the footing I'd intended. It was my turn to blush, though in my defence, Olivia's back view is very watchable.

'No, Sophie. I also work for the security services.'

Her hand flew to her mouth. 'Why? Rod's a farmer. He's not a terrorist.'

'Terrorism is only one of our interests. You'll have to give a statement to the police in the end, so it would help you — and me — if we just had a chat first.'

Down in the yard, breathing apparatus was being removed and hoses reeled in. Vicky and Eldridge seemed to be having their first argument, if the hand gestures were anything to go by.

'What do you want to know?' asked Sophie.

'Two things. First, tell me everything that happened today.'

'I got in at eight. I came on me bike from Grange.' She paused, uncertain about whether that was too much information. I nodded to show that I was interested. 'Rod brings me a cup of tea. I never drank tea until I came here. Doesn't half warm you up. Rod makes a great cup of tea.' She paused. 'He made one. Is he really dead?'

'I'm sorry. You must have liked him.'

'He was dead kind. I mean ...' She took a moment and another tissue.

'Did he have any family?'

'His wife died of cancer three years ago. He has a daughter and grandkids in London. She's nice, but the kids are a handful. They're not used to the country, and the cottage isn't that big.'

'Tell PC Smith her name. He'll need to notify her as soon as possible. Now, what happened after the cup of tea?'

'You can tell what Rod's up to by his trousers. He was wearing his indoor trousers this morning. It's funny, 'cos I asked if he were expecting visitors, and he said no.'

'Did you see him again?'

'Another cup of tea at ten o'clock. I was mucking out when Mrs Bentley arrived.'

This was the awkward part. 'Was there a delivery to the cottage?'

'Yeah. I didn't see it, but I heard the van engine stop here.'

I tried to keep a straight face. 'And that was before Mrs Bentley arrived.'

'No. I mean, I thought she came first.'

'Are you sure, Sophie?'

'Not completely.'

'Best stick to what you know when you talk to PC Smith. Just stick to what you're certain about. Presumably Mrs Bentley came running to warn you.'

'She did. She said that she'd found him dead and there was a fire. We waited for a bit, then the first fire engine came, but they couldn't get the fire under control and the smoke started blowing into the stables and the horses started to panic.'

I looked back to the cottage, and saw Vicky putting on overalls and a hard hat.

'That's excellent, Sophie. Now for the other question, and I need you to tell me the truth.'

'I have!'

'I know, so keep going. Who really owned that mare in foal you took to Mrs Bentley's stables?'

Mark Hayden

She looked down at the cottage, at the fire engines, the ambulance and the police car. It was starting to sink in that her ride to Fellside Farm this morning had been the end of something. I decided to give her a nudge.

'Sometimes a secret can be dangerous. If you tell me, it won't be a secret anymore.'

'Dermot. It sounded like Dermot. Rod used to make a joke that it was spelt *Diarmuid*.'

'I take it he was Irish.'

'Yeah. He had a black pickup and it had a Duddon Valley Eventing sticker in the window.'

'That's very observant of you.'

She shrugged off the praise. 'I notice things to do with horses. When I checked over the mare, I don't think she can have travelled very far and the Duddon Valley's not very far.'

'Even better. These horses will be okay up here for a while. We need to get you warmed up and sorted out. Have you told your parents yet? They'll be worried if they hear about the fire from somewhere else.'

I started to walk down the hill; Sophie fell into step next to me. 'I left my phone in the tack room.' She smiled. 'See? Millennials don't *always* have their phone on them. I'll call when we get down.'

'Good. Who was Mr Bristow's vet?'

'Mr Kerridge in Cartmel.'

'Does Mr Kerridge have a lady colleague?'

She tsked. 'You mean a woman?'

'I do. Sorry.'

'You're as bad as me dad. No, he doesn't.' She'd noticed that I was lurching a little over the rough grass. 'Did you get kicked before when you did your rescue act?'

'No. It's an old injury.'

'But you still ride?'

'I'm not too proud to use a mounting block when I need to.'

She finished my thought. 'And when you're on horseback, nothing matters.'

I gave her a smile. 'Same when you're flying. Unless someone's shooting at you, of course.'

We were in the yard, and the stench of burnt, wet building blew over us on the breeze. Sophie swallowed hard. 'I think I might see if Mum can come up.'

I handed her my card. 'If anyone gets in touch, other than PC Smith, you might want to give me a call. Any time. Thank you, Sophie, and good luck.'

The card disappeared into the back pocket of her jeans, and she disappeared into a building well away from the fire.

Vicky and Eldridge came out of the ruined cottage as one of the fire appliances pulled away. The team leader from the other engine and PC Smith

58

converged on the hard-hatted pair, as did I, as fast as I could over the slippery wet concrete.

Before Vicky could make eye contact with me, I spoke up in my loudest voice. 'Excuse me, it's Victoria, isn't it?'

Everyone turned to look at the talking lamppost, including Vicky, who picked up on my use of her Sunday name and knew that there was something wrong. 'Yes?' she said.

'If you want a lift back to your car, I'll be waiting over there with Mrs Bentley.'

'Thanks,' said Vicky, turning away quickly.

Eldridge frowned. He didn't like it, but he didn't say anything, either.

Olivia didn't look good. She was sitting at the back of the ambulance clutching her phone like the end of an anchor rope. 'They need to go,' she said, pointing to the paramedic. 'The police surgeon is on his way to deal with Rod Bristow, and I don't need to go to hospital, so they need to get on.' She was wittering, and she knew it. She shivered and forced herself to look up. 'Conrad, I've had a phone call.'

I took her hand and helped her down the steps. 'Let's be useful. I'll drive both of us into Cartmel and buy a bucketload of coffee. If there's somewhere that does take-out, that is. Give me your keys.'

Before we left, I did a pantomime for PC Smith's benefit to show what I was up to. He nodded enthusiastically while the firefighters shook their heads to decline my offer. That would save me a few quid.

There was just enough room to squeeze Olivia's Range Rover past the remaining engine. As soon as we got free, she turned round in her seat to face me. 'What's going on, Conrad? While I was talking to Rod this morning, when he was still alive, someone was picking up his horses from FERC.'

This wasn't making me feel any better, though I couldn't say that I was surprised. 'What happened?'

'I don't know, and what's worse, Becka doesn't know either.'

I paused at the junction. 'Eh?'

'Becka. My head groom. She said that someone turned up, gave them the paperwork, and the next thing anyone knew, the horses were gone *and they'd mucked out the stalls.* No horses, no manure for a DNA sample. Nothing. What have I got myself into this time?'

I had a strong suspicion that FERC had been visited by an Occulter, someone who'd used magick to twist the staff's senses just enough for them to perceive the event but not the details. They hadn't forgotten, they'd just not known what was happening. I wasn't going to share this suspicion with Olivia unless I had to. It was time to try out a cover story I'd been thinking about while Vicky was convalescing at Elvenham House.

'Olivia, I think they may have been given a sedative. A very mild one, nothing to worry about. I don't suppose your visitors left any paperwork behind.'

'Becka says she must have binned it by accident. All she could find was a blank piece of scrap paper where the dockets should be.'

I could see the ambulance coming up behind us in my mirror. 'This is very important, Olivia. Was Julian there when this happened?'

'No. He's at the racecourse.'

'Good.' I pulled away from the junction, heading for the village. Julian – Olivia's husband – would be immune to the Work used on the FERC staff, and Fylde Racecourse is only five minutes away. 'Ring him now. Tell him to get home and get hold of that piece of paper. Tell him to do it this second. I don't care if he's hosting a birthday lunch for A P McCoy, understand? Get him back to FERC.'

'Why?'

'Do you want to stay out of trouble or not? And when you've called him, ring Becka and tell her to hold on to that paper as if her life depends on it.'

I'd had to drive, navigate the bends, avoid the stone walls and shout at Olivia simultaneously. And they say men can't multi-task. We were now in the tiny village square, outside the Cartmel Village Shop, of Sticky Toffee Pudding fame. Very nice it is, too. I left Olivia in the car making calls and went to stock up on coffee (and tea for Sophie). When I got back, Olivia looked warmer and less lost.

'Julian's on his way. Becka is searching the office.'

'Good.' It was time for part two of my newly minted cover story for mundane parties. 'Look, Liv, you need to know a bit more.'

She sighed. 'I was hoping I wouldn't have to, but this is getting a bit too close to home.'

'My partner, Vicky, is a highly skilled scientific officer. Together, we look at things that shouldn't happen. We investigate tech companies and university research labs. They follow the rules, mostly. When they don't, we step in.'

'Give me a fag. I can blame you if Julian smells it in the car.'

I waited for her to ask awkward questions. Olivia sipped her coffee and smoked. A very wise monkey.

There were only four people at the farm when we got back. Sophie was talking to PC Smith while Vicky and Mr Eldridge talked on their phones from opposite corners of the yard. Everyone gravitated to Olivia's car when I put the tray of drinks and bag of pastries on the bonnet.

I got a good look at Vicky while Barney outlined what was going to happen now: police surgeon, private ambulance, boarding-up service. My partner was a little sooty round the edges but otherwise none the worse for her experiences. Sophie was now wearing a big woolly hat that had *Grandma's knitting* written all over it. Metaphorically.

The party was about to break up when Olivia got a message. 'Julian says he's finally found that paperwork you were after. Becka had put it in the fire basket.'

'Tell him to put it in a safe place, preferably at the racecourse,' I said, trying not to look at Vicky while I said it.

Everyone, even Eldridge, thanked me for the drinks and cakes. The Langdale Assessor was in his forties, average height and had that healthy outdoor look which said that the Lakeland Fells were not just scenery to him. His face had lines and a perpetual frown. Whether that was from too much squinting against the sun or from a habitual bad temper was hard to say.

When it became clear to him that I wasn't going to strike up a casual conversation, he made his apologies and left, shaking hands with PC Smith and ignoring Vicky completely.

A minute later, I offered "Victoria" a lift back to her car and said goodbye to everyone. I don't think many adults had shaken Sophie's hand properly before – you know, firm grip, smile, eye contact, key word. When I did it, she looked as if I'd handed her a winning lottery ticket and she nearly curtsied.

'You've made a friend there,' said Vicky when we were completely out of earshot.

'I wasn't trying to make friends with Eldridge,' I responded.

For the first time since her *cardiac event*, Vicky tried to kick my bad leg. It was then that I knew she was truly recovered. She missed, by the way.

'Howay, man. Are you thick or what?'

I stood out of range of her swing. 'Yes. No. About what?'

'That rosy-cheeked stable girl. She's smitten with you.'

'Sophie? She's seventeen! And she's in shock.'

Vicky shook her head. 'Whatever, Uncle Conrad, but I wouldn't offer her a lift anywhere on your own.'

'Shut up and get in the car.'

While we got comfortable, Vicky's words did niggle a bit. A teenage girl? Really? Then again, Vicky was no great judge when it came to affairs of the heart.

'Where are we going?' she asked.

'The Swan at Newby Bridge. It's lunchtime.'

'I don't know about lunch, but I could do with a drink.' She loosened her coat. 'Why didn't you want the police to know we're together?'

'Instinct. How did you get on with Eldridge, and was that the Boss you were on the phone to?'

'Badly, and yes, in that order. Long and short, we've got a case, but no leads.'

'I think I might have one. Go on.'

61

She looked out of the window for a second. 'When I told Hannah about the Union Assessors working openly with the police, she went mental. Last time I heard her that angry was at you. She lost it big time.'

'It's easy to forget she used to be a detective inspector.'

'Aye. I heard some new Yiddish swear words before she'd finished. I think they were swear words. Anyway, she says we haven't to rock the boat.' She smiled. 'Then she said, "That especially applies to Mr Wrecking Ball." And she also said well done, to both of us.'

Mr Wrecking Ball? Charming. 'So what happened in the cottage?'

'With Eldridge or with Rod Bristow?'

'Gossip first. Is Eldridge really that bad? I saw you arguing before you went in.'

'I'll tell you what, he's a right plonker, and no mistake. He got all humpy about safety gear and fire risk accreditation.'

'But you won him round.'

'I was gonna threaten him with you. I was gonna say, "Don't make me call the Watch Captain." Then I thought: a) that's no way for an independent woman to behave, and b) What if he's not scared of you?'

In professional terms, I try to think of us as interdependent, but never mind. 'So what did you do?'

'Said we'd seal the cottage and wait for the Invisible College to send someone.'

'And he took that?'

'I did tell a porkie. I said I could declare it a radiation hazard. I've got a fake Geiger counter on me sPad.'

'Neat. I'll have to remember that. How did it go when you got inside?'

'He was professional enough. He waited until I'd finished and listened to what I said. In the end, he didn't argue. He wasn't happy, mind, but he took it.'

'That's because you're good at your job. What *did* you find?'

'That Rod Bristow was killed by the same Work that Adaryn used to give me a cardiac arrest. It was horrible.' She shivered. 'I didn't tell Eldridge that I'd once been on the receiving end of one. I just took me time and a lot of deep breaths.'

'I'm sorry, Vic.'

'I know. I'll have to live with it. At least I am still alive, unlike that poor sod. Instead of a mad partner and a handy Druid to bring him back to life, all Rod got was the magickal encore: a very powerful Pyrogenesis Work. I'll tell you what, Olivia was lucky that only her scarf caught fire. If she hadn't been so quick to scarper, she'd be toast, too.'

There was just a hint in her voice, just something not quite as it should be. The joke about Olivia getting burnt to death was a lot more tasteless than we usually run to. I let it be for now. Instead, I focused on the job. 'And Rod was no Mage?'

'Categorically not. He was a mundane victim of magickal attack. Our case, and butt out Mr Eldridge.'

We were in the car park at the Swan Hotel and Vicky undid her seatbelt. 'For the next part, you need a crash course in Cursing, and no, I don't mean naughty words. I'm going to get washed, you get me a large mojito and a killer burger.'

'A squirrel burger? They don't sell them here. I think it was the Famous Wild Boar.'

'Stop messing. You're doing me head in. Squirrels? Wild boars?'

'There's a pub called the Famous Wild Boar. They offered squirrel burgers as a gimmick.'

'I want a gourmet burger. Made from beef.'

8 — The Luck of the Irish

It was a disappointed but much cleaner Vicky Robson who sat down to a plate of sandwiches and bottle of sparkling water. Naturally, she focused on the important things.

'Where's me mojito? And why no burger?'

'No alcohol on duty, and have you seen the prices in here? I could never claim a burger on expenses.'

'Three nights ago, we were staying in a Michelin starred hotel.'

'That was a personal gift. This is work. What did you say about cursing?'

She pouted. An actual pout. 'And this is me lunch break, so you can wait. I'm starving.'

I waited until she had her mouth full before I said, 'You never did tell me about Li Cheng.'

She paused in mid-masticate, took a deep breath through her nose, then carried on chewing. A glug of water. 'Sod off.'

'Fair's fair. I didn't ask you about him last week because you were convalescing. You couldn't wait to grill me about Mina, to say nothing of gift-wrapped condoms. Spill.'

She put her sandwich down. 'Mina cares about you. I've met her. I've heard it in her voice on the phone. I can't wait to see you together, especially if she wears flat shoes. Right now, I can take the mick because you're happy and she's safe.' She shrugged. 'You've met Cheng.'

'And he doesn't care for anyone as much as he cares for himself.'

She shook her head. 'You don't understand. He's great company out of the office. He makes me feel like a princess. He's had a really hard time in Merlyn's Tower – the first ethnically Chinese Watchman. He wanted to be the Deputy, but the Vicar of London Stone wouldn't let a non-Captain apply. And then there's the pressure from his family.'

I held out my fingers to tick them off. 'Hannah is Jewish, Tennille and Rick are Afro-Caribbean, Annelise is Dutch. You're a Geordie. I'd say that Cheng fits right in.'

'Let's not go there, okay?'

I held up my hands. 'Sorry.'

'I'll forgive you in exchange for pudding.'

While I got the dessert menu, Vicky took out her sPad. She ordered sticky toffee; I ordered a pot of coffee. Business done, she turned her sPad to show me something.

I rotated the screen in several directions, but it still looked like a toddler had tried to draw a proof of Pythagoras' Theorem then scribbled all over it in a temper. 'I give up.'

'It's me Enscripting coursework. I passed.'

I handed back the sPad. 'Enscripting?'

'Putting a magickal Work on paper. That's only a photograph, mind. The original was Enscribed with a quill pen, hand-made ink and enhanced paper. I hated it, and I was rubbish at it, too. Another reason I couldn't take to the Inkwell Bitter, even if it is made with water from your well. Too many memories of indelible stains on me fingers and ruined nails.'

'What did your coursework do?'

She looked round the bar. There was no sign of dessert, or of other patrons. With a confident swirl of her hands through her hair and a tingle of magick, she turned her dark brown locks a vivid green with a hint of phosphorescence. 'What do you think?'

'Impressive. I can just see you in a mermaid costume.'

She wiped away the colour. 'In your dreams. Ooh, pudding.'

When the waiter had gone, she continued. 'I showed you the Enscripting because that's the basic technique for creating a hex – a curse on someone delivered remotely by spell. The actual writing is called a Malaglyph.'

One of the things I hate about magick is the jargon, and the fact that there are two different sets doesn't help.

'Slow down, Vic. You know I can't take too much new stuff at once.'

She closed her eyes in sticky toffee heaven. 'Mmm. This is good. Have you heard the old saying that magic used for evil will return to the sender threefold?'

'Not since I joined the world of real magick.'

'Right. Lux is just a force, like gravity. You don't have evil gravity, so no evil magick either.'

'I'd guessed.'

'But a curse is still a curse – magick used to cause bad things to happen to someone else. Talking of Li Cheng, he once cursed a guy's car so that every time it came to traffic lights, they turned red. Even the pelican crossings.' She suddenly remembered who she was talking to. 'Don't tell anyone that, please.'

'I won't, but I won't forget, either.'

'I know. Sadly. There's two basic approaches to cursing. You can Bedevil your victim by getting some kind of Spirit to do your dirty work. Very difficult and very dangerous. Remember Deborah was an ace Necromancer, but even she didn't try it on you.'

'There's always a risk to using mercenaries. I've seen enough of them.'

'I never thought of it that way. Hmm. The other sort of curse is a hex, and for that you need Imprint targeting. Are you gonna pour that coffee?'

'There you go. Imprint targeting?'

'If you can get a key to someone's Imprint, you can combine it with some nasty Work. You can use vellum, but most use Parchment.'

'Aren't they the same thing?'

'In the mundane world, yes, they're both animal skin, but Parchment with a capital "P" is thick paper treated to hold patterns of Lux. With the right ink, you can theoretically Enscript any Work.'

'In theory?'

'In theory. In practice, they act as a special record rather than a live Work. Like a blueprint. You can't live in the blueprint of a house.'

'Then how...?'

'...That's why I asked Mrs Bentley about the seal. That's where you store the Lux. There are books on how to do all this in the Queen's Esoteric Library, but you have to get special permission to read them.'

'Why haven't I come across them before?'

'Because they're very difficult to create and because, to a more experienced Mage than you, they look like this.' She showed me a cartoon drawing of a bomb: sticks of TNT, wires and an alarm clock. 'Would you mess with that? Poor Rod Bristow had no chance. To him, that paper was just a document. If you want to use a Malaglyph on a trained Mage, you have to trick them into opening it.'

I took my coffee and said that I was going for a smoke. When I got back, I had a question for Vicky. 'Can you work back, forensically?'

'If the Malaglyph hasn't been incinerated, yes.'

I told her about Diarmuid the horse dealer and about Julian Bentley having custody of the blank piece of paper – or Parchment, as I shall now have to call it.

'How far is it to this Duddon Place? *Where* is this Duddon place?' asked Vicky when I'd finished.

'It's a rather beautiful estuary out to the west.'

'West, shmest, as Hannah might say. Is it on the way back to Clerkswell?'

'Definitely not.'

'Then we'll start with Diarmuid. How do we find him?'

'Let's go and ring Hannah from the car.'

I settled the bill and led Vicky through the door by the bridge. When we were next to the water, I pointed left. 'See up there? It gets wider.'

'Aye.'

'That's the bottom of Windermere, England's biggest lake. The top is eleven miles away, and beyond that are the Langdales. This river in front of us, flowing out of Windermere, is the Leven, so that's why the local Union is called Langdale-Leven.'

'And you're telling me this because?'

'If I have to learn about Enscription and Malaglyphs, you can learn some geography.'

She looked at the fast-flowing river, admired the swans that give the hotel its name and shook her head. 'Nah. When you can Enscribe, I'll go on a map reading course.'

We had to wait for Hannah to call us back, then give her the update. I'd barely started asking if her twin sister in the City Police could search for Diarmuid when she cut me off.

'Talk to the Duddon-Furness Union. If Diarmuid's a Mage, they'll know him. If not, then call Ruth.'

'I'm not sure that tipping off the Union is a good idea, ma'am.'

'They won't dare mess you about. They'll want you off their turf asap.'

'Yes, ma'am.'

'Will you stop ...' She sighed. 'It's like this, OK? I got so angry after Vicky told me what they were up to with the police that I fired off an angry email to all the Union chairmen. They know we haven't got the staff or the power to do anything about it, but while there's an active case, they'll be on their best behaviour.'

A classic case of email in haste and repent at leisure. Vicky had a different take.

'Are they all men, these chairmen?' she said.

There was a micro-pause before Hannah responded. Just enough to let Vicky know that she was out of order, though whether Vicky picked up on it is another matter.

'One of them is a Gnome,' said Hannah. 'The other seven are a variety of sexes and genders.'

Vicky groaned. 'Please tell me it's not a Gnome in Duddon.'

Again, the micro-pause. My antennae were starting to twitch. Hannah's voice dropped several degrees in temperature. 'Clan Skelwith are based in Langdale-Leven. Their scion is Chairman. Ask Maxine to email an up-to-date directory of the Grand Union.'

I dived in. 'Thank you, ma'am. We'll get straight on it.'

Maxine Lambert, Clerk to the Watch, is the only other smoker in Merlyn's Tower. She likes me. I sent her a quick text while Vicky was trying to get a 4G signal on her sPad.

'We'll head towards Barrow,' I said. 'With a bit of luck, we can do this by phone.'

We hadn't been on the road long when Maxine delivered the goods. Vicky sorted a number for the Duddon-Furness Union secretary and put in the call. An older sounding man with a local accent answered.

'Hi. I'm Watch Officer Robson, with Watch Captain Clarke. We ...'

'... The sheep crapped in our square, did it?'

'Erm...'

'The Chairman said that you were on the hunt for someone, somewhere in the Particular.'

Vicky was still trying to get her head round the ovine reference.

'That's right,' I said. 'We're investigating a homicide in Cartmel. We'd like to speak – urgently – to a man, first name Diarmuid. He's connected with horses, he's probably Irish and may or may not be a Mage.'

'Diarmuid Driscoll is a Mage alright, and he's produced more winners in the Waterhead Chases than any other breeder. He's as Irish as a leprechaun, too.'

'And where can we find Mr Driscoll?'

'Blackthwaite Stables. It's just off the Millom Road. Take the Hallthwaites turning.'

Vicky immediately started to look it up, so I asked the secretary the obvious question. 'Do you know of any reason for us to take extra precautions?'

'With Diarmuid? Wellingtons, perhaps. Do you want me to notify the Assessor?'

'That shouldn't be necessary.'

'What if you arrest him? You'll not be taking him to London, and you won't get in the Esthwaite Rest without an escort. I'll tell her to be on standby in Millom, shall I?'

'That would be good, and text us her contact details, please.'

'Will do.'

Vicky leaned over to re-program the satnav, then said, 'What in Nimue's name was that about the sheep crapping in his square?'

'It's a thing they do at some village fetes, like a lottery. You put some hurdles round a piece of grass, mark out squares on the grass and sell tickets for each square. At a suitable point in the afternoon, you put a sheep inside the hurdles. Whoever bought the ticket for the square where it first leaves a dropping wins the prize.'

She looked at me as if I were insane. 'Don't the sheep run under the hurdles?'

'Different sort of hurdle. They're … never mind.'

'Is that what passes for entertainment in the countryside?'

'Why do you think we invented cricket? Longer attention spans.'

'Can we go back to London before I lose touch with reality altogether?'

'It's worse up here. Look up the World Gurning Championships and Cumberland Wrestling to see what the natives get up to in Lakeland.'

We were well on the way to Millom before Vicky surfaced from surfing her sPad. 'Conrad, they're mad. Completely mad.'

'And that's what they think about the rest of us.'

She shook her head in mock despair. 'How come you know so much about the place? I thought you went straight from Clerkswell to the RAF.'

'I did, and the RAF sent me to Air Sea Rescue in Wales, which isn't far by chopper. I specialised in Lakeland rescues. Did over a hundred ops, so I know it pretty well topographically. I also spent a week with a mountain rescue team, just to get a feel for their part of the operation. Believe me, flying a chopper in a blizzard to pick up a casualty is a lot easier than climbing the mountain to find him in the first place. Once, I rescued this tech guy. A multi-millionaire. He held a big dinner for everyone at the Samling, so I took a week's leave to explore further. Look, over there, that's the Duddon Estuary.'

'It's beautiful.'

It was afternoon, so the valley was lit by uninterrupted sunshine. I pointed across the water. 'Blackthwaite Stables is over there. Only a mile by chopper, but a long way by road.'

'Is that not … Oh. It's a railway bridge. I can tell that by the choo-choo going across it.'

Blackthwaite stables was exactly where you'd expect a magickal operation to be – down an unmarked track off a quiet lane; there was no board announcing their presence or featuring their website. Two hundred yards down the track was a gate, then a pasture, then a cluster of buildings, fenced off and protected by a second gate.

'We're off the public road,' I said. 'Would you mind driving – I need to get the Hammer out of the boot, and I might as well do gate duty. The walk will do me good.'

Vicky jogged round to the driver's side while I fastened on my holster. I didn't activate my Ancile (shield) because I don't have enough Lux to keep it up for long periods, and it gives me a headache.

I let her through the gate, and she waited until I'd closed it before driving slowly towards the buildings. When I'd opened the gate, I'd got a whiff of magick, just enough for a Ward to discourage the mundane or to trigger an alarm. Or both.

The next gate was the entrance to a complex consisting of stables, a bungalow and some sheds. It was altogether newer, cleaner and better appointed than poor Rod Bristow's hand-to-mouth operation. If Diarmuid wasn't a murderer, I might try to get Sophie a job here.

There was a gravelled area for staff and visitors' cars (empty), and no sign of human activity from the stables. I pushed the well-made and well-maintained gate open and glanced at the buildings. A man came out of the bungalow on my right. A man carrying a shotgun. A man raising his shotgun. A man firing his shotgun.

By then, I was already diving to my left and hoping that Vicky would put the car between me and the man (I'll call him Diarmuid for now).

None of the first shot hit me, but he was tracking me like a pro, and the Volvo hadn't started moving. I had a choice: stay still and reach for the Hammer to activate my Ancile, or take evasive action.

I considered the distance. At that range, so long as I protected my face, he'd be lucky to do terminal damage, so I pressed my left arm over my head and felt under my coat for the Hammer just as he fired.

Owww. Ow. Fuck. Ow. That hurt.

He'd have to reload; I was not disabled was and now protected. For once, my bad leg didn't spasm as I got up. Diarmuid was fast, but his hand had stuck in his pocket when he reached for more shells. I sprinted towards him as Vicky belatedly entered the fray. The Volvo hurtled through the open gate, and I saw the look on Diarmuid's face as the car smashed into him and he was catapulted over the bonnet and off the other side.

Oh, Vicky, what have you done?

She slammed on the brakes. Diarmuid was out of view behind the car, so I ran round the back as she got out. She kicked him. Hard.

'Get the gun,' she screamed.

'Captain Robson! Stand down!' I shouted.

She stopped kicking, bewildered.

'Vicky! Stop. Stand back. That's an order.'

She took two steps away from the writhing figure, and Diarmuid let out his first scream. Then another.

'Vicky, get over there, by the wall. Call that Assessor and get her here. Then call an ambulance. Say no more than that there's been a serious accident.'

'Conrad. You're bleeding. You've been shot.'

'And he's got a compound fracture. Move. Now.'

She stumbled backwards and bounced off the car, then staggered over to the stable wall. When I'd seen her take out her phone, I knelt down to check on Diarmuid. I was lying about the compound fracture, but something was definitely broken.

'Hold still, Mr Driscoll.'

'I can't. Jesus, Mary and Joseph, God it hurts. Can you not numb it?'

'Sorry. I don't carry anaesthetic.'

'With a feckin' Charm, you eejit. Use magick.'

'Sorry. Beyond me, I'm afraid. I really do need you to hold still. If you've ruptured an artery, there will be internal bleeding. I need to know.'

'What?' For a second, he lay still.

I pressed down on his shoulder with one hand. 'Tell me where it hurts.'

I squeezed gently on his hip joints and thighs. Nothing. The fracture must be at his knee or below. His life wasn't in danger, so I peeled off my coat. My shirt sleeve was already soaked with blood.

'You're under arrest,' I said to Driscoll.

'Time and a place, you feckin' eejit,' said the prisoner.

'The time is 14:50 and the place is Blackthwaite Stables, and you're still under arrest.'

'If that was supposed to be funny, I swear to God ...'

'I can't hear Rod Bristow laughing, Diarmuid, can you?'

He had nothing to say to that.

Vicky came slowly round the car, clutching her phone in trembling hands. 'They're on their way,' she whispered. 'Both of them. Assessor and Ambulance.'

'Move the car, Vicky. The story's going to be that Mr Driscoll was kicked by a horse and that you discharged the gun accidentally when retrieving it.'

'But ...' said Vicky.

'Are you on board with that, Diarmuid?'

'Just hurry up that feckin' ambulance.'

I held out my good arm, and Vicky helped me to my feet.

Her face was stark, paper white with black tears of mascara forming. 'What have I done, Conrad?'

I pulled open the driver's door. 'You were nearly fed to a hungry Dragon. Your heart was stopped, oh, and you narrowly escaped being mauled by a psychotic lion. All you've done is come back to work too soon. You need a proper rest, and soon, but right now you need to move that car. I'd do it myself, but I don't want to get blood on the seats.'

'How do you...'

'Car. Move.'

I snatched my coat off the floor and snagged a cigarette as Vicky finally moved the Volvo. I could only draw one arm through its sleeve, and draped the other over my left shoulder. Diarmuid wasn't the only one who needed an ambulance.

Vicky was going to ask me how I could get shot and still function. I'll explain it to her later, when I've dealt with the woman speeding down the track on a motorcycle.

9 — A Reasonable Force

You never quite know what you're going to get with a biker (unless they're wearing Angels colours). This one spurned Hi-Viz clothing for black leathers, which told me something, as did the understated but powerful black Yamaha. She stared at Diarmuid and me as she drove slowly past. When she took off her helmet, she gave me her back view, and didn't turn round until she'd scraped shoulder length silver hair firmly away from her face.

Petra Leigh had a sharply pointed, inverted triangle of a face, pale lips and striking blue eyes that had to be magickally altered or coloured contacts.

'So this is how the mighty King's Watch operates,' was her opening salvo, delivered with the sort of cut-glass accent that even the poshest boarding schools were discouraging when I was a lad. Oh dear.

'Assessor Leigh,' I nodded in return.

'Assessor? It's not a rank, you know, it's a job. So, what's Dodgy Diarmuid been up to, and who called me?'

'My partner.' I jerked my head towards the Volvo, and Petra frowned over my shoulder.

'What's up with her?'

My car had been parked askew against the blank rear face of a stable block. Slumped on the floor, back to the wall, Vicky looked like she'd need the ambulance, too.

'You're dripping blood,' said Petra.

'And I've got two broken legs,' said Diarmuid. 'Petra, for the love of God, can you help me out?'

She dropped down next to Diarmuid and peeled off her gloves. There was no sign of the ambulance, and my plan was falling apart by the second. While Petra did something to Driscoll, I stepped back and pulled out my phone.

'Boss? I've got a problem.'

'Is anyone dead?'

'No, but…'

'Baruch Hashem. What have you done now?'

'We've arrested Diarmuid Driscoll, but he needs to go to hospital, as do I. The story…'

'Stop. Whose arse are you covering? Yours or Vicky's?'

'The Union Assessor is here. We don't want to…'

'Shut up, Conrad. Just for a second.'

I wasn't expecting that. Petra had her hands underneath Diarmuid's shirt, reaching round to his back. What on earth?

Hannah came back on the line. 'You are going to behave like an officer of the law, not a Deadwood Sheriff. Do you hear me?'

'Yes, ma'am.'

'What's she done?'

'How do you know it wasn't me?'

'You'd have killed Driscoll and lied about it afterwards.'

That was very hurtful, but probably true. I told her the story in two sentences.

'Then it goes to Scotland. The Depute Constable will investigate. Vicky stays on indefinite sick leave, and you'll be on desk duty when they've dug the pellets out of you, not that you need to worry about the Depute's enquiry if you've told me the truth.'

'Hannah, I'm worried about Vicky, not myself. She's too good to sacrifice.'

'Sacrifice?'

'If you order an investigation, she may never come back.'

There was a long pause. Could I hear a siren over the estuary? If that was the ambulance, it wouldn't be here for another ten minutes.

'I don't want to lose her, Conrad, I really don't. I brought her into the Watch. I sent her into the field. I want her to be the Watch's second female Captain one day soon, I really do, but I want her to enforce the law, not be above it. We can't be the solution if we're part of the problem.'

'Yes, ma'am. What about Driscoll?'

'You arrested him, yes?'

'Yes.'

'Then transfer him to the custody of the Union for now and get yourself to hospital. You're supposed to appear before the Occult Council on Wednesday, but you can do that by video link. Can you get to London by Thursday? Iain Drummond needs you to go to the Undercroft, and I'll come and get you myself if I have to.'

'I'll sort it, and I'll be there, ma'am.'

'I know you will. Take care, Conrad.'

I was starting to shiver, and my arm was going numb. I could see where Hannah was coming from. I'd faced similar dilemmas myself, in a twisted sort of way. I used to smuggle vodka into British bases in Afghanistan as a sideline, and one day my co-pilot reported for duty under the influence. I wasn't going to let him fly. No way. But if I'd reported him, there'd have been an investigation, so I pushed him off the steps. Somehow, that wasn't an option here.

Driscoll wasn't smiling, but he wasn't in agony either. Petra clearly had a gift for anaesthesia.

'Ms Leigh, can we have a word?' I said.

'It's Miss Leigh. What about?'

'The King's Watch would like to transfer the prisoner to your custody, and our Scottish branch will be conducting an investigation into his arrest.'

She chortled with laughter. 'You've changed your tune. What happened?'

73

'Hey!' said Diarmuid. 'I'm still here. There's no need to get the girl in trouble. She used reasonable force, and after all, I did shoot you. Why weren't you wearing your Ancile, man?'

None of the people who have ever shot at me – and there's been a lot, if you include the Taliban – have ever asked that question or regretted that I wasn't immune to their fire. I'd read this situation wrongly, somehow, and I needed time to work out how. Time I didn't have because the ambulance was arriving.

Petra made two of my choices for me. She pointed a finger at Diarmuid. 'Mr Driscoll, I am accepting you into the custody of the Duddon Union and releasing you on bail for medical treatment. Do you swear to present yourself for arraignment when required.'

'I swear.'

'Good. Mr Clarke, I'll order you a taxi, before you faint.'

'Thanks. I'd better see to Vicky.'

'Hey, tall guy,' said Diarmuid to my back. 'Why are you limping? I'm the one with the broken leg.'

I gave him the finger without bothering to turn round. When I got to the car, I took a bottle of water out and leaned against the bonnet. If I'd got down to Vicky's level, I might never have got up again.

'Howdy pardner,' I said in best Deadwood sheriff mode.

'Not for much longer. Can I have a fag before you arrest me?'

I lit one for her and groaned as I passed it down. 'Give me your phone.'

'Why?'

'Procedure.'

She handed it over without question, and even unlocked it first. She didn't twig what I was doing until I'd found *Mam* in the contacts and made the call.

'Erica? It's Conrad Clarke.'

'Howay man, what are you doing?' said Vicky.

'Is she okay?' said her mother.

I blocked my left ear with a bloody finger and turned my head away. 'She's fine, but she's had a shock. I'm going to put her in a taxi.'

'From Gloucester?'

'Sorry. I thought you knew. We're in the Lakes. Three hours, max.'

Vicky was trying to get up and grab the phone. I backed away.

'What's happened?' said Mrs Robson.

'Nothing. Honestly. It's just that I can't look after her any more, and she can't go back to London.'

'Why can't I speak to her?'

'You can. I called because she's stubborn.'

'You're not wrong. Put her on.'

I handed over the phone and lit my own cigarette.

74

The Millom taxi driver nearly fainted when he saw my arm, and definitely wouldn't countenance a trip to Newcastle. He did, however, deliver us to Furness General Hospital and recommended Arthur's Long Distance Cabs, who took the job but only for cash, and not until five o'clock. Vicky waited with me in A&E while they prepped an operating theatre. The pain in my arm had got so bad that I couldn't move it without gurning like a native.

'Have you any idea what officer training is like?' I said.

'A lot of shouting and running around,' she responded without taking her eyes off the poster telling us that fighting infections was everyone's responsibility.

'That just about sums it up. It's the same in all three services, but there's more mud at Sandhurst and more water at Dartmouth.'

She finally turned to look at me 'Is this supposed to help? I'm in deep shit, Conrad.'

'Shit, yes. Deep, no. Imagine we're driving to Clerkswell and the only choice is listening to me or listening to Classic FM.'

'I'm not getting in that taxi unless the driver lets me choose the music.' She sighed. 'Go on, then.'

'Officer cadets – of which I was one, obviously, are shouted at a lot. Really a lot. We were deprived of sleep, made to do pointless tasks endlessly and pushed to our physical limits. And you know why? I called it *non-destructive testing*. None of it was truly dangerous, and if you can't survive training, you shouldn't be allowed to have men and women depending on you.'

'Aye. I found that out today.'

'Think of Blackthwaite Stables as a training exercise. No one gets it right first time.'

She was appalled. 'You got shot. I broke a man's legs for no reason.'

'We'll both recover, and so will you. You're a brave woman, Vicky. You took Driscoll out to save me. That's priceless. Go home to Newcastle. Chill. Get your story straight for the Scottish investigation. And that's an order.'

Her phone pinged. 'Me taxi's here.' She stood up. 'Don't move.' She bent down and kissed my bald patch. 'I'll be back.'

'I'll try to keep out of trouble.'

'No chance of that.'

She slipped out of the cubicle and left me with nothing to distract me from the pain. I thought about calling my own mother, and had my phone half way out of my coat when the curtain twitched and PC Barnabas Smith appeared. He didn't have a bunch of grapes with him.

'Mr Clarke. How are you?'

I was, of course, wearing a hospital gown, a garment designed for maximum indignity. I abandoned my phone and rolled back, moving the covers in the process. Barney Smith's eyes nearly popped out when he saw the scars on my leg.

'Have you ever been shot?'

'I ... no.'

'I'm still at the thankful to be alive stage. It'll pass after the operation, when the anaesthetic wears off. Millom isn't your patch, is it? I was expecting the police, but not you personally. For some reason, the triage nurse wasn't happy when I said that there was no need to report it.'

He tried not to stare at my bad leg and said, 'I was on my way home when I saw another Assessor case on the log, near Millom. Then a walk-in gunshot victim appears in Furness General, so I put myself down to attend. Now, either you're a very fast worker, Mr Clarke, or you and Victoria Robson already knew each other. I saw her coming out of here.'

I laughed so hard that my left arm moved and reminded me why I needed surgery. Oww. 'She calls me Uncle Conrad, you know. She's single at the moment. Would you like me to give you her number?'

He went bright red, poor lad, and he knew he'd completely lost the initiative. He tried desperately to claw it back. 'Why isn't your shooting listed as an Assessor case? I checked the CCTV out front, and the taxi that brought you here was from Millom. I don't think that's a coincidence.'

I covered up my leg. It wouldn't hurt to test the waters. 'Would you really let a *shooting* be covered by an Insurance Assessor?'

Barney's cheeks had only just calmed down from my crack about Vicky's love life. They coloured up again. 'Not my place to ask, sir, but you must be connected to them.'

'Must I? I'm more connected to you than I am to them. You and I are both sworn public servants, as is Captain Robson.'

'Captain? She doesn't look ... I mean ...'

'Royal Military Police. On attachment, as am I.'

The curtains parted with a practised swish to reveal a nurse and a porter with a trolley.

Barney bounced on the balls of his feet in that way that police constables do. They must teach it at the police academy. He opened a Velcro pocket in his oversized yellow coat with a decisive rasp and took out a card. 'I'll write it up as an accident,' he said, tucking the card in my coat, next to the phone.

'Thank you. I won't forget.'

He left with a nod to me and the nurse. They took thirty-four pellets out of my arm, back, neck and side, leaving eleven in place. The surgeon said they'd probably work their way out eventually. No one came to visit me, though I did have long conversations with my parents, Mr Joshi (priest), Maxine Lambert (Watch Clerk), and even Helen Davies (Druid, still worried she'd done the right thing).

I avoided talking to my sister because she's after me for something, and the highlight, although painful, was a short conversation with Mina. It's difficult to be frank when your call may be monitored.

All Hannah said was that I should go to BAE Systems in Barrow when the hospital discharged me on Wednesday morning. I didn't dare ask about the Bristow case.

And Vicky? She got home safely and told me that she had appointments with a private cardiologist on Saturday morning and with the Depute Constable in a week's time.

The Devonshire Dock Hall dominates the skyline of Barrow in Furness. Compared to everything else in the town, it's huge, just like the contribution that BAE Systems makes to the local economy. You need a huge building to churn out nuclear submarines, and they don't come cheap.

As well as being huge, it's also a complete rabbit warren, and I didn't even know which rabbit hole to go down. I stood forlornly outside the main gate, staring at the impenetrable site map until a familiar black Yamaha pulled up down the road and a pillion passenger dismounted. Without raising her visor, Petra waved, gave me a thumbs-up and rode off.

There was no mistaking the passenger when she took off her helmet. It was the royal blue eyes that struck you first, then the sharp chin. From her father had come fuller, brighter lips and not quite so sharp a nose.

'Mr Clarke?'

'Conrad, please.'

'I'm Laura. Laura Leigh.'

'I'd guessed your last name already.'

She laughed. 'Mum tries to pass me off as her sister sometimes. She said you'd been in hospital. Is everything OK?'

'Getting there.'

'Good. The Union Chairman asked me to escort you through the BAE maze and help out with the video. It's a high-security link, but we need to keep out mundane snoopers. I don't suppose you've been here before.'

'I'm RAF, not Royal Navy. I have been to BAE Warton and Samlesbury a few times, mostly as an air chauffeur for the top brass.'

She looked confused. Laura was about thirty, and relaxed and happy in herself, though she had little of the poise and presence that her mother still radiated at twice her age. She also spoke like a Barrovian. It was then that I twigged why she was confused.

'I've only been a Mage since last Christmas. We'd better hurry.'

'Oh. Right. This way.'

It took over forty minutes to cover the forty metres from the pavement to a blacked-out Portakabin. I won't bore you with the details. Laura locked the door behind us and fiddled with her laptop just as I got a very agitated text from Hannah.

'Where are they?' I whispered when a large table surrounded by empty chairs snapped into focus.

'Hidden. Only Members get to see other Members. For everyone else, it's audio only. I'll put the sound on.' She tapped a key, and a woman's voice filled the Portakabin.

'… budget for research should be linked to …'

I didn't catch the rest because I wasn't interested, and stared at the Council Chamber instead. It was ornate but not excessive, with the self-confidence that Empire gave to Victorian architects and designers.

However, none of the similar spaces I've ever visited has had the portrait of an Elven king on the wall. I assume it was an Elf of some sort. Before I could squint more closely, there was a tap of the gavel and a figure appeared at the head of the table.

'Now we come to the matter of Enhanced Firearms. Do we have Watch Captain Clarke on the line?'

'One second, Mr President,' said an invisible young man's voice.

The President of the Occult Council was male, grey of suit and hair, and blue of tie. If you'd have told me that he was the Right Honourable Member for the Prosperous Suburbs, I'd have nodded in agreement.

Laura had informed me that a red light would go on when they could see and hear us. It blinked into life over the screen, and I stood to attention and saluted. My senior officer was there, somewhere, and even invisible officers must be saluted.

'Take a seat, Mr Clarke,' said the President. 'You're rather close to the camera.'

'Sir.'

'We've asked you to address the Council for several reasons. For one thing, we're very keen to hear about this Dragon. How did it begin?'

His questions led me through the Dragon Brotherhood case in a brisk fashion, and he finished with an observation. 'I sincerely hope that any other eggs remain undisturbed for another two thousand years.'

'You'll be lucky,' said a throaty voiced woman. Was that the Custodian of the Great Work from Salomon's House? I think it was.

The President gave a sharp look at one of the empty chairs before thanking me and disappearing back into invisibility. Seconds later, the red light went out.

'I'm still not sure that I believe it,' said Laura.

'Believe what?'

'I'd heard about the Dragon. I thought it was a story, you know. A bit of truth…'

'You're saying that I don't look like a Dragon slayer, is that it?'

'Oh no. I didn't mean that. Mum said that you knew what you were doing.'

'Don't worry, Laura, I don't take it personally. The half-naked Druid with rippling muscles and a spear was a much better poster-boy for Dragon Slaying. It's a shame that he was blown up.'

78

She smiled tentatively and took out what looked like a child's toy from a deeply disturbed horror film: a ceramic eyeball, complete with red veins, on top of a conical spring. She stared into the eyeball and placed it gently on the trackpad of her laptop. 'Mum said that you'd want to hear the firearms licensing debate. Now I know why. This little Charm will keep the cover video running while I get us some coffee.'

If I'd had magickal rounds at Bardsholm, the Dragon business would have gone very differently, so yes, I did want to hear the debate.

Hannah had sent me the draft Order and her game plan in advance, and I sat back in the Portakabin to watch an empty table debate my professional future. One thing I'd made very clear to Hannah was that no gun meant no more Watch Captain Clarke.

I couldn't see them, but I could hear well enough. Hannah presented the draft Order and gave a short speech commending it to the Council. After my testimony, no one was going to oppose the principle of firearms, but the devil, of course, is in the detail. Or should that be *the Dæmon is in the detail.*

Laura reappeared just as the scary eyeball had started to bounce on its spring, not something I wanted to see again in a hurry. Down in London, they'd got on to amendments.

There were two sticking points before I could get my ammunition back from Hannah's safe: accreditation and rules of engagement.

Hannah had pushed for any relevant service (e.g. the RAF) to give firearms accreditation, but no, the Council wanted something more specific, and they didn't want the Peculier Constable to have it all her own way. Typical committee.

The Watch needed the support of Salomon's House, and Dean Cora proposed accreditation by the Metropolitan Police at the firearms training centre in Gravesend. That would be a pain, but I could live with it.

The rules of engagement were a trickier matter. A woman whose voice I'd not heard before wanted a full enquiry by the Council to set the rules, and I was so outraged by this that I didn't at first notice how attractive her voice was. 'Can we be responsible for putting guns in the Groves and Tunnels of magick until we know how they will protect and not destroy the peace?'

If you ignored the words, her voice sounded like an invitation for dinner *a deux.* 'Who's that?' I said to Laura (who was checking her phone).

'What? Who? Oh. No idea. Sorry. Wait for the minutes to be published and look her up.'

Hannah fought hard, and Cora finally got off the fence. The Council agreed to adopt the ACPO Guidance for now and review it in six months. If you didn't know, ACPO is the Association of Chief Police Officers. I'd read that, too, and it wasn't really relevant to magick. Never mind...

'Heard enough?' said Laura hopefully.

'Thank you so much for your patience. Can I buy you lunch?'

'Some other time. Mum's babysitting, and she's not the best influence on the older one. She said you can pick up your car from Blackthwaite Stables whenever you're ready.'

Laura shut down the equipment and escorted me back to the street. She checked her watch and said, 'You're best off getting the half-past one train to Millom. Much easier to pick up a taxi there.'

'Thanks again. Do you know how Mr Driscoll is?'

She shook her head. 'Mum didn't say. I was never into horses, but I am surprised.'

We crossed the enormous car park of an enormous Tesco Extra. 'Surprised in what way?'

'We called him Dodgy Diarmuid for a reason. You don't call someone that if you think they're going to kill you. Fleece you, yes; murder you, no.' She pointed to a mini-roundabout. 'Go right there and keep going up Abbey Road. The station's about ten minutes. Quicker with your long legs.'

It took nearly fifteen minutes, with a stop to buy coffee and a sandwich. A map on display at the station showed me that I could get off at The Green and walk up to Blackthwaite. I ate my sandwich on the train and admired the scenery, especially the Duddon viaduct.

It was a big hill with a heavy rucksack. Shattered, I collected the Volvo and avoided contact with the young women working at the stables. The satnav told me it was a four and a half hour drive to Clerkswell.

I had a lot to think about on the drive, and some rather haunting oboe music by Sibelius was the perfect backdrop as I left the Lakeland Particular behind. I could just about accept that Petra would enjoy Granny time with Laura's kids, and maybe she didn't have the skills to do what Laura had done with the video equipment. What I couldn't accept was that Petra Leigh had not told her daughter, a Mage of some talent, what was going on in a case where her daughter would be assisting the officer who arrested the prisoner. She'd told Laura about my injuries, and told her enough to make her concerned, so why not update her on Driscoll's recovery?

Not just that. Petra could have waited thirty seconds to talk to me when she dropped Laura off. It would have been completely off the record.

Hannah had ordered me to stay off the Bristow/Driscoll case, and she'd come through for me big time in the Council. For now, I'd follow orders. It wasn't as though I didn't have enough on my plate worrying about Vicky and about going to London tomorrow. At least now that I was on my own, I could smoke in the car. Sibelius gave way to Mozart and I made myself as comfortable as I could.

10 — *All we know who lie in Gaol/*

is that the Walls are Strong.

Iain Drummond had told me to meet Annelise van Kampen at Blackfriars Pier: we were going to the Undercroft, the magickal prison. I got there ten minutes early, switched off my phone and turned my face to the weak sunshine. At 0959 a police launch pulled up to the dock, and Annelise jumped athletically on to the pier — it could have been her natural grace or it could have been her Amsterdam childhood.

Vicky and Annelise are Officers of the Watch, junior to Watch Captains like me. Vicky ended up with me because she has the magick and I have the front line experience. Annelise has a law degree and works for the Deputy PC. Physically and temperamentally, Vicky and Annelise couldn't be more different.

I could not imagine Vicky jumping off a boat, for one thing, nor imagine Annelise giving a Nāgin a clip round the ear for another. Then again, ignoring Annelise had got me in trouble with Iain Drummond, so perhaps it was time to give her a second chance.

'Sorry, my train was late,' I said after handshakes. 'I'd have bought coffee if I'd had the time.'

'Save your money,' she replied, with just a hint of that Dutch accent. 'I don't drink it, but you can get some in the Undercroft.' She wagged her finger. 'No smoking downstairs, though.'

'I'll have one while we walk. Is it far?'

She made a face and pointed up the side of Blackfriars Station. 'All the rebuilding has been hell for us. We had to move the entrance four times.'

'Has the Undercroft really been here since the dissolution of the monasteries?'

'Yah. When Shakespeare was performing *Macbeth* upstairs in the theatre, there were real Witches in the basement.'

I gestured at the enormous glass and iron bulk of the station. 'This was a theatre?'

'Yes, yes. It was Shakespeare's winter theatre for years. It had a roof and lights, unlike the Globe.'

We had arrived at the taxi rank and I disposed of my cigarette. Annelise led us to dirty door under a concrete overhang, completely out of sight unless you looked for it. Behind the locked door was a plain concrete passage — no tiles, no flooring, no plastic cladding, just concrete and LED lights. Annelise walked up to a large sliding door of riveted steel and no visible lock. On the wall was a notice saying *Secure Storage. For access, call 07700-900717.*

I know two things about the Undercroft: Mages fear it and no one has ever escaped. It took Annelise nearly a minute to work the lock before she slid back the door on well-maintained rollers. Beyond it was an empty store room with more bare concrete walls. I crossed the threshold and felt the magick, and did my best to see through any Glamours hiding the next level. *There.* Another door, opposite the first, revealed itself.

The second door concealed a functional but well-engineered goods lift of the kind you see in hospitals. We went down a long way, and the shutters opened to a corridor that mixed ancient rough stone with smooth modern plaster, had arched and shadowy Gothic ceilings but a smooth vinyl floor with occasional black marks from rubber wheels. More and more like a hospital.

There was a bend ahead, but we stopped before it to go through a door marked *Bailiffs' Wardroom.* The interior reminded me of a submarine. There were desks, settees, a well-equipped galley, two pairs of bunks with curtains pulled back, and a door to the bathrooms beyond. The one thing submarines don't have is a view. Above us, the London sky was rendered on the ceiling in live Ultra-HD magick.

'It keeps us sane,' said a middle-aged man, pointing at the ceiling. He came over to shake hands. 'Septimus Morgan, Bailiff to the Undercroft and Sergeant to the Cloister Court. You must be Squadron Leader Clarke.'

'Conrad, please. You wouldn't be ex-Navy by any chance?'

He roared with laughter and stroked his Captain Birdseye beard. 'It shows, doesn't it?'

'On your own?' said Annelise.

'She's on a split shift,' he replied, adding for my benefit, 'I have several deputies to share the load. Coffee?'

'Yes please.'

He poured me a mug from a filter jug, then filled two flasks and headed for the door. 'I'll leave you alone, Annelise. You said you had some business with the Watch Captain.'

The pointed reference to my status over Annelise did not escape her. She blinked twice in annoyance, but nevertheless thanked him, held open the door for him and even brought my coffee over to the table. It was very good.

'What's this about Keira's mother?' I began.

She grimaced. 'I'm glad I wasn't around when she was at the bar. She's a hard woman.'

'Like mother, like daughter.'

'For sure.' She sighed. 'The big problems are that you weren't a Watch Captain when Keira was going postal, and most of the crimes were committed at Lunar Hall. The Sisters won't co-operate with the Cloister Court, and now you tell me that Keira didn't murder Lika.'

'What about joint enterprise?'

Annelise shook her head. 'Doesn't apply in magickal law. When Augusta Faulkner left here on Tuesday, Keira said that she'd contest every charge, including damage to the farmer's wall, unless you agreed to talk to her. That's why you're here.'

I was stunned. 'Criminal damage? Is that all you've got? What about attempted murder of me?'

'Can you see what she wants, first?'

'It must be a trick. She'll try to escape.'

She looked blankly at me for a second. 'You really have no idea, do you?'

'This job is one long learning curve for me. You grew up with this stuff. I didn't.'

She led the way down to the bend, then things got very creepy very quickly. Ahead of us was one long, wide corridor with a number of bays and doors leading off. In the first bay was a pair of hospital trolleys.

'We bring them down under sedation. And there are a lot of deaths.'

I stopped and stared. There had been two deaths in custody at HMP Cairndale. I know because I'd looked it up. Two deaths in ten years.

'For sure. About one in three take the short route and kill themselves,' added Annelise in a matter-of-fact way. I didn't know what to say about that, and Annelise wasn't in the mood to share. 'This way.'

She picked up speed. We passed a couple of store rooms, then a huge picture window (in darkness) next to a trolley sized metal door. Clearly a cell. Annelise was nearly running now, and even my longer legs were struggling to keep up, and I couldn't stop to look in through the two illuminated windows that we passed. They were followed by two more empty cells and she finally stopped.

'In there. I'll be waiting in the Wardroom.'

'Key?'

She was already retreating down the corridor. 'They're not locked. Not the outer doors. Take your time. If you can.'

I moved to peer through the glass and saw what the tabloids would no doubt call the lap of luxury. Never mind the tabloids: I'd call it the lap of luxury, too. Yes, it was painted stark white with little art to relieve the blankness, but it had everything I'd want from a five star suite: king bed, couch, fridge, hotplate, dining table and more. I would complain, however, if my room came with its own ghost.

When I'd knocked Keira down and captured her, she'd been a lean, mean, running machine who fizzed with magickal power. The skeletal figure who shambled around this little slice of luxury had lank hair, a twitch in her arm and a jerky shuffle. The baggy tracksuit did nothing for her either.

I watched as she walked twice round her couch before I twigged that the window was a one way mirror. I moved to the steel door and found a whiteboard next to it with a simple legend: *Keira Faulkner. Day 46.*

The steel door was heavy, and on a heavy spring, but it wasn't locked. On the other side was an ante-room with a big enough empty space to manoeuvre a trolley and a few cupboards on the left. On the right was a coffee table and an armchair on my side of what I can only describe as a portcullis, made of thick stainless steel tubing and engraved with runes. At the edges, steel bars were attached at right angles so that they could be locked into the wall. On the other side of the portcullis, waiting for me, was Keira.

'You didn't do the training, did you?' she said.

We were both standing, despite the matching armchairs on either side of the portcullis. Keira didn't wait for an answer. 'Since Queen Victoria, Watch Captains have had to do a week in here as part of their training. Just to see what it feels like. You lucky bastard.'

Her left arm twitched while she spoke (she's left handed), and what I'd thought was a long-sleeved undershirt on her right hand turned out to be a medical dressing. She wiped the dressing against her face and blood came away from where she'd rubbed her cheek raw.

I pointed to her bandaged hand. 'You broke that when you punched my head. It's been dressed. It will heal. Mother Julia, a truly good woman, has only one arm because you blasted the other one off. I'd say that you were the lucky one, not me.'

I flinched when she grabbed the bars and tried to grab me. I hadn't been stupid enough to stand close enough for her to reach.

'There's no magick in here. No Echo, no Lux, no magick. DO YOU KNOW WHAT THAT FEELS LIKE?'

I've said it before: the reality of magick is brutal.

'So? You tried to kill me four times, not to mention the other stuff. I reckon you deserve nothing less.'

She collapsed into the armchair. Not with guilt, you understand, but with exhaustion. She took a couple of deep breaths. 'You saw me, didn't you, in Bank Station? You saw through my Glamour. Why haven't you told van Kampen yet?'

'Haven't got round to it. Been busy dragon-slaying. Why? Are you eager to confess to everything?'

'The Bank Station business is the only thing that will keep me here. The Cloister Court doesn't like it when civilians are in harm's way.'

I don't like it when I'm in harm's way, but if it took the threat to civilians to keep her here, I'd go with it. 'Do you want me to tell her now?'

'I wanted to catch you before then. If you tell them, I'll testify that Victoria Robson attacked me in Guildford, without warrant and without provocation.

Then I'll tell them about the work she did before you turned up. I've got the receipts and the charts in her handwriting.'

I didn't bother to deny this. We both knew it was true, even if we also knew that there were mitigating circumstances.

Keira hammered the point home. 'Robson will get kicked out of the King's Watch, rusticated from the Invisible College and sentenced to some time in here. Let's see how she copes.'

It suddenly came to me: the reason Vicky was an Officer not a Watch Captain was that she couldn't face the Undercroft. Her mild arachnophobia was an inconvenience next to her fear of underground spaces. I know – I've seen it first hand, and I had a good idea that Keira's mother had been doing her homework on us and that Keira knew it too. That wouldn't stop me bluffing, though.

'I think she'd rather be busted than dead. If you walk, we'll be watching our backs forever.'

'I'll go into Exile.'

'Who'd have you, and what would stop you coming straight back?'

'An oath on the London Stone would stop me coming back, and I can petition the French for sanctuary. If I keep my nose clean for two years, I'll be free to roam – outside the UK, of course.'

She couldn't last much longer in here, that was clear. The only thing stopping her taking the *short route* was hope. Maybe she'd panicked in the Tube. Maybe. She hadn't panicked at Lunar Hall, though.

'Lika. You let Deborah murder that poor kid in cold blood.'

She shook her head, and kept shaking it. 'Oh no I didn't. That was all Deborah. You have to believe me – she would have stopped at nothing. I put a Silence on Lika, subdued her and bound her. Deborah killed her. You have to believe me.'

It was plausible. Under a Silence, with surprise and her full strength, Keira could have taken out the young Witch easily. I had to draw the line somewhere.

'I'll deal. If you answer a question first.'

'*I don't know* is the answer to the question.'

'You don't know the question yet.'

'You want to know where Debs got the scroll with Helen of Troy's Imprint on it. I don't know. We were working on some stuff, working well, then one day she went off. Two weeks later, she had the scroll. Told me she couldn't tell me where from, and that it was dangerous for me to know. That freak Rothman came on Friday to ask the same thing. She had the same look in her eye when she asked it.'

'A little respect. Hannah Rothman is my boss.'

I paused.

'Sorry.'

'Good. I'll see if the Deputy PC will accept a deal for Exile. I'll be in touch.'

When I passed the observation window on my way out, Keira was already moving round her room again, jerking from side to side and muttering to herself.

I stopped at the next cell: *Myfanwy Lewis. Day 17.* Annelise hadn't forbidden me from talking to the other prisoners, so I heaved back the door and went in.

Relative to Keira, Myfanwy was doing much better. If Keira was dangling over the abyss and hanging on by her fingernails, Myfanwy was standing on the edge and looking down. Her hair was still blond, but it had lost its life, and her cornflower blue eyes had lost their lustre. Unlike Keira, she'd also put on weight.

'What are you doing here, Mr Clarke?'

'My job. How's things?'

'I've lost my life's work, my friends, my homeland and you blew up the only man I've ever loved. Things are just peachy, thanks.' She gave me a wry smile and collapsed into the chair. 'Enough about me. How's Victoria?'

'Vicky? She's doing well, thanks to you.' Myfanwy had been the one who re-started Vicky's heart. I owed her big time. 'She blames you for the scars. A price worth paying, I think. How's your case coming along?'

'Four more days. I'm due in the Cloister Court on Monday. Iain Drummond says the Crown will argue for mercy, so you're spared. You won't have to break me out to keep your word.'

'Having seen the security here, that's a relief. Too much to do on my own. How's Gwyddno doing?'

The third prisoner was another Druid like Myfanwy, both members of the Dragon conspiracy.

'He's bearing up,' said Myfanwy. 'Bailiff Morgan plays a lot of chess with him, which helps.'

'Don't you play?'

She snorted. 'No chance. With me, he brings paper – it's forbidden in here – and we do designs for his garden. I think he lives in a flat, really, but it passes the time and keeps my focus on the future.'

I looked at my watch and wished her luck.

Annelise didn't understand my deal with Keira, which isn't surprising because I had to keep my motivation a secret for Vicky's sake. She even went to see Keira on her own to check, but with the prisoner willing to plead guilty to some things, Annelise was sure that Iain Drummond would accept Exile, and I left to get on with other business. During my whole time in the Undercroft – and before, on the pier – Annelise hadn't once asked how Vicky was doing. That's the sort of thing I remember.

I didn't have to leave the Undercroft via the lift. There is another exit, possibly designed by former Navy Officer Septimus Morgan, in the style of a two-valve airlock. On the other side of its outer door is the series of tunnels under London that are known as the Old Network. Once the door has closed behind you, it's completely invisible.

It's not just me who's ignorant about some aspects of magick, especially magickal history. The current form of the Old Network is maintained and was finished by Dwarves. Who began it is another matter. If I had to guess, I'd say that some of it was at the original street level of Roman Londinium, but no one has asked me, so I'll keep that to myself. I was on a branch that led a short distance to one of the major junctions, en-route to my meeting with an expert from the Invisible College.

I switched on my torch and set off towards Salomon's House, only to stop when I saw a light coming in the opposite direction. I've been down in the Old Network half a dozen times, and the only stranger I've met was the late Lord Mayor of Moles. I didn't feel worried, but I was disconcerted.

The oncoming light was magickal, big and bright. I can't do that. After being ambushed by Diarmuid Driscoll, I was determined to be more prepared, so I switched my torch to my left hand and activated my Ancile before setting off myself. I saw him first, a man in his twenties, wearing an academic gown. Statistically, that must be a common sight this close to the Invisible College. He, of course, saw a tall guy with a limp wearing country casuals and carrying a torch. Statistically unique, I imagine. No wonder he slowed down and stared.

Being British, we said a polite *good morning* to each other and carried on our way.

With no roads to cross or pedestrians to dodge, I arrived at Salomon's House in short order. This was my first solo visit, with no Vicky to hold my hand and stop me straying off the beaten track. I was quite looking forward to having a nose around, or at least I was. I couldn't get the door open.

I took out the string of Artefacts from round my neck. One of these doodads identifies me as a Master of the Art of Alchemy, and should get me inside automatically. I deactivated my Ancile and clutched the disk, felt the heat of magick and tried the door again. No joy.

There is a rudimentary mobile phone network down here, courtesy of Hledjolf the Dwarf, if you don't mind him logging the calls you make. I called the guy I was supposed to meet, and waited for him to descend the umpteen stairs to the South Basement. While I waited, I retreated to the junction and had a smoke.

Chris Kelly is the closest thing I have to a friend in the world of magick because he's not a comrade in arms, just a Mage. A very very tall, very lean, very bald and very clever Mage, yes, but he's a Professor at the Invisible College and not a member of the King's Watch. Chris is the Earth Master, an expert on Geomancy, the art of creating, mapping and tapping the Ley lines that shunt Lux around the country. As I said to Sister Theresa, it's the only branch of magick for which I have any real aptitude, and Chris is the go-to guy for dowsing rods.

The doors opened and I moved to greet him.

'Hi Conrad, what's the problem with ...' He stopped and stared at my Adjutant's bag. 'My God. What have you got in that briefcase?'

'It's not a *what*, it's a *who*.' I loosened the straps and drew out the Hartshead Hotel towel, placing it on the floor. 'Chris, meet Madeleine. She was a gift from a Witch I know. A Memorialist by trade.'

'No wonder you couldn't get in. Bloody hell, Conrad, that thing's almost alive. The College Wards won't let something like that across the threshold unless it's in an Egyptian tube.'

He held out his hand and touched the towel. 'Ouch. There's a lot of pain in there.' He scratched his chin. He leaned to one side. He rubbed his neck. Finally, he shook his head. 'Sorry. She won't leave you. Hark at me – I called it a "she". I've never seen anything like it. Go on, unwrap the towel.'

I peeled back the folds. It still looked like a stick to me.

'Touch it,' said Chris.

I grasped the thicker end, and nearly dropped it when my arm was yanked violently round.

'Wow,' said Chris, quite unnecessarily.

There is a lot of Lux near Salomon's House. One of the thickest Ley lines in Britain ran under our feet, and the stick was now firmly aligned with the direction of flow. I closed my eyes and tried to use my Sight to explore the stick. It was like walking blindfold into a tiny compartment on a ship in a storm and finding that someone else is already there. A real person. Madeleine.

There were no words between us. It was almost as if the magick was too loud for us to talk, and I realised that I was sensing the flow of Lux in a completely new way. I've always felt it as heat (even if I don't always describe it to you like that), but now I could hear it, a crashing noise, like water flowing over the slipway of the Kielder Dam in winter. I felt a mental bump as Madeleine and I manoeuvred around each other in the tiny headspace of the branch. When we were comfortable, and I'd got the measure of the flow of Lux, I backed my Sight out of the rod and looked at Chris.

'Never seen anything like it,' he said. 'Unique. I don't know whether to feel jealous or relieved.'

I put Madeleine down on the towel. 'What's the bad news?'

'She's looking for something, or the path to somewhere. I think she'll be in touch one day. Until then, she's biding her time and making sure no one else gets close.' He shook his head in wonder. 'Wasn't expecting that. Anyway, congratulations, Conrad Dragonslayer. From what I hear, that was epic.'

'Don't you start, but thanks. I couldn't have done it without your teaching, and your help, Chris. Here's the student dowsing rod you lent me.'

'And you're clearly a good student. I was just glad to be of service. Ooh. What's up with your arm?'

'Long story. I'd tell you over a pint, but I need to get going.'

'If you're doing field work, you can't take … Madeleine with you. Not like that. You might as well carry a big flashing light and a ten foot sign with your name on it. The funniest thing is that I can only sense her when you're not holding her. Gosh, that sounds so wrong.'

'I know. There's a whole world of double entendres looming with Madeleine. What can I do to make her less visible?'

'Nip downstairs and see Hledjolf. He can knock up an Egyptian tube for you.'

'Thanks, Chris. I'll be in touch.' We shook hands, and he slipped back through the doors to Salomon's House.

Hledjolf's Hall lies below the Bank of England's bullion vault, just down the stairs and along another tunnel. But not today. I didn't have the emotional or financial reserves to deal with Hledjolf. I'd come back some other time. I wrapped Madeleine carefully in the towel and headed for the surface and a taxi to the Tower of London.

I didn't linger at Merlyn's Tower because Hannah was with the City Police, trying to sort out my firearms course, and I wanted to get on my way as soon as possible. Maxine fussed over my arm and helped me get the files for my project into a suitcase. I fell asleep in the train on the way home.

11 — Let the Punishment fit the Crime

One day, I will go to Lancashire and it won't rain. Friday was not that day, nor was Saturday. On Friday night, I'd rented a lodge cabin near Cairndale for the weekend and stocked the fridge. On Saturday morning, I was outside HMP Cairndale bright and early to collect Mina, there being not enough staff for the minibus run into Cairndale. I think they paid for taxis to take the other women to the station.

She appeared with a big black bag, and something must have changed inside her, because she dropped it right there, outside the gate, and grabbed me for a proper I-haven't-seen-you-for-six-days kiss.

'Again?' I said.

'Once is enough. I just won a pair of jeans.' She turned and waved at one of the distant windows visible over the fence (walls are for men's prisons).

Sod that. I grabbed her and made sure she really *was* glad to see me. I think she was.

I opened the car. 'What's in the bag?'

'Laundry. There is a washing machine in this caravan, isn't there?'

I chucked the bag in the back. 'Lodge. It's an eco-friendly sustainable wooden holiday home. I didn't see a washing machine, but I wasn't looking. Perhaps there's one in the service block.'

'Suddenly it doesn't seem so important. Come on, let's get going.'

I drove us out of the gates and said, 'Who did you win the bet with?'

'Michelle. Remember her? Doesn't matter. It was a film night on Tuesday, and there was a massive argument. I don't know how it happened, but they asked me to choose. I told them they should watch a Bollywood movie.'

'That was brave.'

'Maybe. I also knew that if the POs liked it, we'd get to stay up late. They're three hours long. I can't believe it, but there was a copy of my favourite film in the library. *Kuch Kuch Hota Hai*. Must have ordered it in for diversity. Good job it had subtitles – my Hindi is rubbish.'

I struggled to picture it. A group of women, some hardened and violent, most damaged and weak, all sitting down and deciding to watch a song and dance marathon. 'It went down well?'

'Everyone cried.'

'And that's a good thing?'

'They want to watch it again next week. One of the girls started calling me *Rani.*'

'Is that a character in the film?'

'One of the female leads. It means *Princess*. Is this it? I had no idea it was so near the prison.'

I slowed down by the service block. 'Laundry?'

'Maybe later.'

'That's what I hoped you'd say. Here. This is us.'

We got inside, and I eased my coat off. Mina was sitting on the end of the bed, struggling with her boots. I bent down and pulled them off for her, then squeezed her toes through the pink fluffy socks poking out of her leggings. She threw her scarf across the room and flopped back on the bed. 'Can you do that for another seven hours?'

I moved up to her knees. 'Use both hands,' she murmured.

'Sorry, not today.'

She sat bolt upright. 'What now? What have you been doing?'

For an answer, I undid the top button of my shirt and pulled it over my head. It had cost me two hours in A&E last night getting the dressings changed. 'Later,' I said. 'I'm fine. Mostly. So long as you go on top.'

She shuffled forward until her dress rode up her thighs, then peeled it off over her head. She grabbed my belt. 'You'll need help with that.'

I didn't argue.

'Half way there already,' she said, looking at the clock by the bed. It was on my side, so she'd crawled over me in a way that reminded me alarmingly of Pramiti in her serpent form. 'I hate this. I want to lose myself in the moment, but I don't want to miss a minute of our time together.'

'I think we've done quite well, so far. I don't know about you, but I've got one hell of an appetite.'

She slithered back to her side of the bed, then rolled off to grab a dressing gown. A silk one that I'd brought with me and laid out on the chair last night. 'Sod the laundry,' she said. 'That doesn't matter, but I want at least an hour for a proper shower. I'll be annoyed if you forget.'

Me? Why is it my job? I got up and opened the fridge. When Mina returned from the bathroom, I told her how I'd got the wounds, and that I was worried about Vicky. 'She's not as strong as you, love.'

'Me? All seven stone of me?'

'You're the strongest person I know. You've recovered from more trauma than anyone should ever have to deal with.'

She was eating smoked salmon and cream cheese blinis. Slowly. She spent several seconds chewing the last one, savouring the freedom it represented. 'Thanks to you.'

'I'm the lucky one.'

'I mean it, Conrad. I had no future until I met you. Even if you'd disappeared before we went to Four Ashes Farm, and Miles had lived, you'd have given me my future.'

'I just hope the Depute Constable goes easy on Vicky.'

'So do I. She saved your life, and for that I will be forever grateful.'

'Look. It's stopped raining.'

'So?'

'Put some clothes on. We're going for a walk.'

'What on earth for?'

'Because you've been locked up. You need to feel the wind on your face. Please.'

'Don't expect me to make a habit of it.'

We took the only path around the lodge park, past the identikit cabins and down to the pool of water that they call a lake. We were far too close to the M6 for it to be truly peaceful, but they'd done their best to scatter bulbs along the path. After a couple of minutes, Mina lowered her hood.

'These are beautiful. What are they?'

'Just crocuses.'

'All the colour, against the grey. And the daffodils, too. Beautiful.'

A cock blackbird, yellow bill bright, dashed across the path, followed by another, twittering loudly.

Mina reached for my hand. 'That's sweet. What lovely birds. How romantic.'

I didn't break the spell. She thought it was an amorous pursuit, so I didn't enlighten her by saying that the (male) birds were engaged in a vicious territorial battle, and that the loser might end up starving to death.

We walked round the site in silence, pausing for a moment at the water's edge. I brushed the hair away from her left cheek. 'The bruise is nearly gone.' I kissed her nose.

'What time is it?' she asked. I told her. 'We've got plenty of time before I need a shower.'

When she'd finished drying her hair, while she waited for the GHDs to warm up, I handed her a box. 'It's not a present,' I said, 'because I used your money. The last of your secret stash.'

She opened the box and took out a new iPhone. 'Why now?' she said. 'I'm not going to risk smuggling it back inside. Thank you. It's very thoughtful, but you could have waited.'

'It's yours. Put your fingerprint on it. It'll be waiting in the car for you on Friday.'

She turned it round in her hands. 'If I put my old Apple ID in, it will download all my old pictures. Miles will be there. And Papa. There's even one of you. I took it when you weren't looking.' She put the phone back in the box. 'I'll need to think about that. Are you staying here tonight?'

'I am. Too tired to drive back down to Clerkswell.'

She began the laborious process of straightening several feet of hair, so I checked my messages. There was one from Vicky: she'd been declared A1 by the cardiologist and also served notice to expect a visit from the Depute Constable. I told Mina and added, 'She sends her love.'

'Give her mine, and tell her we've nearly finished the present she gave us.'

I didn't tell Vicky that, because Vicky hadn't sent her love to Mina. When you're wrapped up in your own troubles, it's hard to think of other people.

Mina and I linked arms to walk back to the car. 'Talking of driving to Clerkswell,' she said, 'I'm not sure I want to spend so long in the car next weekend. And there's the traffic. One of the girls went to Manchester last Tuesday. It's only an hour away, but there was an accident on the way back and the road was closed. She was four hours late. No pass for her this weekend.'

'Is it Clerkswell or the journey that's worrying you?'

'Both, but the journey, mainly. You're so tired, and that arm needs proper physiotherapy.'

Her point was proved dramatically when I tried to open the car door with my left hand and winced. I drove slowly out of the park and slowly back to the prison. I didn't want to arrive any earlier than I had to.

'I don't want any black marks on my parole application,' she said. 'The assistant governor tried to get me to apply for HDC.'

'What's that?'

'Home Detention Curfew, otherwise known as Tagging. You have to be fixed to one place, and when I walk out of prison, I want the freedom to go wherever I want. They don't care, they just want as many bodies out of the door as possible.'

I would have liked her out today, if possible, but I could see her point. 'Are you still on course for release in May?'

'Yes. Two months, or nine weeks if you prefer.'

We said a long, reluctant, goodbye and I pottered back to the lodge for an early night.

On Sunday afternoon, just before it started to get dark, I introduced Madeleine to Elvenham House, starting with the dragon.

I stood before the front doors and gingerly unwrapped the towel. Feeling an even bigger fool than normal, I said, 'Dragon, meet Madeleine. Maddy, this is the family dragon. I hope you don't mind me calling you *Maddy*.' I laid the towel on the bonnet of Vicky's Audi TT and grasped the ... I'll call it *the end of Madeleine's vessel*. Sounds about right.

There was no Ley line running under my feet, and no violent reaction from Maddy. I closed my eyes and felt the other presence inside the vessel. No emotions, no telepathy, just a presence that was politely making room for me. I opened my eyes slowly and tried to conduct an experiment in magick, my very first.

My magickal Sight works best when my eyes are closed. This is fine in some situations, but not ideal for walking around unknown territory or when expecting attack. Vicky had once told me that there is *some* evidence that magick is propagated in the non-dominant half of the brain (the right, in my case).

You'd think that I should therefore close one of my eyes – but it doesn't work like that. What happens in your eyes is that the right half of *both* eyes sends information to the left brain, and vice-versa. Short of wearing glasses that blocked out half my sight in both eyes, that wasn't the answer. What I did do was swap hands, sending any Lux from Madeleine up my left arm into my right brain. I needed my mundane vision to stop falling over, so perhaps I could try to blend the two.

I turned right and walked slowly round the house. Vicky is a Sorcerer – she can look up, down, around and about. She can feel the whole of the Sympathetic Echo. I can't. What I can do is sense the *flow* of Lux, provided that I'm walking over it. I know for a fact that there is old magick in the dragon, and new magick in the King's Bounty, but I only know because I've been told. I got round to the gardens and felt nothing at all.

Across the lawns, past the tennis court and still nothing. I slowed right down as I approached the well. If there was going to be anything, it would be here. Six feet from the well and still nothing. There's a nice gravel surround to the well, so I closed my eyes fully and spiralled inward, towards the stone lip. Still nothing.

It was only when my left leg brushed against the stone that I got a twitch from the rod. Down. I turned to face the well. *Hard down.* Hunh. The well was something I've never felt before: a node. Instead of a current, I was detecting the *end* of a Ley line. The Lux was deep in the ground, but there was no *flow*. The top of the water in the well was like the bare end of a live wire. I made no move to touch it.

'Thanks, Maddy. That was interesting.'

If she heard, I got no reply.

The driving – and other exertions – meant that I was fit for nothing on Monday morning except an emergency appointment with a physio, exactly as Mina had predicted. She did a lot of work on both my back and my shoulders, and it always amazes me how strong they are when they are constantly lifting and moving limbs that feel to me like they're made of lead. She was strong of stomach, too, and needed to be when one of the steel pellets worked its way to the surface and emerged in a small river of blood. She gave me a dressing, told me to slap it on, and got straight back to work. When I got home, I gave in to the temptation of the couch and an episode of *Money for Nothing*. My dad loves that programme; you could say it was the story of his professional life.

I was dragged away by a text from Annelise van Kampen, who wanted me to get out my laptop and talk to her by secure video link.

'Hej, Conrad. I think your ears must have been burning this morning.'

'My arm certainly is. What have you been saying about me?'

'Not me, the Cloister Court. The judge was very disappointed that you weren't there.'

I frowned. 'You didn't ask me.'

'No, no. None of the cases were contested, so we didn't need your testimony. I think she wanted to see what a Dragonslayer looks like. Hannah said, "He looks very tall, My Lady," which is about as funny as it gets in the court.'

'I'm sorry I missed it. What happened?'

'I still don't know what you cooked up with Keira Faulkner, but she took her medicine. If she ever sets foot in Britain again, her life is forfeit. In theory, she can petition the court for mercy in the future, but they only grant that if you're dying or something.'

'She didn't look too well when I saw her last week.'

'She had to be wheeled in to the court. I've never seen anyone look so bad, but she's gone. She'll be on the train this evening.'

'That's a relief. What about the Druids?'

Annelise didn't look happy. She only looks happy when she's getting her own way. 'Gwyddno is under Close Confinement for four years. Scotland have agreed to take him. There was a plea about his children, but the judge said that someone more experienced in family law needed to hear the case. She set a date for six months' time.'

'And Myfanwy?'

'She seemed disappointed that you weren't there, too. I heard her asking her barrister about you.' Annelise arched her eyebrows. 'Something to do with *not needing a rescue attempt*. What's that all about?'

'I take it she was sentenced to Seclusion.'

'Yes.'

'Then you don't need to know. Where's she going?'

Gwyddno was now under *Close Confinement* – he would see no one for four years except the weekly drop-off of rations. He would have no magick except what his talent gave him and no Ley lines to tap into. Myfanwy's *Seclusion* would confine her, yes, but to a much bigger area, and there would be people.

'Another problem. The only group to offer was the Northumbrian Shield Wall.'

Vicky has told me about them. Her words were, 'As mad as a box of frogs.'

'I take it this didn't go down well.'

95

'She wasn't happy. We're not happy. The Shield Wall don't always play nicely with others. That wasn't what we meant when we asked for leniency. She did save one us, after all.'

'She did. What happened?'

'Now that she's pleaded guilty, she gets a less stringent regime in the Undercroft. She asked to wait a couple of weeks to see if there's a better offer. I'll do what I can.'

'Thanks for the update, Annelise. I appreciate it.'

'Welcome. That's not the reason I asked for a video-call, though. There was more, after the hearing.'

She was looking very uneasy now, and shifted a few times in her seat, knocking the camera at her end and giving me a glimpse of the office behind her. Iain Drummond and Annelise are based in another part of the Tower of London. Their accommodation looked a lot less hardcore than Merlyn's Tower.

She picked up the thread. 'The Clerk to the Court said that there was news of a judgement in the Hawkshead session.'

'Oh?'

'Ja. That Man, Diarmuid Driscoll. His case came to court.'

'Surely not. We haven't interviewed him yet. How come this case has got to trial?'

She shrugged. 'They'll have the Assessors' reports from Eldridge and Leigh. If Driscoll volunteered a statement, they wouldn't need anything else to proceed. He pleaded guilty to murder and aggravated assault on a Watch Officer. You, in other words. He was given a sentence of four years in Esthwaite Rest and an order to pay Weregild.'

'But I saw Driscoll being carried off in an ambulance with two broken legs. What's this Esthwaite Rest place like? Can he convalesce there? Are they expecting him to take the short route?'

'I don't know, Conrad. Esthwaite Rest is like the Undercroft but with views over the lake. It's new, only a dozen years' old, apparently. I've never been. Their mortality rate is about the same as ours.' She shrugged again. 'Mages have survived four years. We'll have to see.'

'Does Hannah know?'

'Yes. She wasn't very happy either, according to Iain, and that's why I'm calling. She says she needs to speak to you, but not until after the papers have come in. There's a copy on their way to you.'

'Then I suppose I'll have to wait. Thanks again.'

'I'll see you soon. Probably.'

We both disconnected and I sat back to digest what I'd just heard. Every time I moved my shoulder, I got a reminder of what I'd been through to bring Diarmuid Driscoll to justice, and there was a lot, lot more I needed to know before I'd be happy about it. However, as I'd said to Annelise, I'll have to wait.

I felt sorry for Myfanwy, though. I was missing Vicky enormously, and the thought of her not being around at all was terrible, and if Myfanwy hadn't been there and been willing to help out, I'd have Vicky's funeral to attend as well as Iestyn's. I hoped that something came up for her.

Finally, Keira was gone. Gone for good? All I know is that she will be heading across the Channel to where Adaryn Ap Owain, leader of the Dragon Brotherhood is a fugitive from justice. Would they meet up? Possibly. Would they actually do anything? Probably not. I can tell you this, though: if Mina ever does become Mrs Clarke, we won't be honeymooning in Paris.

12 — *Home Alone*

Sadly, there is no directory of magickally approved cleaning agencies. I had to make do with one that was recommended – via my mother – by the executives of GCHQ. Her opinion? 'If you can afford them, then you're even richer than I thought.'

I'm not, but Mina would be coming here some day. Some day soon, I hoped. Look at it this way: if she saw the house like this, and wasn't appalled, I'm not sure we'd be suited, long term.

I had left the cleaners to it on Tuesday morning and went into town for supplies and to go to an Iyengar yoga class. The physiotherapy had helped loosen some of the joints, but nothing both loosens and strengthens better than Iyengar yoga. You should have seen the instructor's face when she saw all the scars and dressings.

Peace, calm and an early morning walk on Wednesday saw me ready to move, full time, into the library. I am very slowly stamping my mark on Elvenham House, though so far that doesn't amount to much more than claiming the largest guest bedroom as my own. I did that because it has the newest bed and the only en-suite, plus it allowed me to avoid the awkward issue of evicting my parents from the master bedroom.

The rest of the house is a classic mix of restoration and renewal in different stages, all weighed down by unsaleable pieces from Dad's business. Individually, the items are okay, but cumulatively they can be a bit depressing. I tend not to notice, and where would you start?

The house does possess some stunning, genuine items. One is the twenty-six seater dining table, and the other is the giant partners' desk in the library.

James Clarke had inherited a large farmhouse and knocked it down to build the current incarnation, tower and all. He was a successful solicitor, and brought a master cabinet maker down from Worcester to construct a desk in the library, and he made it as one piece. You can move it around, but you can't dismantle it, which is the only reason Dad didn't flog it off in the late eighties.

James Clarke had sired a line of lawyers and my paternal grandfather was the fifth Clarke to sit at the desk. I can barely remember him: he died of shame when I was a toddler, mortified that his only son had gone into the antiques trade and not the law. When he died, Dad moved the desk into a corner of the room and piled stuff on top of it. It hadn't been moved for over thirty years until yesterday, when I got all three cleaners to help me move it back to its original position. I had checked the alignment and left them to it while I went to yoga.

When I got back, it gleamed. All the natural oak had been polished, and they'd done their best to revive the green leather inlay. I had taken the visible side of the desk when we lifted it, and now it was clean, I walked round to the other side to see if there had been any damage from the heating or damp. I was shocked to find that the desk wasn't symmetrical.

One side, the one I was familiar with and which was now next to the window was simple enough: two sets of four drawers on each side and one central. The other side had ornate brass handles, scroll-work inlay and much smaller drawers, making for a much bigger knee-hole. It took me a second to realise that it had been designed for a lady, and that the smaller drawers were not because a lady would have less stuff, but because she could well be wearing a seriously big skirt.

The past is a funny place. Should we condemn it for believing that women need twiddly bits on their drawers, or celebrate the fact that James Clarke wanted and expected his wife to work at the same desk? My grandmother, when she became a relatively young widow, couldn't wait to abandon Elvenham House to my parents. I do not once remember her ever coming into the library.

I unpacked my stuff and settled down at the desk, choosing the distaff side for two reasons. First, my long legs much preferred the extra room. Second, from that side I could see anyone coming up the lane to the house.

Before I could sort the files, my phone rang: Hledjolf the Dwarf. What???

'We hear that you have slain a Dragon,' said the creepy little robot. I don't like Hledjolf.

'You've heard right. Unfortunately, it's classified.'

'We will find out, but that is not the reason for Hledjolf's call.'

'Oh?'

'We have received a transfer of Lux from our cousin Haugstari, the Old Man of Coniston.'

'Hang on, the Old Man is a mountain.'

'Also a Dwarf. He lives under the mountain that bears his name. The Cloister Court has made a payment to you of 500oz Troy as Weregild from a Mage called Driscoll.'

'Bloody hell.' In magickal terms, I was suddenly very rich.

Lux can be stored in Alchemical Gold, like electricity in a battery, and used for magick. It also forms the basis of a magickal currency, measured in Troy ounces. As far as I know, Dwarves have a monopoly on the creation of Alchemical Gold.

'Could you use it to make a couple of Artefacts?' I asked.

'Of course. You mentioned an Artefact to disguise the Hammer.'

'I did. You quoted me 4oz.'

There was a most un-Dwarflike pause. 'We did. Since then, there has been a great rise in orders for our work. We have had to raise our prices. We will

99

honour the quote we gave, but we cannot guarantee delivery in less than two months.'

'How much for a week on Thursday?'

'We can do that for 12oz.'

I could afford it. 'Deal. And how much for an Egyptian Tube, about 50cm long and 8cm in diameter?'

'The price in leather is 24oz, or 48oz in aluminium. The leather will take at least a month because we do not work with organic matter and need another maker's time. Aluminium we can do in the nine days you requested.'

'Aluminium, please.'

'They will be ready.'

'Great. Thanks.'

That was a tremendous hike in prices. Triple. It was a good job I'd just had a windfall. Suddenly, I didn't want to start on the Merlyn's Tower files and pushed them aside to write a letter to Mina.

The Clerkswell village shop does a very nice crusty cob, perfect for lunch. I also fancied another walk, and I could post my letter, too. As I struggled into my new coat, I wondered if this could be classed as procrastination. I was on my way back from the post box when a car pulled up next to me. He recognised me because I was tall (OK, and currently bald). I bent down and saw the Senior Watch Captain, Rick James. He lowered the nearside window and said, 'Hiya Conrad. Glad I caught you: I've got a delivery.'

'Turn right down there by the yew tree. I'll put a spurt on.'

When I caught up, Rick was admiring the family dragon. 'Nice place,' he said. 'Bit too Gothic for me, but nice.'

Rick lives in a Georgian rectory near Wells in Somerset that was restored so tastefully by his wife that she couldn't measure up to her surroundings and walked out on him. It was either that or his lifestyle. By rights, Rick should be the Deputy Constable in Chester, but he chose to stay close to his children in Glastonbury, and who am I to judge him? Hannah made him Senior Watch Captain instead, in an attempt to take some of the load off her own shoulders.

I led the way inside after Rick had grabbed a nylon holdall from his car.

'I suppose this place has been in your family for generations,' he said, looking round the kitchen.

'Something like that. I'll make some coffee.' I held up the crusty cob. 'Lunch? There's soup, too.' I should point out the kitchen is one of the few rooms *not* in need of refurbishment.

'No thanks. I'll take the coffee, though. If I get going, I can be back for the afternoon school run.' He put the bag on the table. 'I had to go to London yesterday and the Boss asked me to bring this over. She thinks that Clerkswell is on my way to Wells.'

'Typical Londoner.'

Rick grinned, stretching the scar on his left cheek. He's 90% South London, 5% St Lucia and only 5% Somerset.

'It's the stuff from that case in Lakeland,' he said. 'Mind if I unload it?' I pointed to a worktop and he unzipped the bag before continuing. 'Hannah told me that you'd been injured up there, and that there's an inquiry into the arrest.'

I turned to look at him. There's very little guile in Rick James. He wasn't trying to make a point, just letting me know that he knew the score. I saw the pile of folders, with what looked like a telescope on top. 'That wouldn't be an Egyptian Tube, would it?'

'Yeah. You never seen one before?'

'No. What on earth's in it?'

'Evidence, I imagine. Let's have a look at the manifest.' He ran his fingers lightly over a blank piece of paper on the side. 'Thought so. It says *One quill pen, recovered from Blackthwaite Stables.*'

The coffee was ready. I put the mugs down and said, 'How did you do that? And how can I open it?'

He put the leather tube on the table. 'It's called a Script Curtain. Not my thing, but to see what's there, I just imagine it's a lottery scratchcard when I rub my thumb across. Don't *actually* scratch it, though.'

I took the tube and closed my eyes. I swapped hands and tried to imagine the paper was covered with foil that my thumb was removing. I opened my eyes, and there it was. Wow. 'I must be getting better at this.'

Rick coughed politely. 'I don't want to rain on your parade, Conrad, but a Script Curtain is self-revealing. All you have to do is touch it with magickal intent. The hardest part is knowing that it's there in the first place. It's not usually as obvious as a blank piece of paper.'

'Another crashing disappointment for my occult ego. I'll live. How do I open it?'

'It's not locked, as such. Twist the top one way with your hand and turn the holding plate in the opposite direction with magick. Sort of like patting your head and rubbing your tummy.'

I extended my Sight into the top and felt a metal plate being pulled tightly down to seal the tube. I imagined that I was in a chopper and doing two different things became a cinch. The top shooped off with a vacuum sound.

'Nicely done,' said Rick.

I shook the tube, and a feather dropped on to the table, thick, black and glossy. It was at least a foot long. 'Is it dangerous?' I asked.

Rick stared at the feather, then flicked it with his finger. 'Only if you try to Enscribe with it. It's a swan's flight feather, and someone went to a lot of trouble to get that from Australia or wherever. They've laced a Work for disruptive magick through the frondy bits, whatever they're called.'

'Vanes. I think. What's disruptive magick?'

'It's like the magickal equivalent of nerve gas. Disrupts the nervous system.'

'I see. Hledjolf put the same thing in my ammunition.'

The end of the feather was sharpened, notched and stained black with ink. I picked it up and felt a faint pulsing push of magick flow down the feather towards the quill end. It felt ominous, dangerous, like the sound of a gun being loaded.

'Can I keep the tube?'

'For a while. Annelise will want it back sooner or later.'

Rick accepted some Hobnobs to go with his coffee, and I asked him a question. 'You escorted some Witches from Lithuania to the Lake District in January, I believe. Can I ask what you made of the place?'

'Escorting is a bit of a stretch. Accompanying would be more accurate. They don't have a central college of magick in Lithuania, and this was a fact-finding mission, to see how it's done over here. They'd done the Invisible College in London and I went with them to Glastonbury, then up to the Lakes. It was my first trip up there, and it bleedin' snowed. I only stopped two nights; they were there for a week.'

'Who did you meet?'

'The President of the Grand Union. She's a Witch in the Sisters of the Water. I also met the Langdale Chairman. He's a Gnome from Clan Skelwith. A few others. I'm not planning to go back, so I didn't take too much notice. Nice food. Great party.'

Something in his eyes told me that he'd got lucky with one of the Witches. Vicky was, once, another of his conquests.

I had one more question. 'Where did you stay?'

'Some place called the Little Langdale Lodge. It's owned by one of the families.'

'Families?'

'Yeah. A lot of the magickal enterprises up there have been in the same family for years. If one generation has no Mages, they marry one. It makes the whole place very cliquey, and that's another reason we let them get on with it.'

'A bit like Afghanistan, then.'

He gave me a funny look and drained his coffee. 'I wouldn't know. I'd better get going.' He put his mug in the Belfast sink. 'Thanks for the coffee. No, don't get up, I'll see myself out.'

The Egyptian tube was a little too big for Maddy, but would do very nicely for now. I took all the files into the library and carefully put Madeleine into the tube. She didn't complain. The feather, I put in one of the desk drawers.

On a whim, I opened all the drawers, and got the faintest whiff of magick. I wonder where (or who) that came from? One drawer stuck a little, and further investigation revealed a hidden compartment at the back. Not locked, just hidden. It was empty, alas, but despite being born and raised in Elvenham House, it seems that there is still an awful lot I don't know about it.

You could say something similar about the Lakeland Particular. I know seven different places to land a helicopter on Helvellyn, and three places to get a decent pint in Ambleside, but far too little about the magick there. I put the Merlyn's Tower files away and opened the bundle on Diarmuid Driscoll.

There were only two items that had any surprises. The first was Diarmuid's statement. I'll let him speak for himself.

This is a voluntary statement made by myself, Diarmuid Michael Driscoll of Blackthwaite Stables near Millom in the county of Cumberland.

In the summer of last year, I did use magick to promote the conception of a horse and did implant the embryo in another mare. In the autumn, I gave the mare into the care of Rod Bristow of Fellside Farm, Cartmel.

When this was discovered, I confess that I did create a Hex Malaglyph, contrary to the law of the Occult Council, and that I did send the Malaglyph to Mr Bristow at his home with the intent of killing him. I acknowledge that I caused his death on Monday 9th March last with murderous intent.

Later the same day, I was visited by a man I now know to be Watch Captain Clarke, who was accompanied by a woman I now know to be Watch Officer Robson. I admit that I fired a shotgun at WC Clarke with the intention of seriously injuring him when he had offered no provocation or threat.

Immediately after this, WO Robson struck me accidentally with her vehicle. I believe that she was in fear of her life from the shotgun and was distracted.

After I was injured, WC Clarke administered first aid, despite being injured himself, and WO Robson called an ambulance for my injuries.

I confirm that I was arrested by WC Clarke and transferred into the custody of the Duddon Union.

(Signed) D M Driscoll.

Well, well, well. How about that, eh? Diarmuid's statement couldn't have been a bigger gift to the Lakeland prosecutor if he'd tied a ribbon round it. He even admitted to murderous intent. This statement stank worse than the stall of a horse with hypersecretion.

I checked the discovery log and, yes, a copy of Diarmuid's statement had gone straight from Hawkshead to both Vicky and the Depute Constable in Edinburgh. If Vicky had any sense, she'd parrot Diarmuid's words and be cleared of any wrongdoing.

The other item of interest in the files was the Evidence Log. The Assessor had searched the stables and found the feather, petri dishes and some equine gynaecological apparatus, all enhanced by magick. What she hadn't found was any Parchment, ink, wax or scrolls relevant to Enscribing and Hexing.

The King's Watch sometimes follows the mundane law, and sometimes we don't. We aren't governed by the PACE rules, for example, and we don't record interviews with suspects or witnesses. If anyone had interviewed Diarmuid, there was no note of it. No one had asked awkward questions. No one had seen the bleedingly obvious: Diarmuid Driscoll was covering for someone.

I needed to talk to Hannah about this and rang Tennille to get her to call me back.

'You got broadband out there in the sticks?'

'Of course.'

'And you got your laptop with Mr Li's software?'

'Yes. I used it to video call Annelise on Monday.'

Tennille sniffed. Not only is she very protective of Hannah, she doesn't always get on well with the others in Merlyn's Tower. 'Three o'clock,' was her only comment.

13 — Walking the Course

When the Boss came online, she was sporting a jaunty red headscarf and sitting in the comfy chairs by the window overlooking the Thames to stop me (or less trustworthy callers) from seeing what was on her desk. She said hello and lifted an old-fashioned crystal ball into view.

'I've been scrying,' she said. 'You're going to ask me to get an interview with Diarmuid.'

Serious Sorcerers do actually use crystal balls. Hannah is not a Sorcerer.

'You've read the papers, too,' I said, ignoring the oversized paperweight. 'He's covering for someone.'

'Of course he is, but there's a problem. There's been no new crime, has there? He's admitted to everything he could be charged with, so any further interviews would be voluntary because we can't arrest him. I got Tennille to call the Esthwaite Rest after lunch.'

'And?'

'Mr Driscoll has politely declined our request for an interview. He says that he wants to put it all behind him and concentrate on surviving his sentence. There's nothing we can do.' She moved on. 'Talking of Vicky, have you heard from her?'

'Not since Saturday, ma'am. I honestly don't know what to think, other than that without her, I'm a very expensive intelligence analyst.'

She gave me her sad smile. 'Don't I know it. I might have a job for you, though: the Assistant Clerk to the Watch is pregnant. You could do her maternity leave.'

My first thought was *poor Maxine*. She was looking forward to retirement. 'What about those interns I met?'

'They both leave at the end of March. It's little more than work experience for them. Neither has the capacity to take over from Cleo.'

'Cleo? I only caught her last name. Is it short for Cleopatra?'

'Cleonea. Awful name. She made us promise never to use it.'

My second thought about the news was wild and dangerous, so I suppressed it for now.

'That's not all. The Watch Captain for the West Midlands has handed in his notice. Three months. I'm still no nearer finding a Deputy for Chester or getting any new recruits. Apart from Helen Davies, of course, and there's only one Helen Davies.'

'There certainly is. We'll all have to hope that Vicky returns to active duty soon, won't we?'

'I'm expecting the Depute Constable's report on Monday. After that, she'll be off administrative leave, but we both know she's had one knock too many in too short a time. We'll have to see.'

'Yes, ma'am.'

'You know, I've actually got used to you calling me that. I just hope it isn't catching. Now, about your firearms course.'

I raised my eyebrows and kept my mouth closed.

'The Gravesend unit won't admit anyone but a warranted police officer, no matter how much I offered them.'

'I'm not resigning my commission again. I have my pension to think about.'

She hooted. 'That's the least believable thing you've ever said. There's no need to leave the RAF. You can be a Special Constable. It's unpaid, of course, but you have the same legal powers, and it's another complication I don't need. Now I have to see the chief constable.'

'Hang fire, ma'am. I may have an idea.'

'Why do I not like the sound of that?'

'Because you have a suspicious mind. Ma'am.'

'Go and get on with that project and look after your arm.'

She disconnected the link and left me to stare out of the window.

I stared for a long time, until the urge for a cigarette got too much. I made myself a cup of tea and took it to the morning room, which I don't normally use because it's bloody freezing, thanks to the French doors leading to the gardens. Mother put a big curtain over them to keep some of the warmth in, and in winter the curtain just spoils the ambiance completely. The cleaners had opened it yesterday to dust behind, and I stood in the draught, looking at the carnage on the lawn where a gang of moles had had one hell of a party. By the time I'd drunk my tea, I'd come to a decision: it was time to shake things up a bit. I grabbed a pen and quick-marched back to the village shop.

They sell a few old-fashioned postcards there, mostly of the village and printed in the nineties. I dug out one showing the Church Well that was neither faded nor curling at the edges and jotted a message to Mina. I was just putting the stamp on when the red van came to collect the last post. It was game on.

The next morning, I started to put my plan into action. After that, I arrested myself for procrastination and sentenced myself to a whole day in the library working on the King's Watch files.

Last Thursday, Maxine Lambert had given me all the official reports into fatalities and near misses involving the King's Watch since 2010, and Dean Hardisty had added a list of Mages from the Invisible College who had gone AWOL or died in mysterious circumstances. It was my belief, shared uneasily by Maxine and Hannah, that there had been a shift, a sea-change in what the

Watch had to deal with. My primary evidence for this was a trail of dead Mages and Watch Captains.

To create a cover story for my researches, Maxine had set up *Project Talpa* on the system, so that anyone who came looking for the files would know they weren't simply missing. If you're wondering, Talpa is the genus of moles, a double joke. I didn't expect to find a George Smiley type mole in Merlyn's Tower, but I did have to do a lot of digging. By Friday morning, I'd barely started.

At eleven o'clock, I scanned my notes into PDF files and uploaded them to the Merlyn's Tower server, then I took all the documents and locked them in the safe. It's an original feature, designed so that James Clarke could work from home. I hid the key in the secret compartment in the desk, grabbed my bag and turned off the heating.

14 — *Family Time*

I've talked about my car being *the Volvo*, and you might have thought it was the XC90 4x4 I mentioned. It's not, it's the XC70, the sort used by traffic police. It's nigh-on indestructible and perfect for me. On Wednesday, I'd left it at a garage in Cheltenham for a major overhaul and today I took the XC90 up to Cairndale. When Mina saw the upgrade, she gave me an extra kiss.

'Why didn't you use this last time?'

'I'm going to sell it. Come on.'

She belted herself in and got out the postcard of Clerkswell. 'What's this all about, Conrad? *Pack your warmest clothes?* Is your heating broken?'

I drove down the valley road and pulled in to a café just before the M6. It was very popular with prison officers and prisoners' families alike. Mina complained very loudly when I told her we needed to talk.

'Do we have to?'

'Yes. Sooner or later, and we need to do it here, because there's a choice to make at the motorway.'

With a cappuccino and croissant to savour, Mina looked a little less grumpy. 'What choice?'

'We need to think about the future. Yours and ours.'

She put the croissant down and wiped her hands. One of the other girls inside had done her nails in a vibrant red that matched her scarf. 'For Ganesh's sake, don't propose, Conrad. We don't want to deal with that Nāgin yet, which would mean I'd have to say no and make you wait.'

'Erm, you've jumped ahead of me there, love. I was thinking more about whether or not you're going to join the world of magick.'

'How can I? Ganesh isn't offering free upgrades, unlike your Allfather.'

'There's going to be a vacancy at Merlyn's Tower. The Assistant Clerk is pregnant. They – we – will need maternity cover.'

She folded her hands. 'Why would a highly secret law-enforcement agency employ a criminal like me? And why would I want to work in a cold, damp mediæval tower?'

'It's only maternity cover at first, but it's a job. You might love it, you might hate it, and a job where everything is bonkers will help you feel normal. They'll have you because, right now, they won't find anyone better.'

'Sounds like you've got it all worked out for me.'

I took her hands in mine. 'If you told me that you wanted to enrol in dance classes and try your luck in Bollywood, I'd back you every step of the way. When you get out, which is only a couple of months, I'll be there for a week, maybe two, then I'll be back at work. This would give you something to get your teeth into, and I think you'd actually enjoy it.'

She rubbed my hand with her fingers. 'Why do I have to decide now?'

'You don't. If you're interested, we're off to the Lakes, if not, we'll head to the Ribble Valley.'

'Please tell me we're not camping. I am not going to sleep under a bush.'

'A boutique hotel. Here.' I passed her a printout from the hotel's website.

She looked at the sheets of paper for a few seconds, then drained her coffee. 'Let's go. I hope you've booked the royal suite. Even the POs are calling me *Rani* now, and not all of them sarcastically.'

'The Lakes are that way. Why are we heading south?'

I swung the car down the slip road. 'You've a better sense of direction than Vicky. She wouldn't have noticed. We're going to pick up some evidence from the Bentleys at FERC, then head back north. Lunch in Ambleside. And shopping.'

I explained the plan until we were near the Blackpool turnoff, then I called Olivia and asked if Julian had managed to hold on to the mysterious piece of paper.

'It's in the safe at the racecourse, but we're in Ireland. Amelia's there, and she knows the combination. I'll text her to expect you.'

Mina immediately sat up straighter. She knows exactly what Amelia once meant to me. I tried to act casual. 'What's Amelia doing there?'

'Daddy. He left her 25% of the shares in the racecourse. She's trying to find herself a job.'

As soon as I'd disconnected the call, Mina said, 'Where's my new phone?'

'In the glove box, like I promised.'

She had it out and working before we got to the racecourse, and I didn't need to peek to guess that she was Googling Amelia Jennings. I didn't ask if she was coming inside with me – she was out of the car before I'd turned off the engine.

Amelia is not a bad person, it's just that she has a taste for married men and got involved with a sociopathic mercenary who wanted to kill me. And she turned down my proposal of marriage, for which I am now grateful. She was waiting for us in the general office, all lithe limbs and jodhpurs. Naturally, she went for the full-body hug.

'You saved me,' she said. 'I dread to think what would have happened to me if you hadn't been there.'

'And you stopped Will Offlea shooting at my helicopter. I think we're quits. This is my partner, Mina Desai.'

The women shook hands. 'Livvi said that you were a Geordie,' said Amelia when she heard Mina's accent.

Mina chose to ignore the racial elements of that remark and responded, 'That's his work partner. I'm his girlfriend partner.'

'Oh,' said Amelia, taking a step back. 'Julian's office is this way. Can I get you a coffee?'

'We're not stopping,' said Mina. It's a good job she'd kept her coat on, because the temperature in here was now very chilly.

Amelia picked up a large padded envelope from Julian's desk. 'What's this all about?' she asked. 'Livvi said something about a suspicious death. Should I be worried?'

Mina stepped forward and, without snatching, took the envelope from Amelia. 'No. You're not important. Thank you for this. Goodbye.'

I had to hurry to catch up with her. 'What brought that on?' I asked.

'She hurt you, and she thinks she still owns you. She needs a few lessons. Here. You'd better take this.'

Mina has seen my magickal Artefacts, and touched them, and has no connection with them whatsoever. If she simply doesn't have the Sight. If she stood in the Sacred Grove at Lunar Hall, she'd feel something – a tingling, maybe, but she wouldn't be able to separate the general atmosphere from the peculiarly magickal elements of the experience.

I dropped the subject of Amelia and, when we were back in the car, I opened the envelope.

'Is that it?' said Mina as I fingered the gorgeously thick weave of the paper. Sorry, *of the Parchment.*

'Oh yes. I've got them now.' I passed her the Parchment, started the engine and drove away.

She examined the evidence. 'How come?'

'When Vicky, or another Sorcerer, has had a look, I'll have proof that magick was used to defraud Olivia. That's a crime. We can investigate.'

She gave me a twinkle. 'We?'

'This is strictly unofficial. I'm not going to put us in harm's way. We're going to have a break in the Lakes, you're going to have a spa day and I'm going to meet Vicky for a spot of Sorcery. The fact that we'll be doing it under assumed names is just so that I can get a feel for how the Lakeland Particular operates for ordinary Mages. I've got it all worked out.'

'Famous last words. Did you say spa day?'

'A luxury one.'

'Just this once, then.'

Mina was still complaining about Ambleside when we got to the Little Langdale Lodge. 'You call that shopping! Nothing but outdoor clothing shops and rubbish that even my mother would turn her nose up at. I'm not going to wear these after this weekend.'

Mina's city boots had been replaced by Gore-Tex walking shoes, much to her disgust.

'You'll fit in better,' I said.

'I'm Indian. Did you see any brown or black faces in Ambleside, apart from mine?'

She had me there. I didn't say that it was much the same in the villages of Gloucestershire.

And she wasn't finished yet. 'What about all those students? I'm feeling old, Conrad. Not as old as you, obviously, but old. I don't like it.' She pulled down the sun visor and looked in the courtesy mirror. 'At least I don't look as old as Amelia. Did you see the lines on her face?'

'You know what you need, don't you?'

'No, oh great master. Tell the poor Indian girl what she needs.'

'A friend. A proper friend. Have you lost touch with all the girls from school and university?'

She snapped the visor up. 'I wasn't planning to have this conversation half way up a dirt track in the middle of nowhere.'

'This isn't a dirt track. This is what all the roads are like round here. Whoops.' I reversed into a passing place to let an oncoming 4x4 get past, and not for the first time since we'd left the A road from Ambleside. 'So you were planning to talk about it.'

'Yes. No. I don't know. Probably. I know more about you, your family and your history than you do about me.'

'That's mostly because you prefer not to talk about it. I get that.'

'I wasn't always an orphan. Once upon a time, I was Daddy's little girl. I had a family. I had two brothers and some cousins in Wembley. I had Kavia Foi and Vanshi Massi and lots more cousins in Gujarat and Mumbai. Now I have a mother who has disowned me because my father brought shame on the family, and a brother in America who will only write to me courtesy of Joshi-ji because he doesn't want to write letters to someone in prison in case Homeland Security come knocking on his door. And you. I have you. Is it any wonder I don't talk about what I've lost?'

We had arrived at the Little Langdale Lodge. I left the engine running so as not to disturb her.

'And friends?' I said, gently.

'Conrad, I had no friends. Yes, we spoke mostly English at home, and I wore western clothes most of the time, and ate English food in the canteen at university.' She made a face at that memory. 'But I am Indian. Indian women don't do friends, they do family. The girls at school were acquaintances, and we had a good time, but they're all married now. I lived at home when I went to university. My parents were touting round for a husband when Joe Croxton destroyed everything. If Miles hadn't taken me in, I'd be a faceless burden on my family in Gujarat.'

She looked around, snapped the visor back down and took another look. 'And now I shall have to repair my makeup before we go in because you've made me cry. Go outside and have a cigarette.'

I walked slowly round the outside of the Lodge. It wasn't huge, but it was lovely. The front was faced in horizontal slate, with a roof that sloped gently towards us and showed off their eco-credentials because it was covered in wild plants. To the side of the main building was a viewing platform – the bulk of the hotel was down the hillside, towards the tarn. Every room had a view, apparently.

'How cold is it?' said Mina when I got back in.

'It's a beautiful spring day. Quite warm. If you're not up for this, we can just enjoy the place.'

'I think you're mad. I think they'll know exactly who you are as soon as you walk in. How many giant Mages are there in this world of magick?'

'More than you'd think. If, *if* word has got around up here, they'll be looking for a Conrad Clarke and a Geordie woman called Robson.'

'Then let's go, Edward.'

The front door took us to an open plan lounge cum bar with a reception desk tucked into the corner. Mina ignored it and was immediately drawn to the view. There were already half a dozen guests relaxing over afternoon tea, all of them enjoying the window tables.

No member of staff was visible, so I rang the bell on the desk. A young lad, no more than nineteen, came out of a back office and gave me a nervous smile that needed a lot more practice.

'Good afternoon, sir. Is it tea or are you checking in?'

'Edward Enderby. I've a room reserved.'

He looked at the small list next to the computer. 'That's right. Three nights on the half-board special. Can I ask you to fill this out?'

He gave me a registration form, pre-printed with my false name and real Notting Hill address. All I had to do was add my car's registration number and write *no beef* in the dietary requirements box. As it happens, Edward Enderby was my mother's father, a man I wished I'd known better. I'd had to tell Mina not to call me Ted.

'And how will you be paying?' said the lad.

I took out an envelope full of twenty pound notes. It's how Mages often pay for things. 'That should cover the food and accommodation, with some to put on account.'

He glanced at the notes and put them aside to count later. 'You're in the Bowfell suite, one floor down. Do you want a hand with your luggage?'

'No thanks. Will there be someone from the family at dinner?'

He looked at me again. 'Of course, sir. I'll ask Mrs Forster to join you. Here's your key.'

Mina had wandered up to join us. It was instructive to watch just how much effort the lad put into not staring at her. 'Sorted?' she said.

I gave her the key. 'You go and open up. I'll get the bags.'

The young lad jumped to. 'Let you show me the way, Mrs Enderby.'

Mina gave her head a tiny jerk, just enough to twitch her nose upwards as if she were butting something. 'It's Miss Mukherjee. Rani Mukherjee. Thank you.'

She followed him out of the lounge, every inch the Bollywood princess, which is what she'd chosen to be. Apart from being her new nickname, Rani Mukherjee is the star of *Kuch Kuch Hota Hai.* Apparently. I haven't got round to watching it yet, though HMP Cairndale enjoyed their second screening even more than the first.

Unbothered by fame, I went to get the bags.

'Good evening, madam, sir,' said the Maître D', a woman who bore a strong family resemblance to the lad who'd checked us in. Her name badge, however, said that she wasn't Mrs Forster.

Mina put her hands together on the breast of her royal blue kameez and bowed slightly. 'Namaste.'

The Maître D' wasn't flustered, but she wasn't sure whether to respond in kind, so she just bowed. 'This way, please.'

The restaurant was on the lowest floor and had multiple sliding doors for warmer weather. Even though it was pitch black outside, we got a prime table with a view. I made sure that Mina faced in to the room.

'Will you be wanting the wine list?'

'Yes please,' said Mina sweetly, and for the next hour, the staff completely ignored me.

'I thought I'd need magick to blend in,' I said, 'when all I needed was you. I haven't felt this anonymous since I had dinner with Defence Secretary.'

She dabbed at her mouth with the napkin and checked for lipstick transfer. The multiple bangles on her arm jingled softly. They were a job lot she'd picked up at a shop for teenage girls in Ambleside, but they were very effective with the gold hoop earrings and fake nose-stud. Not having been to temple, she hadn't put a bindi on her forehead. 'But it's not me you're with, is it?'

I looked around. 'You look like you to me.'

'But I'm not me, I'm Rani Mukherjee, even if they don't know who I am. If that makes sense.'

'I'll try not to think about it.'

She rolled her eyes. 'If you walked into a restaurant in Mumbai and shouted "What ho, chaps," they'd all treat you like an Englishman.'

'But I am an Englishman.'

'I give up. Sorry, I give up *Edward.*'

Mina has a logic that is not Indian, not Gujarati, not anything. It is completely hers. I rarely follow it. She shook her head and drained the last of the white wine.

Mark Hayden

I'd had my eye on a cheerful looking woman for the last ten minutes. She was circulating through the restaurant as if she owned the place, which she (or her family) probably did. I used my advanced navigational skills to figure out that she was plotting a course that would finish with our table in about ten minutes. Time for a smoke.

I slipped back into the dining room just as the woman arrived at our table. I saw her give an exaggerated version of the full Namaste, which Mina returned after first standing up. I took my seat after a brief handshake that came with a tingle of magick. She now knew how little Gift I had.

'Are you ready for dessert?' said Mrs Forster.

'We'll give it a miss, thanks,' I said, 'but we'd quite like a glass of dessert wine. Perhaps you'd join us.'

'Delighted. Won't be long.'

'She was checking you out,' I said to Mina.

'Everyone's been checking me out,' she responded. 'Underneath this, I'm sweating worse than monsoon season. I've never been looked at so much since the Old Bailey.'

'No, well, yes. I mean that she was checking out your magick, that's why she bowed so low.'

'Shall I just wear a sign round my neck? "No Talent Here"?'

I was spared a response when the waiter brought a chair and three glasses. Mrs Forster carried a half-bottle of something rich, golden and full of French sunshine. As she poured, she said, 'Accept this as a token of our hospitality.'

Her words, and the gift, meant that Mina and I were accepted, and acknowledged, and above all protected as guests. We drank to accept her hospitality, and I proposed a toast to the coming spring, which went down well.

'Is this your first time in the Lakes?' asked Mrs Forster.

'It is mine,' said Mina.

'And it's my first time in the Particular,' I said.

Mrs Forster raised her glass again. 'Then doubly welcome. What brings you here? Apart from the usual reasons.'

'I've been working in Iraq,' I said. It was a gamble, but any cover story had to have some unverifiable but totally plausible details.

Mrs Forster put down her glass. 'Iraq?'

'Oil,' I replied, as if that answered everything. 'It was time to settle down, and someone suggested that I should try up here.'

'Not much oil in the Lakes. At least I hope not. It's bad enough with fracking for gas down on the Fylde.'

'But there's always work for Geomancers.'

She frowned at me. 'If you've got something to offer, yes. Have you?'

'While Rani was getting ready, I went for a walk. You take a feed off the Ley line running from Waterhead over to Wasdale. I'm guessing that it was re-woven when the Lodge was rebuilt.'

She inclined her head in acknowledgement. I couldn't have done it without Maddy to help me, but very few Mages could have done it at all. Both Ley lines were very faint, a bit like the broadband up here.

I pressed on. 'I wouldn't normally tout for business in a hotel, but my friend said that I'd need an introduction to the Unions as a starting point, and he said the hospitality here was first rate. He was right about that.'

'Thank you, Mr Enderby. Are you going to be around tomorrow?'

'I am. Rani is booked in to the Brimstone Spa for the day at Langdale. I'll have dropped her off by ten o'clock.'

'Lucky you,' said Mrs Forster to Mina. 'You'll love it. Did you give your mobile number when you registered, Mr Enderby?'

'Yes.'

'Then I'll text you some contact details.' She turned to Mina. 'Rani. That's a lovely name. Where's it from?'

I cringed. If Mina cringed inside, she didn't show it.

I had to steady Mina's arm on the way back to the Bowfell suite. It doesn't take much alcohol to affect someone her size. When the door had closed behind us, she clutched on to me and swayed as she unfastened her sandals. 'You are such a man, sometimes, Edward. Conrad. Whatever.'

'I try to be one all the time. What have I done now?'

'Tell me to pack warm clothes, then bring me here. I have only one kameez. I can't wear that for three nights.'

Sandals removed, she weaved her way to the bed and plonked herself down on the end, then raised her arms. I pulled the kameez carefully over her head, straightened it and hung it in the wardrobe. When I turned round, she was flat on her back. 'Not everyone was checking me out,' she murmured. 'One woman definitely had her eye on you.'

'I'm flattered.'

'Not in that way. Help me up.' I got her vertical again. 'When Mrs Forster stopped at this woman's table, she patted the husband on the shoulder and talked to the woman. They looked right at you. When Mrs Forster had finished with us, theirs was the only table she stopped at on her way back to the kitchen. Trousers.'

I peeled off the skinny jeans that had stood in for the salwar she hadn't packed. 'Good work, love. Could you describe her?'

'English people all look the same to me. Night night.'

15 — *Probable Cause*

'Stop looking round. She isn't here and you're making me dizzy.'

It was a very subdued Mina at breakfast. This time she'd chosen the darkest corner of the restaurant to avoid the sun. We hadn't said much to each other so far this morning.

She kept her eyes and voice down. 'She's not a resident. When they got up to go last night, her husband took out a set of car keys and passed them to her. They weren't staying here.' She tried to eat some of the fruit I'd put together for her and made a face of disgust. 'Get me a bacon sandwich. It's the only thing that works.'

I moved the bowl of fruit to my side of the table and headed to the hot buffet. Mina has never knowingly eaten beef in her life. Not once. The bacon habit she picked up from Miles, though it was always puréed until she got her jaw re-built.

'Mmm,' was all I got for the next ten minutes. I'd finished my porridge and her fruit before she opened her mouth to speak rather than to nibble daintily at the bacon. 'That woman. Witch, I suppose. She wasn't very distinctive. More wholesome in a *Call the Midwife* sort of way rather than distinctive.'

'Would you recognise her again?'

'Of course. I'd spot her hair first, if she didn't change it. That triple plait must have taken her ages.'

'Did it have a fourth strand, sort of appearing half way down?'

Mina woke up a bit. 'Since when are you an expert on women's hair? Or men's, being so follicly challenged yourself.'

'It's a Goddess braid. Definitely a Witch and probably a Sister of the Water. You'll see more tonight, and for that you will need your warm clothes.'

She looked at me suspiciously. 'Why?'

'While you were still unconscious, I went for a walk. I ran into Mrs Forster – Andrea, by the way. She invited us to a special tea this afternoon. Outside.'

'In March? In Krishna's name, why?'

'A surprise. You'll see.'

She slapped the table. 'No! I am not turning up to some Pagan frolic without clear directions.'

'I doubt there'll be frolicking. I've got no more idea than you – I'm a Heathen, not a Pagan, remember? Just wear your new shoes. There may be gardening.'

'Grrrrrrrnh. You're impossible when you're in a good mood. Be more depressed, please. That woman's husband must love her.'

'Which woman? What husband?' I resisted the urge to look round.

'The Witch-woman with the hair. He must have helped her do that. Or a daughter, maybe.'

'Vicky did it on her own, and she's not a Witch. Are you done? I don't want you to be late for the Brimstone Spa.'

'Don't they have fire and brimstone in the Christian Hell? You're not leaving me with a bunch of magickal evangelists, are you?'

'Not to my knowledge. It's just a nice spa at the Langdale Hotel.'

In the upper Lune Valley, just before the river turns to head due east towards its source in Newbiggin, there's a flat plain that slopes up towards Shap. I could have said *at Junction 38 on the M6*, but that ignores the underlying geography. When I arranged to meet Vicky, I just told her to meet in the hotel at Tebay Services.

If you've never stopped at Tebay, I can thoroughly recommend it. Not only is the setting beautiful, it restores your faith in the service industry. The hotel, tucked away behind the lorry park, is just as nice, and that's where we all gathered.

Old Tom was there first and I found him leaning on the bright red Audi TT that we'd taken from Adaryn ap Owain in Wales and which he'd driven up this morning. According to my dad, we may be distantly related to the Thomas family, and they're certainly one of the oldest families in the village. Old Tom (and no, I don't know his first name), used to be an agricultural labourer, and now that he's retired, he'll do almost anything for cash, especially with the Gold Cup coming along soon. I just hoped that he'd worn a clean coat to drive up.

We passed a few minutes until Eric Robson appeared with Vicky in his passenger seat. After handshakes and introductions, Eric headed off to drop Old Tom at Carlisle Station on his way home. Vicky waited until they'd disappeared before she gave me a big hug.

'I've missed you,' she said. 'I didn't think it was possible, but I did.'

'I've missed you, too, Vicky, and not just for your magickal talents.'

'You've got Mina, now. How is she? Where is she?'

'Having a spa day. And yes, it's wonderful to be with her. I still missed you, though. Come on, let's get inside.'

I'd booked a meeting room, and got a good rate because it was a Saturday. We settled in with a pot of coffee, both instinctively choosing chairs with a view outside.

'How's...'

We'd both said it at the same time. I gestured for her to start, and she asked me how my arm was.

'Getting there. I need a few more days, a bit more exercise. I'll feel a lot happier when I've collected my holsters on Thursday. How are you? How did it go with the Depute Constable?'

'Fine. We were both a bit embarrassed by it, especially after Diarmuid's statement turned up. He's going to put a note on file recommending that we plan things a bit more thoroughly.'

I didn't rush to reply. I passed her the plate of biscuits, and she moved them well away. 'And what do you think, Vicky? Are you ready to go back to field operations?'

'Mam and Dad don't think I should. So long as we take it steady, I'll be fine. He had a point though, we should have a bit more of a plan next time.'

'And you're happy to look at this now, even though you're still officially on sick leave and barred from duty?'

'Howay, man, don't be daft. Since when did rules ever stop you doing summat you wanted? Pass it here.'

By way of an answer, I got out the Driscoll material and spread it over the desk.

She started with the quill. She took the glossy black feather out of the Egyptian tube and placed it in front of her. She got her sPad and switched on the camera function. She stared at it. She shivered.

'That's evil, that is.'

I put my coffee down. 'I thought there was no such thing as evil magick. Rick said it has the same Work in it as Hledjolf's ammunition for the Hammer.'

'Aye, he's right, but you can choose what to use your gun for. So far, you've only used it in self-defence. This is different. This can only be used to cause harm. There is no acceptable use for this kind of magick.'

'That tells us something,' I said. 'Any more clues?'

'It's old. It's got some sort of preservative magick underneath, and a layer below that, too. If I tried to dig any deeper, I'd probably destroy it.'

'How old? A couple of years? A couple of centuries?'

'About twenty years old. Possibly a bit older. If we get a sample of script, I should be able to tie it to this pen.'

She glanced at the contents list of the paper bundle, then moved it aside. 'I've read all them. The Depute Constable said it was the most bizarre set of case papers he'd seen since the Dr Hyde incident, back in the eighties. That's the 1980s. He's a good bloke, is Dan.'

Lieutenant Colonel Daniel McCabe, Depute Constable for the Peculier of Scotland is quite a mouthful. No wonder he preferred "Dan".

'What did he make of them?' I asked.

'Same as Hannah, same as you, I imagine. Driscoll is covering for someone. I know I didn't get a close look at Diarmuid after I broke his legs, but he's no great Mage. I can see him messing around with horse embryos, but not Malaglyphs.'

'Leg. Singular. In the small print, it says that only one leg was actually fractured. The other had a hairline. Wouldn't even have needed a cast. Still hurts like hell, though.'

'That I only broke one leg is no great comfort, Conrad. Let's have a look at this Parchment.'

To me, the Parchment was a high quality but very blank piece of paper. To Vicky, it clearly had a story to tell. She repeated the trick with the sPad, then started stroking the paper with her fingertips. 'This could take a while,' she said.

I topped up both our coffees and went outside for a smoke. As I left the room, Vicky had unconsciously drawn the plate of biscuits towards her and started nibbling on a custard cream.

I found the smoking shelter and considered what Vicky had said about planning our operations. As far as I could remember, all the life-threatening situations we'd been in were ones where we had no idea what was waiting for us, and could have had no idea. It was still a good point though. I'd have to give it some proper thought. I finished my smoke and headed back.

Vicky was sitting back, looking at the empty plate of biscuits.

'Are you done?' I asked

'I should really get Cheng to have a look at it. We'll definitely need his testimony if we're going to go to court. What I'm certain of is two things: it wasn't created with that black quill, and it wasn't written by Diarmuid. Definitely a woman.'

'How do you know?'

'She bled on to the Parchment. Must have cut herself trying to sharpen the quill. As for the actual Work that was used, that was pretty well put together, and quite simple really.'

'Explain it in equally simple terms. Simpler if possible.'

'What did Becka think she'd been given on that paper?'

'A Horse passport. They're a bit like the V5 logbook for a car, but with added DNA.'

'Figures. They used a Mirror Glyph, and it only works if you've got the original document, though I imagine that they were copying a forgery, if you see what I mean. You Enscribe the Mirror, put it on top of the original, and it makes an exact copy, right down to the thickness of the paper. A good Enscriber can fake banknotes, human passports, anything. The Mirror Glyph was combined with what we Millennials call a Trash Glyph.'

'And the grown-ups? What do they call it?'

'A Trash Glyph. There is a Latin name, but no one uses it in the beginner classes. There's a time limit on the magick, and as soon as it expires, the Trash Glyph wipes everything, and anyone in the area will want to burn the Parchment, and that was the first sign we're not dealing with a Master, because Becka put the Parchment in the kindling box, not the stove.'

119

'It can't have been completely wiped or you wouldn't know it was there.'

'You're learning fast, Conrad. If it had been an Eraser Glyph, there would be no trace at all. Only a Master Enscriber could do that, and whoever did this is no Master.'

'Presumably a Master wouldn't leave blood spatters on their work, either.'

'You're right. So, where do we go from here?'

'Have a look at this.'

You'd think that the law relating to the use of magick would be written in heavy leather bound books. It probably is, somewhere. Thanks to Maxine Lambert, some parts of the King's Watch have entered the twenty-first century and all the Orders of the Occult Council are available in searchable PDF files.

I took a ring binder from my briefcase and opened it where a Post-it note had marked the place. Vicky took the binder and read it carefully. Then she read it again using her finger to move under the words. '*That you shall not seduce a horse from its master on pain of death.* Does that mean what I think it means?'

'That woman who turned up at FERC either stole the horses or broke the law on equine movement. Both are crimes, and horse theft still carries the ultimate punishment.'

'Great. If we had someone to arrest, we'd be in clover.'

'We are in clover. To be exact, it's Diarmuid who's in deep shit. We now have reasonable grounds to interview him, or as they say in America, we have *probable cause.*'

'Fair enough. What's the next step?'

'You write it up, and I add a few legal references. We email it to Hannah, and see if she lets us off the leash. Do you fancy lunch before you burn up the road to Kirkby Stephen?'

'Aye. Go on. You can tell me all about what you and Mina have been up to.'

16 — *Words over Water*

'Why is there a plant in the back of the car?' said Mina, somewhat dreamily, when I collected her from the Brimstone Spa.

'It's an offering for the vernal equinox. Have you had a nice time?'

'Mmm. Zuzanna was lovely. Her name would get a lot of points in Scrabble, if it wasn't a name. And foreign. I'm going to close my eyes now.'

'You will owe me for this, Conrad. Owe me big time,' she said a while later as she stared at the wardrobe.

'I thought the spa treatment was payment in advance.'

'Can I wear jeans? Do I have to put on ceremonial robes?'

'We're in the middle of nowhere. This isn't a closed order service, so you can wear whatever you want. I'd go with layers because it's warm in the sun, but it might be windy down by the tarn.'

She didn't quite go the full penguin, but she was certainly dressed for all weathers when I led us back upstairs.

'Where are we going? I thought the tarn was down there.'

'It is, but the path starts in the car park, and I need to pick up the offering.'

'What offering?'

I opened the car and lugged out the small shrub. 'This. It's *nandina domestica*, also known as Sacred Bamboo. Native to the Himalayas. Should stand a chance in the Lakes. You're going to give it as a Spring offering. Don't worry, I'll carry it down.'

'And you?'

'I shall make an offering of Lux. A small one.'

'If I join your world of magick, will there be a lot of this sort of thing?'

'If you took the job at Merlyn's Tower, would you still go to temple and make offerings to Ganesh?'

She looked offended. 'Of course.'

'And would you expect me to join you for big festivals?'

She stopped on the path for a second. 'Expect? No. Be honoured? Yes.'

'Then ditto. Look, there we are.'

There was a good view of the tarn from the hotel, which we'd both enjoyed many times since arriving. However, you couldn't quite see *all* of the water, because part of it had been deliberately screened by trees and rocks, which did double duty as camouflage and windbreak. About ten metres up from the water's edge was a south-facing wild garden, full of shoots and life and the feeling that Winter was over. Mina took my free hand and gave it a squeeze.

Half a dozen women and two men were gathered by a small shelter at the top of the garden. I recognised Andrea Forster, the couple who'd stayed at the hotel last night and the Maître D', together with her son/nephew. Three other women made up the party, and it was the middle one (in age) who welcomed us. She was also wrapped up warm, with a high neck to her parka. An open and happy face, full of laughter lines, peered over the top. Like all the other women, she sported the Goddess braid.

I handed the plant to Mina. It was a small detail, but in the world of magick it's important that gifts come from the hand of the giver, not their boyfriend. 'Will you accept this?' said Mina.

'It's lovely,' said the woman. She glanced at the label. 'Very thoughtful – we haven't got one of those. I'm Natasha Bickerdike, Witch of this water.'

Mina didn't give her false name, she made Namaste instead.

'Welcome,' said Natasha. She tilted her head to one side and brushed a stray hair out of her face. I could feel magick in the air, and so could Mina, even if unconsciously. She raised her hand to her face and rubbed her third eye. Natasha pointed to it. 'Is that called a bindi?'

Mina smiled nervously. 'It would be, if I had one. Just moisturiser and foundation today.'

'No, I can see it,' said Natasha. 'You have been touched by the gods. You are more than welcome.'

Mina lowered her head. 'Not me. Him. He's the one.' She pointed to me.

Natasha's eyes didn't leave Mina. 'I know, but that's his business. It's you I'm bothered about. I can see that you lied for him. Often. And that you're doing it here with your name. I can also see that you did it for love.'

Mina's hand shot to her mouth, as it always does when she's nervous. She keeps forgetting that she doesn't have to hide her face any more. She took half a step back, away from Natasha.

The Witch took Mina's hand and lowered it gently from her face. 'Your secret is safe with me. Don't worry. Would you like to join in? Join in properly?'

'How…?'

'Come with me.'

Mina looked at me. 'Go,' I said.

The rest of the company had been out of earshot during this exchange, but they'd all been watching. Andrea came over and asked me to join them. In that wonderfully English way, there was curiosity written all over her face, loud and clear, with not a word said about what she'd just seen.

'We don't have a special tree, or stone, or spring here. It's just the garden and the water. We line up at the edge to make our offerings. Have you done this before?'

'No.'

'Then I'll take it easy on you. Natasha will lead the prayers, her niece will take the offering.'

The snap of a twig drew my eyes back to the shelter. Mina's hat had gone, and in its place was an immaculate Goddess braid with not a single hair out of place. Natasha had a protective hand on Mina's shoulder and looked very pleased with herself.

Mina looked nervously happy, like a bride before her wedding. She came over and stood next to me, beckoning for me to lean down. 'I'll tell you later,' she whispered, eyes gleaming.

We'd been standing around for a while now, the others much longer. Natasha took her coat off and pulled a necklace out from under her white tunic dress.

She was good. The devotions were short but heartfelt and long enough for me to zone in to the present, to feel the wind on my face and catch reflections of the clouds amongst the ripples on the tarn.

Natasha's niece moved along the line with a tiny chalice, a solid gold bowl on top of a silver stem. We each took the chalice and raised it to our lips, not to drink, but to breathe out a little of ourselves and mist the golden bowl with Lux. The young woman's part in this was to hold the stem and work her magick as we breathed, taking no more or less than we could spare. When she came to Mina, she put her finger to Mina's lips and smiled. Mina smiled back.

The chalice was given to Natasha and she took a step to the edge of the tarn. She whispered a final devotion, raised the chalice, then lowered it slowly into the water. An extra breeze whipped up, bending the reeds and taking our offerings from the surface of the tarn. The lightest of fingers brushed against the burns on my head and moved on.

'In peace, let us share your bounty,' said Natasha. She lowered her head for a second, then looked round with a smile. 'Right, everyone. Time for tea.'

Everyone was very polite, no one asked any awkward or embarrassing questions, and the tea was hot, strong and went well with the fresh scones. We were soon on our way back to the Bowfell suite. When we got to the door, it was Mina's turn to put her finger to my lips. 'Everything can wait,' she said.

We were much quicker getting to dinner because Mina left the Goddess braid in her hair. It looked good and went with the all black casual outfit. In fact, we were so early that we went upstairs for a drink first and snagged a window table. There was just a glimmer of light in the west as we sat down.

'I'm in,' said Mina. She grinned and sat back in her comfy chair, almost disappearing into the folds.

'And I'm glad.'

I sat back, too, and waited to see if she could keep quiet. No, is the answer.

'You need magick for the Goddess braid,' she said, leaning forward so that we could keep our voices down. 'Natasha did it for me, and for a short while,

I felt what you felt. A bit. I think. Just enough that I felt the Goddess's blessing when she passed among us. After that, it went back to being a hairstyle.'

That explained a lot. No wonder that the Lunar Sisters and other covens were able to attract non-gifted worshippers. 'How did it feel?' I asked.

'That's the strange thing. The world felt exactly the same – just as cold, just as damp, just as beautiful, but for few minutes, I felt the air moving, not just the pressure of … of gases against my skin, but the whole of the air moving around me. I can't describe it really.'

'Would you want to do it again?' I asked, with just a sneaking worry about addiction at the back of my mind.

'In time and in season. I'd like to know if there's a temple that does the same thing for Ganesh and Krishna. Could you ask for me?'

'I will.'

'Good. I felt something else, too.' She took a deep breath. 'When I was at school, there was a shelf in the chemistry lab that I couldn't reach. It's stupid, but it really annoyed me that they should do that. There was a bench in front so I couldn't stand on a stool to reach it either. That's how I felt when the magick came. I could see it, but I couldn't touch it. I will never be able to do what you do, even though you say it is so little. I simply can't, and no matter how upset I get, I never will.'

We shared a moment, until Mina spoke again. 'What did you find out with Vicky, and how is she?'

I told her, and it took a while. We were downstairs in the restaurant before I finished.

'What now? And what does your boss think about what you discovered on the parchment?'

'She'll be finding out all about it soon. Vicky emailed before we left Tebay, and Hannah doesn't check her emails on Shabbos.

'Now, let's forget about magick. I've been texting my brother with my nice new phone. I'm going to call him tomorrow afternoon. And can you put some more credit on for me?'

Before we went to sleep, I got a message from the Boss: *Promise me to stop involving Vicky now and I'll forgive you. We can discuss it on Thursday. Enjoy the rest of your weekend.*

I promised.

On Sunday, I walked up to Blea Tarn and over into Great Langdale. You get a great view of Bowfell from there. Mina had sharp words with her brother and felt better for it. Andrea Forster was solicitous but not intrusive.

When we checked out on Monday, leaving a stonking great tip in lieu of a 5* review on Trip Advisor, she came to say goodbye.

'It's been lovely to meet you both. You don't need me to say it out loud, but I will anyway. What happens in the Lodge stays in the Lodge. You'll always be welcome. Both of you.'

Before I could say anything, Mina gave her a big hug. There was nothing to add after that.

17 — Orders

'Why did you put in for two days' leave?' asked Hannah on Thursday morning. It was her first question after pouring the coffee. 'You were still on the sick, officially, until today.'

'It's Gold Cup week.'

I might as well have said that it was the world ferret knurdling championship for all she understood. I expanded a little for her benefit. 'The Cheltenham racing festival. Four big days of racing, and it's only five miles down the road from my house. The village cricket club always goes to Ladies Day on the Wednesday. The day before is lads day. Unofficially. I haven't been for years, and a visit to the races while on sick-leave isn't my style.'

She shook her head at me, then grinned. 'Did you lose your shirt?'

'I remained fully dressed throughout, ma'am, as befits an officer and a gentleman. The team captain, however, will have a lot of explaining to do if the village WI ever sees the pictures.'

'Cricket? Racing? Women's Institute? More respectable than hunting, shooting and fishing, I suppose.'

'I've never fished.'

'Hmm. Other than for information, it seems. It shouldn't, but it feels to me like you've been undercover in enemy territory, not the other end of our own country.'

'I got a warmer reception up there than I did in Wales. Apart from the Dragon. She gave me a warm reception.'

She picked up my reports and scanned through them, looking for something. 'There's no expenses claim. Most unlike you.'

'Most of the weekend was pleasure. I was there with Mina.'

She fidgeted. She straightened her skirt. She scratched under her headscarf (green today). 'Mina Desai? That woman you took Vicky to see in prison?'

'Yes.'

Her hands moved around in the air, vaguely pointing at me and vaguely pointing at the window. 'What were you doing with her?'

I raised my eyebrows. 'You want details?'

'No!'

She squeezed her eyes closed and rubbed her temples. 'Please tell me you did not take an ex-con with you on an undercover operation.' She opened her eyes. 'No jokes. Just yes or no.'

'Mina was on weekend release. She did not accompany me to meet with Vicky, and even if she had, I don't see that as a problem. As for the rest, all she did was give a false name at the hotel. She isn't the first unmarried woman to do that.'

She looked out at the Thames, as grey and bleak as her face. 'When is she being released?'

'*Mina* is being released in May. Perhaps sooner.'

'I think that explains a lot. I hope you make a go of it, but I'm not sure that we can have a Watch Captain with someone like that.'

'Someone like what, ma'am?'

'She's not a Witch who got caught selling love potions, she's been convicted of GBH with intent and money laundering *in the mundane courts.*'

We were both leaning forward, both hot under the collar, neither willing to give ground. I decided it was best to go for the nuclear option now rather than later. 'And she's going to be doing maternity cover as Assistant Clerk to the Watch.'

'What! Are you insane?'

'I'm saying it now so that you can get used to the idea.'

'You are insane, or I am, or you think I am. I don't know which.'

I was trying not to lose my temper. It was a struggle.

'I've checked the job description, ma'am. It only says she must not have broken the laws of the Occult Council, which she hasn't. If you get anyone half as suitable, I'll eat my hat. You know it, and so does Maxine. The way things are going, we'll end up like the IXth Legion.'

Hannah threw up her hands. 'I'm not mad, I've just entered a parallel universe where you have to be a criminal to work for the police. I haven't forgotten what you got up to, Conrad, and I haven't ignored the Roman reference, I just don't care.'

It was time for me to shut up.

She closed her eyes again and took two deep breaths. 'We'll pretend we haven't had this conversation. What you do at the weekends is your business, but you will not be going undercover in the Particular in the near future. Is that clear?'

'Ma'am.'

It could have been worse. Not much, but it could have been.

She took off her headscarf and re-tied it as a way of re-setting her temper. 'As for that Parchment you picked up, if that was all you'd done, I'd be a very happy little Constable. That was good work, and so was Vicky's analysis. Li Cheng is going to have a look at it today, and when I get his second opinion, I'll start the ball rolling on getting you and Vicky an interview with our Mr Driscoll. She starts work again officially on Monday.'

I knew that, because she'd told me. I was still trying to work out why she'd asked to base herself at Elvenham House. I'd been planning a return to London.

'Do you think you'll be fit for active service by then?'

127

'Yes, ma'am.'

She picked up a note and stared at it. While she was deciding what to do with it, Tennille stuck her head in and said, 'Cora is here.'

'You'd better go,' said Hannah. 'We don't want to keep the Dean waiting, do we? Actually, you can make small talk with her while I get my wig on.'

I stood up and nodded. 'Thank you, ma'am.' When I left Hannah's office, Tennille slipped inside and shut the door behind her. Hannah's wig is a sight to behold, and she needs it because a great chunk of her skull is titanium plate and she thinks that headscarves are too informal.

The Dean of the Invisible College, Cora Hardisty, is unusual among female Mages in having her hair well above her collar and shaped to her head. She also prefers to dress like a senior academic. Cora is a very capable politician, and according to Vicky, a powerful Sorcerer. We fell out the first time we met, and I'm not saying that we won't do it again.

'Conrad! I wasn't expecting to see you. Or should I add *Dragonslayer* to your rank, Squadron Leader?'

'Dean. Thank you for your work on my behalf in the Occult Council.'

'Shall we drop the status wars at last, and stick to first names? Good. There are a lot of people in Salomon's House who'd love to talk to you about the Dragon, you know. I'd seriously like to arrange a seminar.'

'Of course. Give Tennille some dates and she'll make sure I'm there. I've started work on Project Talpa. Slowly, but I should have Vicky to help next week.'

She looked at the firmly closed doors to the Constable's Office. 'Are you on wig-delaying duty?'

I smiled.

'I wish she wouldn't bother,' said Cora. 'I know you're at the sharp end, Conrad, but do you really think there's one single entity behind these deaths and disappearances?'

I rubbed my chin. 'Entity? Possibly. I'm starting to think that it might be an event rather than an entity, you know, something like the invention of the railways changed the world forever.'

The conversation was interrupted by the reappearance of Tennille. Cora and I shook hands and I headed off to the Old Network for my appointment with Hledjolf the Dwarf.

Underneath, I was seething when I got back to Clerkswell that night. Hannah was the boss, yes, and if she doesn't want Mina in Merlyn's Tower, that's her prerogative. I've put up with far worse situations in the RAF, but that doesn't mean I have to like it.

My mood didn't improve when I got an email from the prison service: due to industrial action, home visits were being suspended this weekend. Mina was going to be locked up and there was nothing I could do about it.

Things got slightly better on the Friday when Tennille called me to say that Hannah was going to see the Cloister Court on Tuesday about getting our interview with Diarmuid. I spent the weekend at a leisure centre in Cheltenham focusing on the truly important things in life: the forthcoming cricket season. Our captain insisted, and who am I to disobey an order?

We picked up another small clue to our equine mystery in the pub. Vicky had arrived on Monday afternoon, we'd gone for a drink in the evening, and I'd had the feeling that there was something she wanted to tell me, but that it might be a few days before she was ready to talk about it. Instead, I broached the subject of Mina and the Watch.

'I'm not trying to recruit you to Team Mina, or put you in an awkward position, but you deserve to know.'

She took a long drink from her dry white wine. I'm still trying to convert her to Inkwell Bitter.

'Bloody hell, Conrad. You don't like a quiet life, do you?'

'I've been trying to achieve it for some years. I sometimes wonder if someone has other plans for me.'

'And Mina's up for it?'

'She doesn't know about Hannah's opposition yet. If she thinks she's not welcome, she won't want to get involved.'

'From what I know of Hannah, she'll calm down, but she won't make it easy. It takes a lot to shift her once she's set against something. You'd have to come up with a pretty damn good reason for her to change her mind.'

'She needs softening up. I just don't know how, yet.'

At that point, we got bumped off the table when a party of four turned up with a reservation and we had to retreat to the noisy end. On the way through, I noticed the old display case.

When Reynold and his then boyfriend bought the Inkwell, it had been pretty much stuck in a horse-brass and stuffed-pheasant time warp. The only thing they'd kept was a collection of quill pens. It's pretty unique, and the pub is called the Inkwell, after all.

I paused at the bar to get Vicky more wine. Reynold himself served me. 'I might have another feather for your collection,' I said.

'Must you? Every year I tell him it's got to go, but he's such a traditionalist. I told him he should take it down and dust them if he loves them so much.' He leaned forward. 'What you got, then? Desert eagle feather from Iraq? Vulture from Afghanistan?'

'A black Australian swan.'

He put the drink on the counter. 'We've got one. Second on the right.'

Weird. All the feathers in the case were white. I took the drink and peered closely at the case. Reynold was right: *Australian Black Swan, flight feather*. White as you like. What's that all about? I pointed it out to Vicky, and she said, 'That would be the underlying Work. Must have dyed it black. Seems like a lot of trouble to me, but some Mages go for the trappings in a big way. Never mind feathers. You never did finish telling me what your pal Chris had to say about that stick.'

'Her name's Madeleine.'

Vicky laughed and we picked up where we'd left off, two weeks ago in Blackthwaite Stables. It really was good to have her back.

Hannah didn't get in touch until Wednesday. We spent Tuesday making some serious headway on Project Talpa once I'd brought Vicky up to speed, and she noticed a glaring omission from the papers. Hannah herself had been nearly killed, and the file simply wasn't there. Perhaps because it would include the details of her husband's death. Vicky knew that it had been bad, but no one she'd talked to had been able to add anything to the plain facts of trauma and death.

We'd also talked about planning better, and started with a plan for Hannah's video call on Wednesday afternoon. The main strategy was that I should sit as far away from the camera as possible, and that Vicky should do all the talking. That lasted for about ten seconds, which was the time it took Hannah to enquire about Vicky's health.

'Conrad, come closer and sit where I can shout at you.'

'Ma'am.'

'Ruth went away for the weekend. With her husband. She left her girls with Auntie Hannah, and do you know what? I had less trouble from them than I get from you, and you're on the other side of the middle of nowhere. I wish I knew what I was being punished for when you were sent into my life. If I knew, I'd could either regret what I'd done or savour the memory. Have I made myself clear?'

'Yes, ma'am.'

'Now, I am going to give you an order. You will carry out this order to the letter, yes?'

'Ma'am.'

She waved a piece of paper to the camera. 'This is a warrant to interview Diarmuid Driscoll. The Hawkshead Cloister Court will give access on Friday morning. You will interview him in relation to the removal of the horses and nothing else. You will then report to me and I will think about it over the weekend. You are not to pursue this in any other way. Do you understand?'

I thought this was going a bit far. I'm used to being torn off a strip, and I can keep my mouth shut when I need to, but did she need to be quite so parental about it? Then again, she hadn't mentioned Mina directly, so perhaps this was her way of re-setting the clock. I decided to take it on the chin.

'Yes, ma'am.'

She couldn't keep it up any longer. 'If you were my Deputy in Chester, I'd send you up there to declare war on the whole pack of them, but you're not. We do this one my way. For now.'

I nodded.

'How's Project Talpa coming along?'

I moved out of the way again, and Vicky took over.

'We're still reading through the files, and we're racking up a list of anomalies that can't be a coincidence. I think we may need to take this to the Esoteric Library for further research.'

Hannah's eyes flicked back to me. 'It's a good job that Dean Cora is speaking to you, Conrad. Things could be a lot worse.'

Vicky cleared her throat. 'We noticed that the Revenant file hasn't been included. Ma'am.'

I still have no idea what a Revenant was, in magickal terms, and it was a Revenant who gave Hannah her catastrophic injuries and killed her husband.

Hannah pulled her lip. 'When you really need it, you can have it. Until then it stays in the safe. I'll send the Cloister Court warrant by special delivery. If you can video-link on Friday, great. If not, phone me. Good luck.'

Vicky and I breathed out. 'We're back on the case,' I said. 'That's a result for me.'

She closed the lid on the laptop and looked at me. 'Is it?'

'Rod Bristow lost his life. His daughter lost her father. Sophie lost her job and an employer who was good to her. You can't tell me they've had justice. Not only that, there's someone out there who's got away with murder and could very well do it again.'

She pointed at the Project Talpa files. 'Wouldn't you rather find out why Helen of Troy and the Dragon and the Revenant are on the loose? If there's something out there that's after us all, wouldn't you rather focus on tracking it down?'

'I don't see why we can't do both. Now that you've brought it up with Hannah, are you ready to tell me what a Revenant is yet?'

She looked out of the window at the afternoon sunshine. 'I don't know meself for certain. I'm ready to tell you what it's not.' She looked back at me. 'All the vampire legends in the world are based on Revenants. They're what our instructors scared us with at school. The reality is far, far worse than anything Bram Stoker dreamt up. Hannah is the only Mage in Europe for well over a century to come up against one and survive. She didn't share the details, but I'm sure she's afraid it'll come back.'

'And how will I know if one knocks at the door?'

'When you feel your soul being dragged down into hell, you'll know about it.' She didn't smile when she spoke, which made me feel very uneasy.

'Come on then. We're going for a walk.'

'Do I have to?'

'Yes.'

We walked up through the garden to the well. Vicky paused with her hand on the parapet for a moment. 'They're still down there,' she said. 'It's the Spirit equivalent of sleeping. They'll be fine indefinitely, so long as nothing changes.'

The path through the wood starts a few metres past the well. Vicky had never been this way before.

'Do you remember the first time you came to Elvenham?'

'Aye. Oof. This is steep.'

'It'll do you good. You said there was a discharged Work in the Dragon. Did you ever find out what?'

'No. We'll have to get a Necromancer down here and get your ancestor out of that well. I'll have another look then.'

I stopped in the middle of the trees. 'The Depute said we should prepare more. I thought an exercise on contact in the woods.'

'Contact?'

'Sorry. It's military jargon for when the enemy start shooting.'

She looked at the damp woods and twitched her nose at the smell of end-stage leaf decomposition. 'On yer bike, Uncle C.'

'Perhaps we'll work up to it,' I said. 'We'll start with a bit of physical conditioning. Like walking up this gentle slope.'

'Gentle slope, my arse. I thought it was all flat round here.'

'Come on.'

I headed off again, giving her the option of following or stomping back to Elvenham House. She followed.

By the time we got past the woods, I could see rain clouds bowling in across the Severn Valley from Wales. We had about half an hour.

Vicky huffed up next to me. 'It is bonny up here. Nice. Have you ever been to the Cheviots?'

'A couple of times on exercise.'

'When I went to stay with the Shield Wall, I drove up to their Hall. Couldn't believe how far out it was. Then we had to walk up to this tree on a hill. God, it was bare.'

'England's forgotten wilderness.'

'You're not joking.'

'Did you hear about Myfanwy? I went to see her. She was asking after you.'

'I heard she pleaded guilty and got sentenced to Seclusion.'

'Did you hear that the only offer to host her was the Shield Wall. She's hoping for a better offer.'

'I'm not surprised. They'd have her cleaning pots in cold water. They're a rather traditional bunch of nutters.'

I didn't float my mad idea past Vicky. One campaign of subversion at a time. I pointed to the path down to the village and we set off together.

'Do you reckon you'll be with Mina this weekend?' she asked.

'I wish I knew. It depends on how many POs are willing to work overtime.'

'Best take two cars, then.'

'Good idea. Let's go and prepare some awkward questions for Dodgy Diarmuid.'

18 — *At Rest*

'T'his is more like it,' said Vicky. 'Proper mountains, proper lakes, proper tourist tat shops.'

I passed her a coffee. It had been strange driving up on my own with nothing but the radio for company. To avoid the embarrassment of chasing each other up the motorway, we'd set off separately and made a rendezvous at the main car park in Hawkshead. The drive along Coniston Water and over the ridge to Hawkshead certainly counted as more of a taste of the Lake District than did our foray to Blackthwaite.

'Still no news?'

Vicky had caught me checking my phone, for the umpteenth time today. 'No. She's saving some credit for when she knows what's happening.' I had no idea whether I'd be seeing Mina or not, or if I did, for how long.

'My car or yours?' she asked.

'Mine. More leg room. The pilot should be here soon.'

'Pilot? I am *not* flying anywhere.'

'Pilot as in ships.' She looked at me blankly. 'When a big ship comes near a port, a local pilot gets on board to guide them into harbour, or in this case, into the Esthwaite Rest without having to mess about breaking Glamours and evading Wards.'

'Mansplaining again, Conrad. I know more about Glamours and Wards than you ever will. Why didn't you just call her an escort?'

'It's a him, and he won't be armed, so he's not an escort. The other stuff I admit to. Sorry.'

She had a point, but she wouldn't normally have pulled me up on it, something confirmed when she put her coffee on the roof of my car and took out a box of Xanax tablets.

Interviews with convicted prisoners serving a sentence have to be carried out in a Limbo chamber. That's what they call the magick which blocks out Lux, as seen in prisoners' cells and the cage in the Cloister Court that serves as the dock. And that's why Vicky was taking a tranquiliser. She was dreading it because she knew what would happen. I was dreading because I didn't, and because I was worried about her.

'They said I'd recognise you,' came a voice from beyond the hedge. It was followed by a cheerful, wrinkled chap of advanced years. He introduced himself as Bailiff Gabriel. 'Just *Gabriel*. I dropped the other names a long time ago.'

Vicky looked around. 'Where's your car?'

He grinned. 'I walked. It's only a mile and a half. Shall we?'

He spent the short drive out of the village telling us that soon we wouldn't be able to park here at all on account of the tourists. 'From Easter onwards, it's like Blackpool in here. You can use the car park at the Cloister Court, as you're official.'

'Where's that?'

He laughed. 'You've driven past it. Just up the road there. It pretends to be a farmhouse. Turn right here.'

Esthwaite is a stunning little lake, set in perfect rolling fields and much loved by aficionados of Beatrix Potter. He took us half a mile down the little road on the western side of the water. To our left, walkers and fishermen were making the most of the outdoors.

'Slow right down here,' said Gabriel, 'and look out for a gap in the hedge on the right.'

He touched his chest and closed his eyes. I focused on the road and, round a slight bend, I saw a narrow opening in the tightly bound hawthorn. There was just enough room to swing the Volvo through and up the stone track towards a wood.

'Into the trees and swing left.'

The track divided twenty metres into the trees. I took the left fork and came across a clearing I hadn't seen from the road. A battered Ford Fiesta was parked away from the track, and I pulled in next to it. The track dead-ended at more trees ahead of us.

To the left was a grass promontory sticking out from the slight slope. It reminded me of ... aah. The grass roof at Little Langdale Lodge. Of course. One of the Lakeland magickal families must specialise in construction. The bulk of the Rest would be underground, leaving only the windows to be Occulted. Neat.

We got out of the car, and I said, 'Did Driscoll's lawyer walk, or did you fetch him?'

'Didn't you know?' said Gabriel. 'He doesn't want a lawyer. This way.'

He led us through the trees a short way, then turned round. Behind us, a set of steps had appeared which we hadn't seen on the way past. We followed him down the steps and through a substantial but not steel door. Already, the security here was less than at the Undercroft.

Inside the Rest was a reception area with two doors. Bailiff Morgan had used the Navy term *Wardroom* for his lair in the Undercroft; up here the sign said *Bailiff's Bothy*. The other, more substantial door had no signs on it. Gabriel opened a cupboard.

'Because you're going into Diarmuid's room, you'll need to deposit all your magick in here.'

The inside of the cupboard was mini-bank of safety deposit boxes. I stood aside to let Vicky go first.

She opened one box and looped the Artefacts from round her neck. After placing them in the box, she took the stamp and manipulated the lock. 'Level 5,' she whispered. 'Do you want me to lock yours when you're done?'

'Please.'

I dropped my own Artefacts in another box and checked to see if Gabriel were watching. He had turned away and didn't see when I deposited the Hammer and its holster. That left me with one more magickal item – the other holster. Unfortunately, there wasn't room in the box for two handguns, and as the SIG isn't magickal, I stuffed it in my back waistband and dropped the holster in the box. Vicky did the honours with the lock.

'Ready,' I said. I wasn't sure if Vicky would ever be ready for this, but if we wanted answers, we had to ask the questions.

'Do you want more coffee?' said Gabriel.

'We're fine,' said Vicky, shaking her hair loose and bracing herself in front of the unmarked door.

Gabriel unlocked the door using an Artefact. From the way that he pushed the bronze disk into the door plate, I think it was a combination of his Imprint and the Artefact that worked as the key.

While the Undercroft is all patched-up mediæval stonework, Esthwaite Rest is unequivocally modern. A straight corridor of poured concrete, about 15m long, was punctuated by three openings on the left, towards the lake, and four on the right. It ended in a door like the one we'd come through. Gabriel pointed right. 'Those are the short-term lock-up. Up to three nights. They're all empty at the minute, and we've only got Diarmuid in the long-stay rooms. He's at the end, next to the kitchen. I'll need to lower the grille for you.'

The cells in the Undercroft had their one-way mirrors and lobbies. The ones in the Rest all opened straight off the corridor; they were much bigger, too. The entrance was protected by a 2m square bronze grille set into a steel frame. Beyond it was an antechamber with cupboards, on top of which lay the remains of Diarmuid's breakfast, cups and bowls neatly stacked on a tray. The main part of the cell was beyond the antechamber and in shadow.

Gabriel took four Artefacts out of his pocket; they looked like duty-free shop fridge magnets. 'Been on holiday, Gabriel?' I said, trying to lighten the atmosphere for Vicky's benefit.

'Bit gaudy, aren't they?' said Gabriel. He offered me one. 'That's a North.'

I inspected the little plaster souvenir, and I could feel the magick. That didn't detract from the awfulness of the Viking longship and flag of Norway, though. He showed me another with an elephant and the flag of South Africa. 'Don't spoil the surprise,' I said, passing him back the Norway souvenir.

'It's just so I don't make mistakes,' said Gabriel. He put the two North magnets on either side at the top of the metal casing surrounding the grille, put the two Souths at the bottom and put a physical key in a hidden switch box. 'The Artefacts are to maintain the Limbo status when I do this.'

He turned the key and the grille dropped slowly into the floor. If it had gone upwards we'd have needed to be three metres further underground. Gabriel stepped over the threshold and said something. I don't know what he said because despite the fresh air blowing into the room, no sound came back. He picked up the breakfast tray and stepped out. Now that the grille was gone, I could see down a short passage into a bigger, brighter room beyond with daylight pouring into it. I could just make out a white plaster cast.

'He's waiting. I'm bringing some coffee for Diarmuid so I'll make a pot anyways and you can suit yourselves. There's three green buttons inside; press any of them if you need me. Press the red ones for a genuine emergency.'

He took the tray through the nearby door and I caught a glimpse of a small kitchen. I turned to Vicky. 'Together?'

She nodded and we crossed the threshold.

For just a moment, I was straight back to a storm over Helvellyn. The climber had no broken bones, so we'd winched him up instead of trying to land. The guys in the back were busy securing him and I got us a bit more height. Then an updraught took the chopper towards a sheer drop and a sidewind pitched us round. For that moment, I didn't know which way was up and which way certain death.

In the chopper, I'd pulled the stick left and prayed. In the Esthwaite Rest, I staggered into the antechamber wall, gripped it for dear life and checked on Vicky. She was holding her head as if she'd just been whacked with a cricket bat and was sinking at the knees. I felt drunk, seriously legless and incapable of walking in a straight line. I fixed my eyes on Vicky's hair and took a step towards her.

She let out a moan and sank further. I put my arm under her shoulder and lifted her so that we could cling on to each other in the storm. She put her free hand round my back and whispered, 'Conrad, I can't see. It's all gone black.'

I moved my left arm and pulled her hand away from her eyes. I rubbed my fingers around the orbit of her right eye and said, 'Can you feel that? Can you feel my fingers?'

'Aye. I'm scared. I don't want to open me eyes.'

'Think of blue. Think of my RAF uniform.' I tilted her head and put my face down until our noses were nearly touching, keeping my fingers moving. 'Open your right eye now.'

She did, and jerked back. I kept hold of her enough for both of us to stay upright. She took a deep breath.

'You are an ugly sod, close up. I don't know how Mina does it.'

'She closes her eyes, too. You're no oil painting, either. How do you feel?'

'Hurt. My self-image may never recover. I can see, though. How about you?'

'Tipsy. Disoriented. I'd ask you to hold my hand only Diarmuid will get the wrong idea.'

'Everything's faded all of a sudden.' She held up her hand. 'These fingernails look white when they should be pearl grey.'

'I'll take your word for it. Let me try and stand on my own.'

We backed away from each other, and I reckoned that I could manage to walk. 'After you,' I said.

Vicky led the way down the short passage with doors on either side. The one on the left was ajar, and showed us a white tiled bathroom with a towel on the floor in a pool of water. Showering, on your own, with your leg in plaster is not easy. Been there, done that. I didn't blame Diarmuid for the mess.

His sitting room was very nice, or it would be if the walls didn't move slightly. The picture window was twice the size of the grille and the lake views were indeed stunning. Better than we got at the Little Langdale Lodge. The rest of the room was in awe of nature, subdued and submissive by contrast, and only the obdurate black face of the wall-mounted television made an effort to draw your attention away from the Lakeland vista. Diarmuid didn't get up to shake our hands.

He was in a wheelchair, and had placed himself in a position to swivel easily between the TV and the view. A comfy armchair had been pushed out of the way in a corner, leaving two dining chairs facing the prisoner for us to sit on. A small coffee table sat between them and a bigger one was at Diarmuid's right hand. His table had a TV remote, a notebook, a paperback and a little black box with two buttons on top, one red and one green; I'd noticed the same unit fixed to the wall in the bathroom.

The room was well ventilated and just the right temperature for sitting in your shirt sleeves. I'm glad it was ventilated, because I did get a waft of *eau de bachelor* on the way through. I wouldn't want to be cleaning this place in four years' time.

'Mr Clarke! Good to see you. How's the arm?'

'Getting better. How's the leg?'

'Ditto. Have a seat.'

I waited for Vicky to sit down. She moved one of the dining chairs firmly away from the window. 'Sorry,' she said. 'It's easier if don't face the light.'

'You'll be a Sorcerer, then,' said Diarmuid. 'Always gets the eyes.' Vicky said nothing and plonked herself down.

I did the same and took a deep breath. The walls took pity on me and stopped moving, and I turned my head slowly to look at Diarmuid, trying not to set the nausea off again. I took a moment to adjust my posture because the SIG was digging into my back.

Keira Faulkner had clearly been going insane in the Undercroft; Myfanwy Lewis had been dying slowly. Diarmuid Driscoll seemed hardly bothered at all, and you couldn't tell whether his discomfort came from lack of access to Lux or from his broken leg. He'd even shaved this morning.

'I would have wrote you, if they'd let me,' he said. 'Not to help youse out, you understand, just to ask if you'd pop into the charity shop and buy some DVDs.' He pointed to the television. 'No cable or Freeview in here. Just DVDs. What I'd give to see the Grand National in a couple of weeks. I've a cousin with the back leg of a horse running.'

'Sorry?' said Vicky.

'My cousin's a partner in a syndicate that owns a racehorse,' said Diarmuid. 'You both had a good journey, then?'

We had planned a strategy for this interview, but left the final decision on roles until we'd crossed the threshold. We had no idea who would be affected most by the Limbo chamber, but the basic plan had been for me to be bad cop because I'd been shot, and for Vicky to be good cop because she'd broken his leg. Now that we were here, I chose good cop/no cop because Vicky was disappearing by the second.

'I don't bother much with the National,' I said. 'Too random. I did have a good couple of days at Cheltenham, though.'

'Were you there?'

'Yes. I had time to spare, what with being off sick.'

'Sorry about that. I hope you put your shirt on JJ's Auntie in the Mares' Hurdle.'

Say what you like about Diarmuid, he knows his horses. 'I did. She certainly has stamina.'

'Beautiful horse.'

'Apparently you've something of a name yourself, Diarmuid.'

'Ach, not that anyone outside the Particular knows it.'

'What is the Waterhead Chase, exactly?'

'It's ours, that's what it is. Nothing else like it anywhere. That's what I'll be missing the most. I'm telling you, Conrad, I'll be in tears all through next winter.'

You'll have noticed his switch from *Mr Clarke* to *Conrad*. We were in no rush. So long as he kept talking, I was fine. I moved my legs and caught a glimpse of Vicky. Oh. Perhaps we wouldn't be fine. Her nostrils were dilating and her pupils were fixed on some point in the mid-Atlantic.

'Go on. It must be very special.'

'It happens on the first full moon after the Winter Solstice, over three nights. It's the Skelwith boys' gift to the Particular, a sort of thank-you-for-having-us thing, what with them being Gnomes and all. They spend a week hiding a route from all the way up at Moss Leigh at the top of Great Langdale to Waterhead. Eight miles it is, eight miles of dry stone walls, fences, woods, snow if you're lucky, and becks raging down the fells. And all for the chase.'

'Chase? As in hunting?'

'Sure. Folks line up all along the route to have a go at the chasers. It's all a bit of fun now, but there's a monument to the fallen at Moss Leigh.'

'Is it worth buttering someone up to get an invitation.'

'For you, Conrad, a pleasure. I'll send you some names in the summer. Give you a chance to work on them.'

I glanced at Vicky. Still somewhere else.

'Was that what you were breeding the horses for?'

Diarmuid looked down. He knew we were moving towards the formal part of the interview and he made himself more comfortable in preparation. He also looked slightly guilty.

'Greed. My last winner was a lovely stallion, all ready to be the making of my little stud. Then the eejit girl rolled him down a fecking cliff. She wasn't too bad, but by the time we got to the poor horse, it was too late. I'd been working on a Charm to capture his Imprint and I had a go just before we had to put him out of his misery.'

'Then what did you do?'

'I bent the rules a bit. Cloning and surrogacy aren't banned in magick as such, but they're not allowed for horses.'

'So why did you ship the mare out to Olivia?'

'Who?'

I gave him a hard stare. 'You know who.'

'I was never going to put the colt to the Chase; that would be stupid. I was going to put him to stud, and if I could pretend I'd bought him in, no one would check too much.'

I took the Cloister Court Warrant out of my adjutant's case and placed it on his coffee table. The smell of aftershave made me sit back sharpish and I banged the gun into my spine. Ow.

'That's a warrant, Diarmuid. Just a formality. You don't want a lawyer?'

'No. Where's Gabe with that coffee? I'll give him a buzz in a minute.'

'Don't bother on our account. Were these horses registered?'

He could see where I was going from miles away. His body language started making distinct *fight or flight* movements, somewhat hampered by the cast on his leg. His eyes flicked from me to Vicky, and he must have taken some comfort from her appearance because he settled down and answered my question.

'Sure, the mare was registered good and proper. Not my horse. I just borrowed her.'

I had my notebook out. 'Who from.'

'You wouldn't know him.'

I left my pen poised and said nothing.

'Cousin in the old country. Eamon. Shipped her over specially.'

'Eamon Driscoll?'

'That's the one.'

I wrote down the name. 'Of…?'

'Narraghmore. County Kildare.'

'And the colt?'

'What about him?'

'You sent someone down to take the DNA sample.'

'We didn't really sample him. He's not going on the national register. I just did that to keep Mrs Bentley happy.'

'Who did you send?'

'A friend of mine has a daughter wants to be a vet.'

'Friend's name? Daughter's name?'

He shook his head so sadly. 'I'm sorry, Conrad, but it's that notebook of yours that's doing my head in. It's like this, see? You London folk will go everywhere checking everything and talking to Mrs Bentley, and before you know it, the poor girl's name is being dragged through the mud and she won't get into vet school. I'll blow the trumpet and summon the archangel, shall I?'

He broke eye contact and looked down at his table. Taking his time, he picked up the box. He looked at Vicky again and nodded to himself. He knew she couldn't keep this up much longer. With a flourish, he pressed the green button and placed the box back on his table.

'He shouldn't be long,' said Diarmuid. 'Where were we?'

'More to the point, Mr Driscoll, where are the horses?'

'They're …' He stopped, caught in a dilemma. He folded his hands and said, 'They're still at Mrs Bentley's, aren't they?'

'I'm afraid they've been removed. Without horse passports.'

His manufactured outrage was transparent, but at least he made an effort. 'That's a terrible thing! Stolen, you say?'

'I do. Do you have any idea who might have taken them?'

'How could I when I'm stuck in here?'

Vicky shifted in her seat. I kept my eyes on Diarmuid, until Vicky screamed.

'Contact!'

I dived to my left, away from the opening to the corridor and rolled. Vicky threw herself flat on the floor and started crawling to the right. Diarmuid had no choice. He had to sit there as a terrible roar of thunder reverberated around his prison cell and blood blossomed out of his chest.

19 — The Luck of the Irish (Part Two)

I had the SIG out of my waistband just as Diarmuid slumped forward. I stood up, using the rush of adrenaline to get me upright, propped against the wall and out of sight from the passage to the antechamber. Vicky had had the same idea and was on the other side of the opening. I raised my gun and made a motion for her to get down so that I could shoot anyone who came after us. I strained my ears for sounds, but heard nothing over the aftereffects of the gunshot.

What did we know? I knew, and was very grateful for the fact that it was a hunting rifle. The distinctive sound and the single shot said that. If the shooter had had another weapon, he or she would have come in and attacked all three of us, but they had chosen to use their one free shot to kill Diarmuid. Even a novice, in a panic, would have reloaded by now.

I made eye contact with Vicky and mouthed the word *mirror* to her and pointed to her bag on the floor. She rolled her eyes at me like a total teenager and reached into her pocket. She took out her phone and unlocked the screen. She hit a button and lay on the floor, stretching the back of the phone to the corner of the passage, angling the screen so she could see it. Of course. A camera.

I waited while she tried for a better angle. She pressed the screen, then turned to show me. I could just make out an empty passage with no one in sight. I stood up, and motioned for her to do the same, and at that moment we did hear a noise: the sound of the grille being raised.

If that grille got to the top of its casing, we'd be well and truly stuck. I raised my gun and dashed out, and then dived into the open bathroom. There was no one in sight behind the grille. I grabbed the towel off the floor and limped up to the entrance, keeping my gun raised. Still nothing. The towel was wet, giving it just enough weight to be a missile. I slung it at the shrinking gap above the grille and it landed on the mesh as the motor pushed it home. The metal compressed the towel, but it hadn't slotted completely home. The motor whined, then stopped. I'd hoped it had a safety feature that would lower the grille again, like a garage door that hits an obstacle, but no. It just stopped.

Vicky was checking Diarmuid for signs of life. In vain. She wiped away a tear and stood back. 'Poor sod. Didn't stand a chance.'

I stood next to her, moving her out of the sight line to the entrance and taking her right hand in my left so that I could keep hold of the gun. She squeezed my hand, and we gave Diarmuid a moment. I let go and glanced down the corridor. The grille was firmly stuck and no one was sticking a rifle through it.

'Take it from the beginning. What did you see?'

'I wasn't really looking. Or listening. I was just trying to hold it together. Still am. Can I have another Xanax?'

'In a bit. You saved our lives, Vicky. Again.'

'I didn't realise at first. I'd seen Gabriel walk past, just normal like, heading to the front entrance from the kitchen. A bit later, two shapes appeared. I couldn't work it out at first, then it hit me: they were using a camouflage glamour. I perked up a bit, and I was gonna say something when one of the shapes stuck a rifle barrel over the line of the Limbo effect. That's when I screamed.'

'You didn't scream. You shouted a warning. You said *he*. Are you sure?'

'One of the shapes was bigger and taller than the other. It was a bloke or a freakishly tall woman. Are you sure I can't take a pill?'

'Give us a hand, first.' I moved to the armchair and, with Vicky's help, we moved it to face the entrance. 'Sit there and keep watch. I'm going to start to get us out of here. I take it you don't have a signal on your phone.'

'No chance.'

The first thing I did was press the red button. Several times. I even did SOS in Morse code. 'I'm not expecting Gabriel to come and get us,' I said, 'but there might be a backup – if the alarm isn't cancelled, it might summon outside assistance. Here. It'll give your thumbs something to do.'

My next job was to approach the entrance, slowly, and examine the grille. I edged up to the metal, ready to shoot or take evasive action. Nothing. The corridor outside was empty. I shoved the gun in my pocket.

The towel had done a stand-up job. There was about 5mm of gap above the grille, and if steel bars do not a prison make, then bronze is even less effective. All I needed was a lever, and I knew the very thing. They were propped in a corner of the antechamber: the late Mr Driscoll's crutches.

One of the (aluminium) crutches was bent to nothing, and we'd had to dismantle his wheelchair to get some steel parts, but the motor on the grille finally gave up the ghost and I forced it down half a metre. Vicky was lying down on Driscoll's unmade bed by then, the second tablet having sent her to sleep. With the sense of triumph from a job well done, I reached through the gap and grabbed the two North magnets. In a heartbeat, the ground became more solid, the walls became straighter and a tiny rush of energy swept up my arm. Good.

After that, it would just be a matter of time, and I took the chance to have a smoke, standing next to the grille and enjoying a Diet Pepsi from the fridge I'd found under a worktop in the antechamber.

I stripped off my shirt and attacked the grille where it ran in the casing. I slowly worked on distorting the grille until I could push it out, gaining me another half metre at one end, enough for me to get out when I was ready. Vicky was still asleep, so I left her there and turned over Diarmuid's lair, looking for evidence. When I'd opened the last DVD box and found nothing, I gave up.

The first thing I'd checked was his notebook, and had been crushingly disappointed. All it contained was alternating sketches of the view from his window and some rather beautiful pencil drawings of horses' heads. It was time to go.

Vicky slowly stirred from her slumber, and allowed me to put my shoulder under her arm to get her to the entrance. When she got near the grille, she opened her eyes a bit. 'That feels good.' She pointed to the bent metal. 'How long did it take you to do that?'

I checked my watch. 'An hour and a half. Can you stand?'

'Aye. Just about. Did you have to smoke in here? It stinks.'

There was a mobility stool in the shower which I'd avoided mangling because I needed it on the other side of the grille. I passed it over the top and placed it on the floor. With a chair on the inside, I managed to get through and felt even better. Vicky just about followed me without tearing strips of herself on the sharp points of bronze. Now we just had to hope that the stout doors between us and the outside weren't locked.

'Give us a minute,' said Vicky, drawing deep breaths of Lux laden air.

'What are the chances of a magickal booby trap?' I asked.

'Do you think Gabriel's involved in this?'

I had a fairly good idea of what Gabriel's involvement was, and he was more likely to be a victim than a conspirator. 'No.'

'Then we should be fine. There's a hell of a lot of Works woven all through this building. Setting a booby trap on top of them would be nigh-on impossible. I'll still check, though, as best I can.'

'Start with the kitchen. You never know, there might be an emergency exit through there.'

'I don't think it's our lucky day, somehow.'

'Hey, Vic, we're alive, aren't we? That always counts as a lucky day in my book.'

'Stop being so bloody cheerful.'

She ran her hands over the door. Without her Artefacts and her sPad, she had to get close and physical to figure it out. That's where I'd have put the booby trap, on the outer surface, knowing that it would be touched. Our luck held. No sudden explosions.

'It's not locked at all,' said Vicky.

I took out my gun and moved to the front. I placed my right boot on the door and balanced carefully. 'You bend down and work the handle, then drop flat and scan the room.'

In one co-ordinated movement, the door flew open and I dived to the floor while Vicky looked around with mundane and magickal senses.

'Clear,' she said. 'And nothing detected.'

The stainless steel worktop was at the right height for me to lever myself up again. I checked the room and decided there wouldn't be anyone hiding in the commercial kitchen fridge. The storeroom was a different matter, and we repeated the manoeuvre with the door. Clear. The only access to outside was a pair of small, high windows that didn't open. On the way out, I took the largest kitchen knife I could find.

The door to reception *was* locked, but not magickally, and was easily opened using the large red button to the side. This time, Vicky didn't cry.

When she saw Gabriel's lifeless body on the floor, she set her jaw and moved straight to the outside door to check that first. 'Unlocked,' she said. 'Now let's see if I've got enough left in me head to work that safe-deposit thingy.'

'Wait. Let's make sure we're completely alone first.'

'No. I think you're wrong. The best place to use that rifle would be from the trees. I'm not opening the door until I've got me Ancile back working, and nor should you.'

'Good point. Get cracking.'

It was a good point, and one that I should have thought of. It took Vicky nearly five minutes to work her own lock, and considerably less for mine after she'd restored her Artefacts. She passed me the box and I loaded up. There was no one outside, and that wasn't the only thing missing. There was no mobile signal, either.

'Bugger,' said Vicky. 'What do we do? The Wards off the road are so strong I might not find our way back if we drive into Hawkshead to get a signal.'

It was my turn to have the good idea. 'There'll be a landline in the Bailiff's Bothy. I'm going to make us some coffee while we decide who to call first.'

I didn't have to make the coffee because there was a perfectly good flask of the stuff on a tray in the kitchen. Making it had been Gabriel's last action before he answered the door and let his killers in. Now, did they knock, or was he expecting them? I took the coffee outside to Vicky, who didn't want to spend a minute underground that she didn't have to. It meant I could stand downwind and have a cigarette.

'We should phone Hannah first,' I said.

'Why? Don't forget, that'll show up on the call log.'

'You heard her. She's paranoid about this case. If we call anyone else, she'll say it was the wrong decision. She's our CO and she can take the flak on this one.'

She gave me the first smile since we'd come outside. 'Yes, sir. Whatever you say, sir.'

'Good. Let's walk around a bit. There might be tyre tracks.'

It took me two minutes to find, not tyre tracks, but hoof prints.

145

'Tell me they didn't come here on horseback,' said Vicky.

'Of course they did. They came from over the hill, somewhere on the way to Coniston Water. Brantwood's in that direction, I think. That's something else we've learnt.'

'Something else? What do you think we've learnt, other than that Diarmuid and Gabriel were killed by two camouflaged blobs?'

'Is that Xanax still in your system?'

'Magick metabolises it more quickly. What are you trying to say?'

'Think about it. Go on, tell me all the things we can figure out, no matter how blindingly obvious.'

To prove my point, I got out my notebook.

'There's at least two of them, for starters. And they're Mages, obvs.' She paused. 'One of them, probably male, has access to a rifle and can use it.' She looked around. 'They can both ride horses. That's it.'

'Those are all facts. What about their knowledge and intentions?'

'Oh. I see. They know the Rest. They know it fairly well. They knew the routines and what to expect.' She looked worried. 'Do you think they knew we'd be there?'

'I do. It can't have been a coincidence. They must have heard about the warrant for the interview from somewhere, and that begs more questions. Did they arrive late, not expecting us to be there? Did they have an electronic bug in there? Did they hear what Diarmuid was saying? And above all, why didn't they come mob-handed and try to take us out as well? I'm glad they didn't, of course.'

Vicky threw the dregs of her coffee in the sprouting bracken. 'It smells mouldy out here,' she said. 'Too wet under all these trees. I think I know the answer to that.'

'Go on.'

'I think they could only get one firearm. They're not like you. They don't drive round with an arsenal in the boot of their car and two guns strapped to their belt. And they had to take the shot from outside the Limbo chamber or I'd have seen them. If more than the rifle barrel had crossed that threshold, they'd have had to kill all three of us. That was your contribution.'

'Eh? You've lost me.'

'Conrad the Dragonslayer. In a completely non-magickal fight, I don't think they fancied their chances against you. They did what they had to and legged it.'

'Don't flatter me. You might be partly right, though. They must have been desperate to silence Diarmuid, though. And they must think that all the shit that's going to rain down on them for murdering a Bailiff is worth the risk of leaving two Watch officers alive.'

She picked up the tray from the roof of the Volvo. 'So let's go make some rain. You can call Hannah.'

Before facing the music, I tried the boxes and filing cabinets in the Bothy to see if there was any more evidence. No, was the answer.

I made myself comfortable in the Bailiff's chair and picked up the phone. I'll spare you the *sturm und drang* from Merlyn's Tower. It wasn't pleasant, though Hannah did agree to my one request in the end.

The last thing I said to Vicky before we were arrested was, 'Don't, whatever you do, mention the SIG.'

'Sign there, Mr Clarke,' said the bad cop.

'In a minute, Matthew,' I responded. 'I just need to add some bits at the end.'

'What on earth for? We've gone over it twice.'

The Assessor for Langdale Leven, Matthew Eldridge, last seen at Rod Bristow's farm, wasn't bearing up too well. Out of rank or policy, they'd decided to interview me first, with Petra Leigh from Furness playing the good cop and Eldridge the bad.

When they'd finished with me, they'd done a turn with Vicky, then me, then Vicky, then finally a session to write it all up. I don't know what Eldridge did for a day job, but it didn't involve sitting down. He clearly had a headache after a couple of hours, and was visibly wilting after four. Petra had gone to finish off with Vicky, leaving Eldridge to my mercy. Poor bloke.

We were in a meeting room at the Cloister Court, Hawkshead division. The room was not a Limbo chamber, and apart from taking the Hammer off me, I'd been treated fairly well.

'Let me see,' I said. 'You've missed out the bit about the post-mortem, the sharing of information and the involvement of specialist forensic officers.'

'That has nothing to do with your witness statement.'

'It's at the heart of my witness statement. I have asked you to ensure that the rounds used in two murders are tested by ballistics experts and the results passed to the King's Watch. Unless you're telling me that you'll work directly with the Lancashire and Westmorland Constabulary?'

'It's none of your business who we work with. The Cloister Court has asked Miss Leigh and myself to conduct this investigation, not the King's Watch, and certainly not you or Ms Robson. You are material witnesses, as I've said many times today.'

'Eventually. You started by treating us as suspects.'

He finally snapped. 'Just sign the form! We've been here hours.'

'I know. You didn't take my watch off me, so I can tell the time. Have you tracked those horses yet?'

The crimson flush had spread up from his open necked shirt to his all-weather tan. I could actually hear him grinding his teeth. Bad habit. He closed his eyes.

'The Rest will be open again this evening. Would you like me to lock you up so that you can finish your statement in there?'

'Five minutes. Go and check on Petra and I'll finish it off for you.'

He left me to it. If he'd really wanted to push me, he'd have threatened to lock *Vicky* up for the night. I picked up the pen and made my point.

The first thing we did when we got outside was check our phones. I had a voicemail from Mina saying that she was being locked up for the weekend again, but that all home visit prisoners would be given six days over Easter to make up for it. I also had a text from an unknown number: *Worried about you. Text this number to say you're OK. Guppy. XXXXXXX.*

For that to make sense, you have to know that a guppy is a little fish, and that (amongst other things) "Mina" means "little fish" in Gujarati. I responded with, *Fun times in the Lakes. Will write. Can't wait for Easter. Igor. XXXXXXX.*

You can look up Igor Sikorski if you want.

Vicky didn't look happy. 'What are we gonna do now, and are we gonna do it straight away?'

'What's up, Vic?'

'It's me gran. I'd like to get back to Newcastle if possible.'

'No problem. I'm not going to do anything without authorisation. Well, not officially. Hannah won't move until after Shabbos tomorrow, so you get yourself off. Do you want a lift to the car park?'

'For once, I think I'll walk.'

'I'll come too, it'll help me find out whether I can get back in to the courthouse building.'

The Hawkshead session of the Cloister Court takes place in a building known as *East Grange*. From the main road, it looks just like a substantial, modernised farmhouse. And when you walk down the gravel drive, that's all you see. Instead of trying to deter hawkers and postmen, the Wards make you want to stick to the path and ring the front door bell. To get to the courthouse, you have to walk backwards round the side of the house, treading carefully on stepping stones through a bed of roses. No, I don't know who thinks of these things. Perhaps wheelchair users have a separate entrance.

Behind the farmhouse is a metal roofed cowshed, as seen on Google Earth. That Glamour hides a light and airy modern office building with a covered walkway back to the main building which, I think, is where the actual courtroom is located. I don't know, because I was stuck in an office all afternoon.

We walked out of the front gates, and I asked how her interview had gone.

'I had the easy job. All I had to do was tell the truth and not mention the SIG.' She laughed. 'For some reason, they kept coming back to check details of what you'd said. I hate to say this, Conrad, but I don't think they believed you all the time.'

'Good. That's what I'd hoped.'

She stopped before we crossed the road. 'How is that good? I know you couldn't afford to be caught with a loaded gun, but why do you want them not to trust you?'

'So they'll trust you. If we need to spin them a line, they'll be more likely to believe what you say.'

She shook her head. 'I give up. I just want to go home.'

We sauntered across the empty twilight road. 'How are you feeling now?'

'Fine. I think. Just a bit like a wrung out dishrag. I wouldn't have wanted to be down there with no tranquilisers, though. They took the edge off it. How about you?'

'Annoyed. Pissed off. Frustrated. Probably a good thing Mina's not here.'

'Shall I tell Hannah we're out?'

'No, you get on the road. The sun will already have set in London, so there's no point calling her.'

Vicky looked at the disappearing orb. 'How do you know that? No. Don't tell me. I really don't care.'

We were by her car. She clicked the locks and dropped her bag on the passenger seat. 'What are you gonna do now? It's a hell of a drive to Clerkswell.'

'Hannah said, and I quote, "I don't care what you get up to at the weekends." I'm going to take her literally. Hope you've got your credit card handy. It's eight quid for all day parking. Daylight robbery.'

'I saw the cameras, so I put a Glamour on the car. Their server thinks this is Mike Ashley's Bentley.'

'Who?'

'Mike Ashley. Billionaire who bought the Toon. Me dad hates him with a passion.'

'Damn. I wish I could do that.'

She opened the driver's door. 'Be thankful you can't. You get in enough trouble as it is. See you later.'

I stepped back and turned to leave. As I walked back to the road, a sleek black luxury motor glided past me with a big fat bloke at the wheel. I stopped in my tracks, not because of what Vicky had done, but why Driscoll's killers had arrived on horseback. They must have been avoiding CCTV somewhere.

I sent Hannah a text: *No surprises. Ah gutten Shabbos. Talk Sunday. Conrad.*

They were waiting for me at the top of the slope, just visible in the last of the daylight. The Little Langdale Lodge does not have exterior lights so as to preserve the natural darkness. Andrea Forster was dressed for entertaining in the restaurant, with added wellingtons and a coat. Natasha Bickerdike had gone for the outdoor priestess look, with full cloak and hood. I'd called ahead and asked for sanctuary. I limped over to meet them.

'We're only doing this for Rani's sake,' said Andrea, with a tight mouth. 'And I thought she'd be with you.'

'Mina. Her name's Mina, and she can't get out at the moment. I take it you've heard the news.'

Natasha spoke first. 'The Union Secretary forwarded the email, with comments. It took all of five minutes to join the dots.'

'I've never seen a message from the Peculier Constable before,' added Andrea. 'I didn't even know that there was a woman in charge. Who is she?'

'I'll tell you later, if you'll let me.'

'Let's go down to the tarn,' said Natasha, diplomatically. 'Do you need a light?'

'Not yet. Perhaps on the way back.'

She led the way, I followed and Andrea brought up the rear. Natasha paused at the entrance to the garden to point out the Himalayan bamboo and said that it seemed to be thriving.

That email from Hannah to the Union officers was my doing, of course. I had convinced Hannah that the only way to stop the Assessors and the Cloister Court from covering up what had happened was to tell everyone. Hannah had been sceptical at first, but I'd convinced her that I was the expert on country matters. The Lake District is huge, but everyone knows everyone across two counties, and that's just in the mundane world. In the world of magick, it's even worse.

Hannah had emailed the Union chairmen and secretaries to say that the King's Watch was offering its full support to the Court in its investigation of this terrible crime. Etc Etc. She had told me that it would cause a huge stink, and I had said that that was my objective. After all, we have nothing to lose.

'So, you're this Conrad Clarke who got shot at in the Rest,' said Natasha when we got to the water's edge.

'No one shot at me today. Only Gabriel and Diarmuid Driscoll got shot at. In prison. Where they should have been completely safe.'

'This is just London propaganda,' said Andrea. 'A naked attempt to discredit the Particular before abolishing it.'

'Did Gabriel have any family?' I asked. 'The Assessors wouldn't tell me.'

Natasha lowered her hood. 'I know his great-niece. She'll be devastated.'

We were interrupted by a great beating of wings as a pair of swans flew over the ridge, banked to port and executed a perfect landing on the tarn.

'Ooh, they're back,' said Natasha. 'I wondered if they'd be coming.'

The birds settled themselves in the water before disappearing in the direction of some reeds, where the land was already in full darkness.

I turned to Andrea. 'Someone murdered Diarmuid Driscoll in front of my eyes. They did it to shut him up. They did it because they're doing something so bad that Gabriel became collateral damage, an obstacle to jump over on their way to Diarmuid.'

'Then let the Assessors deal with it. It's our mess, so we'll clean it up.'

'Natasha, do you know why Driscoll was in gaol?'

She looked down. 'I only found out today. He confessed to killing a mundane farmer. In cold blood.'

'Except he didn't. I knew it, the Cloister Court knew it and the Assessors must have known it, too. They just didn't think we'd come back with more questions. The Assessors didn't investigate Rod Bristow's murder properly, so they won't do any more for Gabriel, will they?'

'What do you want, Mr Clarke?' said Andrea. 'You came here under a false name, and now you're back. Why?'

'I came here for Mina. To let her see the world I've come to live in. You made her welcome, and for that I will be forever grateful. If you turn me away, I won't hold it against you. All I want tonight is sanctuary. A bed, a meal in my room and some peace. And I want to ask Natasha a question.'

Natasha gave me a half-smile. 'Now you're here, you might as well ask.'

'Who's big? Who's powerful? Who will be furious that this has happened?'

The smile changed to a frown. 'A lot of people. And a lot of those people could have done it, too. I don't want to name names. That would be wrong.'

I couldn't argue with her, nor did I want to. I clutched at the only straw I had. 'What about Clan Skelwith? Are they as powerful as I think they are?'

She shuddered and drew her cloak closer. 'Gnomes. Yes, they are powerful. Very powerful. They're also my number one choice for any dirty tricks.'

'Not them,' I said. 'This was amateur work, or Vicky and I would be dead. Thank you, Natasha.'

Andrea broke her silence. 'I'm freezing. You can have your sanctuary, Mr Clarke. We've got vacancies tonight, and Mina will always be welcome, but if you come back on official business, we're full. No room at the inn. Are we clear?'

I bowed and thanked her in the formal way. She said goodnight to Natasha and clumped back up the path.

Natasha looked over the tarn, towards the swans' refuge. 'We had a bad winter,' she said. 'The tarn froze a couple of times, and they disappeared.

151

They won't have gone far. One of the wetland centres in Lancashire, probably.' She turned back to me. 'Would you join me in vigil for a while?'

'It would be an honour.'

We stood next to each other, watching the tarn, listening to the wind and the evening sounds from the hotel. The air was clear here, clear and fresh and full of life. It was good to breathe.

Natasha spoke a prayer to the Goddess and I joined in at the end.

'Let's go,' she said. 'I'll light the way back.'

They gave me an upgrade at breakfast. Not all the rooms at the hotel are equal, and the Bowfell Suite which Mina and I had enjoyed was a palace compared to the tucked-away single that only had a view of the tarn if you employed a series of mirrors. When they'd come to take away my supper tray, the lad had knocked on the door and told me that I would be welcome in the dining room in the morning.

Just to confirm my rehabilitation, I was briefly joined by Andrea. 'Why didn't you say that you were a Dragonslayer?'

'At the risk of false modesty, I was just doing my job. The Welsh affair was only my second encounter with magick. How did you hear about it?'

'Once I knew your name, I made a few calls.' She tilted her head. 'There's a Druid order up here, you know. Very small. They claim continuity with the original kingdom of Rheged. Not sure anyone believes them.'

'I'll make sure to give them a wide berth. These sausages are excellent, by the way. As is all the food here.'

'My boy is the chef. I'll tell him you said so. Can you answer me a question?'

'If I can.'

'Are you planning to do up here what you did in Wales?'

That was a bit of a googly. 'I'm sorry. In what way?'

'Charge in and shake things up. The Welsh Druids got knocked right back on their heels.'

I took a moment to mop up the last of my breakfast with the last of my toast. 'Are you scared of harbouring a Witchfinder, or do you want to bet on the winning team?'

'No one knows you're here except Natasha, and she's only interested in the tarn. I don't want to turn away a good customer unless I have to, but this is the last time you can stop here as Edward Enderby.'

'Could you recommend a good mundane hotel?'

'I could, if you could answer the question.'

'Shaking things up is for senior officers. I'm just a field agent. Did you ask about Hannah as well as about me? She's the one who makes the policy.'

She leaned back. 'I had a guest from Salomon's House last year. We've kept in touch. He says that the Peculier Constable has got a lot on her plate.'

'And he's not wrong. Hannah could reassign us anywhere next week.'

'Us? I did hear that you were with a Sorcerer.'

'Who's gone home for the weekend. I'm going to take today to ask a few questions, then I'll be off, too.'

'Are you going to see the Gnomes?'

'I take you don't share Natasha's low opinion of them.'

'I don't. They put a lot of business my way, including Rick James and his party. I take it that's how you heard of us.'

I nodded my head.

'Those girls know how to party, that's for certain. Perhaps they learnt it from British hen parties going to Tallinn.'

'I thought they were Lithuanian.'

'So? It's all Baltic to me. They're coming back, or they are back. Some of them. They've rented a barn this time.'

'A barn?'

'We get a lot of visiting Mages up here, and not all of them want to stay in mixed accommodation. The specialist places are called barns. Some barns are mansions, some are actual barns. Rick James rented one for their big do.'

'Rick recommended you highly. If you know one of the Clan, not the top people, but someone with their ear…'

'I do. I'll bring you some more coffee and make a phone call.'

'Thank you. Make sure you tell him that it's "Edward" who wants to see him, not "Conrad".'

'I shall.'

Just to the south west of Ambleside town centre is a field. That's what you see if you look over the wall or check it out on Google Earth. If you take the side turning near a private house, on the other side of the road to Borrans Park, you'll find a field, yes, but you'll also find an old air-raid shelter, grassed over and not on the way to anywhere.

If you're bloody-minded and have some latent magickal Gift, you'll wonder what an air-raid shelter is doing in the middle of Ambleside (not a prime target for the Luftwaffe), and perhaps you'll go closer. Unless you have a real Gift, all you'll see is grassy sides and nettles. Lots of nettles, or in winter, dead brambles. I have just enough Gift to see that there's a big rusty iron door, like a hatch, set into the slope on the side away from the lake. As soon as you walk round the back, you're invisible to the mundane world.

I hammered on the metal and stood back. On smooth hydraulic arms, the doors opened out to reveal stairs heading down into the dark. The doors closed above me as I walked carefully down the steep concrete steps. As the daylight was shut out behind, Lightsticks on the walls blossomed into life. The bottom of the stairs was a corridor leading to the right and sloping further underground.

Opposite the end of the stairs was an elaborate sign. The centre was a heraldic shield that had four elements. At its heart was a fire, a blacksmith's brazier, and above it was crossed a mattock (big spade) and long handled axe. I don't have many genuinely authentic sources of magickal lore, but I had come across an appendix to the Proceedings of the Occult Council which explained this, and Vicky had grudgingly added a few details on one of our road trips.

Dwarves are older than Dragons. The official definition is *as old as the Gods*, which means that no one knows where they come from. We do know that their entire existence is reliant on Lux. No Lux, no Dwarf. They are also universal: there are Dwarves in every place in the world where metal has been worked. Gnomes are different.

Gnomes are exclusively northern European and made their way over here with the Angles, Saxons and various Scandinavians who turned Albion into England. If you see a sign with a hammer and anvil, that's usually a Dwarf. If you see a spade, pick or shovel, that could be a Gnome, especially with the brazier. All of this I was expecting. What surprised me was the waves at the bottom of the shield. Gnomes are not noted for their affinity with water.

The heraldic shield was surrounded with text in impenetrable German Gothic lettering. It's a good job I did German for GCSE (and had a relationship with a German spy, but that's another story). Above the shield was the Clan name: *Skelwith*. Below it was the motto, *Eisen über Wasser*. That's *Iron over Water* in English. No, I've got no idea, either.

The one big no-no with Gnomes is gnome jokes or references to fishing rods and toadstools, so all I could think as I stared at the shield was *this isn't very gnomely…*

'Mr Enderby?'

Gnomes can move very quietly when they want to. He was standing in the middle of the passage, legs firmly planted apart. He was blocking the way, physically and socially. His face was neutral rather than hostile, and he stuck out his hand in peace.

He – and Gnomes are 98.4% male – was taller than the other Gnome I'd met and looked a lot less like a B movie gangster. Gnomes *look* human, and can have children with humans, but they're not human, and this isn't a metaphor for racism or scapegoating of the "Other". They really aren't human. He was a lot younger than me, too, or at least he looked it. The leader of Clan Octavius in East London looks younger than my dad but is well over 300 years old. This Gnome was still a lot shorter than me, though.

I shook his hand and said, 'We can stick with Edward Enderby or use my real name. We've both got plausible deniability.'

'Why should we need that?'

'I don't want to get into trouble with my boss, and Clan Skelwith don't want official contact with the King's Watch. Not here, not now.'

He studied me carefully, as I'm sure he'd already done on his way up the passage. I returned the compliment. He was wearing jeans and a white shirt that showed off his shoulders and didn't emphasise his thick neck. His black hair was gelled and naturally curly. Either that or he lives with a hairdresser.

He made up his mind and said, 'Let's not confuse things, Mr Clarke, shall we? A Dragonslayer is always welcome.'

'Conrad, please.'

'I'm George Gibson of Clan Skelwith. Welcome to our home over the water.' He turned to lead us down the slope. 'Are you enjoying your visit to Little Langdale Lodge?'

'I am. I enjoyed it more when I was with my partner. She got a day at the Brimstone Spa as well.'

'Lucky girl.'

Did you spot it? He called Mina a *girl*, which she only is when she's amongst a load of other girls, on a *girls' night out*, for example, or with *the girls from the Ribble wing of the prison*. Gnomes have a somewhat old-fashioned view of women. In their defence, they are trying to change. Some of them.

The corridor zig-zagged a couple of times. We were now a *long* way underground, or, by my reckoning, we were very nearly under water, the water being Windermere. One final turn presented the open valves of a marine grade bulkhead, designed to keep water out of your submarine, or in this case to stop water flooding out of your underground cavern if there's a leak from above.

'Some place, George.'

'Impressive, isn't it?'

It was. I've seen much bigger caverns, but to have your own personal hollowed-out underground space, complete with random rock formations is quite neat, but neatest of all was the waterfall.

The cavern was cigar-shaped and not that high, perhaps twenty feet. At the far end, water ran out of cracks high up in the rock and cascaded over the ground to form a small stream that ran down a slope to the left and disappeared into a hole in the wall. To the right of the rivulet was a stone table with stone benches and, to the relief of my aching bones, a group of easy chairs round a glass-topped coffee table. George led me over.

'When you spend five minutes in here, you realise that it's cold, damp and very uncomfortable. I've got a real office down there, and a kitchen. Coffee?'

'Please.'

I noticed something else on the table: a used ashtray. Goody.

He returned with coffee and said, 'According to Andrea, you're pretty much a fish out of water up here.'

'A fish in unusual waters. I'm not planning to die of oxygen starvation.'

He smiled. 'We'd best not push that metaphor too far. How can I help?'

I passed him my card, the one with the badge of the Watch on it.

'Watch Captain at Large? I thought that was Rick James.'

He was teasing me, just to let me know that he knew more about me than I did about him.

'Rick is the Senior Captain. The others go to him for advice. When something special comes up, they send for me. That's the theory. Hasn't worked out like that yet. Just so I don't embarrass myself, where do you fit in to Clan Skelwith?'

'I'm fourth, and I mostly deal with offcomers.'

Offcomer is the local word for anyone from outside Lakeland. 'People like me, you mean. I presume that this place is designed to keep offcomers at a distance.'

'Among other things. The Clan base is on the other side of the Brathay, near Skelwith Falls, as you'd expect. This chamber was dug out by some mad ancestor of ours, who was looking for something in completely the wrong place. The Clan was going to back-fill it until the same mad ancestor decided to make it a showroom.'

'For what? Uncomfortable furniture?'

'Have a guess.'

Gnomes do like to test you. This was a gentle introduction, an amuse bouche over coffee. He offered me a cigarette, just to show that he'd been told everything about me by the owner of the Little Langdale Lodge. The last time a hotel owner had been free with my personal details, I'd gone back to exact vengeance with an axe, but this was different: I'd hung out a sign for everyone to see. So long as there weren't cameras in the bedroom, I don't care what Andrea Forster shared with the locals.

'Mining technology,' I said. 'We're well below the lake surface here, and I imagine that's Windermere pouring out of that spring, so the little hole over there must lead to some sort of pump. And there's the air, of course. You can smoke in the Old Network under London, but only because there's no one there to stop you. This air is much fresher.'

'Very observant. There's more, but we'll come to that later. I'll get some water to go with your coffee.'

He took two squat glass tumblers from a stone sideboard and went to the little rivulet. He scooped them both half full and brought them back. 'Please accept the hospitality of Clan Skelwith.'

'You are most kind.'

I sipped the water, expecting it to be cold, but not expecting it to have magick running through it. The last time I'd tasted water like that was at my induction to the King's Watch. Underneath Merlyn's Tower is a well, and in the well is Nimue, a Nymph. I had drunk from her hand, and tasted the first water to run off the glaciers at the end of the last ice age. This water had the same taste, but more of an echo than the full flavour. There was magick in the water, but not much. Enough to calm, to restore and to refresh.

George Gibson had been watching me closely. 'This isn't Windermere,' I said.

'You're right. This is being squeezed *up* from the rock, not being forced down from the lake. There is a pump next door, but it stores the water in tanks, then pumps it to the surface for all Mages and creatures in the Particular to share from. You can find the fountain over the meadow.'

I wonder what Nimue would think if she knew that the Gnomes of Clan Skelwith were tapping into the source of Lux from which she herself had once flowed. Perhaps she did know and was cool about it. It was unlikely I'd be seeing her again soon, so I filed it away and smiled at George.

'Again, thank you.'

'My pleasure, Conrad. So far you've been respectful, and you've been acknowledged by a Witch of the Water, yet you've also been at the centre of the biggest incident we've seen in years, and that's hot on the heels of a Dragonslaying. Shall we get down to business?'

I crushed out my cigarette and finished my coffee. 'You wouldn't be talking to me if you thought that Eldridge and Petra Leigh were going to make an arrest in the near future.'

'We might, just to see what you're up to.'

'What if they don't?'

For the first time, he looked away, shifting in his seat. 'It's very early days.'

I press on. 'This is the key time. For you as well as me.'

'How come?'

'Because of what Diarmuid said.'

'Oh? I thought he denied everything.'

That was interesting. Clan Skelwith clearly knew exactly what was in my statement to the Assessors.

'He did deny everything. There's one thing he said that's not in either of our statements.'

Gibson had reached the limit of his brief. He smiled and said, 'I wouldn't know, would I? And even if I had read the statements –'

'– which you haven't –'

'Of course. Even if I had read the statements, how would I know whether Driscoll said it or not?'

'Because I'm telling you he did. He was talking about the Waterhead Chase. Did you ever meet him?'

'Only briefly, during and after the Chases. I'm part of the team that lays the course, so naturally he tried to bribe me.'

'That sounds like Diarmuid. Do you ride?'

'None of us do.'

'I ride. Diarmuid and I bonded over horses, and he said he'd give me some names. People who could get me an invite. That's not in my statement because my partner was suffering a bad case of Limbo syndrome. She wasn't listening at that point.'

'Give her another spa day.'

'Wrong partner. If I bought Vicky Robson a spa day, my girlfriend wouldn't be happy.'

'Why does she need to find out?' he grinned. As I said, some Gnomes are making an effort, but they just can't help themselves. He saw that I wasn't laughing and moved on. 'If you're really interested in the Chase, I'm sure Andrea could be persuaded to sell you a package including a place on the course. Tickets for the finish at Waterhead are only available to Union Members. But that's not for months, Conrad, and I don't see how any of the Chases are worth killing Gabriel for.'

'Chases? Plural? Is there more than the Waterhead meeting?'

'All the Unions have one, and there are some in Yorkshire and a big set in Scotland, but Waterhead is the biggy. Or so the experts reckon.'

That was interesting, but probably not relevant. 'The key thing is what Diarmuid said when he issued his invitation: *I'll give you some names in the summer.*'

'So?'

'So, he doesn't want me around before then. Something's going to happen before the summer. Between now and the end of May, I reckon. And the people responsible couldn't take the chance of him keeping quiet, so they silenced him.'

Gibson poured more coffee. Half a cup this time. I offered him a cigarette.

'We've heard nothing,' he said.

'I know. If you had, you wouldn't be talking to me. You'd be dealing with it. That's what Henry Octavius in London would do, and I'm sure your clan are just as pro-active.'

'I asked them about you, and Henry did me the honour of calling back in person. Another reason I was happy to meet. You're right, though: we haven't heard any rumours. What you say makes sense, and I'll ensure that our Clan leader takes it on board.'

'I was hoping for more than that. There's a case in our jurisdiction that's still open.'

'Oh?'

'Theft of horses. That's definitely in my statement. Diarmuid said they were stolen from him, and in the theft a fraudulent instrument was used.'

He frowned. 'I wouldn't know where to start with that.'

'I do. Swans and quills are easy to come by, if you don't mind a bit of blood and plucking. It's the paper, though. Where would I go for Parchment?'

He laughed. 'You'd go where the Daughters of the Goddess go: to Sexton's Mill at Linbeck Hall. They're one of the biggest Parchment makers in Britain, if not Europe.'

'And where would I find them?'

'In the Kentdale Union, between Kendal and Staveley. Look for Linbeck Farm and find your way to the dairy.'

'Thank you,' I said, standing up. 'You've been very generous with your time. If this is your office, the Clan home must be a spectacular place.'

He stood up, too and joined me in looking round. 'We've been very lucky,' he said. 'I wish you the same luck in your ventures.'

He escorted me as far as the heraldic shield by the stairs, and a mad question came into my head. 'Something odd came up when I was dealing with the Dwarf Hledjolf last week.'

'Rather you than me. Haugstari is a very different creature.'

'Glad to hear it. Hledjolf said that he was having to raise his prices significantly. I wondered if you'd noticed anything similar.'

It was the first time that George had looked genuinely perplexed. 'As a matter of fact, we have, especially at auctions when outsiders are present. As a Clan, we only do commissions for Union members, but a lot of goods have been heading south recently at prices way over expectations.' He considered me again, gears engaging behind his eyes as he wondered why the Watch were interested in the value of Alchemical gold. He decided not to pursue it, and we shook hands. 'Let me know if you find anything out,' he said.

'I will.'

The visitor centre at HMP Cairndale is a place with an identity crisis. The Prison Service gets it that small children shouldn't be brutalised. It also knows that some prisoners wouldn't think twice about using their infants to smuggle in drugs, phones or tobacco, so you get a weird compromise between family fun and intimate searches.

I let the grandmothers and husbands take their small charges through the search and security checks before I got out of the car to wander inside. After the school rush of young visitors, the lobby was a haven of quiet. The PO on duty was one I knew that Mina had a lot of time for, and she, of course, recognised me. Everyone recognises me.

'Hello Mr Clarke,' she said, frowning. 'You do know it's family day?'

Before Mina was allowed home visits, I had been forced to see her during the week, when more staff were on duty to handle adult visits. Only women with children got visitors at the weekend in this prison.

'I do. Just come to make a donation to the library. And deliver a letter to Mina.'

I passed over the cream envelope, unsealed, and the PO scrawled something on it before putting it in the post tray. Then I handed over a package from Amazon. I'd already opened it, just to check, and because it's never a good idea to have a sealed package in a prison. They get very twitchy about things like that.

She peeled back the cardboard. 'DVDs. Oh. And they're all in…'

'Hindi. With English subtitles. They'd better have subtitles or I'll want my money back. Have you seen her today?'

'No. The overtime ban has hit hard. The governor only scraped together enough staff to run the family centre. There'd have been a riot if she hadn't. All the senior managers are in, looking after the others. I know that Mina was gutted when they cancelled her visit.' She sighed. 'I'll make sure these get to the library.'

'Thanks.'

I drifted out to the car park, mission accomplished. It was a grey, nothing sort of day in the Cowan valley. The trees couldn't be bothered to come in to leaf, the clouds couldn't be bothered to rain. Only the wind was making an effort, dragging the heat out of any exposed extremities, especially my less than well covered head.

I lit a cigarette and walked round the car park, trying to catch a glimpse of Mina's room. I missed her so much it hurt, and I remembered saying the same thing to her on our trip to Little Langdale. She'd replied, 'It's easy for you.

You have Vicky and Hannah and all the others to distract you. I only have four walls and a picture.'

Conrad... A whisper in the wind. It made me turn round and see some women emerging from one of the smaller buildings. One of the women was shorter than the others and wearing a thicker coat. She turned to look at me, and long black hair lifted off her shoulders when she lowered her hood. I waved, and she waved back, frantically. Two of the other women turned, and the little figure pointed. I gave them all a huge semaphore wave, my arms stretching out of their sockets to get the maximum windmill effect. Mina waved back, as did some of the others. At the front of their little party, a man in dark blue realised what was going on and made a gesture. I didn't want Mina to get in trouble, so I moved out of sight. When I looked back, they were gone, as was my tiredness. There's nothing like a shot of love to get you going.

The ridge between Esthwaite Water and Coniston Water is home to Grizedale Forest, numerous adventure trails and not a lot else. I put on my walking shoes and packed a rucksack. It was only a couple of miles, but even on the lower hills, you can get hit by all sorts of nasty weather. I strapped on both guns and took the path most likely to lead to the Esthwaite Rest.

For the first kilometre, the path was actually a forest road, half-metalled and built to take logging waggons. It was after that things got interesting.

I had crested the rise, and if I weren't standing in the middle of a forest, I'd have a good view of the lake. I checked back over my shoulder to see if the clouds were thickening in a rainy sort of way. Not yet. I had only seen two other people on the way up here. At least, I assume they were people. Two man-shaped lycra missiles had shot past on bikes, tinted goggles fixed firmly on the track. What a wonderful way to enjoy the countryside.

Even though there were a couple of hours of daylight left, all the walkers were at home, in the pub or on more serious walks than were offered here. I had the forest to myself.

I shook Maddy out of her Egyptian Tube and into my gloved hand. I gave her a moment to wake up and said, 'Good afternoon, Madeleine. Welcome to Grizedale.' That was another reason I was glad to be on my own: talking to sticks is considered eccentric even by locals. I took off my left glove and grasped the end of Maddy's willow home...

...And got the peace of the ocean. Nothing but the gentle waves around me. There was not a sniff of magick up here other than the general swell of background activity that is Maddy's perception of the Sympathetic Echo. I hadn't expected the Geomancers of Lakeland to run a Ley line over this hill: the obvious route was down from Hawkshead. Still, we use the tools we have to hand. I walked along the track, dowsing for Lux and keeping one eye to the right for bridle paths down to the lake. After 300m, I had two to choose from.

The path up from the main road was too well finished to show hoof prints, but the second track down towards Esthwaite had a whole bunch of them, overlaid and mixed together. There was no flow of Lux along here, so Maddy couldn't find anything. I straightened up and found a comfy tree to squat against while I had a cup of tea and a fag.

Refreshed, I took it very slowly from there. The path wandered along the edge of a field until the wall turned left to avoid a wood. Naturally, I didn't climb over the wall because I respect the rural infrastructure, so I followed the footprints until I got a good view of Esthwaite Water. I might walk back to Hawkshead and drop into … Damn. Those bloody Wards. I'd just walked right past it, hadn't I?

Footprints. I shouldn't be following the booted prints of walkers, I should be on the trail of shoed horses. I backtracked, and it took me two goes to get there: in the corner of the field, the horseshoes stopped. They didn't mill around, as they would have done if the riders had dismounted, they stopped four feet short of the wall, going *and* coming. I gave myself a smile for having discovered that our assassins were very good on horseback – even before damaging my leg, I would have thought twice before jumping that wall.

I was sweating by the time I flopped over the stones, having pushed against a great wall of magick to get past the Wards. From there, it was a gentle stroll in the wake of the horses to the cleared area at the top of the Rest. This time there were no cars in evidence, and I didn't knock at the door. What I did do was check the ground where the killers had dismounted and where I'd found their prints yesterday. I could see my size 13s and Vicky's new shoeprints, but nothing else. Humans leave a much clearer trace, and no human had been here to track the horses. Very remiss of the Assessors, especially after I'd gone to the trouble of telling them it was important. I could do nothing more today, so it was time to head back and find somewhere to eat and sleep.

I had got as far as the forestry track when my phone rang: PC Barnabas Smith was on the line.

'Squadron Leader Clarke?'

'Yes. Hello Barney, what can I do for you?'

'Are you still in the Lakes?'

'Yes.'

'There's been an RTC – a traffic fatality. It's Petra Leigh. Her pillion is going to be airlifted to Preston.'

'Is it Laura?'

'Who? No. It's the other Assessor, Mr Eldridge. I don't like the look of this, Mr Clarke.'

'Neither do I. Where are you?'

'At the scene. On the A592, just up from Newby Bridge. Near Fellfoot. Do you know it?'

'Yes. I'm in Grizedale, but not at my vehicle. I'm on my way, Barney. I don't want to get you in trouble, but...'

'Don't worry. I'm doing this one by the book. Our book, not theirs.'

'I'll be as fast as I can.'

I had to choose between a steady jog and making calls. I chose the jog because the car ride would be long enough. Sweating profusely, I piled into the Volvo and, while waiting for my phone to bond with the car, I sent Hannah a message: *Mega shitstorm. Pikuach Nefesh. Matthew Eldridge. Am acting on initiative until told otherwise. C.*

I once spent an idle afternoon looking up what would provoke or permit Hannah to break her Shabbos. I'm willing to bet that last Saturday she did it quite happily to keep her nieces entertained, but she'd deny it to me. The one universal exemption is *Pikuach Nefesh* – saving a life. This has to be an actual person, not a principle, and that's why I'd named Eldridge, and because this is Hannah we're talking about, I'd added the bit about me acting on initiative. That was far more likely to get her attention.

Vicky answered on the first ring. 'Hi,' she whispered. 'I'm in the RVI. The hospital.'

'Is it your grandmother?'

'Aye. She's had a fall. Bad, but she should be OK. We're waiting on evening visiting.'

'Petra Leigh is dead and Matthew Eldridge is waiting for the air ambulance. I got tipped off by PC Smith, so I'm on my way to look into it. I've texted Hannah.'

'Do you want me to come down?'

'Yes. I don't want to drag you away from your family, but duty really does call sometimes.'

She sighed. 'I know. At least I saw her this afternoon. I'll make me excuses and leave.'

'I don't want to stop in the Particular tonight. Head for Cairndale and I'll sort somewhere out.'

'I'm on me way.'

At the Newby Bridge roundabout, there was a matrix sign saying *Road Closed after Fellfoot*, and a mile up the A592 there was a police car across the road. I tucked in to the side and activated my Ancile. If this had been an ambush, the killers could easily be waiting to clean up the relief party. It had been thirty minutes since Barney Smith's phone call.

Two large yellow figures were having an argument in the middle of the highway, between the road block and the open rear doors of an ambulance. The older figure, sergeant's stripes on his shoulder, turned to shout at me. Barney said, 'That's him. The Secret Service guy.'

The sergeant didn't shout, but he did stick out his hand and demand my ID. I gave him my RAF badge and a blank card with a phone number scrawled on it. 'That's the Security Liaison office,' I said. 'Call them.'

'Wait behind the car, please,' said the sergeant.

'No,' I said. 'You call the number and if you're not happy, arrest me. You could always take your officer's word for it...' The sergeant was caught between a rock and a hard place, and I really think he would have arrested me if the paramedic hadn't come round the ambulance.

She looked very worried, and there was blood on her latex gloves. 'We need to move him quickly,' she said, then pointed east, beyond a screen of trees to an open field. 'There's no way we can lift him over the wall if the chopper lands in that field, and it's full of sheep, anyway. We need to get him down to Fellfoot, and that needs to be cleared.'

The sergeant had a life to save and he couldn't delegate that to Barney; he would have to take the lead or risk serious consequences. He stuffed my ID and card in his jacket and said, 'Smith, secure the scene. If this idiot removes anything or contaminates the evidence, I will have your balls. Understand?'

Barney nodded.

The sergeant wasn't done yet. 'And keep trying the Grand Union secretary. Try the President, too.' He looked to see if my car were in the way and got out his keys. 'Right. Let's move,' he said to the paramedic. She nodded and went round the front of the ambulance. Barney and I followed.

The scene of the accident was bracketed by the ambulance and a second police car. A member of the public appeared to be doing the job of telling the southbound traffic to turn round. We were in the middle of a wood, bare trees sloping down to the lake on one side and rising to a rocky cliff on the other. The perfect place for an ambush.

On the left, the western side, was the entrance to some sort of access road, and that's where the action was. Barney spoke up, 'We've no idea when it happened. The bike was heading south and came off the road there.' The access road was fenced for the first twenty metres, and about five metres in was a gaping hole. He continued, 'They went through the fence and stopped at the trees. Invisible to passing cars. It was called in by an American tourist on a coach – he had enough height to see down, and enough presence of mind to identify the location. I was the nearest patrol officer.'

'This could be crucial. Can we take a look?'

'Yeah, come on. I'm in enough trouble anyway, so I might as well give you the chance to do your job. Whatever your job is.'

'This is exactly my job. How's Eldridge?'

Barney took me round the gap in the fence, skirting the track of the bike. Eldridge must have come off first, because he was being treated in the open. Further away, I could just see black leather and black metal sticking out of the undergrowth.

Barney answered my question. 'Bad. Unconscious. Unknown spinal and head injuries. I was a bit suspicious when I found him, and when I'd identified him and Petra, then I got really worried. Have a look at his helmet.'

'Have they taken it off? I thought they left it in place to prevent spinal trauma.'

'There's an emergency release. It separates the shell from the lining so they can make sure he can breathe. It's on the ground there.'

We edged closer to the stretcher. The paramedics were getting ready to lift the Assessor into position. Something about him wasn't quite right, and I don't mean the multiple dressings and neck brace. 'Here,' said Barney.

A plain white helmet lay on the ground, and a portion of the upper rear shell was missing. I linked my hands behind my back to avoid the temptation of touching and bent down. It took me two seconds to realise what was wrong and celebrate Barney's instincts as a copper. 'Help me up, will you?' I said.

He pulled, I rose, and the female paramedic said, 'Three, two, one, lift!'

I had to see Eldridge before they took him away, especially his coat. I took a step closer and saw that his waxed jacket was open to the chest. 'Barney, did you find him like that?'

'What? On his back?'

'No. With his coat open.'

'Yeah. You'll see the same with Petra.'

'Then it was an ambush and murder. That damage to the helmet was done after the crash, as you'd already worked out. Well done. Most coppers would have been too panicked to notice that.'

'Perhaps. I only saw it when I'd seen Miss Leigh and got suspicious. No biker puts leathers on and leaves the zip down. There's something else, over there.'

'Hang on.' I turned to the paramedics, who were finishing with the straps. 'Do you need a hand getting to the trolley?'

They looked at me blankly. They'd been so focused on their patient, they hadn't noticed the giant stranger ambling about. The woman flexed her biceps with a smile. 'Thanks, but no thanks. We're good.' And with that, she zoned back in to the patient and forgot I'd been there.

Barney showed me a police evidence bag with a rock in it. 'This was half-embedded in the helmet, but when I pulled it out, it was obvious that the hole's much bigger than the rock. He didn't hit his head on that – someone smashed the helmet, then dug the rock in. Horrible.'

We watched the paramedics get the trolley to the ambulance. They got the trolley up the lift and the man closed the doors before jumping in the front. Seconds later, he was reversing into the access road before heading south with his lights flashing. I held up my finger to Barney. 'Incoming chopper,' I said. 'Let's hope he's OK.'

'The sergeant will be back in ten minutes. What else do you want to see?'

'Her satnav. I need to know where they were going, and I know that she had one mounted on her handlebars. I'd also love to know why Eldridge was riding pillion and not in his comfy Land Rover Discovery.'

'What's going on, sir?'

'You're not in the forces, so call me Conrad. What do *you* think is going on?'

'Either some billionaire has bought and sold two police forces, or there's some sort of mad conspiracy thing going on where a secret society has taken up residence in the Lakes. I don't believe either theory, not really, but I can't make sense of it any other way.'

'You're half right. There is a secret society, but not one you've ever heard of.' I was at a loss. Now was not the time to risk a demonstration of magick, nor did I have the authority. I waved my hand. 'Think of it as the wild west. The Assessors have been here a long time. They're mostly good at what they do and your Commissioner doesn't have the budget to pick up the slack if they were abolished. Now, that satnav.'

I let him lead me on a long walk round the back to approach Petra's Yamaha. It meant I didn't have to have a close look at her body. When we got near the bike, Barney took out a pair of latex gloves and held them up.

We paused to hear the sound of a helicopter engine dying as it settled on to the open field at Fellfoot park.

'Do you promise not to delete anything?' said Barney.

'My word as a Clarke.' I gave him a smile. 'You'll never hear a more solid promise.'

He dropped the gloves into my hand and stood back. I snapped on the latex and got to work.

'I'd send a colleague to the Ship Inn, Bowness, if I were you. That's where they started, and that's where Eldridge's car will be. Now let's see where they were heading.' I checked further. 'Does number 4, Fell Court, Grange over Sands mean anything to you?'

He looked worried. Very worried. 'Sophie, that lass from Rod Bristow's stables. She lives there.'

'I'll go. I'll go straight away.'

'Shall I call for backup?'

I turned away, took the SIG out of its magickally concealed holster and showed it briefly. 'I'll be fine. I just hope she is. Look, Barney, you may not have an answer to this, but is there a more senior police officer who isn't keen on the Assessor situation?'

'My first boss. Inspector Ross. I heard he got into some serious bother about Assessors. Some sort of scandal that got hushed up. He got promoted, just out of area. He's the Commander of Cairndale division now.' He saw my face. 'Why? Is that a problem?'

'He may arrest me for theft of a vehicle. And shooting someone on Cowan sands, not to mention criminal damage to the golf course. Thanks, Barney. I'd better get going.'

His eyes bulged. 'That was you? Bloody hell. Good luck, and keep me posted. If you can.'

'As much as I can, I will. See you later, as they say up north.'

The North West Air Ambulance must be good, because it was back in the air before I'd turned the Volvo round and found Sophie's address for myself. On the way back down the road, I came face to face with the police sergeant's BMW. He stopped in the middle of the road and started to get out. I did likewise.

'Are you done?' he said abruptly.

'Did Eldridge get in the chopper OK?'

'Yes. I phoned that number.'

It was yet another thing I'd get in trouble for. Hannah had told me only to use it in case of emergency, and I had no idea what the consequences might be. I also had no idea whose number it was.

'Good.'

The sergeant reached into his pocket and took out my ID badge. 'They said, "We can confirm that this man is acting with authority. Please refer to your chief constable." I'm not on first names with my chief constable, so I haven't rung him yet. Did you touch that crime scene?'

'I observed, I asked questions, I offered opinions, but I have not laid a finger on a thing.'

'Then bugger off, and before you interfere again, get permission *first*. Is that clear?'

I held out my hand for the ID. When he'd passed it over, I said, 'If PC Smith gets in trouble for this, I shall most definitely be back. Is *that* clear?'

He got into his car and reversed out of the way. I put my foot down and headed for Grange.

22 — *Believers and Sceptics*

The sun was setting over Morecambe Bay as I wound through Flookburgh towards Grange over Sands. Hannah clearly hadn't checked her phone, or if she had, she didn't want to interfere. Knowing Hannah, she wouldn't have checked her phone. I had used the journey to make the one call I thought might swing things in my direction. Would Petra and Eldridge be alive if Vicky and I had been on the case? Too soon to say.

The Fell Court development was down a lane on the hill behind Grange. The lane had houses sprouting out of one side all along it, from Victorian cottages near the main road, past 1940s council houses, 1980s boxes and finally a group of six modest semis with no room to park until you got on top of them. It was the usual balance of risk: did I go halfway to Cartmel and cross umpteen fields, or did I just stick on my Ancile and march up to the front door? I paused outside Fell Court and activated the magick. I'd done enough tramping over fields for one day.

Sophie's dad answered the door, and I could see why she'd compared us. He went grey when I announced myself and showed my ID.

'Sorry. She's not here.'

He went to close the door, and I was very glad that I hadn't changed out of my walking boots when I shoved my foot in and he tried to crush it.

'She's behind you, and I need a word. Your daughter may be in danger, sir. Let her decide whether to see me, and please feel free to call the police.'

He continued to press the door. 'Why don't you wait outside?'

'Because I've seen one dead body already today, and I don't want Sophie to be the second.'

He flung the door back and went for me with a rugby tackle, thinking I'd be off balance. I wasn't.

'Dad! Stop it!'

His daughter's voice had no effect, because I'd just swung him into a headlock and dumped him on the drive. He rolled, bounced up and came back for more, until Sophie jumped in front of me and put her hands up. 'Wait! Give him a minute. Please.'

'Out here,' he said. 'We'll talk out here, where there are witnesses.'

'Suits me,' I replied. 'I have nothing to hide.'

'I do,' said Sophie. 'I'm not standing out here like this in me old jumper. Come in, Conrad. I'll get the kettle on.'

I wasn't going to let the father go in first: he'd have done the routine with the door again. I followed Sophie through a lounge strewn with weekend detritus into a kitchen-dining room where someone was in the middle of chopping onions.

'Eurgh,' said Sophie. 'Me eyes. I'll just get rid of these.' Clearly not the cook, then.

The onions disappeared into a Tupperware and the kettle was switched on. I kept an eye over my shoulder as her father came in and leaned on a worktop, folding his arms and glancing at the chopping board to make sure he knew where the knife was. I got the message.

'What's happened?' I said when Sophie had poured water into three mugs.

'We've had a visit,' said the father.

'Dad. Let me tell the story.'

Sophie was indeed wearing a very tatty pullover of extreme vintage, along with dirty jeans and stripy socks. There was something about her face, though. Aah. She was in the middle of putting makeup on. I reckoned that I'd knocked on the door half way through her right eye.

'I won't be long,' I said. 'I can see you're going out.'

'Staying in,' said Sophie. 'Me brother's bringing his fiancée round for tea.'

'He doesn't need to know all our business,' said the father.

'Dad. Be nice.'

When I'd last seen Sophie, she was in shock and grieving. Here, on her home territory, she was much more confident. It made me admire her more for having got out of her comfort zone and struggled up that huge hill to Cartmel at eight o'clock every morning.

'Pass the milk, Dad. Sugar, Conrad?'

Father clearly wasn't going to move from his sentry post by the knives, and the fridge was next to me. 'No sugar, thanks. I'll get the milk.'

I put the plastic bottle near Sophie, and she made a point of handing my mug over in person. Her dad's, she left next to the chopping board.

'You had a visitor,' I prompted.

'An old woman on a motorcycle. She even wore leathers.'

I remembered Rachael as a teenager, and thought I'd better make adjustments. I risked a question to the father. 'Would you say *old*, sir?'

'Call him Jerry,' said Sophie, grinning over her mug.

'Older than me,' said Jerry. 'Not that old, not really. She had white hair, though.'

'Definitely too old for leathers,' added Sophie.

'Pointy face?' I said.

'That's her.'

As casually as I could manage, I said, 'What about her accent?'

Father looked at daughter. Daughter looked at father. 'Didn't really have one,' said Jerry. 'Sort of posh, I suppose.'

I stood up straighter and thought of an Air Vice Marshal at Cranwell. 'Did she by any chaaaance talk like thisss? My name is Petra Leigh?'

Sophie snorted her tea laughing. 'No way. Just sort of posh. Like … like your *friend*, Mrs Bentley.'

Oh dear. Looks like Vicky was right. *Sophie was flirting with me in front of her father.* Oops. 'What did Miss Leigh want?'

Doubt appeared. Sophie lowered her eyes, and Jerry spoke up for his girl. 'She wanted to check if Sophie had any pictures of that horse. Or its foal.'

I went very still. 'And did you?'

'Yeah. She paid me five hundred pounds to delete them. In cash. I had to hand over my phone for her to do it completely.'

I looked at Jerry. 'What else did she say? You can't have attacked me for no reason.'

Sophie went even redder. 'She said not to trust you. She said you had something to do with Rod getting killed. Said you were part of a cover-up. I didn't believe her. You were dead sad about Rod. You wouldn't have had anything to do with his death.'

'What time did she call?'

'About five o'clock,' said Jerry. 'Sophie had only just got home from her new job at the Co-op. Her mother's the manager and won't be home until eight. Sophie was supposed to help with the cooking tonight.'

I took a good slurp of tea. It was too good to waste. 'One final question. Did either of you see the motorbike?'

'No,' said Sophie. 'She was already in here when I came downstairs.'

'Me neither,' said Jerry. 'She appeared at the door with her helmet in her hand. I think she must have left the bike on the road. I don't remember seeing it.'

'Thank you. Sophie, Jerry, I'm afraid the police may well come to see you. Answer all their questions as truthfully as you can.'

'Why? What for? What's going on?' they said, sharing the dismay between them.

I finished my tea and put the empty mug next to the sink. 'At five o'clock, Miss Leigh was lying dead in a wood by Windermere. Mr Eldridge was next to her, seriously injured.'

'What? No,' said Sophie. 'What if they ask about you? And what about the money?'

'Keep it. You earned it. As I said, tell them the truth. What I wouldn't do, if I were you, is volunteer information. Especially about her accent. Thank you for the tea. I hope I don't have to come back. This business has nothing to do with your family, and I'd like to keep it that way. You've both been very helpful, and I'll let you get on with your cooking.'

Sophie whipped her phone out of her back pocket and fumbled with the screen. My own phone pinged in my pocket. 'I've just texted you my number,' she said. 'Just in case you need to talk to me.'

'Thanks. I'll pass it on to my partner. You met her at Rod's place. Vicky Robson.'

'Oh.'

Sophie was clearly disappointed, and immediately jumped to the wrong conclusion. Vicky (and Mina) would forgive me. I hope. Jerry spared me further embarrassment by escorting me out personally. He was looking very troubled, as well he might. I was about to reassure him when Monti's *Czardas* started up in my pocket. Hannah must have looked at her phone. I waved to Jerry and took the call.

'Is it true?' was her first question.

'Yes, ma'am. Assessor Leigh is dead, Eldridge is in hospital and they were attacked magickally.'

'I meant, Is it true that you've got into bed with the Gnomes of Skelwith?'

Typical Hannah. She always tries to keep me off balance. 'Ma'am?'

'I got your first message. While I was thinking about what to do, my landline rang. Only Ruth and the Cabinet Office have that number, and it wasn't my sister calling. Why did you use that emergency number? And don't say it was an emergency. It wasn't.'

I'd been walking through Fell Court and reached my car. I got in and turned on the engine. The phone bonded seamlessly with the console and I drove off.

'It fell into that yawning chasm between a genuine emergency and speeding tickets. Until we get proper, mundane authority, I have to improvise. If I hadn't investigated that crime scene, some bloody Assessor from the back of beyond would have crawled all over it and declared it an accident. Case closed, nothing to see here.'

'And you're sure? It was murder?'

'Yes. Petra Leigh is an experienced biker. She knows the road. It was dry and daylight. She's used to pillion passengers. Our enemy is good, very good, at Glamours. They put one on the road, to make it look like a bend. She took the bend and drove straight through a fence into a wood at full speed. After the crash, they stole their Artefacts and bashed Eldridge on the head for good measure.'

'You have evidence?'

'Without Vicky, no, and Glamours don't leave a trace. I do have evidence for the post-crash assault, and for the theft of Artefacts.'

'Right. I understand. I get all that, and you did the right thing at the crash, but why did you bring the Gnomes into this mess?'

'Do you want the truth?'

'I was born to suffer. Make me suffer more.'

'I was thinking of the Roman Empire. I ...'

'Stop. I don't care any more. After the Cabinet Office, I had the Clan Father on the line. His call I took, may Hashem forgive me. He wants you to sort it out. Personally. He said that the Convener of the Cloister Court in Hawkshead won't accept our involvement, and will insist on another Assessor taking over the case, but he wants you to stop this … this slaughter. Before it's too late.'

'That's what I hoped he'd say. That's why I called them.'

'Can you do it legally? Can you do it without me summoning the Occult Council?'

'Yes. If you let Vicky and I investigate the theft of the horses, we'll find them. I just hope we're in time.'

'Then go with my blessing. This has to stop.'

'Ma'am. Thank you.'

'Is there anything I can do to help?'

'I'll let you know.'

'Where is Vicky, by the way?'

'On her way from Newcastle. Went back for a family emergency. She'll be here tonight. I hope. And don't worry, ma'am, Mina's home visit was cancelled.'

I wasn't going to give up. Not while I had a chance. I heard a sharp intake of breath down the line, then a pause.

'Be careful. I'm going to Edinburgh soon, to see if I can poach any Watch Captains from Napier College. Until then, I can't afford to lose either of you. Goodbye.'

I call that a result. Not only was I off the leash, she'd made no threats about my relationship with Mina. One step forward.

I made my way to the A590, the main artery through the South Lakes. When they say *one road in and one road out*, that's the road they mean. There's total chaos when it gets blocked.

There was a tribute to the great Russian pianist/conductor Vladimir Ashkenazy on the radio (bear with me), and amongst the short pieces was that haunting oboe of Sibelius again. This time I was paying attention when they gave the title: *The Swan of Tuonela*. Memories stirred and joined together. I had other business to deal with first, but I was going to look that up later.

Lights were on in the villages when I swung round the Bretargh Holt roundabout and climbed out of the Lakeland Particular. My next stop was a gamble, but a calculated one.

Where do you find a police commander on a Saturday night? In the rugby club, of course. Commander Allister Ross of Cairndale Division is a big fan of Cairndale RUFC, and they'd played at home today. Unless Mrs Ross had put down a three line whip, he'd be at the back of the lounge putting the world to rights with his mates. That's where I'd be, and that's where I found him.

He'd left the Scots Guards as a captain, so he should have been saluting me, but I know who's boss. I snapped my best salute and said, 'Excuse me, sir.'

'Who the bloody hell are you, and why are you interrupting my quality time?' The voice was both sharp and rich. It echoed the glens and lochs, rawness tamed by the parade ground. He did a lovely line in irony, too. I doubt that *quality time* was normally in the Ross vocabulary.

'Sorry sir. My card.'

His glasses were on the table, both the empty whisky glass and his pair of ready readers. He picked up the specs and frowned. 'It can't be you, can it? Bloody maniac on the golf course?'

'The same, sir.'

'How did you get back in to the RAF after that little stunt?'

The climax of Operation Jigsaw had involved hijacking a police helicopter, dumping it without fuel on a golf course, a shootout on the sands and "borrowing" a Land Rover Defender. I was gone before the local police had arrived on the scene, leaving poor DCI Morton to make my excuses.

'They'll take anyone in an emergency, sir. Could we find somewhere private?'

'Get me a Glenmorangie and I'll see you out there, by the pitch.'

I was starving by now, and the temptation to join Ross in a single malt was almost overwhelming. I resisted temptation because I knew it would be very hard to stop at one. Perhaps later. I chose an energy drink to go with the scotch and worked my way to the pitch-side exit. While ordering, I'd looked carefully in the mirror behind the bar. Ross was on the phone, and it wasn't to his wife. He'd chosen to meet outside in case he needed to arrest me. Wouldn't do to have an altercation in the lounge.

'I take it you won,' I said when he finally appeared.

'Aye. Handsomely, for what it's worth. The season's nearly over and we're no going to win anything this year. Do you play?'

'Too tall, sir. Cricket's my game.'

Ross was only an inch shorter than me. 'Too tall,' he snorted. 'I've heard everything now, including my control room telling me that officially, you've never been to Cairndale. How in God's name did you get that wiped off the record?'

'I come here a lot, sir. My partner is staying nearby. For work.'

'Is she, now? Or he.'

'She.'

'And you've ignored the bit about the shooting.'

'Not my decision. I did my bit, and I'm not sorry.'

'I can see that.' He shrugged and drank his whisky. 'What do you want, then?'

'Assessors in the Lakeland Particular.'

He stiffened. Not fully on combat alert, but definitely wary. 'What about them?'

'I was told that you don't like them by a constable who shares your views.'

173

'It's no great secret. What's your interest?'

'I work for one of the under-the-radar outfits. We'd like to get rid of them.'

'Would ye now?'

He wasn't going to give anything away. Don't blame him. We didn't need to have a full sharing session to work together.

'We would. You should check the logs for South Lakeland Division. Assessor Leigh was killed this afternoon and Assessor Eldridge is in the ICU at Preston. It'll be marked down as an accident.'

'I didn't know Petra Leigh was still around. Never heard of the other one. It was Leigh I fell out with.'

'What about, sir?'

'Doesn't matter now she's dead. I'm not getting involved over the border. I made a promise.'

'And I respect that. I'll bet one of your friends is a magistrate.'

He laughed. 'A cliché, but true. Aye.'

You'll note that he didn't say which one. I pressed on. 'Under regulations, you're a designated chief officer of the Lancashire and Westmorland Constabulary.'

'I am.'

'Make me a Special Constable. Assign me to a crime.'

'Any crime in particular? I've plenty for you to look at.'

I took out a folded note. 'This one. Think it over. If you're willing, give me a call when your friend is sober. You've got my number.'

He took the paper and pocketed it without looking at the contents. 'As easy as that, eh?'

'It's the first step, sir. If you give me a police warrant, I can pull the first brick out of their wall. It would be a real start, even if someone else finally pulls the whole thing down.'

He turned to go back inside. 'Timescale?'

'Monday would be good.'

'I'll think it over. Good night, squadron leader. If you go straight ahead, you won't need to go back through the bar.'

'Thank you, sir.'

I'd known he wasn't alone. A shadow had appeared behind me while Ross was still in the clubhouse, and now he'd returned, it quietly disappeared. It was time for me to disappear, too. I yawned and lit a cigarette before strolling round to the car.

Vicky was leaning against the Volvo, hood up and trying to look inconspicuous.

'Did you see him?' I asked.

'Aye. Tricky bugger.'

Vicky had followed me into the clubhouse in a light disguise, then used magick to get my back when I went outside. 'In what way?'

'He snuck out of that bar like he was invisible and took the best vantage point. I had to double round and only caught half the conversation.'

'Description?'

'He was on Ross's table, sitting in the corner. He definitely recognised you as soon as you walked in.'

I knew the one she meant. Tall, stocky, older than most of the men and looking as if he still worked out regularly. Ross made a big thing of being an old soldier; this guy preferred to keep it quiet, most of the time. 'Thanks, Vic. Let's head off. We're back over the bridge at the Red Roses hotel. They're keeping us a table.'

'Good. I'm starving.'

23 — *Peace and Tranquillity*

The Red Roses hotel isn't the sort of place that has a dress code. It caters 50/50 to people who are away on business and coach parties away on pleasure. Tonight it was almost deserted, and I was tempted not to change. When Vicky said that she had to, I made the effort. The receptionist had informed us that only a limited menu was available after nine o'clock, and I suspect that the Polish waitress would take our order, go directly to the freezer and shove whatever we wanted in a microwave. We both opted for the vegetarian lasagne and decided to split a bottle of house red.

'What's the latest?' she asked.

'Barney Smith is off duty, and I don't have an official interest. Yet. The last he heard was that Eldridge is still alive but may need surgery. He's in an induced coma. Preliminary results of the investigation are treating it as an accident.'

'Surprise, surprise.'

'I know. How's your Gran?'

'Broken hip. She's eighty-eight, and we all know how dodgy that can be. The sooner they get her out of hospital and back to the nursing home the better.' She gave me a bitter smile. 'We're still having to pay while she's not there.'

It was the use of *we* that grabbed me. Vicky is on a good salary for someone of her age, yet is perpetually pleading poverty. I'd put it down to Millennial extravagance until it suddenly struck me. 'You're paying the fees, aren't you?' I said.

She looked uncomfortable. 'Aye, well, not all of them. You should have seen the place the council wanted to put her in. When I got into Salomon's House, I told me Mam and Dad that I'd be on good money sooner or later. They convinced Gran to use her savings. She was nearly skint when I got the Watch Officer job.'

'It can't be easy.'

There was just a trace of bitterness when she said, 'We can't all be landed gentry. Some of us have to be peasants.'

That was my cue to say nothing and suck it up, so I did. Marzena brought the lasagnes and some very unhappy salad in a separate bowl. We both prized apart the layers of pasta to let it cool down.

'Why?' said Vicky. 'Just generally, *why*? Why were the Assessors heading to see that bairn Sophie? Why did the opposition ambush them? Why did she disguise herself as Petra Leigh? Why were those photos so incriminating?'

'You missed a question.'

'I missed loads. Which one?'

'Why is Eldridge still alive?'

She tried her lasagne, found it edible and took the edge off her hunger. I did the same.

'Do you think Eldridge is one of them?' she asked.

'I think that Matthew Eldridge is out of his depth, well out of his depth, and I don't like him, but I don't think he's guilty of anything. Let's go back to yesterday, when Petra was questioning you at East Grange.'

'God, was that only yesterday?'

'I know. They made a big thing of double-teaming us at first, then when it came to statements, I got lumbered with Eldridge. I just wondered if she thought you might have seen something that I didn't.'

She waved her fork at the salad and speared a cherry tomato that I'd had my eye on as being one of the few edible things in there. 'Are you trying to say that as a weak young woman, I might give in to pressure?'

That had been in the back of my mind, yes, but I wasn't going to admit it. Let's be honest here, Vicky hasn't been interrogated by the RAF police, assorted gangsters, MI5 and my mother. All of them are a lot scarier than Petra Leigh.

'No, Vicky,' I said. 'You're the real Mage here, as Petra knew full well. Did she ask anything on her own that she hadn't asked when Eldridge was present?'

That seemed to mollify her a bit. 'Now that you mention it, she did. Sort of. She kept going back to the Glamours they used. *What sort of edge did they have? Could you smell anything?* Questions like that. She and Eldridge had already asked, obviously, but Petra went on about it for ages in that far back voice of hers. Got right up me nose.'

It was another piece of the jigsaw. I was starting to get the picture, now, and had just one more question for tonight. We were both shattered, and any planning could wait for tomorrow. 'Tell me. Could this woman pretending to be Petra have interfered with Sophie in other ways?'

Vicky frowned. 'What do you mean?'

'She went to a lot of trouble to get in Sophie's house. She spent a lot of money to delete some pictures. What if there were other memories to be got rid of? What if she did some Occulting while she was at it?'

Marzena returned, looking even more tired than we did. To her evident relief, we both skipped dessert and Vicky skipped coffee.

'It could be,' said Vicky. 'Or she could have been checking to see if Sophie remembered something else. Or it could be something really simple.'

'Such as?'

'The pictures. Sophie took pictures of the horses, but what if she took pictures of something really incriminating, like the killers? They could have been having a picnic with them. Let's face it: who checks back in their pictures unless you're looking for something. I'll bet Sophie wouldn't notice they've gone.'

It was an intriguing thought.

'One last thing, Vic,' I said. 'Have you ever heard of the Swan of Tuonela?'

'As in a Tuonela Pen? Desi sent me some stuff about that. I must say I've been a bit busy to follow it through. Is Tuonela a special breed of swan?'

'You could say that. It's a piece of music, but forget that. The music is based on the Finnish legend of the Swan of Tuonela. It swims along the river outside the Finnish underworld. Some say it's got black feathers.'

Vicky was too tired to high-five, and went for a fist bump. 'Well done. This is my reward for putting up with that awful music. It fits. That black quill is definitely a Tuonela pen. We'll keep our eyes peeled for Finns, shall we?'

'There are some Lithuanians about, somewhere.'

'Eh?'

'Never mind. Time for bed.'

We agreed to meet in the morning, and Vicky said, 'Not too early, eh?'

'No rush. I'm not looking forward to this next bit. Sleep well.'

We didn't even get over the threshold at the late Petra Leigh's house. Laura answered the door, saw who it was and said, 'Wait there.' Then she closed the door in our faces.

'Nice view,' said Vicky.

Petra had chosen location over size for her lair: the ancient cottage couldn't have had more than one bedroom. As it was dug into the hill, there was no room behind, but what it lacked in square footage it made up for with a view of infinity.

We turned round to soak it in. Perched high above the Duddon Estuary, Petra's cottage had a square of grass with a token border as a garden, a garden which seemed embarrassed next to the extravagantly equipped outdoor living area. From the western gable end, a cluster of all-weather furniture clustered round a patio heater and barbecue. High on the gable was a big metal cassette holding a giant awning for those less than dry Lakeland summers. I reckoned that you could stand under the awning and still work the barbie.

I could imagine a lot of parties here with no neighbours to annoy. All the seats had been angled to get a glimpse of the estuary, the Millom peninsula and the Irish sea beyond. It was heaven.

The front door slammed and Laura appeared, wrapped in a long, chunky cardigan. She caught the breeze and pulled it closer, wrapping her arms to her chest. 'This was my birthday present, two years ago,' she said, indicating the cardigan. 'Mum said I had to keep it here so that we could go outside on cold days. Her way of trying to get me to come round.'

Instinctively, we'd all turned to face the view, like actors in a badly directed play who faced the audience and not each other.

Laura wiped her eyes. 'It didn't work. If she'd wanted to see more of me, she should have bought a sandpit, or got a TV, or a slide, or anything to keep the kids amused.' She made an effort to face me. 'The Eden Valley Assessor's coming over later. He made a point of saying that the King's Watch is not investigating. It was only when I put the phone down I realised who it was.'

She zoned out for a second.

'Who what was?' I prompted.

'The Assessor. I used to babysit him. He can't be any older than … Sorry. I don't know your name.'

'Watch Officer Robson. Vicky. I'm so sorry for your loss.'

'So am I,' said Laura.

The poor woman was in shock, and Vicky's body language was pointing to a fast exit. 'We'll go,' I said to Laura. 'You need time.'

'Don't go yet,' she replied. 'That'll mean I have to go back inside, and I can't face that. You're a good excuse for me to stay here. You can smoke if you want. How's Matthew? The Eden Assessor either didn't know or wouldn't tell me.'

I moved downwind and lit up. 'They're operating on Matthew this afternoon to relieve intracranial pressure. Anything could happen.'

She shivered again. 'He didn't have anything to do with it, did he?'

'I very much doubt it, Laura, and we're not investigating what happened to your mother. We just want to know about Diarmuid Driscoll and his friends. How well did your mother know him?'

'Ask me no questions and I'll tell you no lies. That could have been her motto, you know. I got all sorts of stick at school when she turned up in her leathers. I was a weekly boarder, and at the weekends there'd be a different aftershave in the bathroom. Her conquests were always gone when I came home, but they always left a trace behind. One spring it was a fridge full of Guinness. A couple of months, perhaps.'

'That can't have been easy,' said Vicky. 'Girls can be the worst, and that was before social media.'

'Yah,' said Laura in a wonderful impersonation of her mother. 'We only had wex teblets to wrate on when I was at school. I got over it.'

'Nothing more recent?' I asked.

'Mother was great at keeping people onside. Women, too. I once heard that she never had affairs with married men.'

The thought of hearing about one's mother's affairs in any circumstances was quite stomach-churning. 'So Diarmuid was never married?'

'No. It was fifteen years ago that he had a fling with Mum, and that wasn't a thing to make me want to see very much of him.'

'You're not joking,' said Vicky.

'I saw him about a bit after that. As you know, it's a small world in the Lakeland Particular. I got the impression that he could never commit to putting another woman before his mares, and he was never short of female company.'

I tried to be casual. 'You didn't have a horsey childhood, by any chance?'

'No. I'm 100% geek, in the mundane and the magickal worlds. I even married an engineer. There's a lot of them about round here.'

'So you don't know who Diarmuid's pals are. For example, who his jockeys are in the Waterhead Chases.'

For the first time, she laughed. 'They're not jockeys, Conrad, they're *riders*. The Waterhead Chase isn't a flat race, or even the Grand National. It's mythical, it's epic and it's bloody dangerous. You have to be very talented and very bonkers to attempt it, not that we'd know. They all wear masks.'

'You what?' said Vicky. 'How does that work?'

'Making a mask of your hero or heroine is part of the madness. I only go for the party afterwards. The last winner to ride one of Diarmuid's horses was Boudicca – she could have been any one of a hundred young Mages from here or somewhere else.'

'I have to ask this, Laura, but you don't have to answer. Did your mother give any hint that she might know who killed Diarmuid and Gabriel?'

'No. She was round at our house when it happened, I can tell you that much. She went as white as her hair when she got the call. She knew Gabriel, too, of course, and she'd been telling me how stupid Diarmuid had been as if she still had a really soft spot for him. When she put the phone down, she didn't know whether to get mad or burst into tears. I think she did both, inside. I made her wait ten minutes before she got on her bike. I got a text message on Friday night saying that she and Matthew would be working together until they'd cracked it, and that she was staying at his house. That was the last I heard from her.'

'You need to get inside,' said Vicky. 'Anything else, Conrad?'

I shook my head and we left her to her grief.

'What did we learn?' asked Vicky when we got back to a decent road.

'That Petra wasn't a member of the opposition, though I reckon that she had her suspicions.'

'I agree about the first part. What makes you think she had her suspicions?'

'Mostly the fact that she's dead. Plus the fact that they were on their way to see Sophie, though that could have been a trap. There was no connection between Sophie and Petra. They'd never met. They obviously don't move in the same circles. The only connection is Matthew Eldridge.'

'You don't suspect him, do you?'

'Definitely not, but I'm still trying to work out whether Matthew was also a target or whether he was collateral damage. We may never know why he got on the back of her bike. I'll try to talk to Barney and see if there was damage to Eldridge's car.'

'I don't want to be a wet blanket, but that doesn't take us any further.'

'Unfortunately, I agree.'

'It was a hell of a lot easier when we were chasing that Dragon. We had a clear enemy and we could just track them down. This is like trying to catch a will o'the wisp.'

'Have you tried? Are there such things?'

'Oh, aye. I've never been so drunk that chasing one was a good idea, though.'

'Glad to hear it. You're right, though. We have no clear idea of our enemy, their intentions or their plans. All we know is that there might be a timetable. All we need to do is keep looking for that Black Swan. They've been pretty reckless over the last twenty-four hours.'

'But they've gotten away with it so far.'

'Only because it's been Assessors and not the King's Watch on their tail.'

'Go Team Merlyn's Tower. Not.'

I don't expect my work partners to be positive and upbeat all the time. That would be very annoying, and probably make me want to throttle them. On the other hand, Vicky was definitely on a downer today.

'Vic, how many Xanax did you take on Friday?'

She looked out of the window when she answered. 'Two. You saw me.'

'And since?'

'I can't tell you it's none of your business, can I?'

'No.'

'I had one yesterday morning in the hospital. I hate them places and it reminded me of when I died.'

'You're not dead yet, but you are suffering from withdrawal. I should know.'

'You've never taken Xanax in your life.'

'You should try oxycodone. Now that *is* addictive.'

'When did you … ? Oh. Your leg.'

'Yes. I've still got the ones they prescribed when I left the rehab centre.'

'Are you gonna report me?'

'To whom? We're nothing if not a team, Vic. I could see that you wouldn't have survived the Limbo chamber without them. I get that. Totally. Think of the Limbo chamber as a bar. How far below that bar will you need to be before you take the next one?'

'I don't know. It's not something you can plan for, is it?'

I didn't push her on it. Now was not the time. 'Promise me this, please. Tell me before you take one. I won't judge, but I need to know, OK?'

'Aye. Fair enough. What now?'

'We're not going to look into the Parchment today. Too late and too Sunday. We're going to grab a sandwich in Ulverston and then we're going to go for a long walk.'

She snapped back. 'What the fuck for? I'm not a child.'

'No. You need endorphins, and as your partner, I'm prescribing a long walk. We both need to clear our heads.'

We talked about the case as we worked our way up from the little town of Ulverston, but mostly we talked about the Lakeland Particular and its irregular arrangements for law enforcement. Vicky was starting to understand that I really didn't like it. And then she asked an awkward question.

'I heard Commander Ross talk about some serious stuff you got into. How does that fit with wanting to kick the Particular off their perch?'

Hannah had made me promise not to tell Vicky about Operation Jigsaw, but the truth has a habit of coming out in all sorts of awkward ways.

'It's because of that business I'm so worked up, Vicky. I saw what happens when things break down. I'm not saying that what we did in Afghanistan was right or wrong, but it definitely warped a lot of people, including me. I got out alive but damaged. Several people didn't get out at all, including one I respected a great deal. How many Rod Bristows have there been up here? How many mundane victims of magickal crime have had their cases brushed under the carpet of deniability?'

She laughed. 'Carpet of deniability, eh? Is that like a flying carpet that needs an overhaul?'

I let her laugh for a second, then pointed to a hill. 'Up there. You won't believe what's at the top.'

'Do we have to?'

'Yes.'

'I still don't get the bit about the Roman Empire,' said Vicky when we got to the Sir John Barrow Monument, also known as the Hoad. It looks like a lighthouse and stands proudly above Ulverston. It wasn't the highest point of our walk, but it did have the best views. We'd been going over all the conversations we'd had, separately and together, to see if we'd missed anything. I was just explaining why I'd brought the Gnomes of Skelwith into the mix.

'That's how the Romans operated. If they had their eye on a piece of prime barbarian territory, they'd wait until it was in turmoil. One side or other would be desperate enough to bend the knee to Rome and before you know it, there are legions marching everywhere and the new king has to pay tribute.'

'So … we're the Romans in all this, and the Particular is like a load of barbarians?'

'Pretty much.'

'That puts us on the side of slavery, autocracy, torture and genocide, to say nothing of what the emperors got up to.'

Fair enough. I deserved that. There was only response. 'What have the Romans ever done for us?'

'Eh?'

Straight over her head. Never mind. I mentally put *Life of Brian* on the playlist for the next time we were holed up somewhere. It's a lot shorter than *Kuch Kuch Hota Hai*.

We both leaned against the monument and looked at the view. We'd exerted ourselves a fair bit to get this far and we needed a moment to relax. I closed my eyes, then jumped upright when I heard a skittering of claws nearby. I looked around, half expecting an ambush. When you've been attacked by magickal lions, you learn not to discount four legged enemies. I couldn't see anything, and Vicky hadn't noticed, so I closed my eyes again.

'You could be right,' said Vicky after a long pause. 'I mean, you could be right about the Xanax. I've just remembered something I should have said last night.'

'Go on.'

'I asked around, like you said, about the paper. Well, to be fair, I asked Desi to find out. She said that a lot of the Circles use Linbeck Hall Parchment. I still don't see that it gives us a strong enough lead to go on.'

'Whoever created that Malaglyph didn't go to a shop in London and buy the Parchment. They sourced it locally, and you reckon there aren't many Mages capable of Enscribing with that degree of skill. We just need to know who their local customers are.'

'And if they won't tell us?'

'They will. Or they'll be in serious trouble. I was thinking...' I stopped when my phone rang. It was Commander Ross.

'Right, laddie. Cairndale Magistrates Court tomorrow morning. Eight thirty sharp.'

'Sir.'

'Who was that?' said Vicky.

'It was my ticket to Gravesend, and perhaps to finally tracking down this Black Swan. Do you fancy an Indian tonight?'

'Not as much as you fancy Indians. One in particular...'

'Shut up and give me a hand. My leg's gone to sleep.'

24 — The Press Gang

All police constables, including Specials, have to take their oath in public, and it has to be a matter of record.

If you've never been to a magistrates court, you won't know that even in these days of terminal decline for local newspapers there is always a reporter on duty. No matter how far-flung the court, there will always be a journalist of some sort present to take notes and publish your shame in the local paper (or on the local website). This poor person will scan the lists every morning in the desperate hope of seeing a famous name appear and being able to call London with a scoop. I sometimes think they'd be better off working in a bar and spending their wages on lottery tickets.

Naturally, there are ways to game the system if you're in charge. The reporter would turn up at half past nine this morning, when the first case is normally scheduled. She would look at the lists and notice that an item had been added: at half past eight, while she was still organising the school run, a Special Constable was sworn in. She will ignore it and move on. I'm making this up, by the way. For all I know, the local reporter is a bearded hipster. Whatever he/she looks like, at 08:30, the place was deserted.

A gownless usher ushered me to Court One and fumbled around for the lights. He lit up the court and disappeared, leaving me to look around a cold and empty room. In all my misadventures, I've never actually ended up in a court. For obvious reasons, I couldn't offer Mina any support when she was sentenced, though I imagine that the Old Bailey was a bit more imposing than Cairndale Magistrates. This one was all pale oak and durable fabrics with network ports at the desks. Very 1990s. I was contemplating the unchanging royal arms above the bench when the now fully dressed usher reappeared.

He took up a position by the doors and was joined in the room by a clerk who took his place at the front. The clerk remained standing, as did I, so the usher didn't need to tell us to rise when the magistrate walked in from the back. A creak from behind me said that Commander Ross had entered the room as well.

The magistrate was Ross's sneaky friend, the one who'd crept out to keep an eye on me at the rugby club. As soon as he got to the bench, I saluted and said, 'Apologies for not being in uniform, sir.'

He grunted and returned my salute from force of habit. Good. 'Let's get going,' he said.

The clerk stood up. 'Take the card and take the oath. You might want to read it through first.' He offered me a big laminated card with big writing on it. A lot of writing. I read it through.

I, ... of ... do solemnly and sincerely declare and affirm that I will well and truly serve the Queen in the office of constable, with fairness, integrity, diligence and impartiality, etc. etc. etc. according to the law.

I inserted my name into the blanks and read the oath in my clearest voice. A shadow passed by the window, high up in the wall. Everyone turned to look. Perhaps the officials wondered what such a big bird was doing near a building. Perhaps not. I knew what it was doing, and something on Ross's face told me that he knew, too, even if he couldn't put it into words.

It was the shadow of Odin's raven we'd seen. The Allfather, my some time patron, would know of my oath and would hold me to it.

'Warrant card,' said the magistrate.

Ross came forward and nodded respectfully in front of the bench. He was in uniform, every crease as sharp as his haircut. He took a small card from his pocket and passed it to the clerk, who passed it to the magistrate. The magistrate signed it and it came back down the chain to Ross. Along the way, the clerk copied something down in a book.

Only then did the magistrate seem to wake up completely. 'I hope you know what you're doing, Allister,' he said.

'So do I, Will, so do I. Are you going to welcome the laddie or what?'

'I suppose so. Welcome to the Lancashire and Westmorland Constabulary, constable. Commander Ross will see to your needs.'

He stood up and turned round before I could salute, leaving the clerk stranded half way out of his chair.

'Come on,' said Ross. 'Colonel Shepherd is always grumpy on Mondays.'

'Colonel Will Shepherd?' I said. 'Ex Military Intelligence?'

Ross gave me a knowing look. 'Aye.'

Shepherd knew exactly who I was and what I'd done. No wonder he wasn't thrilled. I followed Ross out of the court.

He held the warrant card in the air. 'I don't know who the hell you answer to in London, Clarke, and I hope they're keeping an eye on you, but the second you take this card out of your pocket, you become one of mine. Is that clear?'

'Yes, sir.'

'And I expect you to meet the highest standards at all times or you'll be answering to me.'

'Also clear, sir.'

'Good. Your warrant number is on here, but don't tell anyone. For all official purposes, use your collar number. They get recycled. If you ring the control room, they'll know you're a Special because the collar number begins with a 7. Most of the time, call my secretary if you need help.'

He passed over the warrant card and took out a piece of paper. It had four things printed on it: the direct line to the control room, his secretary's number, his mobile (which I already had), and a crime number for the stolen horses.

I accepted the paper and considered what I'd done. Odin is a god. He is as scary as a god can be. Somehow, Commander Ross was a lot scarier right now. I put the paper and warrant card in a safe place and saluted my new (part-time) CO. 'I won't make you regret this, sir.'

He accepted my promise with a nod of his head. 'Do you think you'll make a difference?' he asked, almost casually.

'Yes, sir, I do. Whether it'll be enough is another matter.'

'Then good luck.'

We shook hands and I headed back to the hotel for breakfast. Vicky was pouring her first cup of coffee and trying to blink herself awake. I showed her the warrant card.

'Did I miss much?' she asked.

'Not really. It's one of those things that only matters if you're taking part.'

So far during my time in the Lakeland Particular, I've seen a prison disguised as a hill and a courthouse disguised as a farmhouse. Finding a paper mill disguised as a dairy shouldn't be a problem.

The citizens of south Lakeland do enjoy giving epic names to their roundabouts (Bretargh Holt, Meathop and Plumgarth to name but three). It helps keep them amused during the long winters, I suppose.

The Plumgarth roundabout is just north of Kendal, and just north west of this monumental piece of civil engineering is a parcel of land marked on the maps as Linbeck Farm. Things only get interesting when you've parked in front of the modest farmhouse.

'Hang on,' said Vicky. 'This is familiar.'

'In what way?'

'You reckoned that the same architect had done the Esthwaite Rest and that Little Langdale hotel, yeah?'

'I did.'

'This driveway is the same as East Grange, only more powerful.'

'A powerful driveway? You've lost me.'

'A powerful Work of magick. All your attention is focused on the drive and the farmhouse. You don't notice the rest of the place. I hope we don't have to walk backwards through a rose bed.'

'I still reckon that was a joke played on offcomers. Let's try the front door.'

Vicky and I had agreed that if a non-Mage answered the door, she'd speak first. I've grown used to all sorts of weird people answering the door in the world of magick. This was an old farmhouse, so ... what? A Troll? A talking sheepdog? A robot?

No. An old lady, complete with apron and flour on her hands. She had a slight stoop, and plenty of outdoor wrinkles burnt into her face, but there was no disguising the calm and peace wrapped round her. It suited her better than the apron. Vicky stayed mute.

'Can I help you?'

'Watch Captain Clarke and Watch Officer Robson. We're looking for Sexton's Mill.'

Her eyes opened wide, and I couldn't help thinking of the grandma in Little Red Riding Hood. If there was a wolf inside this woman, I'd be almost relieved.

'The King's Watch?' she said. 'What on earth are you doing here?' She smiled. 'Are they all as handsome as you and as pretty as her?'

This was so not the conversation I'd been expecting. Vicky was busy blushing.

'I couldn't possibly comment, ma'am. Would you be one of the Sextons?'

'I am. Evelyn Sexton. Come in and don't bother to take your boots off.'

She turned her back on us and disappeared into the farmhouse.

'Lead on, O Handsome one,' said Vicky.

'Careful, pretty wench. We don't want to end up in that pie she's baking.'

It wasn't a pie. It was a batch of scones, and she was busy rubbing in the butter. This much about baking I know, because it was all my mother ever bothered to teach me.

The one concession to her age was a stool by the ancient farm kitchen table. Evelyn perched half on, half off the stool and carried on rubbing. I knew what to say next.

'What a lovely kitchen.' It was lovely. Completely lovely. Someone had tried to bring it into the twenty-first century and given up. I pointed to a large wooden and cast iron machine in the corner. 'I haven't seen one of those since I don't know when.'

'It's a cheese press and it shouldn't be in here by rights. It should be in the dairy, but my daughter insisted it would look good. Waste of space if you ask me.'

'Is that dresser original?' said Vicky admiringly.

'Depends what you mean by original. It's older than me, that's for certain.' Evelyn stopped rubbing for a second. 'You're in for a surprise one day, Mr Clarke.'

She said it so matter of factly and with such authority that she might have been quoting the short range weather forecast. 'A pleasant one, I hope?'

'I couldn't say. You cast several shadows, you know. One of them carries a spear. If you take that door over there, you'll be in the back yard. The mill is down by.'

I was still in shock. *You cast several shadows* was not a comment to pass over. Before I could ask about it, Vicky said, 'Down by what, ma'am?'

Evelyn laughed. 'Down by. You'll see. Nice to meet you both.'

Vicky had to grab my arm and propel me out of the kitchen. 'Leave it,' she whispered to me. Out loud, she said, 'And you, Mrs Sexton. Thanks for your time.'

I fumbled open the latch, and we stepped out the back of the farmhouse. 'Aah. That's what she meant,' said Vicky, closing the door behind her.

'About what? About the future or about the shadows?'

'About *down by*. It just means down the slope. See?'

The farmhouse was on top of a meadow which sloped down to a marshy valley that almost certainly flooded on a regular basis. That hadn't stopped them putting up a low stone building at the bottom. Did they keep the water out using magick, or did they just let it flood and come back later?

It had been getting warmer, and the grass was starting to grow properly, turning most of the view into a vivid green carpet that stretched from horizon to horizon. I looked behind and saw a couple of stone sheds tacked on to the farmhouse. Bleating from one of them suggested a late lamb was being born.

I turned back and had to hurry to catch up with Vicky. 'What on earth was she on about?' I asked.

'Search me. Looks like she's got a touch of the Diviner about her.'

I thought I'd come across all types of Mage by now. 'What's a Diviner?'

'They're rare. It's a Sorcerer who can see movement in the Sympathetic Echo, can see where things are heading.'

'You mean they can see the future?'

'In a way. To me, the Sympathetic Echo is a bit like a photograph of a motorway junction. I can tell you a lot, but I can't tell you what's going to happen next. A Diviner sees it in little glimpses, like five second videos from a camera. If you had those, you could predict a lot about where the traffic is going.'

'But not what its final destination is or the reason for the drivers' journeys.'

'Good. Spot on, Uncle C.'

I thought about calling that comment *Magesplaining*. Perhaps if she did it again.

'Precautions,' I said. 'Better safe than sorry.'

Vicky nodded her agreement and I activated my Ancile. We had come down a footpath from the farmhouse. As we got nearer the mill, I realised that we were approaching the workers' entrance and that most of the building was hidden by a fold in the meadow. There was a side door at the end of the path which looked firmly locked from the inside, so we went round the front.

'There you go,' said Vicky. 'The regular entrance.'

A farm road led away from the mill, curling round the hill to a point at the back of someone else's premises. Another part of the Sexton patrimony? An understanding neighbour? In front of the mill was a packed stone forecourt which had two modest, utilitarian vehicles: a black pickup and an unmarked white van.

'Where's the 4x4s?' I said.

'They won't be far away,' said Vicky. 'What's those over there?'

She pointed to what looked like really cheap swimming pools, rough concrete rectangles set close to the ground.

'No idea,' I said. 'Paper making is not an area of expertise.'

The white van stood in front of double doors; a smaller door, propped open, was near the pickup. On a nod, we moved further apart for safety and I approached the door. Something skittered away from us and took refuge under the pickup, but it moved too fast for me to see it properly. When I got close to the door, I could hear the hum and clank of machinery. There was no point knocking, so I just walked in and looked around.

The far wall was lined with galvanised steel vats, the middle was full of tables and presses, and the bottom held a pile of … old clothes? Yes, very much like the reject pile in the sorting centre of a charity shop but on the scale of a warehouse. It was only when I looked up that I actually saw any paper.

On long strings running half the length of the mill, white squares hung heavily. What impressed me most was the size of the sheets – sheets being the operative word. You could have tucked yourself up under one of those.

There was no sign of human life at first. The hum of machinery came from pumps near the water tanks, and the clank had stopped. A movement by the old clothes caught my eye as a young man stood up, surprised. I could only see the top half of a sleeveless blue boiler suit and a mop of dark hair, but I heard the call clearly. 'Dad! Visitors!'

'Hello,' came a voice from behind me.

I turned and saw a tall man heading into early middle age. He wore dungarees and a black tee shirt with some design hidden under the bib. Unlike his son, he'd tamed his hair into a long ponytail that showed the lines on his face and emphasised the blue of his eyes. Two well-muscled arms were devoted to carrying steaming mugs of tea.

'Good morning, sir. I wondered if we could have a word.'

Given that he was armed with nothing more dangerous than a cuppa, Vicky had joined me inside. The man shouted, 'Leo! Tea! I'll leave it on the bench.' He put one of the mugs down and said, 'Follow me.'

The western end of the mill had been divided off into an office and workroom. The door which led to the farmhouse path was in the middle. The man ignored the horribly messy desk and took us to a cast-off settee. 'It's clean,' he said, having seen the look on Vicky's face. He took an old dining chair for himself, Vicky grabbed a swivel chair and left me to disappear into the soft furnishings. But only after introductions.

'Watch Captain Clarke,' I said, offering a handshake.

'Karl Winter,' he replied, shaking hands. He shook with Vicky, then said, 'You're a long way from home.'

We sat down, and I had to shuffle to get my holsters away from the cushions. I made a mental note to institute Standing Orders on who sits where during interviews.

'What are you doing here?' said Winter. 'It can't be anything to do with what happened to Petra Leigh, can it?'

'You knew her?'

'Everyone knew Petra. Legend, she was.'

Vicky coughed. I think both of us had just had a vision: the teenage Laura coming home to find a man's hairband in the bathroom.

Karl must have spotted the look. 'Not me. Not like that. I was married then.'

'You're not married now?' said Vicky.

'Well, yes, but I was married to Diana then. I'm married to someone else now. Someone mundane.'

Vicky gave me a funny look. Was that because of Mina, or something else?

'Diana?' I said.

He took a sip of his tea. That we hadn't been offered any was a notable event.

'Diana Sexton,' he clarified. 'Evelyn's daughter. Didn't you know?'

'We met Evelyn at the house. She pointed us down here. We know nothing else.'

'Oh. Then …' He stopped, self-mystified. 'When you said you weren't here about Petra, I thought you'd come to buy Parchment, in which case you'd want Diana. We don't have customers here unless they ask for a tour.'

'I think we should start again, Mr Winter. Who does what round here, and how does it all fit together?'

He put his tea down. 'Why do you want to know?'

'Curiosity. I never said we weren't here about Petra. You just assumed it. We're here in relation to a serious incident on the Fylde.'

'The Fylde? I know nothing about that.'

'We'll come to it in a moment. Just run the operation by me first. If you wouldn't mind.'

'You really know nothing about us?'

'Nothing. Start with Evelyn. She's a Sexton, yes?'

'Married on the Sextons. She's from Borrowdale, originally. The Sextons have been making paper and Parchment here since just after Caxton brought the first press to England. Before that, they were growing flax in a small way, and they had the water. We grow our own flax and buy in used cotton and linen. Our products are 100% wood-free. Best in Britain.'

'So I've heard,' said Vicky. 'Not that I'm an expert.'

He nodded and pressed on. 'Leonard Sexton was no Mage. He married Evelyn and they ran the business together. He was a smashing bloke. Taught me everything I know about fibres, presses, the lot. He left a huge hole in a lot of lives when he died.' He drank some tea to give himself a moment. 'Diana and I run the mill together. Leo – my lad outside – is apprentice to me. Diana was never that keen on getting her hands dirty. Or wet.'

Vicky had been nodding attentively and picked her moment. 'Leo's not a Mage, is he?'

'No.' said Winter, daring Vicky to push it further.

She didn't, so I picked at a loose end. 'Was Diana an only child?'

'No. She has a younger brother, Guy. He's no Mage either. He went abroad and renounced his legacy. Now he's back, he's very supportive, and his lad is going to take over the farming side from Evelyn. He's been doing the hard graft for a couple of years.'

'Is he doing the lambing? I heard one coming on the way down.'

'No. He's at college today. A Hungarian lad from the farm shop is covering for him. The sheep are just to keep the grass down, really. Most of the farming is flax.'

A thought struck me. 'Those outside tanks. They're for the flax, not the paper, aren't they?'

'That's right. We do tank retting. Smelly business.'

Vicky shifted in her seat and looked at me with raised eyebrows. I've known her long enough now to translate: *If you start talking about flax instead of customers for Parchment, I will kill you slowly*. I might have exaggerated the last bit.

'You and Leo must be busy. Where can I find Diana?'

'The Hall.'

'What Hall?'

'Linbeck Hall.' It was Winter's turn to raise his eyebrows at me. 'If you go back to the farmhouse, turn right and go round the lambing shed, you'll see the open path. You can't miss it after that.'

Vicky got up and stuck out her hand – to me, to help me get out of the settee. I took it gratefully.

'Thanks for your time, Mr Winter. We'll let you get back to work.'

'That was just getting interesting,' I said, outside the mill.

'To you, maybe. When he brought up the flax and the tanks, I couldn't stop thinking about frogs. And sex.'

Wow. I had not seen that coming. 'I thought he was too old for you.'

'Eurgh. Not him. Seamus Heaney.'

I had to stop. 'I am so looking forward to this. Go on.'

She carried on up the hill towards the farmhouse, and I had to hurry to get my explanation.

'GCSE English. We had to do Seamus Heaney's poetry. *Death of a Naturalist* is all about rotting flax in this Ulster bog, only the frogs spawn in it, then the tadpoles grow up. Sort of like an Irish version of the birds and the bees, only with frogs.'

'I bet that went down a storm with a bunch of teenage girls.'

'Why do you think I wanted to get out of there?'

'I still think we could have got more out of him. He can't spend his whole life in that mill.'

'He obviously doesn't have much to do with his ex, and there were kids' drawings on that desk. He's got a mundane second family.'

'Well spotted. I hadn't noticed.'

We turned past the lambing shed. 'Aah. They're so cute,' said Vicky. Two little lambs were suckling greedily on their mother's teats. In the dark at the back of the building, a second ewe was complaining loudly. I hurried her on before she noticed.

Past the farmhouse buildings, we both shivered as we pushed through the vector that was keeping the rest of the farm hidden. Beyond the wall of magick, a raging torrent assaulted my ears, and I looked around for a waterfall. I also looked for the cliff (no cliff, no waterfall), and realised why Vicky had gone quiet.

Linbeck Farmhouse was a nice, if modest, traditional building. Newly revealed, half way up the hill was a proper Mage's residence: Linbeck Hall. It wasn't a mansion, and it didn't have Elvenham House's neo-Gothic flourishes, but it was a fair bit bigger. Made of local stone in the local style, Linbeck Hall was stout, well-proportioned and comfortable in its surroundings. It had its back to the hill and the west, protecting it from the worst of the prevailing weather and allowing a decent sized garden out front.

'More landed gentry,' said Vicky. 'You should fit right in up there.'

'Knock it off, Vic. I'm a tradesman, that's all.'

'Yeah, right, and I'm the Queen of Sheba.'

'Did you get that from your Dad?'

'Aye. Along with a lot of things that only make sense in Geordie. Shall we go and doff our caps?'

'I want to look for this waterfall first.'

'What waterfall?'

'Can't you hear it? It must be hidden. Be careful we don't go over a cliff.'

'You've lost the plot. There's no cliffs round here. Other side of the hill, perhaps.'

'Over there. Come on.'

'Oh my life!' said Vicky. 'It's not a waterfall, it's Aqua Lucis. I can smell it.'

'Smell it?'

'Madeleine must be rubbing off on you. You heard the Lux flowing from all the way up there. I'm impressed.'

We came to a small rise, and below us ran a fairly healthy stream, or *beck* as they say here. Go for a walk other than during a dry summer and you'll cross a dozen becks without noticing them. That's where the name had come from: the Lyn Beck runs through the grounds of Linbeck Farm.

I took a step closer, and the noise of a waterfall wasn't all that I heard. 'Who's singing, Vicky?'

She stepped carefully towards the beck and looked upstream, towards the Hall, the hill behind it and the wood on top of the hill. 'I might be wrong, but that has to be a Dryad's song. It makes sense.'

'Not to me it doesn't. I don't speak that language, whatever it is.'

'No. Not sense in that way. I don't speak it, either. It's the water. The Aqua Lucis.'

'Tell. All of it.'

'No need to get humpty. I've never seen one so powerful. She must be very old.' Vicky glanced at the wood again. 'Hold me hand. I'm going to take a drink.'

'Is that wise?'

'No. That's never stopped you, though.'

She took a step closer to the small drop above the beck and held out her left hand for me to steady her. We hadn't been invited to drink by the Sextons, and I wouldn't have tried it, but Vicky knows these things better than I do. I grabbed her wrist.

She bent down and scooped up as much as she could, holding it in the palm of her hand and staring. She closed her eyes and whispered something to the water, then sipped the few drops that hadn't run through her fingers. 'Pull me up.'

I heaved her back from the edge and let go. 'Well?'

'Dryad is a Greek word for oak tree and the spirits of oak trees. We use it to mean any Spirit who lives in and comes from a living tree. I'm getting visions of white flowers and red berries with this one. Trees aren't my thing, though.'

'Rowan. Mountain ash.'

'If you say so. There's a whole grove of them up there, where the beck rises, and Lux comes down the water. Only Spirits can do that. No wonder the Sextons' Parchment is so good. Not only is the flax soaked in it, they use it to press the sheets.'

'Why?'

'Who wouldn't make use of a resource like that?'

'I get that, Vicky, but what's in it for the Dryad?'

'Protection. I got a whiff of perfume, too. The sort me Gran uses, and so does Evelyn Sexton. She must be some sort of guardian.'

'Excellent. Well done, Vic. I got nothing like that.'

'Well, you should give up smoking while you've still got a nose left.'

Touché. 'Anything else?'

'I'm not going in that wood with an axe. You shouldn't, either.'

'Right. I'll leave it in the car.'

'Let's go up to the Hall and give Diana Sexton a surprise.'

I steadied her hand as we regained the path. 'She won't be surprised,' I said. 'She'll know exactly who's on the way.'

'How come?'

'Her mother. I'm sure that Evelyn really is a sweet old lady. She's also as sharp as a tack. Why do you think she laid on all the flattery?'

'Eh? I thought she fancied you.'

'I'm not that vain. She did it to put us off the scent. She sent us to the paper mill deliberately, knowing that we'd get nothing out of Karl Winter or Leo. You'll notice that she didn't mention the beck, the hall or the Dryad when she knew we'd be heading up there sooner or later, and that gave her the chance to tip Diana off.'

'You have a very suspicious mind, Conrad.'

'It's a good job one of us does.'

The path up to Linbeck Hall was steep enough to keep both of us quiet until we got to the steps that led to the formal garden.

'Tell me something, Vicky. If Mages are mostly so rich, who does their cleaning? Do they have house elves?'

'You wish.'

'What?'

'You want to hire some to look after your stately home.'

'It's not that big. I'll make do with the contractors for now. So?'

'Eastern Europeans, I'll bet. Front door?'

'No. Tradesman's entrance. I only use the front door when I've got an axe to grind.'

We found it round the back in a dark gap between the house and a retaining wall that held up the hill. A Range Rover Sport and two small hatchbacks were clustered nearby. One of them had L plates. Vicky pointed triumphantly at the Range Rover. 'See. I told you the 4x4s wouldn't be far away.'

'That'll be Diana's. I wonder who the other two belong to.'

'Let's find out.'

Before we could ring the bell, the back door opened and a young woman emerged.

'Oh! You gave me a shock. Sorry.'

She was quite dark, with brown eyes and curly dark hair. She was about Vicky's age and wearing exactly what Vicky would be wearing on a day off: jeans, trainers and heavy sweatshirt. The lack of coat meant she must be about to get in one of the cars.

I made the introductions.

'Wow. The King's Watch!'

The surprise in her face couldn't have been faked: this woman definitely wasn't expecting us. She brushed some hair away and looked at us again, her eyes moving slowly rather than darting. She gave the impression of considering things carefully, and didn't speak until she'd got the measure of us.

'I'm Miss Sexton. People call me Rowan.'

'We'd like a word with your mother, please.'

A flash of pain, barely visible, showed in her eyes. 'Not my mother. Diana is my aunt. I'm Guy Sexton's daughter. Come in.'

She stepped back into the house and led us along a refurbished below-stairs passage and into the posh bit: a double height entrance hall with a giant carpet over a flagged floor. I didn't get a chance to look properly at the designs woven into the carpet or the oak panelling because we were straight through to a small sitting room.

Rowan knocked at an imposing set of connecting doors and stuck her head in. 'Diana, I've got the King's Watch here .... What?' She disappeared into the room and left us to study the sitting room.

Vicky was examining the soft furnishings and didn't notice when a black shape slipped past the window. Oh dear. Diana had just sent her niece out of a different exit so that we couldn't talk to her again. Before I could draw this to Vicky's attention, the connecting doors opened and Diana Sexton came out to meet us. She closed the doors firmly behind her.

Diana was very clearly her mother's daughter. She was shorter than average and looked like she came from a long line of farmers. She had a healthy glow, wore pastels over tight jeans and had her hair tied back in a conventional braid. It was obviously dyed. She was also worried. You didn't need to be a Mage to see that.

We shook hands and she offered us a seat where we were. This time, I beat Vicky to the comfy chair.

'How can I help?' she asked, planting her hands on her knees.

'I think you know why we're here,' I said.

'What makes you think that?'

Fair enough. Diana was worried, but not frightened. We weren't going to get a free ride.

Vicky spoke next. 'We're investigating a serious offence committed in the mundane world and outside the Particular.'

'Oh?'

My turn. 'A fraudulent instrument was used in theft of two horses. We're investigating both crimes.'

There. In her eyes. *She knew.* Diana Sexton was implicated in this business somehow. I stood up and opened the door to the entrance hall. The last time we'd been in this position, our witness had been shot. I didn't want that happening again.

'What theft is this?' she asked. 'And what has it got to do with me?'

'Two horses belonging to Mr Diarmuid Driscoll were stolen from a stables on the Fylde.'

'Stolen?' That was a surprise to her.

'Yes. Stolen. Mr Driscoll reported them stolen to us. He may have been killed, but a crime's a crime.'

'Can you investigate a crime where the complainant is dead?'

'How well did you know Mr Driscoll?' said Vicky.

That put Diana right off her stroke. 'Nothing. I mean, not really at all. Hardly.'

'Do you own horses?' I said.

'Me? No. I did pony club as a girl, never since.'

We had her off balance. Just one more push…

'Everyone speaks highly of your family's Parchment. Have you, or Rowan perhaps, any skill at Enscription? I can easily check with Clan Skelwith. They've been very supportive of our investigation.'

'No. Not me. I couldn't Enscribe *Happy Birthday*. And Rowan's just a child.'

Damn. Damn and blast. I'd asked the wrong question. I looked at Vicky, and she gave me a grim smile. Then again, Diana had just sent her niece packing.

'Rowan's hardly a child, Ms Sexton,' said Vicky, nodding towards the back of the house.

'Who? Oh, you mean *Pihla*, the one who showed you in. You weren't to know.'

'Know what?'

'My daughter is called Rowan. My niece's name is Pihla, which means Rowan. She pronounces it something like *Bihla*, which is impossible unless you're Finnish, so she sticks to Rowan outside the family.'

I felt rather than saw Vicky sitting up straight. I'd done the same. 'Finnish? That's unusual.'

'My brother married a Witch from Finland.'

She was getting nervous again. 'And does your sister in law practise Enscribing? Or anyone else in your extended family? This is a very serious matter.'

'Tui did. Guy's wife. She was killed when Pihla was ten. For the record, Pihla is apprenticed to an Enscriber, yes, but she is bonded to the Sisters of the Water. She wouldn't, she couldn't steal horses or engage in anything like that. You've met her.'

'We need to speak to her, and to the Master Enscriber. Where can we find them?'

'Pihla's on her way to Keswick. I can give you the address of the scriptorium if you want.'

'Please. And have you ever heard of the Swan of Tuonela?'

'That's the bird, not the piece of music,' added Vicky.

'Are you saying that someone has used a Tuonela Pen in this?'

I thought she was a bit quick to jump to conclusions there. I paused. 'If that's what a black swan quill is called, then yes, we are.'

'Then someone's trying to frame her.'

'How do you figure that?' said Vicky.

'Have you met any Finnish Witches before?' said Diana. 'No? I thought not. It would be like leaving a katana lying around.'

I waited until I was sure that Vicky had no idea what she was talking about. 'It's a Japanese sword,' I said. 'If there were a famous Japanese warrior in the neighbourhood, one might start with asking them for an alibi.'

'Might one?' said Vicky. She was not impressed by the way things were going. Neither was I.

It was time to tie Diana down to some specifics. We had time and numbers on our side. I made a point of getting out my notebook. Vicky got out her sPad. 'When is Rowan – Pihla – due back?' I asked.

'A couple of days. Wednesday or Thursday. She's gone to see a woman about some oak trees.'

'And your daughter?'

'She boards at the Waterhead Academy.'

'Does your brother have any other children?'

'I don't see why that's relevant.'

Vicky had the good sense not to butt in while I waited for an answer.

'Twins. Tarja and Toivo; they're twenty. Tarja – she's a girl – is with the Northern Sisters. Toivo lives with Guy at Sprint House. He's combining a mundane course at Newton Rigg agricultural college with an apprenticeship to a Herbalist.'

'Karl Winter mentioned that Toivo was going to run the farm.'

'I hope so,' said Diana, 'and the sooner the better. You've met my mother. She still feels responsible.'

'Hang on,' said Vicky, making a note. 'Guy and … could you spell his late wife's name?'

'T-U-U-L-I-K-K-I. Tui for short.'

I made a correction in my notebook, as did Vicky on her sPad. She had another question. 'So, if I've got this right, Guy and Tui had three children and all of them are Mages?'

'Yes.'

There. Again, I'd seen something. Diana had stopped herself adding a comment. I don't know why this was significant, and Vicky didn't see the need to enlighten me yet. She lowered her head and left me to it.

'Apart from being a single parent, what does Guy do? Karl said that he renounced his legacy.'

Diana sniffed aristocratically. 'There was nothing to renounce. He chose to make his future in the Baltic, not here.'

I looked at Vicky. She shrugged. Time to wrap things up.

'Thank you for your help, Ms Sexton. I need contact numbers and full addresses for all those people.'

She hesitated, torn between co-operating, to get rid of us, and refusing to help at all. I did nothing to make her choice any easier.

'Excuse me. I'll be back shortly,' she said, then disappeared into her den behind the doors.

'What's with the bit about the children being Mages?' I asked Vicky.

'Probably nothing. It's just very unusual for a non-Mage to have three Gifted children, no matter how powerful Tui was. She's definitely hiding something.'

'Tell me about it. I wish I knew what.'

'What did you reckon to Pihla?' she asked.

'Innocent,' I said decisively. 'She was curious and surprised when we turned up. Her aunt was shifty.'

'You're not joking. I just wish we knew what questions to ask.'

Diana returned with a note. 'Rowan – my Rowan – doesn't have a phone at Waterhead. No signal of any description. She'll be home for the Easter break on Wednesday evening.'

I studied the list. It all seemed to be in order. She'd even added contact info for her ex-husband.

'Thank you for your time.'

Diana took us into the main hall and opened the front doors. When we got to the corner, one of the hatchbacks had gone. In its place was a van.

'That's who does the cleaning,' I said. 'See?'

Vicky looked at the van. 'Particular Domestic Services,' she read out to herself. 'Sounds about right. Let's follow the drive and see where it leads.'

The drive from Linbeck Hall swept to the right, away from the rest of the farm.

'Your brothers and sisters are all older than you, aren't they?' I said.

'Thanks for not calling them half-brothers. Aye. The closest is twelve years older than me.'

'So you're an only child in some ways.'

'I guess. So are you, really, with Rachael being ten years younger.'

'She was very advanced for her age. Your family didn't have as much to fight over as mine.'

She stopped on the track. 'Really? Ooh, do tell.'

'Some other time. I was just thinking about Evelyn Sexton.' I started walking again. 'She has two grand-daughters called Rowan. I wonder which one will get to look after the Dryad.'

'Now there's a thought. The one with the Finnish name must be favourite. She's the oldest.'

'But her father is younger than Diana, and Guy is not a Mage. It could pass through the female line.'

'Perhaps. Do you think it's relevant?'

'It could be. I don't think Pihla is involved directly, though she is the only Enscriber we've come across.'

'But she's a bairn. There was a lad in my year at Salomon's House — Anthony, his name was. He was the most gifted Occulter they've seen in years. More naturally talented than Li Cheng. He couldn't do half of what Cheng does because he's still got a lot to learn. Mages who can do really heavy stuff at that age are only born once a century.'

'All the more reason to track down that Scriptorium.'

The track from the Hall ended with a cattle grid that let on to a very minor public road.

'That's enchanted,' said Vicky.

'I'd guessed. We're a long way from the farmhouse by road. Shall we go back the way we came?'

'Aye. I'm hungry. And thirsty.'

'I know just the place.'

We walked back down the drive until I spotted a path over the fields that took us directly to the farmhouse. There was no sign of Evelyn, and if there had been, I don't know what I'd have asked her.

I drove us round the corner – literally, to Plumgarths Farm Shop, or the Two Sisters Café, to be exact. The clue is in the name.

We started with a pot of tea. While I was ordering, I casually mentioned that we'd been to Linbeck Farm.

'Oh yes,' said one of the sisters. 'Where's that?'

Now that's what I call a low profile: a business not two hundred yards from Linbeck Farm had never heard of it. Way to go, Sextons.

Vicky wasn't surprised when I told her. 'Unless they've got a good reason, why should they?'

'I'd say that the cooking here was a good enough reason. Never mind. Have you finished putting that list in your sPad?'

'Aye. Who should we start with?'

'Guy Sexton.' I poured the tea. 'Let's enjoy the tea, order some lunch and you can go out to call him while I wait for the food to be prepared.'

'Why should I have to go outside? All of them places were freezing except Evelyn's kitchen. I haven't warmed through yet.'

'Fine. I need a fag anyway. I'll have the quiche and salad.'

'Share fries?'

'I had a cooked breakfast. So did you. No fries.'

'You might regret that.'

'I won't be long.'

Guy Sexton answered on the first ring: as expected, his sister had been in touch. I asked him for a meeting.

'I'm not in the Particular at the moment. I'll be home for Easter. Is there anything I can help you with over the phone?'

'What can you tell me about this scriptorium where your daughter is apprenticed?'

'Is it true you've found a Tuonela Pen? I can't believe it.'

'I take it you're familiar with them.'

'Yeah. Sort of. Where was it found?'

Now, why was he asking that question? Why should he care?

'It was used in connection with the horse theft.'

'You should know that I'm Chairman elect of the Kentdale Union, so I've been getting copies of some of the correspondence about these events. If this was the pen used in the murder of that horse guy in Cartmel, then the Assessors are looking into that. And quite right, too.'

'Mr Sexton, *these events*, as you put it, include four murders and an attempted murder.'

'I know. That's why I can't understand why you're farting around with an alleged horse theft. Bit of a come-down from Dragonslaying, I'd say.'

'Perhaps you could take that up with the Occult Council. In the meantime, what can you tell me about that scriptorium? How many people work there? What do they do? That sort of thing.'

'That's precisely why the Assessors should be left to get on with things. Do either of you know anything about Enscripting? If someone is really trying to frame my daughter, I'd rather someone who knew the area looked into it.'

Vicky appeared at the door and made eating signals. I waved her over and put the phone on speaker.

'Mr Sexton, we have the resources of the Invisible College to draw on, if we need them. The Eden Assessor has his work cut out with the murders. If we can come at this from another angle, we can clear your daughter's name much more quickly. Alternatively, I could start taking members of your family in for questioning.'

'Stop making empty threats. You'd never get a warrant from the Cloister Court.'

'This is a mundane crime. I'd use the mundane law.'

The phone went quiet. Vicky looked at me nervously.

Sexton came back on the line. 'Your threat has been noted, Mr Clarke. What do you want to know?'

'The scriptorium where your daughter works. Tell me about it.'

'It's where her mother worked, too. Don't ask me for the details. I'm a politician and administrator, not a Mage. Do you want the address?'

'Something more useful than *High Wray Repository, Wray Holme via Low Wood Water Sports* would be helpful. Your sister clearly thought that would make sense to us.'

'That's Di for you. Did she give you the co-ordinates?'

'Why would we need those?'

'It's in the middle of the lake. You have to hire a boat to get there.'

Vicky couldn't help herself. 'You're joking, aren't you?'

'I'm afraid not. I'm back in the Particular on Thursday if you want me to arrange a visit.'

'Will there be anyone there today?'

'Yes. Not Pihla, obviously.'

'So what do we do?'

'Go to the boat hire at Low Wood Marina. Hire a boat and navigate to the co-ordinates. I'll text you straight away.'

'Thank you, Mr Sexton. We'll be in touch.'

One of the Two Sisters stuck her head out of the door to check if we'd run off without paying. I waved and shouted, 'Sorry. Back in a second.'

I put my phone away. 'Well, Vic, are you up for a boat trip?'

She started walking back to the café. 'Are sure it's wise? Couldn't we pick this up on Thursday, when everyone's back?'

'We could, but we can't hang around in the Lakes until then. We'd have to ask Hannah what she wants us to do. I get the feeling that things might happen quickly if we wait until then. At least we can keep moving this way.'

We sat down at our table. 'What about the Gnomes?' said Vicky. 'If you've made friends with them, surely they could supply a list of Enscribers.'

'Worth a try. If you drive to Low Wood after lunch, I'll call George Gibson. Right now, I'm starving.'

As you'd expect from a Gnome, George was rather cagey when I asked about scriptoria.

'You've put me in a difficult position, Conrad,' he said. 'The Clan Father wants this business sorted, but not at the cost of the King's Watch tearing all round the Particular. Hang on.'

I waited while the background sound effects changed. The echoing of a large room was replaced by wind noise over the microphone, then the click of a cigarette lighter.

'Did you mention our name when you talked to Guy Sexton?' he asked.

'Give me some credit, George.'

'Good. Sexton is going to be Chairman of the Kentdale Union after the Summer Gathering, and the President of the Grand Union is stepping down in the Winter. Probably. The Clan Father wants to be the first of our people to be President. If word gets around that we're dealing with you, things could get very difficult.'

'Hang on,' said Vicky. 'It was your leader who approached the Constable.'

'To get the spotlight off the Particular as quickly as possible.'

'Even more reason to help us now,' I said.

'Go on. What do you want to know?'

'Start with the place where Pihla – Rowan – Sexton works.'

'Used to be based at Staveley, moved to Wray a few years ago. They do a lot of work with ancient texts, and Guy is abroad a lot. Still has contacts in the Baltic. It's run by a woman called Jasmine. That's all I know.'

'Thanks. That's a help. What about other places?'

'The biggest is near Penrith. I doubt it's them. They don't have a lot to do with the west coast, and they're very religious. There's one in Borrowdale, one towards the Solway Firth and one near Ravensglass, and that's just the ones I know of. A lot of Enscriptors work alone.'

'Thanks, George. I'll let you know if we need their details.'

'This is it,' said Vicky, slowing down by the ever-growing Low Wood Hotel and turning into the marina. 'I'll let you sort out the boat hire while I get changed. At least it's not blowing a gale or lashing down with rain.'

I've flown light aircraft, small, medium, large and extra-large helicopters, but in all my thirty-seven years, I've never piloted a motor boat. Just not my thing. I paid very close attention while the nice man showed me what to do.

'Almost unsinkable,' he said. 'Not completely, but almost, and no *Titanic* jokes. There's not enough power in the engine to destabilise it. Just watch out for the other boats. Especially the sail boats. They don't like it if they have to take evasive action, and they love to complain.'

'We're really not sure when we might come back. Is that a problem?'

'Not really. It's a lake, not the sea, so you can't sail off with it. Even if we've all gone home, so long as you tie the boat up and put the keys in the drop-box, you'll be fine. We're not exactly rushed off our feet, and we've got your credit card number.' He gave me a big smile which said that he didn't expect me to behave like a man on a stag do, then handed over the keys. 'Enjoy the lake.'

I unfolded the map and checked the co-ordinates from Sexton's message. Then I double checked them: NY 37855 00522. The scriptorium at High Wray Repository was in the middle of the lake. Not the middle, exactly, because it was quite close to High Wray Bay, but there was no island marked there. If this was a wind-up, I'd be making my first arrest: for wasting police time.

'Steer or navigate?' I asked Vicky. She was doing a fair impersonation of Mina, insofar as the number of layers was concerned. 'Are you sure you'll be warm enough?'

'It's cold out there. I stood on the jetty and got frozen in seconds. I'd get your thick coat if I were you.'

'Fair enough. You get some water and I'll get set.'

Vicky didn't just get water, she even filled our re-usable coffee mugs. 'You can smoke on the boat, if the wind's right. Let's get this over with.'

She handed me into the boat. That's right, the young woman helped the pilot down the step, because the pilot has a dodgy leg. I asked again if she wanted to drive.

'No thanks. If ever there was a job for you, it's this one. Where are we going?'

I pointed south-south-west. 'There. Make yourself comfy and watch out for other boats. We don't want to get barred from the lake.'

'Or crash. Do you want me to cast off?'

'Great. I'll start the engine.'

The little hire boat had a windshield, for which we were both very grateful when we left the marina. There was a strong breeze out there. Once past a little headland, I could see where we were going and throttled back to minimise the swell and give me time for a cigarette. Within a few minutes, we were well out on the lake, heading in the right direction, and I was completely mystified.

'Vic? Can you sense an occulting?'

She peered over the shield. 'Where?'

'Dead ahead. Just to the left of that castle.'

'What castle?'

Mark Hayden

She must be joking. Surely? A great Gothic pile sat on a promontory, surveying the world and announcing its supremacy. 'That castle. There.'

She squinted. 'Oh. Gotcha. Where am I looking now?'

'Left, just past the wood.'

She concentrated. 'Yeah. It's a Dispersal Glamour. We'll be able to see through it in a minute.'

'How does that work?'

'It's the basic Work for hiding things from a distance. Works a treat with aerial photography and satellites. It bends light round itself. Once we reach the lens point, the effect stops. That's how come you can see Merlyn's Tower inside the Tower of London, but not from outside.'

'And when we get there, which thousands of people must do every year, we shall say, "Why isn't this island marked on the maps?" Or something similar.'

'Let's see, shall we?'

We chugged on for another quarter of a mile, until the wind was making my eyes water. I blinked away some tears, and there it was. A small but perfectly formed wooded island, sitting in Windermere as if nothing was unusual. I scratched my chest and turned to Vicky. She was peering down the top of her jumper. I slowed the boat even more.

'That's weird,' she said. 'Did you feel it?'

'Whatever it was, no I didn't.'

'There's something linked to our Persona medallions. Wish I could figure it out.'

The very first magickal Artefact I picked up was a Persona, given to me by Mother Julia at Lunar Hall. It smudges the edges of your Imprint a little, especially from a distance. It stops nefarious Sorcerers from tracking you down.

'Is it dangerous?' I asked.

'Don't think so. I reckon that it flips things on their head – if you're *not* wearing a Persona, it triggers a more powerful Work. Probably makes boats steer round the island without noticing it. That's quite serious magick, and it obviously works all the time.'

'They do stick out a bit here. It's different in the countryside.'

'I suppose. Do we have to swim? If we do, you're on your own, partner.'

'No. We tie up there, next to that little powerboat.'

'Thank the gods for that. What do you think this place is called?'

'Wray Holme. I should think. I'd forgotten that most of the islands on Windermere are called Something Holme. Hen Holme, Rough Holme and so on. Can you tie us up?'

'Yes and no. I'll wrap the rope round, but you better check me knots.'

I'd got the hang of the boat by now, and glided us gently in to the little mooring. There was barely room for two boats, even though the other one was only a dinghy with an outboard. I killed the engine, pocketed the key and finished Vicky's rope work.

'I'm guessing it's that way,' she said, pointing to a dressed stone path through the trees. 'After you.'

Wray Holme is little more than a teardrop in the vastness of the lake, with the mooring at the thinner end and a ring of trees surrounding a squat stone building with no windows and a door down a shadowy passage. There was just enough room in front of the building for a plastic picnic table and chairs. The table was actually tied down, so they must use it all winter. I approached the doorway, and to the right was a slate plaque with *Wray Repository* written in the most beautiful script. The stone around it was lighter, and four holes showed that the new plaque had replaced something

The castle we'd seen on the way here is not a castle in any meaningful sense. It was built in 1840 by a couple from Liverpool, I believe, as their retirement home. Beats Mum and Dad's villa in Spain, though whether they'd swap their heated pool for open water swimming in Windermere is another matter. I mentioned the castle because it's easy to fake age in a building. I examined the stones closely, and they told me nothing. You could go to a new build in Bowness and find exactly the same construction techniques being used – irregular slate blocks built into courses.

Just inside the entryway was a niche containing a wicker basket with a leather pouch inside. A large notice in red on the door offered an explanation, if you could speak Latin. 'Vic? What the hell does *Aedificatrix Operans, non Commaculate!* mean?'

We both squeezed in, and she read the note. Or glanced at it, because she'd seen it before. 'It means that we have to leave our Artefacts in the basket. It's quite common with a workshop, especially where there's an open Work. It's a bit like wearing a hat in a food factory. Not that you'd need to.'

'I still have hair. For now. What if we don't?'

'Best case, we'd piss her off something rotten. Worst case, we'd get turned into frogs. It has happened. We could stand here and hammer on the door until she comes out.'

'Is that someone else's stuff in that leather bag?'

'Most likely to be hers. There's several strong Wards on it, and it's been made specially. It's what you'd do if you worked here every day.'

'We don't have a nice leather pouch.'

Vicky looked theatrically round the small island. 'I think we should be safe from passing thieves.'

There was a small log store round the side, next to a brace of propane cylinders. I went over and started removing my magickal gear. 'Call me paranoid if you want,' I said.

'You're paranoid. I'll put mine there, too. I'll even put a Misdirection on.'

As at the Esthwaite Rest, I was left holding the SIG. I didn't leave it outside because it's a loaded gun. You should never do that, so it was back into the waistband. We returned to the door, and I knocked hard, waited a few seconds, then pushed it open. A loud bell tinkled overhead.

'Hello?' I said.

'Hello back,' said a woman from below whose voice I hadn't heard before.

Only when I'd stepped inside did I realised that it wasn't just the front which had no windows. Lights flickered on. Magickal lights, glowing on the end of bundles of twigs in wall sconces. They revealed a comfy sitting room, with easy chairs arranged around a wooden railing that protected a set of steps down. The start of the staircase was at the other end of the room, by a desk, littered with books and writing equipment.

'Down here,' said the voice.

I walked round the stairhead to the start of the steps, and found I couldn't see the bottom. The end was clearly beyond the wall of the building around us, well into the island. I looked at Vicky. She shrugged and said, 'She ain't coming up, is she?'

I took hold of the rail and started down. My head had cleared the overhang, and I could just see a passage at the bottom when the lights went out and I was sucked down and tripped over at the same time.

Rehab saved my life. When Helga the sadistic physio had been teaching me to use the stairs with crutches, she'd included a module on how to fall down. When my legs went from under me, I relaxed them and curled up, grabbing my head with my arms. The idea is to roll like a ball.

I hit the side, step after step, more side then the bottom, all too quickly for the pain to register. Unlike the kick in the stomach I got at the end. That registered very clearly. Thank Odin they couldn't get at my groin.

'Ooof,' I think I said.

I tried to roll around in agony, but someone stood on my bad leg and shouted at me. I relaxed a little. Enough to turn my head and focus on what they were saying. Oh. Right. The rifle barrel pointing at my chest said it all. I flopped back and tried to see what had happened to Vicky.

'Come down slowly or we'll shoot him,' said a woman's voice. The same one that had summoned us downstairs. Only it wasn't her holding the rifle.

There were two of them. A man in a hoodie was pointing the rifle at me, and a woman was pointing a shotgun up the stairs at Vicky.

I had to say it. I hated to say it, but I had to. 'Run, Vic! Run like fuck! Aaargh.'

That last sound was me having my bad leg twisted. For some reason, Vicky ignored a direct order and emerged from the dark staircase with her hands in the air.

'Lie face down,' said the woman. She was also wearing a hoodie, and there was something about that voice now that we were down here. Yes. It was too low. Some magick was distorting her words.

Vicky got to her knees, then lay down. I'd been glancing at the rifle from time to time. It never wavered, not even when the bastard kicked my leg. I was not going to risk that.

The woman put down the shotgun and whipped out a pair of handcuffs. Before Vicky could do anything, she was cuffed and had a floral pillow case pulled over her head. The woman turned her attention to me. 'Roll over.'

'Can't. I think I've broken something. Can't move my shoulder.'

She grabbed my right arm, and I screamed. As loud as I could. Right into her face. She flinched back, and I let my arm drop before screaming again. She made a half-move towards me, drew back and turned her head to the man.

'Let him crawl,' said the man. His voice was even lower, like a slowed down record (look that up if you need to). 'Cover his head and let him crawl.'

She put a pillow case on my head and said, 'Wait.' I heard her dragging Vicky upright and shoving her down the passage. When her footsteps returned I heard the man move away. 'Right, you, crawl forwards. If you can. I'll get a rope and drag you, if you want.'

All of me hurt. Badly. Except my head and my right arm, which I'd faked on an impulse. That meant I had to crawl one-armed on a very painful knee. It took me a lot of time to cover the distance, and a lot of pain. I nearly put my right hand down at one point, and that would have been very bad news.

'Stop. Turn left.' Two more crawl steps. 'Lie down.'

I was bracing myself for something, and it came. Strong hands rolled me over like a log. I remembered to scream when my right shoulder hit the floor, then the floor was wood, not stone, and I bumped into something soft.

'Mind yourself,' said Vicky. I moved to get my right shoulder in a comfortable position. Even I was starting to believe it hurt.

Heavy footsteps joined us on the hollow, wooden floor. 'OK,' said the man. With a rumble, we started to drop. The rumble was purely mechanical, with no electric motor.

It took about ten seconds to go down, then the man stepped out. 'On your feet, Clarke,' he said. I made a meal of getting up. 'Walk towards my voice.' I did, for five small steps. 'Stop.'

I heard the woman doing something with Vicky, then more footsteps. There was very little light getting through the pillow case. Either it was pitch black down here or they'd used 1,000 thread count bed linen.

Then came the shove. I was pitched forward with some violence, and for a fraction of a second, I thought there was no ground, that I'd fall forever down an old mine shaft. I made a ball, hit the floor and rolled. A scream from Vicky and she thudded next to me. I was already ripping the pillow case off my head.

'Let's do it now,' said the woman, her voice even lower. I did not want to be *done* now, and my left hand was reaching round to my waistband.

'Are you sure the water's turned fully off?' said the man.

I blinked lint and brightness out of my eyes and saw a very depressing sight. We were in some sort of chamber, and the man was on the threshold, pointing the rifle at me.

'Yes, it is,' said the woman. 'I'll put the seals on. North at the top, South at the bottom.'

Shit and double shit. We were about to be locked in a Limbo chamber. Again. I slipped the SIG into my right hand, keeping it behind my back. I levered myself up to a sitting position and watched the rifle sights follow me. Vicky had recovered from her fall and was groaning. A red stain had appeared on the top of her pillow case. Oh dear.

'Just stay still,' said the man. 'Someone will find you sooner or later.'

There was a Lightstick in our chamber, and I could see him clearly in the doorway. When they put those seals on the door, two things would happen. I braced myself, feeling the floor and trying to prepare myself mentally for the disorientation that was coming.

I felt a wave of nausea when the first pair of seals went on. Vicky felt it too, and bucked violently. I raised my left hand to my face and started to shake. The Lightstick dimmed, then went out.

I pitched left, brought up my right hand and aimed to the left of the rifle, which was outlined against the doorway. That guy was right on the threshold, his Ancile pressed up against the Limbo seal. The Ancile uses magick to detect incoming missiles, but it wouldn't see my bullet until it crossed over. The rifle started to withdraw, and I fired.

The man staggered back and dropped the rifle. If he screamed, or if she screamed, I wouldn't know: the magick kept all noise out of our room. Vicky, however, definitely screamed. 'Conrad!'

'Roll right,' I shouted as I started to get up. 'Roll right and keep rolling.'

I tried to focus on the doorway, but it was wobbling alarmingly. All I could see beyond it was shadows, then one shadow got bigger. I aimed and fired again. The shadow disappeared, then everything became shadow because the door was slammed shut, putting us in total darkness. I heard a skitter of metal on stone as the hunting rifle was pushed into the room by the closing door. Good.

That left them with a shotgun, if there was a way of using it. I had to get to safety, and staggered along the wall until I got to the corner. They'd never hit me from here. But Vicky...

I fumbled in my coat for the torch I'd shoved in when I got changed. You can get a lot of light from a very small LED these days. I found it and hesitated. Wherever Vicky was, I couldn't see her, and if I couldn't, they couldn't either. If I switched my torch on, they'd have a target. At least they couldn't hear us.

'Vic? You OK?'

'No. I can't breathe, Conrad. Help me. Please.'

'I'm here. I'm coming.' My eyes had adjusted enough for me to look around at the darkness. I knew where the door was and stared hard. There was nothing round the edges and only a faint lines round a square high up. Good. The observation hatch was closed.

Keeping my eyes on the door, I squatted down and scooted backwards along the floor, making soothing noises as I went. When my back bumped into Vicky, I stopped, took one last look at the door and reached round.

She was on her side, curled into a foetal position and hyperventilating. I reluctantly put the gun down and found her head. I drew off the pillow case and sparked a coughing fit. 'There, there. It's OK, Vic. I'm here. Don't worry.' A glance at the door. No light. 'We're going to breathe together. Ready ... In, deep breath ... hold it ... out, all the way ... In, deep breath ... hold it ... out...'

It took her a few goes to realise what was happening and what she needed to do. I was lying on my back, next to her, gun in hand and watching the door. Nothing.

When she was getting there, I stopped the commentary and gave her a few breaths on her own. 'I'm going to help you move, Vic. We need to get out of sight of that door, OK?'

'Aye. Yes.'

'I'm going to sit you up and help you shuffle. Just follow me.'

We edged to the corner, well out of the line of fire. 'What now?' she asked.

I put my arm round her shoulder and said, 'We wait.'

'How long? What for?'

'We wait until we think we've had enough, then we wait some more. I don't want to start moving around and get a shotgun blast.'

'What makes you think they won't sit there all day and all night?'

'Because they could have done it before, and because that guy will need medical attention. You can't put a sticking plaster on a bullet wound. I should know. I'll bet they're already gone.'

'Somehow I find that less than comforting, 'cos it means we're on our own.'

'I can think of only one person I'd rather be locked underground with, if that's any comfort.'

'It's not, and it's also cheesy and inappropriate. But thanks anyway.'

'Good.' We were both quiet for a moment, and that's when I realised just how much I hurt. 'Oww. That bloody staircase was hard.'

'How's your arm. As you've put it round me shoulder, I'm guessing it's not too bad.'

'It's the only part of me that doesn't ache. My left knee is the worst, as are my right ribs, my left hand and my right hip. They're all the worst. How about you.'

'Me head really hurts. Inside and out. I'm trying not to think about it.' She took a deep breath. 'I'm especially trying not to think about me bag. She took it off me, and it's got me Xanax in it. I don't think I can last until Thursday, Conrad.'

'Yes you will. Have you figured out where we are yet?'

'Under an island on Lake Windermere.'

'It's not called Lake Windermere. Just *Windermere*. There's only one Lake in the Lake District, and that's Bassenthwaite.'

She groaned. 'No. Please stop. No geography lessons. I can't even see the sodding map, can I?'

'Wouldn't do much good, would it? We're not on the map. Regardless of the name of the body of water, I reckon this is the old gaol. The Esthwaite Rest is new, and I thought they'd re-built on the same site. Evidently not. I reckon that Wray Repository was the old one.'

'Makes sense. Wonder why they moved.'

'Too exposed, on the lake. Too old fashioned. Too Harsh. Too expensive. Who knows.'

'Any chance of the cavalry arriving?'

'Did you text anyone?'

'No.'

'Me neither. Hannah knows we're investigating the Sexton mill. She's the only one who'll worry. I suppose she might get on to Clan Skelwith eventually, and George knows we were heading for Wray Holme.'

My right arm was going to sleep. Not good for accuracy. 'I'm going to see if I can hear anything through that door.'

When I moved, I felt the room lurch, and Vicky whimpered.

'Come back,' she said. 'Touch me again.'

I found her hands behind her back, and immediately felt better. So did she.

'I only fell into the pit when you left me,' she said. 'Don't do it again unless you have to.'

'How come? What's going on?'

'I have no idea. Now I know why all cells in the Undercroft are single occupancy.'

'I really do have to check out that door. Brace yourself.'

I let go again and took a breath, until the room stopped spinning. I crawled along the wall, found the door and put my ear to it. I flinched back when I felt cold metal, then tried again. Complete silence. I stood up slowly, leaning on the door and decided it was time for a light. I gave Vicky fair warning and switched on my torch.

The first thing I examined was the door. A sheet of steel covered the wood and fitted snugly into the frame. It was broken only by a six inch by nine inch hatch at eye height for a normal person. The flap was steel, too. I turned my attention to the rest of the chamber and moved the light slowly round.

The room was about five metres by four metres and lined not with stone but brick, as was the barrel vault above. At either end of the vaulted ceiling were pairs of holes, covered with mesh. Air in, air out. Good. There was no distinctive smell in here, just a slight edge of plaster from the mortar.

A few things broke the brick monotony. There was a dog-sized arch in the same wall as the door, an opening in the far left corner, a few useless Lightsticks in sconces and a pile of stuff in the far right. I put the torch on the floor and took out my phone. It may not have any apps, but it does have a little light. I switched it on and moved back to Vicky. She was already sweating. I put my hand under her mass of hair and rubbed between her shoulder blades.

'Mmmm. Thanks, Dad.'

Whoah. I didn't know whether to be flattered or scared that she was losing the plot completely.

'He used to do that. When I came home from school, when the magick was growing, he'd rub just there. Poor bloke thought it was period pains.'

Phew.

The cut on her head had stopped bleeding, and most of the blood had gone on to the pillow case. It would be a big bump later.

'Vic, can you watch the hatch while I check things out?'

'Keep rubbing and I'll think about it.'

I rubbed a bit longer, then balanced the torch on her thighs. It had a better light, and safety was still priority number one. 'Open your eyes, Victoria.'

'Sod off.' She opened them anyway. 'Hurry up. Anything you can do about the handcuffs would also be appreciated.'

'One thing at a time.'

I started by picking up the hunting rifle, carefully, holding the barrel not the stock. I propped it against the wall next to Vicky and moved on to the small arch. It was about eighteen inches high and nine inches wide at the bottom. In former times, that's how the prisoners had received food. Someone had bricked it up since then. Great.

Next, the opening to the north. How did I know it was north? In the Esthwaite Rest, I'd lost all sense of direction. Had I oriented myself before the Limbo seals were put in place? I shrugged and shone my phone into the opening.

It was bigger than I expected, about three metres square, and had a big hole in the floor. In fact, it looked nothing like I expected. The skirting area had six holes, just like mouse holes, but deliberate. Each one had a channel running to the hole in the ground. Something to do with water. Bathing? Toilet? I peered into the hole.

It was four foot deep, perfectly circular and had a six inch hole set into its bottom. The smaller hole appeared to be lead-lined. Stranger and stranger. The chill and smell of damp stone said *bathing* rather than *toilet*. I moved on to the pile of stuff, glancing at the main door on the way, and at Vicky, too. She'd closed her eyes. I decided not to say anything negative, and just made a big groan when I knelt down. She opened her eyes and blinked uncomprehendingly for a second, then re-focused on her duties.

Our captors had obviously wanted to take the edge off things for us. There were three five litre bottles of water, two lilos, and two plastic storage crates. One contained an LED camping lantern and assorted foodstuffs. I shoved it aside and found a wooden hatch in the floor. I lifted the hatch and recoiled from the crusty acid odour. This was the toilet.

Under the wooden hatch was a small, lead-lined hole in the ground that presumably once contained chamber pots. It now had a bucket with bleach splashed in the bottom and a packet of wet wipes. I replaced the lid and checked out the other storage box. It had a gas stove, lighter, two small pans and two metal cups. I checked back in the other box. Only the British could shove someone in a dungeon and leave tea bags, just to show it wasn't personal.

The camping stove had a metal frame to hold the pots, and that gave me an idea. It was time to form an escape committee.

The steel in the camping stove was strong, heat resistant and, if you took it apart, had pointy bits. Perfect. I switched on the LED Lantern and switched off my phone. Vicky had closed her eyes again.

I coughed and walked over. 'Can you lie on your front? I need to have a look at those cuffs.'

'Rub me neck first.'

I rubbed. She lay down.

Handcuffs come in two varieties – sex toy and security. These were not security handcuffs. They may not have had pink furry linings, but they weren't made of carbon steel either. The chain that held them together was already bending just from Vicky's stress levels, and I soon picked out the weakest link.

'Hold still. This shouldn't take long.'

I pushed the stove prong into the chain link and twisted. I yanked and twisted some more. I pushed down on her hands and pulled up. The link parted. 'There you go.'

I stood up and stood back. Vicky rolled on to her front and sat up. 'The cuffs are still on.'

'Sorry. Maybe later. Move your arms round a bit.'

She rubbed her wrists as best she could and stretched her arms. 'Thanks, Conrad. That's good. Give us a hand up.'

I hauled her to her feet and she clamped her fingers round mine. I made her swap to my left hand and moved slowly round the room, keeping a constant eye on the door and showing Vicky what we did and didn't have. She was most interested in the side-chamber. 'That smells good,' she said. 'I'm getting mint.'

Mint? Whatever.

'Let's make camp over there,' I said, pointing to the corner along from the door. 'If you can stay awake, I'll blow up a lilo.'

It took a bit of negotiation until we found a way of leaning against the wall, Vicky's hands around my waist and me doing the inflating. The handcuffs dug into one of my bruises. Eventually, fully watered, we sat on the lilo and considered what we'd learnt this afternoon. I even folded the pillow cases to use as a head rest.

'I still can't believe we fell for it,' said Vicky. 'This place had trap written all over it.'

'No it didn't. We can't go into every magickal building like a SWAT team. Think about those three buildings at Linbeck, the hotel in Little Langdale, George Gibson's grotto and Petra Leigh's house. This is the first time we've been attacked.'

'Aye, but it only takes once.'

'True. Did you get any clues about the opposition?'

'Not really. I didn't see a lot, and they were using voice shifters.'

'Why didn't you run when I told you to?'

'It was too late by then. I was half way down the staircase after you, and I didn't fancy getting shot in the back.'

'Thanks, Vic. I appreciate it. Next time, run back and hide.'

'Charming. I see what you mean, though. Did you see anything?'

'Trainers. Grey socks. Tell me, could a non-Mage have done what he did?'

'With enough Artefacts, yes. You're thinking of Guy Sexton?'

'Who else? Either he's behind all this or someone has infiltrated his life so completely they might as well *be* Guy Sexton.'

'Fair point. Why, though?'

I shifted the pillow case behind my head a bit. I was starting to get twitchy, and I somehow doubted that Vicky would let me smoke in here.

'The big question,' I said, 'is *why are we still alive?* They've had enough chances. I think I've got an answer.'

'Go on. I'm tired.'

'He wants to keep all the crimes local. Whatever he's up to, there's going to be a huge stink inside the Particular. Clan Skelwith will see to that. They don't want their Assessors to be fair game for anyone, but so long as the King's Watch – us – are kept out of it, he can rely on some things being brushed under the carpet.'

'Some?'

'His sister, for example. She's involved somehow. That woman with him out there was not Diana, I could tell that much. Too tall. Whatever's going on, Sexton thought he could keep a lid on it. Too late for that now.'

'How come?'

'I shot him, and that's what worries me. He's got my bullet in his shoulder or chest. That will prove he was here, as will his blood on that rifle. I just hope his partner is a good healer, otherwise they'll be back to burn the place down and bury us here.'

'Can you not be so objective, Conrad? A little rose-tinting might be good today.'

'Noted. What do you think he's up to?'

'I have absolutely no idea whatsoever. You?'

'About the same. It will happen before Thursday, I'm certain, and it involves Enscripting. Too much of a coincidence otherwise.'

'Not horses?'

'No. We've gone way beyond horses. Sport is a serious business, but this is on a different scale altogether.'

We took a moment to gather our thoughts. The bond between us, maintained through gripped hands, was keeping Vicky's demons at bay for now, but I wasn't confident that it would last. For one thing, I wanted us to sleep in shifts, and I didn't trust her to stay awake when it was my turn.

I spoke up to fill the silence. 'I wonder if they moved here deliberately.'

'Moved? From where?'

'Didn't you hear what Gibson said?'

'No. I was looking for the Marina turning at that point. I heard the bit about Penrith then zoned out. I think.'

'He said the scriptorium used to be in Staveley but they moved. It must have been after his wife was killed.'

'Staveley?'

'Yeah. Little place north of Kendal. Handy for Linbeck Hall and Sprint House.'

'Right. I've just remembered what Desi said.'

'When?'

'Right at the beginning. As soon as we started looking for an Enscriptor, I asked her to remind me about stuff I'd forgotten. You know me.'

I do. Vicky had a good magickal education, then promptly forgot everything she didn't need as soon as she'd passed the exam. Typical.

'What did she say?'

'The Staveley Stitch. It's new, relatively speaking. First real advance in Enscripting for decades. It allows you to put a new piece of Parchment into an existing book. An existing magickal book. It's incredibly hard, and very dangerous. There was some talk of banning it, then it stopped being an issue all of a sudden. I guess that's when Tui died. Not that I'd heard her name before. '

'Could you use it to insert a Malaglyph?'

Still holding my hand, she shrugged. 'Desi said that three Mages died trying to copy the Staveley Stitch, and that was just to do a repair. Anything's possible, though.'

In the world of magick, it most certainly is.

I thought through what else Vicky might have missed and laughed.

'What?' she said.

'There's an issue with the plumbing. Guy asked his woman if she'd turned the water off, and that was after she'd more or less propositioned him. When she said, "Let's do it now," I was worried that she meant to kill us, but looking back, that was her bedroom voice.'

Vicky used her left hand to slap her thigh. 'I knew it. He's an FOW. A Golden Y.'

I waited for the explanation, but Vicky had gone into a reverie. I gave her a nudge.

'He's mundane, but all his kids are Mages. Occasionally, very occasionally, you get a bloke who can't help but father Mages. With another Mage,

216

obviously. They're known as a Father Of Witches – FOW. In Salomon's House they say *Golden Y* in honour of the male chromosome.'

She turned to look at me and said, 'If you promise not to let go, I'll tell you something. Something really personal.'

'All right.'

'That's what I was looking for. With Cheng, and Rick, and a couple of others. Close up and personal, I can spot a Golden Y. I was looking for one because I wanted a baby. Don't judge, please.'

I gave her hand a squeeze. This was getting weirder and weirder. 'Was neither of them good enough for you?'

'No. Neither was an FOW. I stuck with Cheng for other reasons. Don't worry, I'm not so broody now. Just a phase.'

'Does Guy know, do you think?'

'Probably. Only an Imprimatist like me could tell for certain, and only if they got close. His mother's a Diviner, remember, so she might have seen something and got him checked out.'

'Your hidden talents never cease to amaze me.'

'I think I've figured out the holding hands thing, too. I'd have spotted it at Esthwaite if I hadn't popped a pill and you hadn't been running around doing stuff. It's because of my *cardiac event*. I think you and that Druid created a link when you restarted my heart. When we're touching, we can create a current of Lux. We won't power a Ley line with it, but it's enough to keep us centred.'

'Sounds about right.'

She shuffled a bit closer. It wasn't exactly *cold* down here, but we were both glad of our extra layers.

'I wonder if there's any Giant Moles around. You could do your Mole charming trick. That would be handy right now.'

Vicky yawned while she spoke, and a few seconds later she put her head on my shoulder. I shuffled into the corner so that I could lean back, then I let her drift off. It was a good job I hurt so much, or I'd have joined her.

The camping lantern was bright enough to see the whole room, and my eyes wandered all over it many times while Vicky slept. Imagine that this was all you got to see, hour after hour and day after day. Would it look different by torchlight, as it must have done when the place was built? And if it had enough ventilation for torches, could I sneak a cigarette?

My gaze drifted up from the sconces towards the scorch marks, higher and higher until my neck hurt. There weren't any. Someone must have scrubbed that brick for months. No they didn't. There never were any scorch marks. No flaming brand had ever sat in those sconces. So why are they there? For Lightsticks, obviously. Lightsticks that don't work in a Limbo chamber.

But what if they did work? Once.

How could that be? Was there some sort of mini-Ley line that ran through the bricked-up food arch? Nothing I'd read or seen would work like that. What else could bring Lux into a sealed underground chamber? Not underground so much as under water…

'Vicky. Wake up, pet.'

'Eh?'

'I need a word. It's time for some tea.'

'Why did you call me *pet*.'

'You were asleep on my shoulder. I wasn't going to call you *love*, because you're not my love. I'm going to light the gas stove.'

'Can't you stay here?'

'No. Easy does it.'

I moved her bodily upright and tried to stand. It took three goes and the help of the wall.

While the water boiled, and while Vicky chuntered about being abandoned, I took another look at the side chamber with the alleged plunge pool. The toilet was a hole in the ground for a bucket, so why go to the trouble of building a bath? And where did the water go? We were so far underground that it couldn't drain away. In fact, water should be flooding this chamber. I groaned and bent down to check the floor round the hole, in particular the drainage channels. Bingo. I had my answer.

'That's a relief,' said Vicky when I took her hand again. 'And thanks for the tea. Much appreciated. I bet you wish you'd had them chips at lunchtime now. I do. Then again, I don't fancy using that bucket unless I'm really *really* desperate.'

'Vic, I think I know why they moved to the Esthwaite Rest. I reckon this place was too cushy.'

'You what? How do you figure that?'

'Apart from electricity and a flush toilet, all the Rest has over this place is a picture window. You could fit the modern conveniences in here if you wanted. Cheaper than a new build. Look at those wall sconces. I reckon there's a source of Lux down here. Enough to activate Lightsticks. Enough to stop you going mad, or there would be if it wasn't turned off.'

'Go on. I can't wait to hear this.'

I told her, in detail, about my visit to George Gibson's Grotto. About the pumps deep underground and about the reservoir of glacial melt water, infused with Lux. 'That bath in there isn't a bath. It's a fountain. That's why Guy Sexton asked if the water was turned off. He didn't want us to have Lux.'

'That actually makes sense. Good thinking.' She drank her tea. 'Absolutely useless, but good thinking.'

'Where's your stopcock at home?'

'Erm… No idea. That's Dad's department.'

'If this place was built in the early 1700s, they wouldn't have had the technology to route the water to the outside passage and route it back again to that fountain. There aren't any floorboards here. Behind that brick is solid rock. I think the mechanism is in there. At the bottom of that pipe, somewhere.'

'Not in the wall? Doesn't it come out of those little holes round the edge and flow down the middle?'

'Finish your tea and I'll show you.'

I picked up a lilo when we went over. 'What's that for?' said Vicky.

'Lying down on. Right. Which way does the floor slope?'

We lay down together on the lilo, which just fitted into the doorway. Vicky checked the floor.

'Bugger me, Conrad, you're right. It flows away from the hole in the middle. What does that mean?'

'It means that you're going to put your arm down that hole and feel for a stopcock, that's what it means.'

'Why me?'

'Smaller hands. Fewer debilitating injuries. Don't worry, I'll hold your legs.'

She grumbled a bit, then shuffled forward on the lilo until she could reach down. I gripped her round the hips and let her go further. Her right arm had disappeared beyond the elbow before she stopped.

'Bloody hell. You were right.'

'Don't sound so amazed. What have you found?'

'This pipe's about a foot long, then it opens out like a … dome. There's a gap, then a floor. I can feel like a wheel.' She grimaced and shifted further. 'By the Mother, Conrad, I can feel it. Coming through the metal, which is freezing by the way, I can feel the Lux.'

'Try turning it.'

She grunted. 'Stuck fast. Hang on. What is it?'

'What's what?'

'The saying. *Lefty loosey, righty tighty*. I was going the wrong way.'

'Don't, whatever you do, apply for a job as an RAF mechanic. I'd hate to be in the air and find you'd tightened the reserve fuel pipes the wrong way.'

'I think you're safe. None of my future career plans include monkey wrenches. It's moving.'

'Stop. Come back. We need to talk.'

We shuffled and bumped into each other until we were back in the main chamber. I poured a measure of water into a pan and dribbled it down one of the drainage channels. After two pans, it started to back up.

'That was a waste of water,' said Vicky.

'No. I've just proved that the drains are switched off. If we open that valve, the chamber will flood.'

'Oh. I hadn't thought of that.'

Mark Hayden

'I think it's a good idea.'

'Drowning? Can't say it's my preferred option.'

'No. Escape. If we flood the chamber, there should be enough Lux for you to do something to that door.'

'What if I can't?'

'I've made a study of prisons. It's personal.'

'And that helps how?'

'All prison doors open outwards, so you'll have water pressure on your side. The observation hatch is only held by a clasp. Once that's gone, use your Sight to find the lock.'

'You have to touch a lock to work it.'

'It won't be magickal. The grill in the Esthwaite rest ran off an electric motor. In the Undercroft, they use bolts. I think this will be a simple bar.'

'You reckon?'

'Why do they put locks on doors in prisons?'

'Don't be daft.'

'I'm serious. It's to protect the prisoners from other prisoners and to stop mass break-outs. No need for that in here. Locks were expensive and unreliable when this place was built.'

She was shaking her head. 'Too dangerous.'

'It's that or take the chance on Guy being forgiving. I shot him. He's planning something awful, and I think all the food and luxuries in here are to keep the woman quiet. I don't think this is going to end any other way than with us being buried alive. Those propane cylinders could explode. Or he could come back with a couple of petrol bombs. There comes a point when you have to take a risk.'

She looked round our prison. 'If I still said no, would you do it anyway?'

'No. We're partners.'

I was lying. I'd rather be alive and have Vicky never speak to me again than die down here without having tried to escape.

'Then let's do it. Ready?'

'No! There's some preparation to do first.'

I tipped the stuff out of the plastic crates and dismantled the hunting rifle, stowing it carefully. 'We need this for evidence. I'm going to strip off now and try to keep my clothes dry. I strongly recommend you do the same. Don't forget, I've seen you naked.'

'Naked and dead. It's a bit more embarrassing when we're both awake.'

'Hypothermia isn't a good way to die, either.'

I matched action to words and put everything except my underwear in a crate. It was very cold all of a sudden.

Vicky had turned away. When she turned back, she stared. 'By the Mother, how many scars have you got? And have you seen those bruises?'

'Hurry up or the rest of me will turn blue as well.'

220

She unzipped her coat. 'What happens in Wray stays in Wray. Understand?'

'Did no one ever teach you to fold your clothes?'

She pulled her top over her head. 'Sod off. You can do it if you want.'

I started folding. 'You can swim, can't you.'

'Of course I can. It's on the National Curriculum these days.'

'So's geography.'

She finished, and I moved the lilos to the edge of the chamber before placing the crates on top. If the water rose slowly enough, they might float together. 'Let's do this.'

'Ow. This stone's cold,' she said, lying down.

I was more careful where I gripped her this time, keeping my hands away from her underwear (and no, I'm not telling you what it was like. I made a promise).

'Here we go,' said Vicky.

'Open it as far as you can.'

'It's coming. Gods that's cold. Whoah!'

The water poured out like a geyser, pushing Vicky's arm out of the pipe and filling the fountain in seconds, then it poured over the rim and down the drains. We backed out, but not before I got that taste again, the taste of endless winter dissolving into the first spring of Albion, the day the ice age retreated.

The water filled the drains and came into the main chamber, seeping along the floor. With a shudder, it hit our toes, and I realised that we were holding each other's near naked bodies. What happened in Wray was definitely going to stay here.

Vicky bent down to take a sip. 'That's good. That's so good, Conrad.'

I joined her, and immediately felt a lot better. As if on cue, the Lightstick on the wall flickered into life. There was a loud clang from the side chamber and the water gave a great surge.

'Oops,' I said. 'There goes the valve.'

The tide reached all four corners of the main chamber. When it hit the hatch covering the bucket, there was fizzing noise and then a loud explosion, shattering the wood and lifting it into the air. We let go of each other and migrated towards the main door. My feet were already going numb.

Vicky ran her fingers over the observation hatch. 'Not enough Lux yet,' she said. Behind her, the lilos bobbed afloat and started drifting towards us. The water was now up to my calves.

She turned her back to look again at the hatch and didn't see why I suddenly made a most un-Conradlike whimper.

'What...?'

In the centre of the chamber, the water was rising in an unsupported blue column, and that could only mean one thing. I dropped to my knees. 'My Lady.'

'Who?'

'Nimue,' I whispered.

Vicky stared at the column until I grabbed her hand and yanked her down.

When I became a Watch Captain, I was brought into the presence of the first Nymph of Albion, Nimue, in her home under Merlyn's Tower. She's made completely out of water but is otherwise human. Except for the feet. She doesn't have any, and rises naked directly from the flood. Vicky hasn't been in the presence, being only a Watch Officer, not a captain.

As well as the biting cold from the water, a fresh breeze blew across the chamber, carrying scents of lost water flowers and spring blossom, of wet wool and nose-irritating pollen. The Nymph looked around as if she had no idea where she was or what she was doing there. Finally, when the water was getting dangerously near my Calvin Kleins, she looked down.

'I said no more. I said no more of this.' Her voice was the beck running over stones, rivulets lapping the river bank. Now I knew the real reason they'd moved the prison.

Vicky took a deep breath. 'My great Lady, we are nothing before you. We serve the realm in your name and beg our freedom.'

That was quick thinking. I was still in awe.

She flowed towards us, stopping in front of me. 'You have drunk from me before. Would you do so again?'

'If My Lady permits it.'

She held out her transparent, liquid hand and I bent my head to sip from her essence. That felt very good.

'And you?' she said to Vicky.

'I am not worthy,' said Vicky, and sounded like she meant it.

'If he is worthy, then so are you. Drink.'

Vicky lowered her head and took the faintest drink. I heard a rumble deep in her throat that sounded mostly like fear. I wonder why.

The Nymph drew back from us. 'You are free to go.'

She flowed back down into the water with a wave that made the lilos bob up and down, nearly dumping my clothes in the water. I waited for the door to burst open. I was still waiting when Vicky stood up and turned around.

'Bang goes me chance of leaving the Watch for a job in the Circles.'

I joined her in standing. I'd worry about her career prospects later: there were more urgent matters to deal with. 'Why didn't she break the door down for us?'

'Nimue hasn't been the full shilling for a while. She thinks the door is open because Lux is flowing out, and that can mean only one thing.'

'Can it?'

'The seals have denatured. Short-circuited, if you like. We haven't got long.'

'Why?'

'The water's going down.'

She was right. My ankles were now near the surface.

Vicky ran her fingers round the observation hatch. 'Catch at the top. Hang on.' She closed her eyes and grimaced. With a *clunk*, the hatch dropped down, and I could see the wall opposite for a second, before Vicky put her arm through the hole and felt around.

'It's too low down,' she said. I can't feel anything.

'Remember the Rest.'

'Rest of what?'

'The Esthwaite Rest. You used your phone to see round the corner.'

'Duh.' She splashed over to the lilos and dug out her phone. She fiddled for a second and gave it to me. 'Here. You're tall enough to see the screen if you hold it outside.'

223

I put the phone through the hatch and angled the camera down. The door was indeed only barred, not locked, but the bar had been secured with a heavy duty padlock. Damn.

I told Vicky and asked her if she could do anything about it. We swapped places and she tried to get a view and an angle. The look on her face changed from concentration to despair.

'I can't do it, Conrad. I can't get the angle, and the background Lux is running low. Can you shoot it off?'

The answer to that was *probably*, if I didn't mind breaking my arm from the recoil. This was Vicky's department. I dropped to my knees again and made a stirrup with my hands, just off the ground. 'Step into this, it'll give you some height. I'll try to share Lux.'

She withdrew her arm, put her left foot in my hands and raised herself up, resting on the door for friction and additional support. 'Bloody hell, this door's freezing me tits off. Literally.'

She stuck her arm through the hatch and rotated her shoulder. I concentrated on my hands, trying to send a surge of power through my fingers. I thought of what I'd learnt from Madeleine, of how Lux flows like water and sent a waterfall of thought down my arms.

Vicky grunted, then banged her head on the door with a thud that was echoed by a clang from the corridor. Then she screamed. 'Oww! Gerroff me foot!'

I let her down as gently as I could. She took her arm back inside and tried to stand. The flash of pain and quick lift said that something was very wrong. 'I couldn't have done that without you, Conrad, but I really do think you've broken something.'

The lilos were about to settle back down on the floor. 'Sorry, Vic, but you still have to move the bar. Quick, while there's still water to stand in.'

She got to it, balancing flamingo-like on one leg. The last drops of water were finding their way down the cracks when a crash from outside said that she'd done it.

I stood up and steadied her until I could give her a big hug. 'That was epic, Vicky.'

'I can't believe it. I can't believe we've done it.'

'You. You were the one who did it.'

'Nah. It was a team effort. Help me to the lilo before I freeze to death.'

I did, and went straight back to the door. With a shove, it opened on to the passage. We were free, if not yet home.

Vicky's foot was swelling alarmingly by the time she'd finished getting dressed. There was no question of putting her boot on. This was going to be a challenge.

I hauled her to her feet. Foot. 'Remember. I've done this before. My right leg has to become your left leg. We'll swing in time.'

'Eh?'

I put her arm over my shoulder. 'Hold on very tight. Your arm is going to have to take your whole weight when your right leg's off the ground. Let's try in here first.

The first time she put her weight on her foot, she yelped. The second time, she did better until she complained that I was pulling her shoulder out of its socket.

'It feels like that, I'm afraid. Let's go again.'

When she plucked up the courage to swing with me, we managed a few steps. Good. 'You need to check the passage for magickal traps,' I said.

She gave me a grin. 'With a bit of luck, the dumb waiter will still be working.'

'Fingers crossed.'

The passage was clear, with nothing to show but five other cell doors; none were occupied. While Vicky rested against the wall, I examined the lift (it was much bigger than a dumb waiter).

'Looks good. You get in, I'll work the ropes. It's been designed so that you can't ride it and move, which is why our female captor didn't travel with us.' I shoved one of the crates in first then helped her to sit down.

The next level up was clearly where the scriptorium did most of its work. Several modern doors were sealed magically, and without the stamps to open them (or Semtex), we weren't going to get a look in. I scouted up to the sitting room and left Vicky to come up step by step on her backside. It took a while, long enough for me to discover that we were locked in, both with magick and a secure five lever mortice. Vicky made it to the top and lay down on a two seater sofa with a deep groan. She was starting to go pale. Even paler than normal.

I looked round the windowless room. There was something wrong here, and not just the fact that we were still locked up. I rubbed my chin and remembered the mill at Linbeck Farm, particularly the office and break room. It had a second door. A fire door.

I went round the room, clockwise, clearing all the furniture out of the way. Vicky raised an eyebrow but otherwise left me to it. I started by the door, closed my eyes, then walked slowly round anticlockwise, keeping a touch on the wall. When I got to the back, my fingers met empty air. I shoved my arm through and opened my eyes.

'I wondered what you were up to,' said Vicky. 'I was gonna say, *is there a door through there?* But you seemed to be having fun.'

'You could see it?'

'Aye. Still, it's good practice for you. *Is* there an exit?'

There was a tiny galley kitchen, a chemical toilet behind a curtain and, yes, a substantial fire door. This one didn't need a key. I lit the gas, put the kettle on and asked Vicky if she wanted a hand to get to the bathroom.

'That would be great, but shouldn't we get straight off? Have we got time for tea?'

'Tea and biscuits. While you're behind the curtain, I'm going outside to get some fresh air and make a couple of calls. Up you get.'

'You mean you're going for a fag. You can wait until I've finished before you do.'

I waited. She finished. I took my turn, made the tea and pushed the door open. Boy did that fresh air smell good. I took a deep breath and went outside, pausing only to put the doorstop in place. A loud and raucous sound from above grabbed my attention. A raven took flight, leaving the branch swaying in its wake. 'Well, Allfather, what do you make of that?' I said, out loud 'Is the Lakeland Particular something you want to preserve or destroy? Do you care?'

As ever, the silence in response could be interpreted however you wanted. I had one last comment. 'If you're not keen, just text. You've got my number.'

Midges were gathering under the trees as the light left the Lake. We'd been down there for several hours, and if something was going to happen tonight, we'd have to get a move on. I got out my fags and phone. When I'd lit up, the first person I called was PC Barney Smith.

He was waiting for us as we approached the dock at the Low Wood Marina, and yes, he'd brought the items I'd asked for. He waved one of the crutches as we came into view.

'I'd have sunk our boat. Or disabled it,' said Vicky from her throne along the back of our launch. 'Mind, it was very clever of you to take the keys.'

'It's my paranoia. Comes in handy. I showed you the blood stains on the Wray Holme mooring. Guy will have needed a Healer far more than he needed to mess about trying to sabotage an escape that he didn't expect to happen.'

'Aye. You're right. I need a Healer, too.'

'You could try the NHS. I had to.'

'Shut up and steer the boat.'

When I glided up to the dock, Barney lowered a crutch, Vicky grabbed it and I tied us up. We somehow managed to get her out without too many swear words.

'What did you want this for?' said Barney, offering me the extra-large police evidence bag.

He took a sharp breath when I put the rifle inside. 'Keep that in a safe place,' I said. 'I've texted you the crime number to put on.'

'How...?'

I took out my shiny new L&W warrant card. 'If anything happens to me, take that rifle to Cairndale, FAO Commander Ross.'

'Do I want to know what's going on?'

'Not yet. Have this, too.'

He looked at the little badge I'd given him. In the middle was the outline of a castle, and round the edge *Merlyn's Tower Irregulars.* 'What do I do with this? Give it to my nephew?'

'Only if he wants to join an elite band of rebels and renegades.'

He had the good sense to laugh. 'Elite. I like that. Does Captain Robson need any help?'

'Oh yes. Lots. Why don't you give her a hand getting to the car while I deal with the boat keys?'

I took as long as I could putting the keys into the drop box while I kept an eye on Vicky and Barney. He was very solicitous.

I checked my phone (again) to see if my arrangements were coming together. They were. Good. George Gibson had messaged that everyone was in place at eight o'clock, and it was now ten past. Unfortunately for Vicky, my arrangements couldn't include a Healer. I looked over, and Barney had ensconced Vicky in the car. He was leaning in to chat to her. Good. The seed was sown.

I lit a cigarette and limped over. The immersion in Nimue's water had done a lot to heal the bangs I'd picked up rolling down those stairs, but I was still pretty sore. I leaned over the roof and Barney stood up straight.

'We're going off the grid for a bit,' I said. 'At most a couple of days. I really appreciate the risks you've taken, and if I can, I'll let you know what happens.'

'Good luck, Conrad,' he said. He leaned into the car. 'And you, Vicky.'

I stubbed out my cigarette and climbed in. Next stop Linbeck Hall.

'I'm telling you,' said Vicky. 'Leave the effing axe in the car. It won't do any good.'

'Spoilsport.'

'No. I want you ready to catch me if I fall, and you can't do that if you're trying to juggle an axe and a handgun.'

'Selfish spoilsport.' I sighed, and put the axe back in the lockable box. 'Kalashnikov?'

She ignored me. 'Show us how to use these things again.'

I got the crutches out of the back and adjusted them for my height. When I had pins and plaster all through my leg, I used to call moving around on crutches *cromping*. It took weeks to get that good.

I braced myself and said, 'Lean forward. Like this. Then lift your good leg and swing. Lean, lift, swing. Lean, lift, swing. You try.'

I readjusted the crutches and helped her out of the car. We were in the car park of the farm shop, just around the corner from Linbeck Farm. Vicky had insisted on practising before we drove through the Wards and alerted the Sextons.

'I don't know why you couldn't have done this at the marina,' I grumbled.

She levered herself out of the car. 'It's bad enough with you watching, never mind anyone else.'

Ooh. She thought enough of Barney not to want to show herself up in front of him. There was definitely hope.

I gave her some encouragement, and she managed a few clumsy steps, but she did get the rhythm. 'Stop there,' I said. 'Save your ligaments for later.'

I helped her back into the car and we drove off, round the corner and through the Wards that ran through the Sexton's cattle grid. In seconds, I was helping her out and walking up to Linbeck Hall. This time I reversed on to the lawn and we used the front entrance.

I took out the Hammer, activated the Ancile, and used the butt to hammer on the doors. George Gibson opened up and looked at us.

'Get the other one, George, if it opens. It'll save Vicky trying to go through sideways.'

He reached for the bolts. 'Are you sure you know what you're doing?'

'No, but don't worry. If this goes tits up, it's my arse on the line, not yours.'

'Ours,' said Vicky. 'It's *our* arses on the line, and I don't like the expression *tits up*.' She balanced on one leg/crutch and stuck out a hand, the other crutch dangling from its forearm cuff. 'Pleased to meet you.'

'And you. Can you manage?'

'Aye. Stand back.'

George gave her some room, and Vicky swung into the hall. I cringed when she approached the carpet: a well-known hazard for the less mobile. She took it in her stride and pivoted to face us. George pulled the second door closed and shot the bolts.

'Where are they?' I asked.

He pointed right. 'In there. The gods only know what they're getting up to now that I've left them alone. I've put out a straight chair, like you asked. I can see why she needs it now.'

'Then thanks very much. I'm not sure who owes what debts after this, but thanks anyway.'

'We'll wait and see, shall we? The accountants can tally the score afterwards.'

'Careful, George. My girlfriend's an accountant.'

'Good luck,' he said as we shook hands. I'm not sure whether that was in relation to Mina or the coming encounter. Vicky had already taken up a ready position. 'It's a good thing that posh people have wide doors,' she said.

I put the Hammer away and knocked on the oak, turning the knob and walking straight in.

The extended Sexton family had had plenty of time to prepare an ambush, violent or otherwise. I took two steps into the room and swept for danger, leaving Vicky to follow behind. No one attacked us, but they were definitely up for a fight.

Call it family room, drawing room, lounge or whatever you want, that's where we were. We'd come through a door in the bottom right, or south-east corner, and the family were arranged around the fireplace on the west wall. There was an empty chair, straight backed, in a strategic place for Vicky to keep an eye on things; the rest of the seating was squashy and comfortable and had been bought with the *inherited* look that interior designers strive for when they do up old houses.

According to George, Diana Sexton had been mistress of Linbeck Hall for a couple of decades now, ever since Evelyn moved out to the Farmhouse. Diana had had the good sense to leave the original features intact, and although I'm easy to please, there wasn't anything in the room that would have set my teeth on edge if I had to live here. I did appreciate the log fire though, and unless my nose deceived me, there was a strong hint of apple in the smoke.

Six pairs of eyes tracked me as I approached the group, most obviously Diana's. As the mistress of the house, she had taken pride of place by the fire, leaning on the mantelpiece and the only one able to watch me without turning round to some degree. Diana had changed since our encounter this morning, black trousers and a cream blouse with a black jacket. She must be hot in that.

She'd added heels, too. Women and heels are a mystery to me, and I suspect to them as well.

The person with the second best view was in a mismatched armchair that had been pulled in to the circle. It might have been his when he lived here, if he ever did. I'm not sure when they split up, but Karl Winter was still very much part of the Sexton empire. He was the one who spoke first, while Vicky was still making her way to the refuge, and he stood up to do it, subtly pushing his ex-wife closer to the fire.

'Look who it is. Hercule Poirot and Miss Marple have nothing on you two. Who the hell do you think are, getting the Gnomes to drag Rowan and Pihla back here and line us all up like suspects?'

One pair of eyes hadn't turned round, and they belonged to Evelyn. She was on a day bed between two of her granddaughters. I'll call Pihla by her Finnish name to save confusion, and the blond teenager on Evelyn's other side was the 'second' Rowan, looking very nervous.

I made my way to Evelyn and stood at a respectful distance. 'Mrs Sexton, I'm sorry about this, but it involves all your family in some way. I see that your son and ... Tarja, is it? ... are not here.'

Diana spoke before her mother could get her words out, not that Evelyn had made a move to say anything. 'Tarja is on retreat, beyond the reach of human technology. My brother is on his way back from Scotland.'

I kept my focus on the matriarch. 'That's not true, is it, Mrs Sexton?'

This time she answered. 'If you say so, Mr Clarke.'

So, that's how she was going to play it: *I won't lie for him, but I won't lift a finger to help you find him.* Fine. We could work with that.

I shifted my attention slightly, to Evelyn's right, where Pihla was sitting. She was now dressed in a long black skirt with a multi-coloured tunic over the top. I felt a slight pang when I saw her in that outfit, because her build and colouring could have been Mina before she was attacked.

'Do you recognise this?' I took the pillowcase from my pocket and draped it over Pihla's knees. She flinched back in horror when she saw the bloodstains and brought her hand to her mouth.

Evelyn snatched it away and screwed it up before throwing it at my feet. 'You didn't have to do that.'

'Pihla? I think you've seen that before, haven't you?'

Would Evelyn step in to order silence? Now was the moment...

'Whose blood is that?' said Pihla. Evelyn kept her counsel.

'She's alive, but injured. Where have you seen it? At Sprint House?'

Pihla shook her head. 'It's Jasmine's. She's the Master Enscriber at the scriptorium where I work. Is it her blood?'

I pointed to Vicky. She'd brushed her hair over the plaster on her forehead. 'No. It's Officer Robson's blood. How long have your father and Jasmine been in a relationship?'

'They're not.' She blurted it out so unconvincingly that Rowan, who'd been watching open-mouthed, actually rolled her eyes.

You'll have noticed that Diana was conspicuous by her silence during this exchange. She was keeping her powder dry to protect her own, and by that I mean Rowan and, if necessary, Leo. While my back was turned, she'd moved to the other side of the fireplace, away from Karl. It was time to take on the grown-ups.

'Sit down, please, Mr Winter,' I said, moving towards his personal space. This is something that comes much more naturally to men – knowing how far to go before a confrontation becomes unavoidable. I stopped short of that point to give him time to decide whether he wanted a scrap. He didn't, not for Guy Sexton or Jasmine.

I took his place, formerly Diana's, and turned round to face them. I also took the Hammer out of its holster. That got their attention.

'By this Badge, I am notifying you that we seek Guy Sexton and another in connection with a charge of aggravated assault and false imprisonment on two Officers of the King's Watch.' I let them see the mark of *Caledfwlch* that Nimue had authorised me to carry when I first met her, then I replaced the gun. 'Does anyone know where they are?'

There had been silence so far from the biggest couch, where two young men were taking up a lot of space. Leo, I'd met, and he was keeping his face as poker-straight as his father, Karl's. The other lad was Toivo, twin to the absent Tarja. He was younger, shorter and much leaner than Leo, and he had the same brown eyes as his sister, Pihla.

'Dad's got nothing to do with this,' he said.

Our next step was a long shot, and not one we'd wanted to take. I nodded to Vicky, and she hauled herself off the chair. Diana crossed her arms and gave my partner the evil eye; Vicky was too busy trying not to fall over, and didn't notice. When Vic got to the furniture, she had to turn right, around the couch where Evelyn and the girls were sitting. She wobbled a little and leaned right to avoid putting her foot down. The crutch slipped on the floorboards, and she reached down to steady herself. On the way, her hand brushed Rowan Sexton's shoulder.

She jerked it back and nearly fell over. 'Oh my life, Conrad,' she said, then bit her lip.

Everyone turned to look at her, even Evelyn, and when Evelyn locked eyes with Vicky, there was a shudder of understanding.

The Sexton matriarch turned to look at her daughter. 'You should have told her,' said Evelyn.

Diana went pale. 'Told her what? Told who what?' she blustered.

Evelyn sank back into her seat, and I crossed to Vicky. Plan A was now history. My partner took a step back and dropped her right crutch on the floor. She moved her newly freed arm in a big circle and pushed the air down with her palm. Everything went quiet, and I felt magickal Silence wrap round the two of us. Vicky took my hand in hers – the only way to communicate – and whispered in my ear. 'That girl, Diana's daughter Rowan. Her father was Diarmuid Driscoll.'

I glanced at the silent Sexton tableau beyond Vicky's screen. Diana was going red, and clearly facing a couple of awkward questions. I evaluated what Rowan would know, where she had been and the sheer pace of events since Friday morning. We had a fraction of a second to seize the initiative.

'Brilliant, Vic.' I let go of her arm and moved beyond the Silence (after picking up her crutch). I raised my voice a notch to cut across the others and said, 'Sorry about that. My partner has just remembered something.' I pivoted to face Rowan. 'We were wondering who was going to train your horses now.'

Rowan frowned at the abrupt change of direction. 'I don't know. Diarmuid says a cousin of his is interested in coming over for the Chases. Why do you ask?'

Vicky had cancelled her Silence and heard Rowan's reply. We turned to face Diana. She had gone bright red and thin lipped. 'It might be better if you gave up the Chase,' she said. 'You'll have other things to think about when you graduate.'

'Mum! You promised,' said Rowan.

Diana's reaction gave me an idea. I'd never get a sensible answer out of one Rowan, but there were two here.

'We'll be back for you later,' I said to Diana. 'You will be arrested in due course, but first you need to tell your daughter what's happened to her father, and who's responsible.'

'How dare you!' Diana spat out the words.

Rowan stood up to face her mother. 'Mum! What's going on? What's happened?'

I slipped behind Rowan and said to her cousin, 'Pihla, you're coming with us.'

'Why?'

I bent down and picked up the pillowcase from where it had been sitting on the floor. 'Because of this. Because we have questions that only you can answer. You're not under arrest, but I will arrest you if you don't come.'

'Don't even think about it,' said Diana.

Karl was on his feet now, unsure what to do but ready to do it. Leo and Toivo were still watching. Evelyn stared at her hands. I bent down as close to the old lady as I could. 'Evelyn, no one here has an Ancile, do they? Let's not go there, eh?'

She turned to Pihla. 'Go on, love. You'll be fine.'

'Gran?' said Pihla, aghast.

I stood back up and put my left hand on the SIG. I took a step away from the crowd, towards Vicky.

Rowan got into Diana's space and shouted, 'What's going on! Tell me!'

Karl was looking at his ex-wife and her daughter rather than his niece.

'Pihla? Let's go,' I said. She kissed her grandmother and slipped off the couch. 'Get the door for Vicky, would you?'

The innate helpfulness inside her took over, and Pihla stepped round to help Vicky. I walked slowly backwards as the Sextons imploded. Only when the door handle turned did Toivo stand up to look at his sister, and it was too late. I hoped he'd forgive himself for that, one day.

It was too late for the café, but the Gateway Inn was opposite. I pulled in before Pihla had got round to asking where we were going.

'Wait here,' I said to both of them. 'I'll see if there's somewhere private.'

A Monday night in April isn't the busiest time in the Lake District. I bagged a table, ordered a bottle of water and two burgers, then went back to get Vicky and Pihla.

'Pihla wants to know why we've brought her here,' said Vicky when I'd helped her out of the back seat. 'Apart from your love of not cooking, I'm struggling to see why meself. She's also been texting her Dad on account of her not being a prisoner.'

'I'm not. You said so yourself.'

There was something indefinable in Pihla. Something she'd inherited from Evelyn, perhaps, or from her mother.

'Has he replied?' I asked.

She shook her long dark hair and turned away. I helped Vicky with the steps. 'It's been a long day, and it's not over yet. We need building up, and we need to build some trust with Pihla. We're need her to betray her father, and that's not going to be easy. Our only advantage is that Evelyn told her to come with us.'

'I wouldn't say no to a large gin, either.'

'When it's over, I'll buy you a bottle.'

'It's always gin tomorrow with you. Never gin today. Go on, then.'

'What's really going on?' said Pihla when we'd sat down.

Vicky drank her water thirstily. I leaned forward.

'Who's going to become the next Dryad guardian?' I asked. Vicky nearly choked on the bubbles. Pihla frowned. I waited.

'It was going to be me,' she said, 'until Dad gave in to Auntie Di. I've withdrawn.'

'Why would you do that? It's a great honour.'

'It is.' She looked around the room, as if her father might appear and take her away from the awkward questions. 'Ever since Rowan went to Waterhead, Diana's been pushing for her to take the guardianship. Dad said it was up to Evelyn, and Evelyn wanted me.'

'What changed his mind? Was it recent?'

233

'He's been leaning towards it for a while. Suddenly, a couple of weeks ago, he sat me down at home and said, '"Diana won't move out of the Hall for decades. If I move the scriptorium here, and rein in Jasmine a bit, you could live and work in Sprint House." I said yes.'

Vicky said, 'Is it his scriptorium to move?'

Pihla nodded. 'It's his in trust for me. Apprenticeships for Enscripting can take a lot longer than other crafts, and I can't run it until I finish.'

'When was this, exactly?' I asked. 'Check your phone if you need to.'

She did need to. 'Sunday the eighth of March. I rang Tarj to talk about it.'

Vicky looked at me. That was the day after Olivia Bentley had rung Rod Bristow. Rod would have rung Diarmuid in a panic. Diarmuid would have rung Diana ... but Diana had got her own way. Doubly. Not only had she extracted the horses, she'd got her daughter as the front runner to become guardian.

That could only mean...

'Pihla, what sort of Mage is your Aunt?'

'A Weaver.'

'Ooooooh,' said Vicky. 'I see where you're going now. Get us another chair, will you, Conrad? Me foot's killing.' While I manoeuvred another chair to take her foot, she spoke confidentially to Pihla. 'He knows loads of stuff about helicopters and Roman history, but he's only been a Mage since Christmas.'

Pihla looked confused. 'But I thought he was a Dragonslayer. That's what Auntie Di said.'

Vicky waved a hand. 'He got lucky.'

I ignored the jibe and positioned the chair. Vicky put her bad foot up. It was clad in one of my socks, and was nearly filling it. Mages (proper Mages, not fakes like me) can do a lot to suppress pain, but Vicky needed magickal or medical attention on that foot, and she needed it sooner rather than later.

Vicky continued her character assassination. 'What I'm trying to say is that Conrad hasn't had any magickal education except what I've given him. Take pity on the bloke and tell him what your mam – your mother – was like, what this Jasmine's like, what your Auntie can do. That sort of thing.' She looked over my shoulder. 'You're not hungry, are you?'

Pihla shook her head just as the burgers arrived. We tucked in.

The young Witch turned her glass of water round and stared at the bubbles. 'People think Mum was a great Enscriber. She wasn't. She was a great Artificer who also Enscribed, and that's me, too, not that I know from first hand.' She looked up. 'I just remember her as my mother, not as a Witch. I know she was good, because I've seen her work, and I've seen Jasmine struggling to do half of what Mum could do. Now Jasmine *is* a good Enscriber, and good with languages. She's got a beautiful Kotodama banner in her house.'

Pihla looked at Vicky in a different way. 'Was that really your blood on the pillowcase?'

'Yes. She didn't go to Japan to study Kotodama did she?'

'No. Some Japanese practitioners visited. We get a lot of them in the Lakes. Something to do with Peter Rabbit, bizarrely. They came to see her to see if she could re-inscribe part of a document that had been damaged. She could and she did.'

'And you're her apprentice?' I asked, just to show I'd been following.

'At Enscribing, yes. I did a Mastery with an Artificer first, away from Kentdale.'

Vicky nodded and put her half-eaten burger down for a rest. They were very good. 'Tell Conrad what a Weaver does. He's never met one.'

'Really?' said Pihla. She looked confused, and turned back to Vicky for clarification. 'You're Salomon's House and Quantum Magick, yeah?'

'It works for me,' said Vicky.

'And that's what you've taught Conrad?' Vicky nodded. Pihla turned back to me. 'Stop me if I go too far back, OK? It's like this. Witches didn't have libraries, or lectures or a career path like Chymists. The Circles have only been going a few centuries.' She realised what she'd said and thought about back-tracking.

'Don't worry, Pihla. The RAF is only a hundred years old. We're learning to crawl.'

'RAF? I … never mind. To cut a long story short, a Weaver was a Witch who learnt patterns, who learnt to put different elements together. Originally, it was to teach the Craft to other women who had the Gift, but later they became a sort of Jill-of-all-trades. That's Auntie Di. She can turn her hand to all sorts of things.'

I finally got to see why Vicky had coaxed this explanation out of Pihla, and why Guy Sexton had convinced her to stand aside in favour of her cousin for the Dryad Guardianship: Guy (and Jasmine) were planning something that only Diana could have done, and up to now, she had refused. The discovery of the horses in Olivia's yard had set off a chain reaction leading to four deaths so far.

Vicky was running out of ideas, and turned to me. I nodded and pushed my empty plate aside. I had an idea of how to prise Pihla open, and it relied on good old-fashioned jealousy.

'When we were up at the Hall, you didn't want to talk about Jasmine and your father. Why was that?'

'It's complicated.'

'I'm sure it is.'

'Jazz can be a bit intense. She doesn't even let me call her *Jazz* to her face, but that's what Dad calls her. Always has, as long as I can remember. She was at the scriptorium while Mum was alive, and she worships her memory. It's a bit weird, sometimes, like it was Jazz who lost a parent, not me.'

'That must be a bit awkward.'

'Tell me about it. She's always ... revered Dad. Yeah, *revered* him, like he was so wonderful for being Tui's husband.'

Vicky said, 'And you're Tui's daughter.'

'I don't look that much like her, not really, which is a blessing. Tarj keeps away, 'cos she's the spit of Mum and Jazz goes weird when she sees her.'

'You must have put up with a hell of a lot,' added Vicky.

'It sounds worse than it is, because I'm telling it all at once. Most days, I turn up and enjoy my work, and Jazz is a good teacher, really.'

'More water?' I asked. Pihla nodded, and I said, 'Has Jasmine or your father been up to anything unusual or different recently?'

'Like killing people?'

I screwed the cap back on the bottle. 'That's for the courts to decide. We're only worried that Jasmine might have got something planned that you wouldn't be happy about.' She looked very uncomfortable. 'Your father knows people, but Jasmine knows magick. Anything dangerous would be her idea.'

'I don't know! Diana says that all you're interested in is abolishing the Particular, that it's all a smear campaign.'

'Do I look like an agent of Salomon's House? Does Vicky?'

Vicky licked sauce off her fingers. 'Only interested in world domination, me. Not bothered about Lakeland.'

Pihla managed a smile. 'It was about two and a half weeks ago. Jazz came in with a real spring in her step and said she was going down to the basement.'

'Is that where the cells are, or does it go down further?'

'Ohmygod! How do you know about the cells?'

'We were locked in one, we believe by Jasmine. Go on.'

'Really?'

'Really.'

'How did you get out? I mean it. How on earth did you get out of there? It took me two years to pluck up the courage to even go down to that level.'

Vicky said she was going to the bathroom. I leaned in to Pihla and said, 'How long would it take you to get out of HMP Cairndale?'

'The mundane prison?' I nodded. 'About half an hour, I suppose.'

'Vicky wasn't joking about me not being much of a Mage. I just looked at the cell from a mundane perspective. They're not that secure, really, and Mages tend to ignore the mundane when there's a magickal alternative.'

'Dad calls it "The Blinkers of Lux". He says that's why he's good at his job.'

'Jasmine went to the basement...'

'Yes. It's above the cells. A sort of mezzanine with secure storage. She brought out this really old-looking book.'

'Old looking, or really old?'

'I recognised the signature work on the binding: it was all originally developed by Mum. Jazz only left the book on the desk for a few seconds while she got a box to transport it, and I saw that she'd put in a Staveley Stitch and re-covered the boards.'

'Sorry. Boards?'

'Like the cover in a hardback book, only made of real wood and covered in leather. I asked her what it was, and she said that it was a private project. I didn't see inside, but I'm sure I saw her working on the loose leaves before she re-bound it, and that was a few months ago. She didn't hide the leaves then, and that's what's strange. Suddenly, she wanted that book out of the Repository.'

Vicky was on her way back to the table as I asked my last casual question before getting out the thumbscrews. Metaphorically speaking. 'What was the book about?'

'Don't know. Something to do with snakes and spruce trees. Have you got a pen?' I passed one over and she wrote on a drip mat. 'I don't know how you'd pronounce it, but you write it like this.' She showed me the word *Eglė*. 'Perhaps she was trying to spare my feelings, for once.'

'Oh?'

Vicky was trying a three point turn and not really listening.

'Because of what happened to Mum. She disappeared in Lithuania, and this book was written in Lithuanian.'

I stood up. 'Don't sit down, Vic. Can you find your way back to Linbeck, Pihla?'

'Eh?' said Vicky.

'What?' said Pihla.

'Thank you for your time, Pihla. We'll let you know what happens.'

Vicky muttered something along the same lines and made her way to the exit. Pihla stared at us until I turned my back and went to open the doors.

31 — Towards Midnight

Vicky had to sit in the back seat, because her foot hurt so much. As soon as she was comfortable and had taken out her sPad, I drove on to the A591, heading north, and put in a call to Andrea Forster of Little Langdale Lodge. To my great relief, she answered.

'I was expecting you to get in touch,' she said.

That put me on my guard. 'Oh?'

'We heard about Matthew and Petra this afternoon. What's going on, Conrad?'

'Those Lithuanian Witches. Someone's planning to assassinate them. As Odin is my witness, I give you my word that they are in extreme danger. Where can we find them?'

'You didn't need to invoke the Allfather. Matthew Eldridge is a good man, despite what some people think of him, and Petra will be sorely missed, and not just by the menfolk.'

'We've spoken with her daughter. I met her.'

'They're at a barn near Castlerigg. Do you know it?'

'The stone circle?'

'The village. It's not far from the circle. Take the 591 nearly to Keswick and turn off for the village. All I know is that the barn is called the Cuddy Retreat. It's a doughnut.'

'A what?'

Vicky piped up. 'I'll explain. Do you know the owner, ma'am?'

'I do. She doesn't do mobile phones and she doesn't live in the same building as her landline. Don't expect a signal when you get there, either.'

'Thank you, Andrea. If you can think of a way of getting word to them in the next half an hour, please do.'

'And what are they in danger of?'

'Tell them not to touch any books.'

I disconnected. 'Go on. What's a doughnut?'

'It's a big round building with a hole in the middle and no windows on the outside. The Shield Wall have a few of them. Excellent defensive structure, very easy to hide from the mundane world and ideal for outdoor magick in the open centre. Where the hell are we going, and slow down, will you? My foot is killing me.'

I did slow down, but only because we were passing through the village of Ings, which sports a very active speed camera. It was half past nine, very dark and we were one of the few vehicles on the road. I once flew over the A591 on a bank holiday, on the way to a rescue, and it was a solid line of baking vehicles from Staveley to Grasmere. Tonight, we almost had the road to ourselves.

'What can you tell me about Lithuanian magick, then?'

'Almost nothing. Like all the Baltic states, it was badly suppressed during the Soviet era and they've been trying to find their own way ever since. This Eglė was queen of the serpents, and has the same status in their country as ... King Arthur, I suppose, but less political. I'm not gonna find out any more without a lot of phone calls to people who have gone home from work for the day. Why don't you ring Rick?'

'You ring him. I need to drive.'

As we sped through Windermere, past the Low Wood Marina again (we both stared hard at that point) and up to Ambleside, I listened to Vicky's contribution to a one-sided conversation. When it was finished, she went very quiet for a moment, then said. 'You'd better put your foot down.'

We were clear of the one-way system in Ambleside, and the road opened up for Grasmere. Well, there weren't any junctions. This road is far from open.

'Tell me the worst.'

'Rick says that what he told you was true. They did come over to look at different options for magickal education. Most of them, anyway. It was a mixed party from different covens, and two of them went AWOL when they got to Lakeland. Nothing suspicious, he said, and a lot of them made side visits all over. These two, though, they missed the big party and got a ticking off from the group leader. Rick says they looked like the cat who'd got the cream after they reappeared. Their coven calls themselves the She Serpents. Sounds better in Lithuanian. They dedicate themselves to Eglė and consider themselves a cut above the covens from the city.'

I had to brake for a slow moving lorry on the night shift back to Scotland. This was going to be torture.

'Are you thinking what I'm thinking?' said Vicky.

'I'm thinking that this group had something to do with Tuulikki's disappearance, and that Guy Sexton is having his revenge served deep-frozen. Seventeen years is a long time to wait.'

'Not in the world of magick, it's not. Rick said that the one who spoke better English was called Rasa. If Guy or Jasmine have delivered that book, they'll probably hold a ceremony before they open it.'

'Is that normal?'

'No such thing as normal, especially if Diana Sexton has been involved.'

'Give me your take. From a magickal perspective.'

'Do you remember what I said about Malaglyphs being like a ticking bomb?'

'I do. You said that any decent Mage would spot them.'

'The one that killed Rod Bristow was pretty primitive. It didn't need to be sneaky for a mundane farmer. The She Serpents are in a whole different league, and so is the magick. Think of the skills they've got. Jasmine put a really convincing forgery together, and was good enough to put a Staveley Stitch inside it. Then she left the book in the cellar. Why? Because they needed Diana to help create the Tuonela Pen, to combine the Malaglyph with other nasty Works, to enchant the new covers on the book and to seal the whole thing with a gloss of … of spiritual authenticity. I'm betting they've sold it to the She Serpents as being locked and needing a ritual to unlock it. In fact, it probably *is* locked.'

I picked up the thread. 'When Diana got in deep shit about Diarmuid, they had leverage with her. Once we'd found those horses, Diana would know we'd work it back to her and she agreed to help them make the book to stop herself being arrested for illegal breeding.'

'But why kill Rod Bristow?'

'An accident? To eliminate the mundane element? Or to make Diarmuid be the backstop. I can imagine Diana killing Rod Bristow, and making Diarmuid go to prison for it, but I can't imagine her shooting Diarmuid. He's Rowan's father, after all. That must be down to Guy and Jasmine on their own. Presumably Diana had delivered the book by then, so Diarmuid could be eliminated, to stop him talking.'

We were past Grasmere and on our way to Dunmail Raise. The road straightened out enough for me to overtake the HGV and really put my foot down.

Vicky's voice had a slight tremor when she asked the next question. 'Do you think Guy and Jasmine will be there to try and stop us? They must know we escaped.'

'I honestly don't know.'

'How much further?'

'About a quarter of an hour. Then the fun starts.'

Let's be kind and call Castlerigg a hamlet rather than a village. There wasn't a lot going on there.

'I've found the Cuddy Beck,' said Vicky as we drew near the turning off the main road. 'Give it a hundred metres and look for somewhere to park. It's on the right.'

'Thanks.'

'I actually had it figured ten minutes ago. It's you and your built in compass – I was so frightened of getting it wrong, I couldn't remember me left from me right. I've got it now.'

'Good.'

As soon as we turned off the A591, I turned off the headlights and slowed to a crawl. Vicky was trying to lean over the seats. We didn't want to end up like Petra and Matthew, driving into a stone wall because of an illusion. A nice space appeared on the right, next to a gate, and I pulled in. I jumped out of the car and activated my Ancile, scanning for an ambush. All I could hear was a light breeze running over the naked branches. The clouds were a bit too dense for my liking: it wasn't going to rain, but we wouldn't have much natural light.

I got Vicky out and said, 'Let's get in the field and hide you behind the wall. I need to look for the Ley line. We'll never find it otherwise.'

'I'm not sure I can use these crutches over grass. Me arms have just about had it.'

'Hang on, I'll open the gate first.' I hesitated with my hand on the rope latch. 'Can you tell if there are any sheep in this field?'

'How the hell should I know?'

'You're the Sorcerer. Try listening for bleating in the Sympathetic Echo.'

'Pffst. Howay and get that gate open.'

I did, and came back to the car. 'I don't think I can lift you on to my shoulders, but I should be able to manage a piggy-back.'

'No.'

'Yes. Or walk.'

I leaned against the car, crouched and waited.

'What do I do with me crutches?'

'Lean them against the car.'

She faffed about a bit more, then launched herself one-legged on to my back. She didn't get very high, but it was enough for me get my arms under her thighs. I staggered round the car, into the field and found a tussock next to the wall. I let her down and went to retrieve the crutches.

'That's not a long-term option, is it?' said Vicky.

'No. I've got an idea, but I don't want to scare you with it.'

'Why don't we just call for help?'

I checked my watch. Half past ten. 'Because no one who'd be of any use could get here before the early hours. There's no Dragon out there. Don't worry, I'm not going to rush in anywhere. Have you got a signal here?'

'At the minute, aye, I have.'

'I'll start by going up the lane.'

'Take care.'

I got the Egyptian Tube out and slid Madeleine into my palm. 'Good evening. Let's go, Maddy.'

The willow wand twitched as we made contact and my spectral helper oriented herself. I got another sound, another *Oh* when she woke up. Was that a twitch to the south? Whatever issues Maddy had taken to the grave, they were somewhere towards the Ambleside/Grasmere/Windermere axis. The wand steadied and I transferred it to my left hand. I was good enough at this game now to keep half an eye on where I was going.

The road to Castlerigg climbed a little, running due south. I'd gone barely a hundred yards when my arm pulsed and the wand twitched. There. Running from the north east to the south west and crossing the road, a Ley line flowed

241

smoothly from the ancient stone circle towards the middle of a field. I traced the continuation of the line in my head – down the hill to Derwentwater. Given that there was a nexus in Keswick, this line wouldn't go to the lake. The doughnut was right there, somewhere. I got as good a fix as I could and headed back to Vicky.

'Sshhh,' she said when I got to the field.

'What?' I whispered. I thought I'd been quiet.

'That water. That noise.' She looked around. 'It's coming from you.'

I held up the wand. 'Maddy?'

'Oh my god. Is that her?' Vicky looked as if she'd quite like to stand up and go somewhere else.

'I need her. The Ley line is over there. We need to cross the field, in the open. I'd rather you were with me, Vic.'

'How the hell are we gonna do that?'

'Stand up and lean against the wall.'

'Why? What are you going to do?'

'Use a fireman's lift to get your bum on that wall, then go for a shoulder ride.'

'You'll never carry me.'

'I don't think we've got an option. Let's give it a go.'

I helped her up, and chose the highest bit of wall. With some reluctance, she flopped over my shoulders and I heaved her up.

'Oww! These stones are sharp. Hurry up or I'll tear me jeans.'

'Here,' I said, passing her the crutches. 'Lay them across your lap. Ready?'

'No, but do it anyway.'

I squatted in front of the wall and hooked her legs over my shoulder, taking care with the bad foot. 'On my word, shuffle forwards and get ready for a hard landing. Ready … go.'

She pitched off the wall and her weight bent my shoulders. I thought I'd go backwards and break my spine for a second, then the momentum took her past the point of balance and I had to try to straighten my legs before her weight brought us both down. I got my right leg up, then the pain seared through my left tibia, and I overbalanced, caught it, took a right step and another left. Vicky squeezed my neck with her thighs as if she were trying to strangle me, but we were upright.

'Wow,' she said. 'I had no idea.'

'No idea of what?'

'How much your bad leg hurts. It washed over me when you put your weight on it. What's that all about?'

'Don't know. Don't care. I could fall over at any moment. Here we go.' I moved into the field, one cautious step at a time, heading for the Ley line. When we were about ten metres away, I reached into my pocket, wobbling a little and pulled out the wand. Maddy came awake, and Vicky yelped like a dog.

'Put her away.'

'Can't.'

My head went into that strange place like the bridge on a ship, where Madeleine was permanently on watch. Watch. I was getting a visual, something I've never had before. The prow of the ship stretched out before us, all air funnels, brass fittings and teak decking. Beyond the distinctly Edwardian vessel, the sea was not the sea. It was a lake. I pushed my legs into action and mist swirled around distant outcrops of rock and shore line. A chill wind blew up from the lake, and carried damp grass and manure with it. The mist cleared off to starboard, and I saw a spit of land with a tent on it. But where was the Ley line?

Without thinking, I turned to my right, and I saw her. Madeleine was standing right next to me, looking annoyed as the boat started to sway. I thought she was tall at first, until I saw that most of her height was hair piled up under a wide brimmed hat. She was dressed like a Suffragette, with a simple black jacket over a white blouse and straight black skirt. I'd only caught a glimpse of her before, in the Grove, and now I'd got to see her properly, the light in her eyes was fierce and radical with pain. The boat swayed alarmingly as I tried to put things together. Where was the Ley line? How would I find it with all these distractions?

A wave tossed the boat and Maddy staggered back. I tried to speak, but something was blocking my breath. A pressure on my windpipe, like hands around it.

Not hands. Legs. I shoved the wand back in my pocket, and the boat disappeared. I nearly fell over trying to ride a wave of nausea, until I turned right and hit the Ley line.

'Thank the gods for that,' said Vicky. 'Are you still alive?'

'I think you'd know if I wasn't. The doughnut is dead ahead, I think. Can you feel it?'

'I can't feel anything except pain, Conrad. Yours, mine and now effing Madeleine's. I think I'd better get down.'

It was easier to keep moving, so I followed the line of Lux, drawing a tiny amount of power through my feet and gaining a little balance. The field was open, all the way down the slope to a wood. Trees are good for hiding things.

So are grass hummocks. Two of them, right on our path, stood up. Vicky got there first. 'Oh shit.'

They were featureless blobs of shadow, but they had the height and width of people. The one on the left spoke. 'Stop there.' It was disguised, but it was the voice of the man who'd kidnapped us.

I didn't stop. If anything, I widened my stride and tried to suck up more Lux from the ground. I felt something move behind my head, round about

243

where Vicky's groin was. With a grunt, I felt an extra squeeze and the field lit up with magickal light. The camouflage Works dissolved, and I saw them clearly.

Sexton was holding a shotgun and blinking against the light. I flicked my eyes to the other, and saw a tall woman in a combats. She had a large dispatch bag over her shoulder, and she was reaching into it. If this was Jasmine, what could she have in there that would hurt us? Sexton raised the gun and gave us both barrels.

It was the first time I've been shot when my Ancile was up. And Vicky's. The shot blew round us like a wind, barely troubling my balance. Sexton must have been healed, or he couldn't have withstood the recoil; good news, if we survived this encounter. He dropped the shotgun, and I could see fear. Jasmine, however, was not looking frightened at all. I shifted right and tried to jog. No good. I was six steps away when she pulled out a long white ribbon, about ten centimetres wide.

'Conrad! Do something!' screamed Vicky. In that second, she lowered her arm and I saw that she'd somehow turned her crutch into a Lightstick.

Jasmine stared at the ribbon. I got a vague impression of calligraphy, then she spoke. Alien, Japanese syllables rang over the grass like bells tolling at my funeral.

The grass became iced brambles of sharp, slippery glass that cut through my leg to the metal tibia. The pulse in Vicky's thighs beat my ears with great hammers of Dwarven steel, striking sparks off and ramming the smell of burning metal up my nose. I couldn't move through that. Jasmine said another word, and the hammers in my head gripped my heart. It was going to burst. The hammers were going to crush it.

The smell of harsh metal, the clang of the hammers and the piercing ice brambles filled my world and my vision shut down, all except a thin track of gold underneath me. The Lux. I tried to suck it up, but the steam hammers crashed down again, like the smithies of hell. If I could just find a way of moving...

The crashing was joined by wailing, as the demons from above joined in, especially the demon riding my back, the hateful demon pushing me to my knees. If I dumped her off.

Her?

The demon stopped wailing for half a moment and whispered *Conrad???* in a dying voice. Was that Vicky?

She's no demon. She's my partner, and riding is exactly what we need to do.

I took the sound of the hammer and moved my feet up and down, marching on the spot, and each step was a nail in a metal horseshoe under my boots. When I got to eight nails, the shoes would protect me from the brambles, and I could do what horses do, I could charge the enemy.

The Eleventh Hour

I moved forward again, following the trail of Lux. My vision snapped back and I was four steps from Jasmine, who was trying to backpedal away. In my left peripheral vision I could see Sexton coming to intercept. Three steps. 'Crutch! Sword!' I shouted.

Two steps and Jasmine stopped to raise the ribbon of silk characters. Sexton was going to dive.

One step and I felt Vicky lean down. I ran past Jasmine and Vicky used all her magickal power to swing the crutch at Jasmine's head, just as Sexton rugby tackled me.

32 — *The Eleventh Hour*

There was no way of controlling my collapse. I just ended up in a heap with Vicky's legs nearly twisting my head off. She did do us the favour of landing on Sexton, though.

I rolled away from the heap as Sexton elbowed Vicky in the chest, knocking her back and out of things. By then I was on all fours. I crawled a step and launched myself at him like a lion as he stood up.

He beat down on my head, but I had him round the waist and upended him on to his back. He jabbed for my face, caught my shoulder, and then I was up to his neck. My hands closed round his throat and squeezed very hard.

I buried my face in his chest and soaked up more blows until a shadow came from behind me. I thought Jasmine had come back, until Vicky crawled up and grabbed his arms. Our combined weight sent him into the night. I held on for another second, then we flopped down together, and I reached for her hand. We squeezed hard and touched foreheads. Boy did that feel good.

Sexton groaned and coughed, breaking the spell. I let go and got up to kneel. I rolled him over and pulled his hands behind his back. 'I'll tie him, you check Jasmine,' I said. Sexton didn't get cheap handcuffs, he got police grade cable ties. He wouldn't be getting out of that without a knife, and I started checking his pockets to make sure. I found his phone, tossed it away, found a pocket knife and smiled to myself.

I also found two little lumps, and fearing that they were some sort of Artefact, I took them out. Two little brass flowers winked in my hand. A 9mm hollow point bullet opens like a flower when it hits you, an image I tried not dwell on as I shoved them in my pocket. I looked over my shoulder to see how Vicky was getting on.

She was sitting on the grass, her head in her hands, and not moving. I glanced worriedly at Jasmine, but she wasn't moving either, so I left Sexton coughing into the grass and stood up.

'Vic? You OK?'

'Aye. I know now.'

'You know what?'

'What it's like to kill someone.'

'She'll be fine.'

'No, she won't.'

I limped over to Jasmine. Vicky must have used a lot of magickal energy, because the left side of Jasmine's face around the eye socket was crushed like a ripe pear. The other eye stared at the horizon, and for some reason I turned to look, too. There, where before there had been a field, was a wooden building, and some very angry Lithuanian Witches were coming out of it. At that moment I realised that the Ley line had been shattered. No wonder they were angry.

'Vic, can you stand? We've got company.'

'If I have to. Give us a hand. And a crutch.'

I picked up one of the crutches and helped her to her feet. Foot. She was clearly in a lot of pain with the other one. I gave her the other crutch and she wiped the end on the grass before shoving her arm in the holder.

The Witches were marching up the field, Lightsticks aloft and fire in their eyes. I decided that now was not the moment to take out the Hammer.

Witches in England tend to go for loose, long robes. These were wearing long-sleeved blouses under stiff, almost canvas dresses that had bright edging at the bottom and symbols woven or applied at various points around the fabric. They were belted with elaborate sashes that glinted with gold and had one end trailing to the hem of their dresses.

I waited until they were close enough to hear, and said, 'Is Rasa here? I am a colleague of Watch Captain Rick James.'

The lead Witch frowned, and stopped at the head of a V formation. 'I am Rasa. Who are you?'

I quickly gave our names and said, 'If you have a book in there, don't touch it.'

A shout from one of the others, and two Witches rushed to Jasmine. An exclamation, a denunciation, and we were in trouble.

'You are man-thief,' said Rasa. 'You come to steal Saga of Eglė. You kill Yasmine and destroy Lux.'

She said something to the woman on her right. The Witch took her sash and started to unwind it.

'I feel power,' muttered Vicky.

I felt fear. There were a lot of them, and we'd ruined their trip. Me being a man didn't help either. I had one shot to get out of this. I showed my open hands to them, knelt down and rolled Guy Sexton on to his back, then heaved him up to a sitting position. He was about to say something when I shoved a glove in his mouth. 'This man is the husband of Tuulikki Sexton. I think you knew her.'

Cue confusion. And argument.

'Is this true?' was the upshot.

I chucked his wallet at them and said, 'I can call his daughter if you want. Pihla. She'll tell you.'

Rasa grabbed the wallet and passed her Lightstick to another Witch. The one with the sash had separated herself and held it up in both hands, like a weapon. The Witch who'd gone to Jasmine had done the same.

When Rasa saw inside the wallet, she had the decency to go white and flick her eyes to Guy, who wasn't moving because I'd pressed the SIG into the back of his neck. Rasa showed the wallet to her neighbour, who also looked very worried. She said something, and they walked forward. In the light, I saw that a family picture held pride of place in Guy's wallet, and clearly it meant as much to the Lithuanians as it did to Guy.

'Is it true?' said Rasa to me. 'Is it true he has … *sabotažas*??'

One of the others said, 'Sabotage. Sabotage book.'

'Ja.'

'Yes. I believe so. Vicky? Can you explain?'

Vicky explained. Then explained again. Then tried some different words until they were all nodding. Rasa sent two Witches scurrying back inside and stepped up to Guy.

'Let him speak,' she said.

I took the gun away from his neck and put my left hand firmly on his shoulder, just to remind him. He spat out the glove.

'Bitches. Filthy Russian bitches. You'll all drown forever in Hell.' As he cursed, his voice rose, raw from being strangled. 'May your children eat your bones and die from the plague.'

Rasa took it, then looked up to me. 'He is the man,' she said, a trifle redundantly. She squatted in front of Sexton, graceful in her white tunic, and balanced with one hand on the ground and the other gripping her sash. 'If I drown in hell, underneath my feet will be your Sami whore. She killed my mother, my sister, my aunt and my best friend.' She showed him the family photo, then chucked the wallet in his lap. 'Do you want *kraujo kerštas*?' She turned her head. 'What is that in English?'

A shadow from behind said, 'Blood vendetta.'

She pointed to the wallet again. 'Do you want blood on your children? Does her Spirit want that?'

Guy said nothing.

I chipped in. 'He has broken the law of hospitality. He will be taken away for a long time. We will tell his daughter of his crime. Pihla will want no more blood.'

A commotion rose up at the back of the coven as the two Witches delegated to inspect the book emerged. One of them was carrying an elaborately carved box which she couldn't wait to put down in front of everyone.

Rasa stood up. 'So mote it be, as you say here.' She turned to the others and there was a shocked and angry conversation which involved much pointing at the box, Jasmine's body and then Guy.

I was starting to come down from the adrenaline high. I pushed Sexton back to the ground and put a foot on his shoulder. I stowed my gun and lit a cigarette. Vicky moved slowly to join me. She moved her arm and placed a Silence over Sexton.

'Good call,' she said. 'That could have ended very badly.'

'It's not over yet. What the hell happened with those Japanese curses?'

'Kotodama is powerful stuff. It's the Japanese magick of words and essences, and Jasmine must have been given a gift when the Japanese Mages came to see her. I've no idea how it works, but we both got a skinful of pain, I know that much.'

'Did you get the visions?'

She shuddered. 'Give us a fag. If me heart can stand that, it can stand anything.'

I didn't argue, and passed her the packet. 'Do you want to talk about it? About the way you saved our lives?'

She smiled ruefully. 'It was a real team effort. Your back must be knackered.'

She hadn't answered my question. For once, I didn't let it lie. 'If you find yourself thinking about it, find yourself dwelling on what might have been, then please, please, talk to someone.'

'Aye. Point taken.'

The coven had finished their discussion, and Rasa came over. 'We think Yasmine still has our payment. We would like to exchange.'

'Fair enough. What did you think you were buying?'

'A rare manuscript of our heritage that was taken by the Nazis during the war. It looked completely authentic.'

'How close were you to the ritual?'

'Nearly finished. We heard the shots and paused. Then the Lux stopped and we came to see. Just before midnight.'

I checked my watch: 23:15. 'It's nowhere near midnight.'

'It is in Lithuania. We were an hour ahead.'

I pointed to Vicky's foot. 'If you can help my partner, I would be very grateful.'

'It is the least we can do. And you must share our hospitality.'

'Vicky will accept on my behalf. I must deal with Sexton.'

'Eh?' said Vicky. 'You're not gonna leave us here, are you?'

''Fraid so. You keep the book, too, and when George Gibson comes to collect you, hand it over.'

'Really?'

'Yes. We had a deal. That book is evidence of Diana's crimes, and they can sort it out. We've got what we came for.'

The Witches had finished with Jasmine and one of them clutched a small bag, heavy with gold. 'Come?' said Rasa.

'Leave us for a minute,' I said. 'Vicky has one more job to do.'

Rasa came forward and shook my hand, then kissed my cheek. 'You have a welcome in Pakuonis always.'

'Thank you.'

The Witches withdrew to the wooden doughnut, and I took out my phone. There was a signal, and I sent the same message to George Gibson and Barney Smith: *Deliver the package.* To George, I added: *You need to collect Vicky from Castlerigg after sunrise.*

'I have to go with a Gnome?' she said.

'He'll behave himself. Can we make a provisional arrangement to meet at Wilf's in Staveley for breakfast?'

'Whatever.' She sighed. 'I felt it. When I whacked Jasmine, I saw the tiniest shadow. She must have got her reward and conceived during the last few hours.'

I put my arm gently round her shoulders. 'Do you want me to gather her effects?'

'Please.'

'Watch laughing boy here.'

I quickly took Jasmine's Artefacts, and her bag, then returned to Vicky.

'Get your phone out and cancel that Silence, if you would,' I said.

'Right.'

I hauled Sexton to his feet and made sure that Vicky was recording. 'Guy Sexton, I am arresting you on suspicion of murder. You do not have to say anything, but it may harm your defence if you do not mention when questioned something which you later rely on in court. Anything you do say may be given in evidence. Do you understand?'

'Since when have the King's Watch adopted PACE?' said Sexton, clearly more thwarted than worried.

I took out my Lancashire and Westmorland warrant card. 'I am arresting you under mundane law. I am a sworn constable and will be taking you to a police station.'

He pulled at the restraints and hurt himself. 'You can't. What for? Whose murder?'

I nodded to Vicky, and she stopped recording. 'Can you make it to the doughnut on your own?'

'Aye. I'll see you soon, eh?'

I put my arms round her neck and kissed the top of her head. 'Take care, Vic.'

She leaned up and kissed my cheek. 'Thank you, Conrad, for doing something really special.'

'What, in particular?'

'You carried me over that field, and you haven't said a word about how heavy I was. For that I am very grateful.'

She gathered the last of her strength and swung herself towards the door into the doughnut.

I put a Silence on Sexton and pushed him up the field towards the car. When we got there, I belted him in the front and shoved the bloodstained pillowcase over his head.

33 — By the Book

Cairndale was due south of here on a straight road. I headed north. That way, I could stick to dual carriageways and the M6. Much safer. I'd nearly reached Penrith when Commander Ross called me.

'Clarke? What in God's name is going on? A coffin has appeared in the station compound and someone rings 999 and says, "Don't worry, it's not a bomb. Ring Watch Captain Clarke." The duty inspector is all for calling the Army and closing the A6. As it is, he has the station in lockdown.'

'Sorry, sir, it really isn't a bomb. It's the body of a murder victim, and I'm bringing in a suspect. PC Smith from Barrow is on his way to deliver the murder weapon.'

'I have no idea what you are talking about. I am now going to get dressed and go in. When will you be there?'

'An hour or so.'

'I am looking forward to this a lot.'

I drove down the M6 to Westmorland Services and pulled in near a wood, close to where Vicky and I had met to discuss the evidence. The first thing I did was use some rope to tie Sexton to his seat. Yes, I do carry rope in my car. It's come in handy many times. I stretched my legs down to the 24 hour cafe and bought two large cappuccinos. When I got back, I took the ropes, the Silence and the pillowcase off Sexton and helped him out of the car. I made a noose out of the rope and dropped it round his neck.

'Kneel.'

'Why?'

I took out a knife. 'I'm going to cut the cable ties.'

I freed his hands and told him to stand up. 'We're going into the woods so that you can relieve yourself. Then we're going to have a talk.'

When we'd returned from the woods, I made him stand on the other side of the vehicle from me, with the rope almost taut in my hand. I lit a cigarette.

'Is it true? What Rasa said: did Tui kill people?'

'Tuulikki, to you. I don't know. Perhaps. She made Artefacts to order and delivered them. When we got married, the Berlin Wall was just coming down. The Baltic states were in chaos, mundane and magickal. A decade later, there were covens and Circles and groups forming and re-forming all over. We made a lot money from them until things changed, and we decided the kids would be better off growing up in the Particular. Tui used to go back to the Helsinki Market twice a year, and one Christmas she was given a big job. I don't know what it was. I never did.'

He sipped his coffee. I think he knew exactly what it was. I think his late wife invented the Tuonela pen for the precise purpose of assassination, ditto the Staveley Stitch.

'What happened?' I asked.

'She delivered the item in the summer. Something went wrong. Something as stupid as a train strike. She was trapped in the back country, no hire cars to be had. Like a bad movie. She was murdered. It took me ten years to find out where her ashes had been scattered and who had done it. You can guess the rest.'

'You got Jasmine to fake that book and Diana to create the deadly magick to go in it.'

He shook his head. 'Not a fake. Or not completely. Tui picked up some fragments over the years, and no, Diana had nothing to do with it. It was all Jasmine.'

'Not my problem. I'll let George Gibson sort that out. You, on the other hand, are very much my problem.'

He said nothing.

'If you want, Sexton, I can string this rope over a branch. You can jump off the car and be found in the woods.'

'Why would I do that?'

'Or, you can confess to Diarmuid's murder and do time in a mundane prison.'

'Why?'

'Because locking you in the Esthwaite Rest for four years would not be a punishment. You're going to do time in Strangeways or Liverpool like the murdering bastard you are. And in return, I'll walk away from your family and leave you alone. If you still want to pursue Rasa after your parole, you can do.'

'Let me think about it.'

'You've got five minutes.'

I could see it in his eyes, working out whether he could throw hot coffee in my face and jump me. No, was the answer. He thought about what he had left, what was important to him and what the options were.

He finished his coffee and put the lid carefully back in place. 'Jasmine said you were linked to the Allfather in some way.'

'She was right.'

'He doesn't have the same reputation in Finland as he does over here. Much darker.'

'I wouldn't know.'

'He chose you for a reason. I think I'd rather not find out why. What do I have to do?'

'Let's get going and I'll tell you. I'm putting more ties on before we get in the car.'

It was well after midnight when I was admitted to the security compound at the back of Cairndale nick. A variety of police vehicles, including an ARV (Armed Response Vehicle), were parked neatly on one side. No driver in Commander Ross's station would dare park in any other fashion than neat.

The other side had a couple of sheds and, sitting on a rolling gurney, an oak coffin. The angled lamps on the barbed-wire topped walls flattened the oak grain and bleached the steel fittings to a dull gunmetal. The only sign of life was on a raised walkway attached to the station. Two black figures waited for us, one ramrod straight with his hands behind his back; the other was more nervous, hunched into his hi-vis jacket and with hands stuffed into his pockets.

'Showtime, Guy,' I said. 'Don't forget your lines.'

He snorted and looked away from the coffin.

Ross came down from the walkway, trailing Barney Smith in his wake. We met in the middle of the yard. Two steps away, Ross held up his hand to stop me speaking.

'Smith, is your bodycam switched on?'

'Sir.'

'Arrest him and caution him.'

Barney wavered during the caution, but he didn't stumble. When he'd finished, he asked Guy his name.

'My name is Guy Sexton, of Staveley. I wish to confess to the murder of Diarmuid Driscoll, and my confession is freely made.'

'How did you do it?' said Ross.

'I shot him with a rifle.'

'Was anyone else involved?'

Sexton turned to me, then turned back. 'I acted alone.'

Ross nodded to himself. 'PC Smith, take Mr Sexton to the custody suite and get him booked in. Tell the custody sergeant we'll be holding the interview in the morning.'

'Yes, sir.'

Barney gave me the strangest look as I handed over the prisoner. I winked and said, 'Thanks, Barney. Vicky's fine and is with medics.'

He smiled, a proper smile, and led Sexton away, leaving the Commander and myself under the lights.

'Shall we?' said Ross, pointing to the coffin.

We approached the coffin slowly, because I wasn't going to rush ahead of the Commander, was I?

'Could you give me a hand with the lid, sir? It's been unscrewed.'

'Who by? The Fairies?'

'Gnomes, sir. They dropped it off for me.'

He didn't think that was funny, for some reason, but he took up a position at the end of the coffin. 'If this *is* a bomb, my ghost will haunt your ghost for eternity. Is that clear?'

We lifted the lid and placed it carefully on the ground. The body of Diarmuid lay, at peace, in a silk lining. The transportation had moved one hand off his chest. The other hand, stark white under the lights, emerged from a stiff shirt fastened with horseshoe cufflinks. I wondered if they'd been a gift from Diana or Rowan. A gentle odour of aftershave wafted up, spicy with notes of iron.

'I'm not going to unbutton his shirt,' said Ross. 'Time enough for that. Let's put the lid back on and get Scene of Crime out.' He turned, probably to a CCTV monitor, and waved an unseen team out of the building. We put the lid back on and Ross touched my arm.

'I want you out of here, Clarke. Best not even cross the threshold. Fewer questions that way. Will this business change the way things are done in the Particular?'

'I believe so, sir. Not today, or tomorrow, but the Assessors won't have it all their own way in future. Thank you for trusting me.'

'Good, and congratulations on your first collar. Having said that, I am not impressed by tonight's shenanigans, sonny. That is not how we roll in Cairndale. Are we clear?'

'Sir.'

He turned away, shepherding me to my car. 'I've one last question. I personally checked the CCTV, and that coffin appeared from nowhere. One second the yard was empty, the next we had a corpse. I've also checked the CCTV from the last remaining public phone box in Cairndale, from where the 999 call came. During the call, the box was empty. Care to comment?'

'Look at it this way, sir. Either the people you're dealing with have the technology to alter and manipulate computer systems at will, or it was magick. You choose.'

'That sounds like a choice between paranoia or madness.'

The sound of boots on the metal stairs drew my attention. Three paper-suited crime scene technicians, cases in hand, were approaching. They were led by a substantial woman with a cheerful smile.

'Evening, Tracy,' said Ross. 'Thanks for waiting.'

'Evening, sir. We're on overtime, so it's not a problem.'

The techs dumped their stuff and Tracy started directing them.

I unlocked the car and said, 'Sir, one more thing. Barney – PC Smith – took a big risk in coming over to our side. I'd hate him to suffer any comeback.'

'I am not on your side, Clarke. While you have that warrant card, you are on my side. Don't forget that, and don't worry, I'll look after wee Barney. Now, go.'

I saluted and got in the car.

'Full English, Vicky? George?'

'Aye,' said Vicky.

George Gibson shook his head. 'Not for me, thanks, I need to be off quickly. Tea and toast would be good.'

'Coming up.'

Wilf's Café in the Staveley Wood Yard is highly rated for breakfast. Very highly. The only problem is that you have to queue while it's made. I was looking forward to the food, but the biggest thrill was watching Vicky walk to the table with only one crutch.

I'd grabbed a couple of hours sleep after leaving Sexton in Ross's iron grip. I'd have had more than that if Hannah hadn't video-called me at seven o'clock and demanded a full report. The good news was that she seemed pleased and relieved by the outcome. As ever with the Boss, there'd been a sting in the tail. Vicky and I were summoned to London on Thursday, but she wouldn't tell me why until we could call her together.

That piece of news I was saving for later; Vicky deserved her moment of triumph. I'd been at the front of the queue at quarter to nine when Vicky rolled in with George. She took great delight in getting out of his car unaided and in standing on her bad leg for a second. The She Serpents of Lithuania have a very good healer, and the bone was knitted. Vicky had said by text that it should be as good as new in a week.

I took the pots of tea and coffee, and George's toast, over to the table and got straight down to business.

'You're going to arrest Diana and take her away?' I said.

'We are. Gnomes keep their word, too. She will definitely do time in the Rest. How did it go in Cairndale?'

While he munched his toast, I filled them on the details of Guy Sexton's fate. There was one piece of information I was particularly glad to share: Matthew Eldridge had come out of his induced coma and was talking. George stood up and left just as our breakfasts arrived.

'What did Eldridge have to say?' asked Vicky.

'Petra was on to the Sextons. She knew that Rowan was Diarmuid's daughter. Unfortunately for her, she asked her questions in ways that got back to Guy Sexton. Matthew said that Petra got an anonymous tip-off about Sophie. They were in a café, and when they came out, his car wouldn't start. He doesn't remember anything after that.'

'Guy just didn't care, did he?'

'No. How was it in the doughnut?' I asked.

'You know what, I thought the Shield Wall were mad. These sisters could see their mad and raise them a couple of bonkers. They know how to party, though. Real old-school.'

256

We enjoyed our breakfasts. At the end, Vicky said, 'Do we have to do this?'

'We do. Call it closure.'

'Then let's get it over with.'

Leo Winter met us at the front of Linbeck Hall. The doors were firmly closed behind him. He nodded in greeting.

'Grandmother says that if you want to speak to us, you can do it before the Dryad.'

'Have you got transport? Vicky isn't fully recovered.'

'I can walk,' she said. 'If there's a path.'

'There is. Follow me.'

He took us round the Hall, to the north. A cinder track led uphill, and we were soon in the trees. I could feel the magick growing around us. Leo had gone ahead, out of earshot, and I took my time, ready to help Vicky with a few awkward steps over rampant tree roots.

She stopped for a breather, and looked around. I joined her in sitting on the trunk of a giant beech that had fallen years ago. Birdsong was everywhere as they paired and jostled ahead of the full spring. Bluebells were just sprouting, daffodils were in their glory and the pungent smell of rotting leaves came and went, alternating with a clean breath of grass.

'I think I've figured it out,' I said. 'Most of the beauty in magickally preserved woods comes from just that – the preservation. Three or four generations ago, all the woods were like this, full of life and variety.'

'Aye. You could be right. What was it you didn't want to tell me in the café?'

I smiled at her. 'I might have to ask for a new partner. You're getting to know me too well.'

'And vice versa. You've seen me naked more times than is good for either of us.'

'It was Hannah. She wants us in London on Thursday, but I don't think we're in trouble.'

'That makes it worse. She's probably gonna send us on a mission to Outer Mongolia, or somewhere equally desolate, like Sunderland.'

'That'll be it. Come on.'

It was a much reduced Sexton clan who welcomed us to a circle of benches around a mature rowan tree. Evelyn was flanked by men, this time, with Karl at her right and Leo on her left. Rowan and Pihla sat on one bench, with Toivo and Tarja on another. It was the first time I'd seen Tarja, and if Pihla was telling the truth about her sister's resemblance to their mother, I could see why Guy missed Tuuilikki.

Pihla is a very attractive young woman. Tarja is in a league of her own, with sculpted cheekbones and a dancer's grace. As you'd expect, she looked

257

bereft and afraid. Between Pihla and Rowan was a distance that would take some time to bridge. I looked up at the magnificent tree, already coming into leaf, and saw a shadow perched on one of the branches.

I turned my attention back to the group and approached the circle. 'Can my partner take the weight off her feet?'

'Of course,' said Evelyn.

Vicky took a place on an empty bench. I stood behind her. The Sextons waited.

There was no rhetorical bluster, though I could see that Karl wanted to offer some defiance; that's why Evelyn had sat him next to her. The Sexton matriarch was going to hold her fire, or keep her peace, depending on your preferred metaphor.

'Thank you for bringing us to this place,' I said. 'It is an honour.'

Evelyn looked at the two Rowans. 'It's somewhere we should have come more often, and will in the future.'

It must have cost her a lot to say that; it was as close to an admission of guilt as we were going to get, not that we needed one.

'We only want one thing,' I said. 'The courts will have a lot to say in the future, including the matter of Weregild, but one voice will be silent: they won't hear from a young girl in Grange called Sophie. She lost out, too. She lost her job with Rod Bristow, the glowing reference he would have given her and the opportunities she worked hard to make for herself. Don't forget her.'

Rowan, Diana's Rowan, hung her head. She knew who I meant.

Evelyn had noticed and said, 'We won't forget her. Would you hear something?'

'I have ears.'

'I can see something dark. I've known it was there for years, but only now can I see where it came from. Your Grandfather has cast a very long shadow, Mr Clarke, a shadow that goes well beyond you. It's time you came out from under it.'

'Thank you for your words. It's time for us to go.'

When Vicky stood up, the raven launched himself out of the tree and announced his presence as he flew away. Young Rowan frowned and turned to her cousin. Whether they spoke, I don't know, because we were already on our way.

Over the last few days, Project Talpa had come and gone from my thoughts as more urgent matters got in the way. After Evelyn's words, I had a horrible feeling that the long shadow cast by my 11xGreat Grandfather might be connected to what was happening in the wild world of magick.

'Penny for them?' said Vicky when we'd left the trees behind.

'I think that a Summoning of Spectre Thomas has just gone to the top of the list. Do you fancy spending Easter at Elvenham?'

'Why not. Are we going today?'

'No. I've got to go back to Cairndale and find an acceptable statement for the coroner and for the CPS, and I've got an appointment at the prison tomorrow morning. We'll head off after that, and go straight to London.'

When we got to the car, that skittering noise I'd last heard at the mill and on the Hoad in Ulverston was back. They must have some strange wildlife at Linbeck.

34 — The Ties that Bind

Vicky waited in the car while I went through the gates to visit Mina. My partner's foot was good, but not good enough to work the stiff clutch on her Audi. Her father had come down on the train yesterday to find out what his daughter had been up to and to take her car away. John Robson thinks I'm a bad influence on Vicky; Mina thinks it's the other way round.

'If it wasn't for her, you wouldn't keep getting in trouble. She leads you astray with her second sight,' said Mina when I'd brought her up to speed. 'And I'm not sure about this bond you have with her. I am the only woman you should have a bond with.'

'I won't tell my mother you said that. Or my sister.'

'They're family.'

'So's Vicky. We're blood siblings, you could say.'

Mina scratched her arm. 'There is a stupid woman in Nightingale House. She has been feeding a stray cat, and now we have fleas. I can't wait to get out of this poxy place.'

'Are you sure you'll be alright on the train?'

She sighed theatrically and trailed her fingers across the plastic table top, flicking her eyes around to see if we were being watched. I moved my hand over and grabbed her fingers, just for a second. That's a bond you couldn't measure with a Luxometer, even if such a thing existed.

'I'll be fine on the train,' she said when we'd shared the smile that always comes after these moments of contact. 'You just make sure my lift is waiting at the gate. If he's not there, I'm going to turn round and walk back inside.'

'He'll be there. You read my last letter?' I said.

'Only fifty times. I keep count and stop when I get to a hundred.'

Okay. That is weird. Or she's winding me up. Irony and hyperbole are closer in the Gujarati dictionary than they are in the English one.

'And? Can I go ahead with my plan to secure a new housekeeper for Elvenham?'

'If you must. If there's no other way.'

'I can't see one.'

'Then go ahead, but I don't want to talk about that now. Tell me again what's happening on Thursday.'

'I don't know. Really.'

'But Buckingham Palace says it must happen at nine thirty.'

'It's the only space in her diary.'

'And you have no idea who it is?'

'The Duke of Albion. That's all I know.'

That had been Hannah's message: Vicky and I were to get our medals on Thursday morning, and it was going to be a mundane ceremony, so our families could attend. Dad was thrilled.

'Do you think it could be Kate? Or maybe Meghan?'

'They're not of the royal blood. Knowing my luck, it will be Beatrice. I really wish you could be there.'

'Maybe next time, if you can convince this Hannah woman to accept me.'

'I'm not sure I want another medal. I nearly got fried just for a DFC. The next one might be posthumous.'

Mina waved her hand from side to side. 'Mmmh. Not sure. If the Duchesses of Sussex and Cambridge presented the medal, to me, personally, I could cope with a posthumous award.'

'I shall see my solicitor and put an instruction in my will: all medals to be presented to Amelia Jennings.'

'That's not funny.'

'It's as funny as wishing for a posthumous medal.' I laughed, remembering a conversation from last night. 'The one who's really upset is Dad. He was desperately hoping to meet you there. I've told them they can't come down to Elvenham over Easter, but that's never stopped them before.'

'Time!'

We stood up and stood apart. The rules state *minimal physical contact*. If you keep your hands off each other, you get a longer kiss. We leaned forward and I tasted berry shades of her lipstick. There are a lot of women in my life, but only one of them tastes like that.

John and Erica Robson will get to see their daughter pick up her award in person. You can't ask for more than that.

Conrad & Vicky's story continues in TENFOLD, the Fourth Book of the King's Watch.

TENFOLD
The Fourth Book of the King's Watch

By Mark Hayden

Conrad's 11xGreat Grandfather is sleeping in the well where he drowned, 400 years ago.

Before he drowned, Thomas Clarke, Keeper of the Queen's Esoteric Library stole some books, and it's time to find out where they went.

When Spectre Thomas appears, his answer opens the door to a whole new world of magickal peril.

Conrad thought that his biggest problem was explaining why the Druid with the cornflower blue eyes is working as his housekeeper. Now, with Ancient magick on the loose, his trouble have multiplied –

TENFOLD

Is now available in Ebook and paperback from:

www.pawpress.co.uk

Author's Note

The King's Watch books are a radical departure from my previous five novels, all of which are crime or thrillers, though very much set in the same universe, including the **Operation Jigsaw** Trilogy that Conrad himself refers to as part of his history.

A book should speak for itself, especially a work of fiction. Other than that, it only remains to be said that all the characters in this book are fictional, as are some of the places. Merlyn's Tower, Linbeck Hall and Hledjolf's Hall are, of course, all real places, it's just that you can only see them if you have the Gift...

And Thanks...

This book would not have been written without love, support, encouragement and sacrifices from my wife, Anne. It just goes to show how much she loves me that she let me write this book even though she hates fantasy novels.

Although Chris Tyler didn't get to see the draft this time, his friendship is a big part of my continued desire to write.

Finally, thanks to my wonderful cover designer, Rachel Lawston. She put up with a lot on the way to getting here, and I am eternally grateful.

Printed in Great Britain
by Amazon

42526483R00152